I0206242

Behind the Rising Sun

S. O. Mezu

HEINEMANN
LONDON · IBADAN · NAIROBI

Heinemann Educational Books Ltd
48 Charles Street, London W1X 8AH
P.M.B. 5205, Ibadan · P.O. BOX 25080, Nairobi
EDINBURGH MELBOURNE TORONTO AUCKLAND
NEW DELHI SINGAPORE HONG KONG KUALA LUMPUR

ISBN 0 435 90113 3

First published by William Heinemann Ltd 1971
First published in *African Writers Series* 1972

Printed Offset Litho in England by
Cox & Wyman Ltd, London, Fakenham and Reading

To Rose Uregbulam, Chinyere Valerie and my Family
To all the innocent victims of the Biafran War

Ce roman est donc tout objectif. Il ne tâche même pas à expliquer: il constate. Il ne s'indigne pas: il enregistre. Il ne pouvait en être autrement. Par les soirs de lune, allongé en ma chaise longue, de ma veranda, j'écoutais les conversations de ces pauvres gens. Leurs plaisanteries prouvaient leur resignation. Ils souffraient et riaient de souffrir . . .

René Maran, *Batouala,*
Véritable Roman Nègre
Prix Goncourt 1921

Therefore this novel is entirely objective. It does not even attempt explanation: it is a witness. It does not criticize, it registers; I could not do otherwise. On moonlight nights, from my long chair on the veranda, I listened to this poor folk's talk. Their jokes were proof of resignation. They suffered, and laughed at suffering . . .

Contents

The White Market Dealers

It was early afternoon in Paris, the crowning moment of six weeks of frustration, during which Mr Ifedi had tried in vain to charter planes to carry home ammunition and other urgently needed equipment. Each attempt had seemed on the point of succeeding but, at the very last moment, something had always happened to disrupt the arrangement—such as the plane developing engine trouble.

The latest of these charter flight experiences was the case of Arthur Kutzenov, a French citizen whose parents had fled from Russia during the 1917 Revolution. Kutzenov had lived through revolts in Czechoslovakia and Poland. From what he said, it seemed that he was determined to fight the Russians wherever he could. He was also determined to assist any group of people fighting for a right to self-government. As a businessman, the opportunity to assist did come to him quite often.

Arthur Kutzenov had now signed a contract to provide either one DC 7 or two DC 3 aircraft for the airlift of some material stocked in Prague, mostly 7·92 millimetre ammunition, some rifles and a few machine-guns. For the sake of security and coverage, the contract was written vaguely to avoid mentioning the exact location of the materials and the exact port of destination, which was Enugu, in Biafra. Should war conditions prevent Kutzenov from landing in Enugu, the island of São Tomé, it was agreed, would be an acceptable final port of destination for the purposes of the execution of the contract. Because of the flexibility of the contract, an agreed rate per flying hour was fixed, both for the big plane and for the smaller ones.

At the signature of the contract, Kutzenov had insisted on a down payment of ten thousand dollars. There was no choice in the matter. Since there was no money then in the Paris account to meet expenditure which would amount to forty thousand dollars, the Biafra European Bank in London (B.E.B.) was asked to cable the money to Geneva; contacts there would then redirect the money to Paris. In operations of this nature, it is always best to clear any links that might expose entire networks. Obiora Ifedi, therefore, asked that the money be wired directly from Geneva to his personal account in Paris. All this had been completed within one day, and Arthur Kutzenov had received in cash the sum of ten thousand dollars in French francs. He had then departed to arrange the airlift.

Now, in his room on the fifth floor of the Hotel Lutetia, facing Boulevard Raspail, Obiora Ifedi managed somehow to communicate his air of joy and achievement to the men sitting with him: Professor Chancellor Obelenwata, Lawyer Peter Afoukwu, Samson Anele, Chief Tobias Iweka, a former Cabinet Minister, the secretary-typist Ndubisi, Jeff Edu and Freddy Onuoha. Before long, Obiora Ifedi got everyone toasting the success of the war with the drinks he had ordered from the bar. Freddy Onuoha raised a few objections about the contract, pointing out that the wording did not make provision for recovery in the case of non-fulfilment. Mr Ifedi brushed the point aside, saying that he had been signing contracts for governments for the past ten years and that the Kutzenov contract was one of the smallest of them.

Arthur Kutzenov then returned and bought drinks liberally for everyone. He also cheerfully announced that the plane, a DC 7, would leave around four o'clock for Prague. He was there barely five minutes when a phone call from his office summoned him away again. As he left, he said that if the plane left at four, it would just be in Prague at dusk. The phone rang again. Mr Ifedi answered it. It was Jean-Pierre Dubien calling from the reception hall of the Hotel Lutetia, and Mr Ifedi asked him to come up.

A call was booked immediately to Geneva to get in touch with the contact man there, Pat Odoro. Mr Ifedi also booked a call to Lisbon to let the people there know that the DC 7 would be arriving that night, and he advised them to make the necessary arrangements for handling the plane and directing it on to its final destination, Enugu. Pat Odoro would get in touch with Prague since connections between Geneva and Prague were faster and safer. The contact man in Prague was Ruddy Nnewi.

The doorbell rang and Obiora Ifedi went to the door and, in

his usual affable way, ushered in Jean-Pierre Dubien. He offered him a glass and asked him to join the rejoicing. 'Finally, things will start moving this night,' Mr Ifedi sighed. Jean-Pierre Dubien looked up in surprise and asked: 'Really?' Ifedi told him that the contract had been signed with Arthur Kutzenov and that the plane would leave at four o'clock that evening. 'Great!' Dubien exclaimed as Mr Ifedi handed him the contract. The telephone rang as Dubien was reading it. Ifedi picked up the telephone. It was Pat Odoro in Geneva. The call had gone through.

Speaking on the telephone, Obiora Ifedi asked Pat Odoro to cheer up, telling him that things would start moving that night. He explained how hard he had tried during the past five weeks to find something. Now he really had something in hand. At exactly four o'clock, the DC 7 would roar away from Paris for Prague. He said that Ruddy Nnewi in Prague should be informed immediately so that he could arrange to get the equipment ready. Priority, he emphasized, should be given to 7·92 mm ammunition. Obiora Ifedi gave him the approximate time of arrival, but was unable to confirm the registration of the aircraft—he would obtain that information immediately from Kutzenov. Toasts were exchanged over the telephone.

'What do you think of it?' Mr Ifedi asked Jean-Pierre Dubien with an air of satisfaction. 'Great,' Dubien replied. He pointed out a few changes he would like to have seen made in the contract, but later agreed with Mr Ifedi that they were not really necessary. He did, however, repeat a comment he had made earlier when he met Obiora Ifedi .'Arthur Kutzenov is a first-class crook and he can get a plane today to carry all the arms you need if he wants to do so.' Dubien added, however, that he had no confidence in Kutzenov. 'He is a drunkard and when he is drunk, he fumes, he raves and I would not leave my daughter with him on the same block—if I had one,' he added as an after-thought. Dubien indicated that he would be ready to help find a plane in case another was needed next time.

At that point, a few jokes were cracked—mostly about women. Professor Chancellor Obelenwata enjoyed jokes a great deal and the bull session would have continued if it had not been interrupted by another telephone call. Professor Obelenwata, to be fair to him, never told a joke himself, but most of the time prompted other people to repeat this and that joke they had heard in this and that capital of the world. He was a well-travelled middle-aged man who would have liked to look younger. He never missed the opportunity of telling people about the number of academic awards he had received in various academies of the world in connection with his archaeological research.

It was Arthur Kutzenov on the telephone. He was downstairs and wanted to come up immediately. 'What is the matter?' Obiora Ifedi asked him, alarmed. 'No alarm, cool it now,' Kutzenov bellowed over the phone, and hung up. Dubien wanted to leave immediately. He did not want Kutzenov to see him there. The two of them did not get along at all. Dubien said again that Kutzenov was a crook and that he did not deal with crooks. He would discuss his own proposal later on with Obiora Ifedi. With that, he left the room. There were two elevators in the right wing of the Hotel Lutetia, almost, but not quite, side by side. After Dubien had left, Professor Obelenwata commented that Dubien was a well-cultured and refined man. Such a compliment in all fairness could not be paid to Kutzenov. He was rough and coarse. His accent in French was bad enough. His English accent was guttural and he stammered when he was angry. He had sharp proletarian features, coming from a family of miners, from the same village as Nikita Khrushchev; but, unlike his compatriot, he had never got to the top.

Chief Iweka showed his native wisdom by describing how the calm and refined Dubien would be entering the elevator going down just as the rough and callous-looking Kutzenov emerged from the other lift. Chief Iweka had little formal education and could not participate in talks about contracts or in any intellectual or theoretical political discussions. But whenever he had the opportunity, he always showed he had an edge over the others in native wisdom and the Ifedi squad always applauded him very warmly for this.

Arthur Kutzenov entered the room. He was definitely in a bad mood. It was mainly his facial expression, which appeared never to have seen a smile, even a wry one, all its life. He gave Ifedi a document. 'Do you recognize that?' he asked. Obiora Ifedi looked at it and said, 'No, but I know that it is a promissory note issued by my Government. Besides, I see that it is signed by a friend of mine, the highest Finance Officer in the Civil Service of my Government.' Arthur Kutzenov sat down and refused the drink Obiora Ifedi offered him. He then started his explanation. The promissory note for £208,000 was issued to Jean-Pierre Dubien for the rendering of certain services. The amount in question was payable in three instalments and the second instalment was due the day before. Using the note in question as security, Jean-Pierre Dubien, who had visited Enugu privately in February of that year, had raised some money, so Kutzenov said, from the General Business Associates, of which Kutzenov was the chairman. On the due date, the Biafra European Bank in London refused to honour the promissory note, since the services were not rendered and could not be rendered because of the blockade against Biafra. 'Overnight,' Kutzenov shouted, 'I find myself ruined because of Dubien and your Government.' Chief Iweka closed the door a little tighter when he saw that tempers were rising. Professor Obelenwata recoiled as if he wanted to hide under the sheets on the double bed. Lawyer Afoukwu drew his chair and heavy stomach nearer to Arthur Kutzenov. The rest were standing or sitting with their arms akimbo.

Situations of this nature brought out the other aspect of Ifedi's character, that of a negotiator. He had an amazing way of firing dull spirits with optimism and of cooling rising volcanic tempers. When he spoke, his calm, low voice contrasted with the almost hysterical tones of Kutzenov. Ifedi tried to explain to Kutzenov the circumstances of the case, though he appeared not to be sure of the facts. He tried to swear on the sincerity of Dubien, whom he said he knew well. He personally promised that he would stake his reputation to make sure that the money, at least part of it, was paid to him soon. Arthur Kutzenov, he continued, must also demonstrate his understanding of the Biafran predicament by successfully carrying out the airlift that night. There would be other contracts and definitely he would ensure that

Kutzenov had the first option on them. 'Those who have suffered on our account must be given the first bite of the transportation cake,' Obiora Ifedi said. Tempers were cooled and even before he had finished his statement, Kutzenov had poured himself a whisky. Lawyer Afoukwu, who enjoyed drinking a lot, moved to add some ginger ale and a twist of lemon. Kutzenov waved his forefinger and shook his head as he said: 'On the rocks, please.' The entire squad laughed, for Chief Iweka was quick to add 'KU-NET-SOV on the rocks!' It was difficult to say whether they were laughing at the joke or at his inability to pronounce the dealer's last name correctly. But the laugh was healthy, for Kutzenov himself suppressed a smile and said, trying to maintain a serious look, 'Let us come back to business.'

Arthur Kutzenov now told the squad that the DC 7 had developed engine trouble and that the departure would be shifted to about five o'clock that day. That was not serious. He was expecting a call immediately to confirm the departure time. The call did come almost immediately. He was almost sure it was his call, so, without even giving the owner of the hotel room the chance to find out who was on the telephone, Kutzenov took the receiver and answered the call. 'Yes . . . Yes . . . Fine . . . Fine . . . Oui . . . Si . . . Ja . . . Jawohl . . . Entiendo . . . Okay . . . Okido.' He hung up the phone and turned slowly to the group and said that the plane could not be repaired but . . . but that two DC 3s had left Lisbon already to do the Prague run. They would arrive in Prague about two or three hours later than had been agreed, but then they could fly directly to Enugu without having to stop in Europe again.

There was silence in the room, everyone apparently trying vainly to find something to say. Kutzenov regretted the slight change in the programme and said that he had done his best. The following day, perhaps, the DC 7 would be able to fly to Prague, but he could not promise anything. At this moment, Pat Odoro telephoned again from Geneva. He wanted to find out the registration number of the DC 7 plane that was coming over to Prague. With a mixture of disappointment and optimism, Obiora Ifedi told Odoro that plans had changed slightly. Instead of the DC 7, he was going to send two DC 3 planes. He was going on to give him the registration numbers which Kutzenov was trying to dictate when Pat Odoro cut him short. Prague officials had just told him that on no account would they accept two planes in one night. Security-wise, one plane was difficult enough. It appeared that the squad had come to the end of another blind alley.

The deal had to be called off. Arthur Kutzenov was furious when he heard this. Right away he started claiming damages for breach of contract. Because of the offer, he had cancelled other commitments in order to help Ifedi. For reward, he was told that the deal was off. When asked to telex his office in Lisbon or his contacts there asking the planes not to take off, Kutzenov, with greater fury, said that the planes had taken off already and that he could not contact them again except when they were near Paris and then only by radio. By that time, they would have flown about ten hours altogether and their journey back to Lisbon would make the total number of flying hours twenty. Compensation for this must be over and above that for the loss of the contract. He would go back to his office and establish his damages. The way he was speaking, with a mixture of pleasure and fury, seemed to indicate that he was perhaps really play-acting. Some of those around, Jeff Edu and Freddy Onuoha, in particular, even suspected that he had neither a DC 7 nor a DC 3 aircraft to his name. For the seventh time in two weeks, another charter deal had come to naught.

Jean-Pierre Dubien had been right when he said that Kutzenov was a crook. Kutzenov's callousness was apparent immediately the cancellation of the deal was announced. He did not say a word about the ten thousand dollars he had in cash already. All he was interested in was the payment of damages. He knew that the squad was not anxious to go to court to contest the action, and he was eager to play on this and take advantage of the secrecy of the entire deal. He had a weapon against the squad. He had all the details, at least most of the details, about their operations in Prague. With a threat to divulge some of the information at his disposal, he hoped, perhaps, to be able to extract some more money from Obiora Ifedi. He revived his claims on the promissory note and, as he walked out, angrily threatened to hand over the case to his attorney if damages were not paid within reasonable time.

When he had gone, Professor Obelenwata and Obiora Ifedi argued for a while how much should be paid to Kutzenov in compensation. Freddy Onuoha insisted that no more money should be paid to Kutzenov at all and even thought that it might be possible to recover some of the amount he already had. It was agreed that further discussions should wait until the submission of official claims by Kutzenov.

That evening, Jean-Pierre Dubien did not call as he had promised. Forced by circumstance, Obiora Ifedi picked up the phone and called Dubien, whom he had always regarded as a reliable person. He was soft-spoken, but did not hesitate to speak rather bluntly on certain issues. Besides he had the merit of having warned Ifedi. Ifedi's spirits were low, but after speaking with Dubien over the phone, a smile showed again on his face. 'Good . . . Good . . . Excellent . . . Wonderful . . . Great,' were the words with which Ifedi ended the telephone conversation.

He explained that Dubien had said he was absolutely convinced when he left the hotel room that the deal would not come through and had already started making arrangements to find another plane for the squad. Dubien was careful to explain that transportation was not his line of business, but that he had friends who could help on purely humanitarian grounds. His field was actually Finance and Banking, though he had read engineering at Oxford University. (Maybe that explains why he had never practised engineering for one single day: he should have gone to Cambridge perhaps.) He promised to bring more details after dinner. Mr Ifedi at that juncture invited him over to dinner. Such a meeting would also give them the opportunity to examine other outstanding issues.

As Obiora Ifedi reported the conversations later, they were very warm and fruitful. He believed that the squad had hit the right man. Before Ifedi could ask Dubien how the highly secret document Kutzenov showed him that afternoon ever got into the hands of that crook, Dubien explained that his company had sub-contracted General Business Associates to do a small fraction of the deal, knowing that they could accomplish it. Only a copy of the contract was shown to Kutzenov and his associates and the story of its being signed over to them was pure fabrication. This revelation completely won over Obiora Ifedi, especially since he was in the mood to believe anything about Kutzenov.

Dubien had made arrangements for a Super Constellation to do the Prague run the following day. Obiora Ifedi made it clear that he would not pay any advance to him, but was willing to pay seventy per cent once the plane had done the Prague trip and taken off from Lisbon on its way to Enugu. Dubien explained to him the risks involved in the airlift, the expenses involved in recruiting the crew, the insurance, the fuelling and airport fees. However, as a special gesture, he agreed to persuade his friends to assume those expenses just to demonstrate their good faith. This mark of good faith was so touching that Ifedi, according to his own report, was even moved to offer to pay immediately the entire amount involved.

The following day, contact was made with Odoro in Geneva. He announced that Prague officials could not handle any plane within the next few days because of Soviet Bloc military man-oeuvres in the vicinity of Prague. He promised to call back the following day and report. The next day, all was fine and Odoro took the names of the pilots and the registration of the plane, so that he could communicate them to Ruddy Nnewi in Prague. The chances of approval looked excellent. Everything for the first time that week seemed set and sound. Most of the day was calm and Ifedi slept all morning, waiting for the confirmation word from Prague so that a mutually convenient time could be fixed.

Word did finally come from Prague, but it was negative. The Prague authorities would not allow the plane to land because of the nationality of the pilots, who were West Germans. At that stage in the game, it was difficult to tell whether Prague or Paris agents were carrying out this exasperating drill, or even whether they were all participating. Odoro was summoned to Paris for immediate consultations. He regretted that he could not come for a week. He was also asked to bring Ruddy Nnewi to Paris for a general meeting. It was then that Pat Odoro confessed that he had not made contact with Ruddy Nnewi for some two weeks. He added also that he had been dealing directly with the army officers in Prague. The equipment in Prague allegedly cost two hundred thousand dollars, but there were no receipts showing actual payment of this sum. Neither did the buyer, Odoro, go to Prague to investigate the merchandise he was buying.

Dubien was very understanding when he learned about the Prague answer and pledged that he would continue to do his best if his services were needed. He was sad that the plane had been immobilized for two days in succession, but what appeared to pain him most was his inability to send at least ten tons of ammunition for the defence of the country at war. Unlike Kutzenov, he asked for no damages.

In the light of the situation in Prague, some members of the squad, in particular Jeff Edu and Freddy Onuoha, now began to wonder if Prague really did exist, and, if it did, whether there were arms really stocked there, and, if there were, whether they had really been paid for. It was, therefore, decided to try to move the wares in Lisbon, which had been paid for and which really did exist. Jean-Pierre Dubien offered to do the run in question. Obiora Ifedi thanked him profusely, saying that he knew he would always come to his aid. He spent the next few minutes wondering what he would do to recompense Dubien appropriately.

The craft of Dubien's associates was parked at Toulouse-Blagnac airport, not far, Dubien himself emphasized, from the factory that was constructing the Anglo-French supersonic jet-liner Concorde. This association raised in the minds of the onlookers the question of the speed and value of the Super Constellation Dubien was offering. Because of the nature of the operation and for reasons of economy (as a banker and financier, Dubien was very particular about spending money well) he hoped that the plane would not have to come to Paris. It was agreed that from Toulouse it would head directly for Lisbon.

Mr Ifedi and Professor Obelenwata wanted to send some provisions home to their families and Lawyer Afoukwu wanted to go home and look after his property. Before he had left Enugu, as the manager of the British Housing Corporation of Enugu, he had locked up all the houses so that they would not be commandeered for military purposes or for housing new administrations. He was getting worried that his prolonged absence might give the army boys an opportunity to claim the beautiful residential houses on some pretext or other. Dubien suggested to them that one or two people could leave Paris on a commercial flight to join the plane in Toulouse and proposed that they take the Paris-Toulouse flight going out that night. Obiora Ifedi, Chancellor Obelenwata and Peter Afoukwu talked in low whispers for a while and suggested that the trip be fixed for the following day so that the Lisbon officials could be informed in time. The extra day would also give them time to do their shopping in Paris the following morning.

Chief Iweka was not averse to shopping and thought that it was a good way to spend his *estacode*. *Estacode* is the living allowance paid to those in the diplomatic service while they are serving abroad. Very astute diplomatic servants can make lots of money this way. They collect their *estacode* in advance on arrival for a planned ten-day trip. At the same time, they collect transportation allowance. Having received these, they usually get an Embassy official to drive them around in his private car and, on the morning of their departure, because they are in a terrible hurry, they usually rush off in a taxi, leaving their hotel bills to be paid by the Embassy. The Embassy of course pays with a smile, since it booked the reservation to begin with. Besides, these perambulatory diplomatic servants are so powerful that they can get the most efficient foreign-based officer sacked with a stroke of their pen or a word from their mouth. The officer abroad therefore pays the bill with a smile and is given a good pat on the back by the itinerant ambassador, for the sake of his conscience, when he next comes abroad. The 'Code of General Directions' issued in Lagos during the civilian regime by the Nigerian Government stipulated that a junior officer should on no account embarrass his senior officer. Some itinerant ambassadors, the smoother operators amongst them, claim their *estacode* in one foreign post and pass the period in another post where they leave their bills unpaid. Though the responsible officers in charge of the posts helplessly complain to each other over the telephone, no written record is kept of the complaint and such dissatisfaction is not supposed to show when the officer drives the visiting diplomat to the airport or when he carries his luggage to the counter.

So, the following day was spent shopping. Lawyer Afoukwu wanted to shop at the Samaritaine, Professor Obelenwata wanted to go to the Galeries Lafayette and Obiora Ifedi said that he normally did his shopping at Aux Trois Quartiers. Chief Iweka did not have any preference except that he just wanted to send home something bought from the Champs-Elysées. He pronounced the word 'CHARMS EL OASIS', thus setting off a chain of coughing and tearful laughter all round the room. After the laughter had subsided, all of them complained about the difficulty of the French language. They all agreed that English was much easier, a compliment that would have pleased their English friends if they had been around. Chief Iweka's ignorance of French was understandable since his schooling was limited, but he made an effort, even though he pronounced French words like Arabic. Obiora Ifedi used to claim that he could read and understand French, but that he could not speak it at all. Later on, after four days in Paris, he acknowledged that his understanding of the French language had gone down to nil. A week later, when he was shown an article in *Le Figaro* about his visit to the United States, he asked the secretary-typist Ndubisi, who had only been studying French for two weeks, to try to translate for him quotations from his own speech: people around him concluded that he could not read well without his glasses. When this happened again when he had his glasses on, Edu and Onuoha concluded that his reading knowledge had depreciated also. Professor Obelenwata had at least the honesty of not claiming to read, write, speak or understand French. His ignorance was such that he could not even convince his two jaws to move apart and articulate the common phrase, 'Bonjour Monsieur', even with an Arabic accent.

Shopping at the Galeries Lafayette can be quite slow especially when one decides to use the *carnet d'achats*, which entitles the buyer to a twenty per cent reduction if he pays in dollars or some other European currency. The buyer spends some two hours waiting to get his bill and packages and starts wondering if the reduction is worth the time spent. Things moved quite fast at the Samaritaine, but it was exhausting climbing stairs and rushing from one building to another, looking for all the articles Lawyer Afoukwu wanted to buy in one of those five separate stores, which are linked together by a twenty-four-hour traffic jam. The shopping at Aux Trois Quartiers was definitely the easiest, but by far the most expensive. When the personal cars of Edu and Onuoha could not carry all the goods they had purchased to Hotel Lutetia the hotel had to rent a special truck to go and collect them. It was at the Galeries Lafayette that Obiora Ifedi suddenly discovered, after waiting some two hours for his packages, that he had used up his last cheque. He had an account in every European country. It was an embarrassing moment when Obiora Ifedi turned and invited Jeff Edu to help. With more than four hundred inquisitive French eyes staring and watching everything on the counter, it was not right to allow a superior officer to remain embarrassed much longer. Obiora Ifedi thanked Edu and promised to give him back the amount. Jeff Edu smiled and put the government account cheque book back in his pocket.

Bell boys at the Lutetia Hotel started running up and down when they saw signs of affluence, for tips normally followed close behind. A bell boy opened the car door as Obiora Ifedi arrived, dusted his shoes with an immaculate white handkerchief, took his brief-case in one hand, his umbrella in another and still found one to accept the tip. At the door of the elevator, the service boy smiled and held the door until he got his tip, even though the lift was automatic. On the fifth floor, another service boy held the elevator door open for Obiora Ifedi and ushered him to his door and kept it open until Mr Ifedi remembered to hand him over something discreetly. Quite often, the stewards went out of their way to ask Mr Ifedi if he had called for a drink, for with each drink came a compulsory fifteen per cent charge for service. Nor would the visitor forget the receptionist because when he had a phone call, she walked straight down to the lounge and tapped him on the back, saying: 'There is a phone call for you, sir,' as the rest of the common folk sat in the lounge wondering who the V.I.P. so well known in the hotel could be. With less generous clients, the receptionist usually sent a small porter with a bell and a board marked with the name of the person wanted, ringing and inviting him to come and answer his call. Most important, if one of the Parisian girls the client met in the night-club the day before came to keep an appointment in the hotel, the tipped bell-boy could usher her discreetly into the client's room without his having to come down and find her, blushing if he were not too black. Some of the French girls get too friendly. They kiss their customers on both cheeks when they see them in the hotel lobby, as if they had known them all their lives. What makes it more embarrassing is that everyone in the lobby knows who the visiting ladies are. Professor Obelenwata and Obiora Ifedi were very well known at the hotel. When Edu or Onuoha telephoned them from outside, the receptionist, whether they gave the name or the number of their rooms, usually supplied the other, with the memory of a private secretary automatically transferring a call to her boss.

Evening dresses from Dior, perfume from Nina Ricci, shoes from Raoul of Paris, scarves from the Champs-Elysées and women's magazines from the Drug-Store were amongst the smaller articles Samson Anele was to take home for the squad. Though Samson Anele was to take home for the group the packages they had bought and deliver them personally to their families, he was actually being sent home because he was carrying a very important confidential hand-written message for the Enugu Government. Professor Obelenwata honoured him with the title of 'Special Courier'. Whenever he or Obiora Ifedi had some provisions to send to their families, a special courier usually accompanied these. Samson Anele was a relation of Obiora Ifedi.

Everyone was at the airport to see Lawyer Afoukwu and the Special Courier off to Toulouse. A small incident marred the day. In front of Hotel Lutetia, there were several taxis waiting in line for passengers. Obiora Ifedi refused to take the Peugeot 403 in front and insisted on going to the airport in the Black Citroën behind: this definitely looked more majestic and ministerial. To avoid arriving late at the airport, both taxis had to be engaged. The pick-up truck, Edu's car and Onuoha's and the two taxis gave the trip to the airport the air of a motorcade. As luck or fate would have it, there was an ambulance rushing to the Autoroute du Sud to pick up some people injured in a car collision. The Ifedi squad motorcade followed closely behind as the ambulance blazed a trail with its siren.

Monsieur Georges Blanc, Dubien's associate, accompanied the group to the airport and was going to travel to Toulouse with Lawyer Afoukwu and Samson Anele. Tickets were bought for the three of them. The amount paid for excess baggage was enough to give a young couple a Concorde trip round the world and a two-week Cunard cruise on the Queen Elizabeth from New York to the Caribbean islands. But there was a sigh of relief that all the arrangements had been made. Professor Obelenwata was happy that his family would have enough to keep them going for another six weeks.

The group watched the luggage leave the check-in counter and head for the loading platform where a truck would pick it up and carry it to the plane. It was fascinating watching the luggage moving automatically to the loading zone. Somehow, it was difficult for the watcher to overcome the fear that it might end up on the wrong platform, in the wrong plane and at the wrong destination. 'Nowadays,' Lawyer Afoukwu remarked as they looked, 'It appears to be a blessing if this does happen, for the passenger can sue the company for an exaggerated value of the lost material, especially if he knows how to calculate the importance of lost man-hours and the monetary value of mental anguish.'

Those who were not travelling paid one franc each to go out on the upper platform of Orly Airport. The departure of the flight was announced and Lawyer Afoukwu carried his stomach heavily towards the departure area, followed by Samson Anele who struggled along behind, carrying both his own and the lawyer's brief-case. The rest waved goodbye and Obiora Ifedi was moving towards the newspaper stand to buy the *Financial*

Times of London when the hostess who had sold them the tickets ran up to him. Ifedi was surprised when the small pretty Air France hostess touched him on the back. He turned round with his usual gallantry and released a smile as if he had known her for years. Ifedi must have found the cheeks of the lady irresistible, for he bent down and smacked her a kiss. The lady turned the other cheek, apparently obeying the admonitions of the gospel. 'A phone call for you, sir,' she finally told him.

Obiora Ifedi followed the hostess to the information desk on the first floor and there took the receiver. Meanwhile, Chief Iweka had gone to the Duty Free Shop to look at some of the leather goods there, while Professor Obelenwata drew as near to the schedule as he could to survey the time-table for planes. Even with glasses, he was still myopic. Edu and Onuoha went with Obiora Ifedi to help him out with the French if need be. At first, Onuoha thought it was a call from the departure gate from Peter Afoukwu who perhaps had forgotten something or wanted to leave a final message. When Ifedi saw them, he turned and gasped in despair. His face changed and Onuoha rushed to his side.

Ifedi was speaking on the phone: 'You say that the plane cannot leave tonight again ... Because of engine trouble ... The passengers are about to leave already ... Can't they wait in Toulouse while the plane is being repaired? ... You do not advise this then ... You do not think that the plane will be ready within the next ten days ... You mean they should not go to Toulouse then ... But their luggage is already in the plane and they will be leaving any moment now ...'

Ifedi could not take it any longer. He handed the telephone over to Onuoha and asked Edu to go and tell Peter Afoukwu and Samson Anele to come back if the plane had not left. Onuoha asked Jean-Pierre Dubien, who was on the telephone, what the matter was. Dubien was pleased that Onuoha was on the phone and begged leave to explain himself in French. He said that everything humanly possible had been done by his associates but, as the pilots were trying to test-fly the plane which had been immobilized for three days, one of the engines had developed trouble. Immediately the best engineers in the hangar were called out to work on the plane. The entire operation had cost his associates more than ten thousand dollars, but they felt so strongly about the disappointment that they were not even going to lodge any complaints about the expenses. He begged Onuoha to try and explain to Obiora Ifedi what had happened. Dubien said that he was an engineer and knew what problems a faulty engine could cause. 'Surely, you do not want the plane to take off from here and then crash over Sierra Leone or in the Atlantic Ocean,' he concluded. Onuoha naturally said no, adding that such a crash would cause loss of life and loss of valuable and scarce equipment. 'Sure!' Dubien said with relief. He promised to continue his search for a plane. Ifedi took over the phone again and asked Jean-Pierre Dubien if he could come over that night and see him at the hotel. Dubien said that he would be busy all night contacting all his friends to see if he could find a plane to do the run. Concluding, Jean-Pierre said, 'That would certainly be more useful than my sitting with you all evening and drinking whisky!' Ifedi had no alternative but to agree with him and there the phone conversation ended.

Professor Obelenwata had finished surveying the timetable and Chief Iweka had bought a beautiful gold-trimmed leather pass-port-case for his wife—or rather, for one of them, since he had five at home. The reappearance of Peter Afoukwu and Samson Anele told them the story. 'You mean to tell me that you missed the plane. You must have been looking at the hostesses you saw on the way,' Professor Obelenwata said, addressing Peter Afoukwu. He could not believe it when Obiora Ifedi told him what had happened.

The Ifedi squad trooped back to Paris in private cars and taxis. As chance would have it, Ifedi had to ride back in the same Peugeot 403 car he had rejected earlier. Morale was extremely low: no one talked. It was only on Lawyer Afoukwu's insistence that the squad decided to go and have dinner at the Escale à Hongkong, a decent Chinese Restaurant on Boulevard Montparnasse. As they sat down at the desk, Obiora Ifedi, who was well known in the restaurant, told the waiter 'As usual'. Lawyer Afoukwu ordered the 'whole fish' dish with sugar sauce, which was meant for two people, and a bottle of Muscadet to wash it down. The rest ordered various dishes. Though the menu was in English, French and Chinese, Chief Iweka insisted on ordering his dinner in French. But the ensuing laughter did little to revive the appetites of some of them, as they dipped their oriental spoons into the 'potage chinois aux vermicelles'.

The Grey Ghost

The war had broken out six weeks previously. Freddy Onuoha and Jeff Edu were in the small Paris Office, the Biafra Historical Research Centre, on a Friday afternoon, 7 July 1967, when the white telephone on the desk rang. The call came from London. The message was brief. There was no time for questions, details or expatiations. Edu turned round as he put back the receiver and told Onuoha, 'War broke out yesterday on the northern borders. We have gained and lost territory at various points.' 'Any other details?' Onuoha asked him. 'None. The speaker was in a great hurry. He was out of breath. He did not even wait to identify himself.'

A chilly feeling ran through Onuoha as he pondered over the news, sad news indeed. Edu pulled him down as he stood there gazing into space and asked him to kneel for a prayer. It had been a long time since Onuoha had last gone to church. Out of deference, and also overcome by fear—like one about to die—and deep emotion, Onuoha now knelt down with Edu and prayed, prayed for peace.

Onuoha and Edu had seen the war coming. The two sides in the struggle had been preparing feverishly for six months. They saw it coming like the rain, but now a deluge had overtaken them by surprise. Somehow, the mind knew it was inevitable, but the heart daily hoped and prayed that a debacle could be avoided.

It was exactly one month after the Arab-Israeli War, the famous six-day war that saw Israel triple the size of her territory. The average Biafran knew that his new nation could perform the same miracle if it had the means. But Biafra had not the means and its independence was barely one month old, independence that was declared in the dark, independence that started with a total blockade of the country, independence that was celebrated with mourning in every family.

The citizens had no illusions about their strength, but they were not to be discouraged. In the city, the petty trader would tell you that the Biafran Government had twelve Mirage Jet Fighters—the type the Israelis used—waiting in Israel for the beginning of the Nigeria-Biafra War. In the village, the farmer knew for certain that if the Nigerians attacked by sea, the Biafran Navy would line the coasts with the debris of the Nigerian Navy. If they attacked by land, the Biafran People's Liberation Army would push the northern borders to the banks of the River Benue. If they dared violate Biafran air-space with their Tiger Moth Air Force, the Biafran Air Force would carry the war right to the limits of the Nigerian territory. Seasoned Biafran diplomats carried around heavy files predicting the number of nations that would recognize the young nation's independence within two weeks. To support his claims one such diplomat with ten years' experience recounted with little discretion the story of how a British Government representative asked him if Biafra would be embarrassed if Great Britain became the first nation to recognize it. Seasoned in diplomacy, he advised the British official to wait until Russia did so, otherwise the latter would say that Biafran independence was Westerned-inspired like that of the secessionists of Katanga. Sandhurst-trained officers in the Biafran Army would confirm all this by emphasizing the weakness of Nigeria and its ability to muster no more than forty thousand rabble soldiers officered by illiterate sons of Emirs.

Behind this confidence lay the undeclared conviction that the nations of the world would intervene quickly. The African nations had done so during other inter-African disputes between Kenya and Somalia, Somalia and Ethiopia and during the Algeria-Morocco border dispute. The United Nations, as the members had done in the Arab-Israeli War, would move to impose a cease-fire within four days of the start of fighting. Jeff Edu himself was sure that this would happen. Discretion is the better part of valour. The Biafran Army had only enough material to last four weeks for three thousand troops, plus some odd left-overs to hold the cease-fire line for another six weeks if need be.

The war had started and had gone on for eighteen hours before the first word of it reached the outside world. That Friday evening, after hearing about the war, Professor Nwoke, who was on a special mission in Europe, decided to go back to Biafra by way of the Camerouns. 'My fate lies with my people. I must return to suffer and die if I have to with them,' he declared. Friends advised him to wait a few days and see how the war would go. Professor Nwoke refused. Onuoha and Edu were deeply moved and wanted to go back to Biafra with him. He ordered them—he had to command for them to listen—to stay in Paris, for they would have very important missions to fulfil abroad. They had been overseas for the past six or eight years and their experience would be very handy during the difficult days ahead. It was with tears in their eyes that Edu and Onuoha bade farewell to Professor Nwoke at the Paris airport, Le Bourget, from where he took a U.T.A. flight for Douala in the Camerouns. From Douala, he would travel by way of Tiko and Mamfe and along the Ikom road to Biafra, if the roads in question had not been cut off by the enemy before his arrival.

Professor Nwoke was a calm and intelligent person. He spoke French quite well and had an exceptionally sharp mind, able to comprehend without labour, courageous in character, magnanimous in behaviour. He lived in Paris and did very useful work for six full weeks, without a word getting into the press about his movements. He stayed in a small studio in Neuilly, not far from Jeff Edu, did his own cooking and washed his own linen. He was a pleasure to work with and when he travelled, for instance to Germany to build up support for Biafra amongst the nationals there, all he needed was one suit for meetings and a few shirts which he washed every night before retiring. Once when Jeff Edu joked with him about his austere behaviour, Professor Nwoke laughed and said: 'You knew me before all this trouble started, I enjoyed living a comfortable life. I have several houses at home, three cars in the family and when I travel about, I stay in the best hotels. Our nation has suffered a lot. Each night when I sit down to have a light supper, I lose my appetite when I remember the myriads of mothers and children sleeping in refugee camps in Biafra. The war has not broken out yet, but you can assume that we are already in a state of war.'

That same Friday evening, several emissaries had arrived in

Europe from Biafra. Some came to Paris, others were on their way to London and New York. Among them were Obiora Ifedi, Chancellor Obelenwata, Tobias Iweka and Peter Afoukwu. They all held important offices in the newly independent government, advising on political affairs, economic programmes, the establishment of new universities and institutes of technology, the organization of national insurance companies, new airlines and new shipping lines. Their attachment to the cause of the revolution helped greatly to mobilize the people for the days ahead. Their voices were heard daily on radio and television, giving hope and courage to those few who faltered along the way. Having worked very hard for the cause of peace at home in Biafra, when the first shots were fired, they flew out of the country to defend overseas the young Republic whose existence was threatened militarily at home. They would help purchase arms for the fighting men at home and also let the world know, beyond any shadow of doubt, of the unmistakable determination of their people to fight to the bitter end, to the last man. Fortunately, they had at their disposal a handsome treasury of foreign exchange which Professor Nwoke had accumulated for the government before his return to Biafra, most of it raised from his friends and their contacts.

Six weeks had gone by and there was still no cease-fire. Nor had any nation recognized the new Republic. Meanwhile, the borders had changed, but not in favour of the new Republic. The armoury was empty and the end was nowhere in sight.

As the dinner progressed at the Escale à Hongkong, tongues loosened, thanks to the dryness of the Muscadet and the Château-neuf-du-Pape which Ifedi had ordered at mid-course. Peter Afoukwu was deeply worried about not leaving that night. When he had left Enugu, he was hoping the war would be over in six weeks. Peter Afoukwu had clashed with the army boys and certain young members of the Science Group, a group of young university graduates and professors who got together to produce weapons for the war, and salt and drugs for the population. In the absence of living quarters, these young professors had wanted to use as offices and residences some of the houses belonging to the British Housing Corporation of Enugu, since they were empty following the departure of the expatriate staff that formerly had been living there.

Lawyer Afoukwu maintained strongly that the army boys and young scientists were unworthy to live there. He would not mind letting someone like Professor Chancellor Obelenwata, Chief Tobias Iweka or Obiora Ifedi live in the houses because they were men of status. He would never live to see those nonentities step into the houses. Freddy Onuoha was furious when Lawyer Afoukwu made the comment. Onuoha considered it a very unpatriotic attitude. He spoke perhaps a little too emotionally and concluded by saying: 'It is most regrettable that these boys who are fighting day and night at the front for your survival, to save your house and property, are considered to be unworthy even to enter your home. And yet they shed their blood, the greatest gift they have, their lives, for your future happiness.' Lawyer Afoukwu was unmoved and said that if the boys did not want to fight, they should come back from the front. 'Then the Hausas will come into Enugu and occupy your house,' Onuoha added. With infuriating contempt, Lawyer Afoukwu said: 'I'd rather see the house destroyed by the Hausas than live to see those bastards enter and soil a house my company built.'

Peter Afoukwu then spoke about his house in Aba. If the enemy destroyed the ones in Enugu, he could always retire to Aba. Chief Iweka agreed that Lawyer Afoukwu had one of the best houses in Aba. It was fabulous, like the People's Palaces of the civilian government era. Peter Afoukwu did add that he would with joy let the Chief Justice of the country move into one of the houses in Enugu, but definitely not the young upstart professors belonging to the Science Group. Professor Obelenwata, in turn, spoke of his country home, simple but magnificent, and said that he was looking forward to retiring there after the war, that is, if the Government did not force him to represent the young Republic at the United Nations. Ifedi lived in a government house in Enugu and before leaving the country had taken the precaution of moving most of his property into his country house or one of his country houses in the village. Of course, the enemy was still far from Enugu and all well-informed sources, civilian and military alike, agreed that Enugu was impregnable. Besides, the determination of the citizens was such that they would rather die than see their capital fall into the hands of the enemy.

Chocolate ice-cream for Lawyer Afoukwu, cheese for Mr Ifedi, tea for Chief Iweka and Professor Obelenwata and water for the rest—dinner came to an end and they all drove back to their base at Hotel Lutetia. The Secretary-Typist Ndubisi had been there waiting for the group. He had in his hand some telegrams and urgent telex messages. One of them read as follows:

MOST IMMEDIATE

TOP PRIORITY

TOP PRIORITY

TOP PRIORITY

FOR COMMISSIONER IFEDI, REPEATED PROFESSOR OBELENWATA, CHIEF IWEKA, LAWYER AFOUKWU, ENVOY ODORO AND SPECIAL REPRESENTATIVE RUDDY NNEWI—MESSAGE BEGINS QUOTE: SITUATION CRITICAL—NOT A SINGLE LOAD SINCE PROFESSOR NWOKE LEFT PARIS—SHOULD WE GIVE UP—ENEMY HAS BROKEN THROUGH BORDERS—OUR TROOPS HAVE BROKEN ALL BRIDGES TO STEM ENEMY ADVANCE—SITUATION CRITICAL REPEAT CRITICAL—URGENTLY NEED RIFLES COMMA AMMUNITION ALL CALIBRES COMMA BAZOOKAS—CONFIRM ACTION IS BEING TAKEN WITHIN TWENTY FOUR HOURS— DEFENCE SECRETARY—UNQUOTE—MESSAGE ENDS. TOP PRIORITY—TOP PRIORITY—TOP PRIORITY—TOP—

The message came in code. Professor Obelenwata was shaking when he read the message and asked everyone what could be done to save the situation. Lawyer Afoukwu said that if he had known that things would be as bad as that, he would have evacuated some of his property in Enugu. He had more than one thousand bottles of champagne sitting in his cellar. Obiora Ifedi was less moved. He said that the situation was not desperate. He was used to receiving messages like that. People at home believed, he said, that frantic messages like that would make them work harder, not knowing that they were fighting night and day trying to get the equipment moving. Chief Iweka added that it was difficult for people at home to conceive of the amount of exertion and anxiety those of them abroad suffered as they tried to charter a single plane to carry arms and ammunition home. He promised that when he got back to Biafra after the war, he would get everything straight. Those who worked abroad deserved real credit for winning the war.

The war was far from over. It was merely beginning and, before they could start winning, equipment had to be moved to the fighting forces at home. Precautions perhaps could have been taken, long before actual hostilities broke out, to form a government transportation company and a shipping line. A study had been done to that effect by the young professors and officers of the navy and air force, but not a word had been heard about this again. Later on, news filtered out that, faithful to the principle of private free enterprise, a group of leading businessmen had obtained the monopoly for operating the shipping and air freight companies. The Board of Directors of the companies included Obiora Ifedi, Chief Iweka, Pat Odoro and Ruddy Nnewi. Their legal adviser was Lawyer Afoukwu. It was to organize this company that the group had left the country the very day that the first battle shots were fired in the Nsukka, Obudu, Gakem and Eha-Amufu borders. Before long, other overseas representatives were to join them in Europe, once they had prepared the ground.

The war had broken out and it had become more difficult to buy things openly in the name of the unrecognized Republic. At first, the new company thought it would be possible to charter planes from other companies to carry the war materials, like other African airlines that operate with planes borrowed or chartered from European airlines. For a country in rebellion, however, the only open market was the black market of white businessmen. The new company had the money because the new Republic had lent it a substantial amount to help launch the new enterprise. The events of the past six weeks had shown that it would be very difficult. Also, as a private company based on cost-accounting, the board members wanted to make sure that they did not pay so much to the charter companies that they would impoverish for-ever the future share-holders of the company about to be formed. Also, the Board of Directors had to be paid for their services while abroad.

In the face of these almost insuperable difficulties, Professor Obelenwata suggested that they buy their own planes for the operation. The government could advance them some more money and they could pay back to the government by forfeiting a certain percentage of the cost of each charter trip. As if someone had been listening to everything they had said that night, a journalist appeared and told them that he could suggest some very reliable contacts. The journalist was Joel Bouchara. Obiora Ifedi had met him when he had come to Biafra long before the war started to report on the situation and interview all the important members of the government. Ifedi had been very nice to him and Bouchara had reported some of his experiences in Biafra in Euro-pean newspapers, mentioning Mr Ifedi's important role in the government several times in the course of the article.

The day after the collapse of Dubien's scheme, Joel Bouchara appeared at the Hotel Lutetia accompanied by two men, both of whom were black. Joel Bouchara was a *pied-noir*, one of those who returned to France after the Algerian War of Independence. With him came the two men, one old, the other young. The elderly man was introduced as Colonel Ochar Lavignette, one of the West Indians who had served directly under General de Gaulle during the Second World War. Colonel Lavignette had attended the famous meeting in Gabon in 1945 during which the illustrious French General had promised French citizenship to all French-speaking Africans and West Indians. This of course explained the French citizenship of Colonel Lavignette. He did not understand a word of English and spoke French with a military accent. Beside him stood the young Dr Eugene Fresco, lighter in complexion, taller, well-built, well-fed, almost like an American, impeccable in manners. He stood very straight and there was a trace of superiority about him when he spoke. Dr Fresco had an encyclo-paedic memory and seemed to be quite at home in many fields. As he entered the room, he was carrying a bundle of newspapers.

From the way he spoke, he could have passed easily as a distinguished professor of current affairs, but he claimed that he had got his degree from Oxford, though he did not mention in what year or what subject.

Joel Bouchara merely introduced them and left the room. He had to be back in his office and did not seem interested in what followed. As a journalist, business had no interest for him and he only wanted to help because he was sentimentally linked to Obiora Ifedi. Professor Obelenwata was highly impressed by Dr Fresco's manners and the latter reminded him of his very young days as a Doctor of Philosophy, teaching the history of Ancient Greece. For Professor Obelenwata, history was a science and he liked to refer to himself quite often as a scientist. He would prefix several of his statements with the phrase, 'As a scientist . . .' The presence of Dr Fresco in the group revived his spirits and for the first time during his stay in the French capital, he felt that he had met someone who was his intellectual equal, and this created a good rapport between the two of them. Dr Fresco always addressed him with profuse courtesy. Somehow in the course of the discussions, Mr Ifedi was phased out and Professor Obelenwata became the central negotiator for the Ifedi squad, and acted as the middle-man between the squad and the West Indians.

Colonel Ochar Lavignette appeared to have some difficulty pronouncing the name of Professor Obelenwata and decided just simply to call him *Professor*, always with a slight bow of the head. Professor Obelenwata in turn had difficulty pronouncing the Colonel's name, therefore he took the liberty of just calling him *Colonel*, but with all the deference due to someone very close to General de Gaulle. Hence when the Professor talked about Colonel Lavignette to third parties, he always spoke of him as the Colonel and the whole world understood whom he meant.

The Colonel's proposals were simple. Colonel Lavignette spoke in French, Dr Fresco interpreted in impeccable English. Professor Obelenwata, whenever he opened his mouth to speak, tried to recover some of the Oxford accent he had acquired at Trinity College, Dublin, with the result that his diction was slow and premeditated, but not necessarily profound. Because it took him a long time to understand other people, Professor Obelenwata had the tendency of harping on minor points to make himself clear, as if he had some difficulty following his own explanations. It took him a little longer to comprehend people's ideas. As Obiora Ifedi had once remarked in a moment of rare insight, it took Professor Obelenwata archaeological years to understand what any other professor would grasp in a few minutes. Therefore, with the Professor at the helm and with discussions centring on business, it required all the intelligence and patience of Dr Fresco to convey for the Professor's understanding the brief remarks about piloting, insurance and company law made by Colonel Lavignette.

Dr Fresco and Colonel Lavignette presented a very generous plan to help the squad buy their own planes and offered to help in the course of the negotiations. As black people, they were naturally moved by what was going on in Biafra and were willing to help because, deep within them, they felt they belonged to that part of the world. Separated by language and the Atlantic Ocean, they were nevertheless all one in colour. Thanks to the white man, they had rediscovered their identity. Such were the introductory remarks of Colonel Lavignette, embellished and ennobled by the translations and expatiations of Dr Fresco. Professor Obelenwata took the opportunity to deliver a brief lecture on the slave trade across the Atlantic and by the end of his speech, it became quite apparent that probably the forefathers of Dr Fresco and Colonel Lavignette came from the heart of Biafra.

Following the experiences of the past few weeks, Colonel Lavignette's offer appeared fantastic at first. It was Professor Obelenwata's optimism and enthusiasm that got everyone involved in it. Obiora Ifedi was so diffident about the proposal, he decided that his company would stay out of that one. In addition to buying a plane, the Colonel would help in procuring the insurance, spare parts for replacement and pilots to ferry the plane between Europe and Biafra. It was too good to be true and, deep within himself, Ifedi laughed his head off. But the Professor was entranced more by the diction of Dr Fresco than by the logic of the proposals, and monosyllables continued to fall from his lips: 'Yes ... Yes ... Yes ... Wonderful!' His comprehension appeared incredible that day. This impression was marred, however, by frequent questions the Professor asked about what the Colonel and Dr Fresco had explained three times over. Chief Iweka had to come in once in a while to further elaborate the point in Igbo. Colonel Lavignette assured the Professor that the negotiations were to be done secretly and that the negotiations would not start until the Professor had himself seen the plane in question. Besides, the deal would be with a reputable company, directly, without intermediaries. To give the Professor more confidence in the project, Colonel Lavignette promised to take him along that day to see the engineering director of Air Branco. The Professor was enchanted. Even when the two visitors left, the Professor spoke of nothing but Dr Fresco the whole day. The others were a little bit more sceptical and cool to the proposals. But a drowning man will cling to a straw, to anything; in the same way and in the absence of anything else, the Fresco gamble seemed to be worth taking. Freddy Onuoha wanted to go along with Professor Obelenwata, but Colonel Lavignette thought that a crowd of black men at the place in question would attract unnecessary attention. So the Professor had to go along with them.

The optimism of the Professor, instead of diminishing, increased when he came back from the visit. He could scarcely hide his amazement. The plane in question was one of a fleet of discarded but reconditioned Super Constellation G planes, phased out a few years earlier by Air Branco. According to the Professor, Colonel Lavignette took him to the office of the Engineering Director of Air Branco where they drank cocktails and champagne. The room he described sounded very much like the V.I.P. lounge at the airport terminal, but he assured everyone that it was the office of the Engineering Director. He was quick to point out that, for the first time, direct contact had been made with the dealers involved. He had also seen the plane himself and there were more than fifteen engineers overhauling it. The Engineering Director assured him that the plane would receive a certificate of air-worthiness from Air Branco before it took off. While not trying to read too much meaning into its significance, the Professor pointed out that Air Branco was a government-controlled company and the Colonel someone very close to General de Gaulle. Also, to avoid any misunderstanding, the contract was to be drawn up in English and French. After the catalogue of assurances, the Professor spoke on a more serious note. The deal must be concluded by ten the following morning. According to the Colonel, the plane had already been offered to other buyers who had paid a deposit on it, but exceptionally, because of their attachment to Biafra, they would hold off the signature of the contract that night to give Professor Obelenwata the opportunity to make an offer. If the Professor did not react by the following morning, Air Branco would feel itself under no obligation to wait and would go ahead with the delivery of the plane to the other prospective buyers.

The group was still considering the merits and demerits of these proposals when someone knocked at the door. It was Dr Eugene Fresco. Normally he telephoned before coming over, but that night, he just walked in. His eyes were red with anger and he was stammering. He put his hand in his small brief-case, brought out the photo-copy of a document and threw it before the Professor, saying: 'Look at that!' Everyone crowded around the Professor to see what the matter was. Dr Fresco explained that Colonel Ochar Lavignette was attached to the Army Intelligence during the war and through his contacts could get hold of documents of great importance within minutes. 'Look at that,' Dr Fresco continued. 'Look at what these people are trying to do to us.' By 'people' he meant the Nigerians; by 'us' he meant the Biafrans, for, after the Professor's lecture, he considered himself body and soul a son of Biafra.

The story was this. The Nigerian Government had paid about one million dollars for about thirty small fighters of the T-28 model and also for seven B-26 bombers that used to belong to NATO, but were discarded and sold to the French Army as surplus material. Colonel Lavignette had mentioned earlier that day that he was thinking of the possibility of buying two of the B-26 bombers and about five of the best T-28 fighters for the Professor. The Nigerians, it was learned, had just paid in cash for the entire lot. A private businessman had bought over the lot from the French Government and was happy to get rid of it as an entire lot instead of selling it piece-meal. There was agitation in the room, for the reinforcement of the Nigerian Air Force spelled tragedy for the new Biafra. And the question in the heart of everyone was what could be done to stop the purchase or its delivery.

As if he had read the mind of everyone, Dr Eugene Fresco, calmer now that everyone else was agitated, reassured them. Colonel Lavignette was intending to come over that night to the hotel with him, when one of his colleagues in West Germany had called and told him about the deal. He immediately telephoned his contacts in the government and they confirmed it, adding that the British government provided the Nigerians with the necessary foreign exchange. The Colonel had been busy all evening trying to stop the deal and would telephone there as soon as he had some definite information. Dr Fresco had hardly finished telling them this when the telephone rang. It was Colonel Lavignette on the phone. Dr Fresco breathed with relief as he spoke with him. His report of the conversation showed that the Colonel had succeeded in blocking the issue of an export licence for the equipment the Nigerians had bought. Dr Fresco added with wry humour, 'And because they have already handed over the cash, the blocking of the export of the equipment means that the Nigerians have in one day lost one million dollars.' As if further to demonstrate his commitment, Dr Fresco picked up the telephone and called the house of the Nigerian Defence Secretary then in Paris. He wanted to tease him about the deal and let him know that it was no longer a secret. A woman answered the telephone and asked for the identity of the caller. Dr Fresco gave his name and half a minute later, the woman said that the Nigerian Secretary was saying his evening prayers and could not speak then. Dr Fresco hung up the phone and several comments were made about the Secretary who bought war materials in the morning and prayed for salvation at night. 'And then goes to bed,' Lawyer Afoukwu added, 'to sleep with his harem of women.'

There was an air of relief in the house. A big storm had arisen and been quelled immediately. It was as if heaven had brought the

Colonel into the picture that day. Dr Fresco, shaking his head, said 'We must buy that plane, carry our arms home and teach the enemy a lesson they will never forget.' Everyone in the room at that point shared his opinion. A new confidence and a feeling of mutual trust was created between Dr Fresco and the group. Before he left the hotel room, Dr Fresco telephoned Joel Bouchara who was on duty that night at the newspaper office. Though the first edition of the newspaper had been printed, the second edition suppressed an article about revolt in the Stanleyville province of the Congo-Republic and put in a story about the foiled Nigerian arms deal signed with financial credits obtained from Great Britain. The news agencies in turn picked up the article and the next day it was echoed on the local radios and in other national papers. When Colonel Lavignette arrived in the morning at nine o'clock, an agreement was reached in principle and the Professor was even ready to sign the contract for the Super Constellation.

However, when the two parties met later on in the afternoon and sat down to negotiate, a few complications arose. Not being French citizens, Professor Obelenwata and Mr Ifedi could not buy the plane without very great difficulties, which, even if they could be overcome, would delay the ratification of the sale contract for more than three months. Even if they had been French citizens, they could not have bought the plane from Air Branco unless they were duly constituted as a company, operating a legitimate business, recognized in law and registered with the Department of Commerce. If Dr Fresco raised these difficulties, it was because he had in hand ready solutions for them. His solution was simple. He was translating the speech of the Colonel: 'Use will be made of a reputable French company. The company in question,' the Colonel said, 'has a capital of one million old French francs.' Dr Fresco translated that the company in question had a capital of one million, leaving it up to the British-trained Professor to imagine one million pounds sterling. The directors of the company were reputable and straightforward and were also committed to the survival of the new Republic of Biafra. The company in question was called Compagnie Nationale de Recherches et d'Exportations (CONAREX). All transactions would be between Air Branco and CONAREX. The latter, to facilitate transactions, would act as buying agent for Professor Obelenwata. It was understood, however, that the merchandise belonged to the new Republic, but since the latter was not recognized, an individual had to be named. The cost of the Super-Constellation, $220,000, would be paid in cash to CONAREX, who in turn would hand over the money to Air Branco in the presence of everyone. Receipts would be issued by CONAREX to Mr Ifedi, and to the Professor for the amount of money received. The question of spare parts was also discussed. The Colonel emphasized the fact that the planes were out of use and spare parts would be difficult to get. But with the co-operation of the Engineering Director of Air Branco, arrangements had been made to buy spare parts worth about $120,000. That night was the last possible time for the purchase of the spare parts because Air Branco was planning to close down all its Super-Constellation service stores.

When Professor Obelenwata and Obiora Ifedi reported the proceedings of the meeting, Onuoha and Edu had very serious misgivings about having to buy the plane in the name of a third person. Arrangements of that nature often led to complications later. Under the circumstances, it appeared that there was no alternative. The firm belief that the Air Branco administration was selling the plane gave great confidence to Professor Obelenwata and he dismissed every objection with the question: 'Do you know that Air Branco is a government-controlled company and that the Colonel is very close to General de Gaulle?' It was difficult to circumvent such arguments. The Professor firmly believed also that Colonel Lavignette was a philanthropist who had nothing to gain from the deal and that Air Branco had actually broken an earlier engagement to sell the plane, just to make it available to Biafra, due to the special relationship existing between himself and the Colonel. In a meeting behind closed doors, the advantages and disadvantages of the deal were examined. A decision was taken to go ahead and an emissary was sent to the Biafra European Bank in London requesting them to send the amount in question to Paris. These monetary transactions delayed the signature of the contract by a day.

At four o'clock on Thursday afternoon, according to schedule, the contract was to be signed in a beautiful spacious office on the third floor of a giant building on Avenue des Champs-Elysées where CONAREX had its headquarters. The office was a plush one. On the floor were bold newly painted signs marked CONAREX. On the left side of the table was the Engineering Director of Air Branco and one of his collaborators. Representing CONAREX was Monsieur Dodo Urnal, the President and General Director of the company. Colonel Lavignette was there dressed in his military uniform with all his medals and ribbons. It appeared that he had attended a luncheon organized for ex-servicemen, for his pictures appeared that day in Joel Bouchara's paper. Dr Eugene Fresco, as affable as ever, sat beside the Colonel. Professor Obelenwata and Obiora Ifedi sat right in front of them. Present was also an engineer whom Colonel Lavignette had asked to report on the condition of the plane. Before the session, the engineer reported that the plane was in excellent condition. The fact that Captain Wilheim Lang, the engineer, was a retired Air Branco pilot, added weight to his testimony. Later, on the word of the Colonel, Professor Obelenwata assured his friends that Captain Lang was the best pilot in Air Branco. Since the deal was between Air Branco and CONAREX, Mr Ifedi and Professor Obelenwata attended as observers. Also they were able to satisfy their consciences that the money was really handed over to Air Branco representatives.

The deal concluded, the Air Branco officials retired and left with the money. Colonel Lavignette took over from there. He had made arrangements for the plane to be piloted by the retired Air Branco pilot, Captain Lang. Professor Obelenwata remarked to Mr Ifedi that if Captain Lang had agreed to pilot the plane, then the plane must indeed be in excellent condition, since he would be strict in judging it. Colonel Lavignette informed the group also that he had invited three army engineers for interview in order to choose who would be the engineer on the plane. Another retired Air Branco pilot would act as co-pilot. Colonel Lavignette announced also that his pilots would contract to train Biafran pilots how to fly the Super Constellation. Professor

Obelenwata was full of thanks. A sum of ten thousand dollars was agreed upon as payment to the pilot, co-pilot and flight engineer per round trip to Biafra. Four trips a week were agreed upon and the pilots were given a firm contract of three months, payable in advance to CONAREX, who would act as honest broker for the two groups. Dr Eugene Fresco spoke at length on the nature of the sacrifice the pilots were making and how Colonel Lavignette had used his personal influence to convince them that this was a duty to be done for Biafra, for France and for humanity. The cost represented a paltry sum in connection with the great risks involved. The plane would not be covered by any insurance during the trips to Enugu, which was in the heart of a war zone. Those pilots who had already distinguished themselves with Air Branco were running the risk of losing their international licences once it was discovered that they were undertaking such adventures without full insurance coverage. Dr Fresco concluded by saying that the Colonel was using all his contacts to cover up any loop-holes in security and other arrangements.

At moments like this, Professor Obelenwata felt like shedding tears as he began in a very low and soft voice asking Dr Eugene Fresco to convey to the distinguished Colonel his own humble thanks and those of his comrades. He thanked the Colonel for his generosity. At that point Professor Obelenwata was so choked with emotion that Colonel Lavignette waved in understanding and said, turning to Dr Fresco, 'Tell the Professor that what I am doing is being done because of my special relationship with him, for myself also because I feel myself a Biafran and this is our fight for survival, for prosperity and happiness.' Dr Fresco folded his hands and enunciated the translation.

It later came out also that the Ifedi squad would have to pay for the cost of refuelling and necessary repairs as well as airport charges at the ports of call and hotel bills of the pilots while wait-ing in Lisbon to ferry the planes to Enugu and also while in Enugu. There and then an advance was paid for one month with a promise to pay the remaining two months within days of the first few flights.

A little complication then arose. It was brought out by Dodo

Urnal, the President of CONAREX. It was the question of insurance. Before the plane could take off from Orly Airport for Lisbon, international regulations required that it be insured. The insurance would not be necessary between Lisbon and Enugu, since the officials over there were willing to close their eyes over such issues. After some discussion, Dodo Urnal kindly agreed to get one of his friends to sell him a two-day insurance for the purpose of the flight. This was paid for in cash. Discussions revealed also that the pilot and co-pilot of the new plane would not be allowed to fly it out of Orly Airport, since, now that they were retired, they had lost their regular commercial pilot's licences. In actual fact, as it turned out later, one of them was facing a prison term because of fraud and the other had lost his licence because of an assault on an air hostess. These revelations would come later. It turned out also that Air Branco had absolutely no knowledge direct or indirect of the deal and that none of the men worked with the company. But still Lavignette announced that Air Branco would provide the pilots to ferry the plane to Lisbon. They would make a technical stop in Bordeaux and Wilheim Lang and his crew could join the plane there as passengers. There was no argument over this since Air Branco would assume the cost. The Colonel promised to get revalidated that night the expired licence of Captain Lang. Then came another complication: the President-Director-General of CONAREX announced solemnly that the plane could not come back to France once it had left the country since it would be difficult to get registration for it in France. Before the departure of the plane a company must be found in Lisbon to act as the buyer of the craft from CONAREX. It must be a company, not an individual.

The deal was getting more complicated and more expensive with each second that passed. The discussions had to be adjourned to make arrangements about forming the company. It was suggested that the Ifedi company register in Lisbon and 'buy' over the plane. Obiora Ifedi objected, saying that his company did not want to get involved in it. Personally he was unwilling to sign on behalf of the company. None of the others was ready to do so either. They contacted one Everly Nwomah in Lisbon and he agreed to set up a dummy company overnight to buy over the plane from CONAREX. Everly Nwomah came over from Lisbon straight away to present the papers. Professor Obelenwata, who had done most of the negotiations with Air Branco, refused to append his name on the document, even as a witness. He did not want to have anything to do with money or with buying and selling. He insisted that he was a scientist and as a scientist he did not want his name dragged down in the mud by association with businessmen and their agents. Mr Everly Nwomah decided to sign the contract of transfer and append his signature to the documents, though privately he expressed reservations about details and the terms of the contract.

After the signature of the contract, Colonel Lavignette pointed out yet another small difficulty. The pilots of the new plane had refused to take charge of the plane unless they had all the spare parts needed. Colonel Lavignette had spoken earlier about this and Dr Fresco had reminded Professor Obelenwata about its necessity. The cost of the required spare parts was $120,000 to be paid in cash to CONAREX, who would in turn issue a cheque to Air Branco. Legally, individuals could not buy and export aircraft spare parts obtained from Air Branco or government agencies. In short, Air Branco would not sell the parts directly to Mr Ifedi or to Chancellor Obelenwata. The payments were mounting up in an alarming manner for everyone, especially for the B.E.B. in London, which issued a warning that it would not make any other payments on the plane after that. But all agreed that it was unheard of to leave the new plane immobilized because of lack of spare parts. The amount was paid and everything was ready. A final visit was paid to the plane. The inside was repainted and the outside was painted grey. It looked lovely in the afternoon sun. Chancellor Obelenwata was more than satisfied with his debut into the world of contracts and diplomacy and his self-confidence had grown considerably.

At eleven on the following Monday night, everyone—Colonel Ochar Lavignette and Dr Eugene Fresco, Obiora Ifedi and his group, the Air Branco officials and a few air hostesses, the CONAREX group and all their secretaries assembled at the Lido on Avenue des Champs-Elysées to toast the successful completion of the operation. Everly Nwomah had gone back to Lisbon. Champagne flowed, courtesy of Air Branco as very pretty and elegant French girls danced and entertained on the rostrum. Jokes flowed freely across the table about the beauty of French girls, their freedom, their healthy and characteristic lack of complexes about sex. Professor Obelenwata enjoyed every moment of it, but he told no jokes. It was a long night, but finally all of them paired off to their hotels as Edu and Onuoha returned to their homes. Before Edu left Onuoha, he called him aside and said, 'I hope this works. For one thing I know we have paid through the nose.' 'It will work,' Onuoha consoled him, half believing it himself. 'It is a stiff and heavy price,' he acknowledged. 'But time alone will tell if it was worth it.' Immediate means of transport had been required as the military situation at home continued to get more desperate, and it seemed that they now had it.

While Professor Nwoke was staying in Paris, he had made several very quick trips to Germany to address the Biafran nationals in that country. The boys were so fired with zeal that when the war broke out, they collected money, electronic and telecommunications equipment to send home to the fighting forces in Biafra. One of them Mr Madu, an engineer, had left Germany with six Biafran pilots for Biafra. They had travelled by way of the Camerouns. Another was a young Doctor of Physics, Dr Clinton Okeji, who had been making enquiries about the engineering and chemical needs of the armed forces. After he had made a report to the Paris office, he was asked to bring over what he had collected, for onward transmission to Biafra. Dr Okeji had managed to purchase about two tons of equipment, including chemical, glycerine and explosive compounds. He tried to send these by air freight, but the officials at Frankfurt airport refused to accept the cargo for fear of endangering the lives of passengers. Undaunted, Dr Okeji decided to send some of the material by train and carry the rest in a rented station-wagon, which he would himself drive to Paris. His arrival in Paris coincided with the completion of the arrangements for the Super Constellation. Informed before-hand about the chemicals and equipment coming by train, Freddy Onuoha went early on Tuesday to the Gare de l'Est in Paris to make the necessary arrangements.

Clinton Okeji arrived later the same day. A few minutes before the customs closed, towards five in the evening, Onuoha and Dr Okeji arrived at the Gare de l'Est with three vehicles; they went down the ramp and there quietly received their goods from the hands of the affable and smiling customs officials. Some of the articles were very heavy, others had to be handled with extreme care. Everything was safely packed into the cars, and the gates of the customs house closed behind the group as they drove off. Onuoha led the way with his car. Dr Okeji, who had not had anything to eat or drink for the past twenty-four hours, sat by his side. They talked as they drove along the road.

They saw the Biafran struggle as a real challenge and also as an opportunity to build a new state, a new generation of people, strong and united in a common struggle for the good of all. The nationals in Germany were mobilized and ready to come home to defend their people. Meanwhile, they were going to do their best to sacrifice all they could and even more in order to give to the soldiers at home what they needed. Under the circumstances, they agreed that no risk was too great to take. The young Biafrans in England and America felt the same way and were ready also to go home and fight for their country. Several of them had gone over to those countries on Nigerian Government scholarships, but with Biafra's declaration of her independence, the stipends were cut off because the Biafrans refused to sign an oath of allegiance to the government that planned the massacre of their people. Several of them, including medical students in their final year, had abandoned their studies for lack of funds. Their sense of pride and the feeling of injustice were too strong to let them sell their consciences and their people for the sake of a few hundred dollars. Some of the students who had to give up their studies were working day and night in hotels washing dishes just to make enough to live on. They were even then so moved by the war at home that they decided to contribute monthly a certain percentage of their wages to the war fund which they had established.

It was a horrible feeling driving through the crowded streets of Paris and passing through centres like the Place de la Concorde carrying about ten gallons of glycerine on a hot summer afternoon, in the crowded circle with cars heading in all directions and some of them bumping into one another. The trucks rented for the purpose did their best to follow closely behind. An accident could have set fire to the Concorde Bridge facing the French National Assembly. An explosion could have literally destroyed on the spot about one hundred cars and several hundred human lives. Onuoha and his friends meandered through the traffic. They reached the Inno garage in Montparnasse not far from Hotel Michel where Dr Okeji would be lodged, and parked the cars there. As they came out of the garage, Onuoha greased the outstretched hands of the gatekeeper and told him that he would be back at three o'clock in the morning to remove the trucks and the cars.

As they left the premises, Onuoha was continually haunted by the image of the four cars containing chemicals exploding in the middle of the night in the third underground floor of the gigantic garage. The building stood at least twelve storeys high and besides the garage there were stores and restaurants on the ground floor and living apartments on the other floors. Two days earlier, a department store in Brussels, Innovation, belonging to the same chain of stores, was blown up, causing numerous deaths and much damage. That was a clear case of arson, for people were protesting against American policy in Vietnam and the store was owned partly by Americans. Onuoha made a sincere wish that the cargo would not explode over the quiet neighbourhood. As he and Clinton grabbed some sandwiches after dismissing the drivers and giving them a rendezvous at two-thirty in the morning, each bang on the street sounded like the explosion of glycerine in a large garage.

The Super Constellation G, registered F-BGNE, was scheduled to leave Orly on Wednesday morning at five. While Dr Okeji and Onuoha were at the Hotel Michel, getting ready their luggage for the trip home, Ifedi and the rest had gone to Orly Airport to reclaim their luggage that had come back from the unfortunate trip to Toulouse-Blagnac airport. At the Hotel Michel, Edu joined Onuoha and Dr Okeji as they kept vigil waiting for departure time. Dr Okeji had just been appointed a Professor of Physics at a German University. He was very unhappy though, because as he said, he could not in good conscience pursue his private and personal career when he felt that his people faced the danger of extermination. He wanted to volunteer to help as long as his presence was necessary. He was firmly convinced that science and science alone could save the people. Outnumbered ten to one, facing forces fifteen times larger in equipment and number, fighting against a nation twelve times the size of their country, science and science alone could save the people from starvation and extermination. Dr Okeji was quick to add that he meant scientific war, scientific farming, scientific planning. Ordinary means alone could not rescue the people, softened as they were by seven years of a corrupt civilian regime. People must change their attitudes and see the nation first before their own private interests. Dr Okeji added that graft, nepotism and selfishness had led to the demise of the former Federation of Nigeria. He prayed and hoped that the same evils would not beset the new Republic. He lamented the fact that almost the very same people who advised the civilian Prime Minister until his assassination, the very same people who condemned the Prime Minister and supported General Ironsi when the latter came to power, were the individuals, the Commissioners, the Special Envoys advising the present regime.

'We cannot look up to them for our salvation,' Dr Okeji said. 'If we trust our destiny in their hands, they will sell us along the way again and we would have ourselves alone to blame.' 'That must not happen,' Edu agreed. 'These old cronies,' Edu said, 'now realize in the moment of great catastrophe that they need the intelligence of the young generation to survive, that they need you and me.' Edu drew his chair closer to Dr Okeji and Freddy Onuoha and said, 'Did you know that these politicians really believed that Biafra would win the war in four days. They did all the planning themselves. Even the head of the armed forces did not know how many soldiers he had in the army he was supposed to be commanding or how much equipment there was at their disposal. If he asked a question about his own army, he was told that everything was being taken care of, that arms were being bought and that there was enough to vanquish the enemy. The poor commander had to keep quiet, dissatisfied as he was.' Dr Okeji remained quiet as he listened with attention to what Jeff Edu had to say. 'The plan,' Edu continued, 'I believe, was to win the war alone without the people and then impose their will on them. Already the politicians were distributing monopolies to their brothers. Some relations who could not even read or write were sent abroad to negotiate the purchase of drugs and arms, for the country. Where there was any buying to be done, it was always some politician's relation who did it in Europe. No accounts were kept, no questions were asked. The result was that when war started, there were very few arms in the country, in spite of an investment in arms of almost six million pounds.'

Dr Clinton Okeji at that point stopped Jeff Edu and asked him what Ruddy Nnewi was doing trotting up and down in Germany staying in expensive hotels, racing up and down the autobahn between East and West Germany with a blonde-haired girl in a Mercedes 230 SL and spending all the money he could lay hands on. Jeff Edu could only say that Ruddy was supposed to be charged with highly secret missions. He rendered accounts to no one and when questions about him were asked, there were always several relations highly placed to prove his alibi and speak on his behalf.

While Jeff Edu and Dr Okeji were engrossed in this conversation, Onuoha moved aside to write a letter he would give to Samson Anele to mail on arrival in Enugu. The letter was addressed to Yvette Okonkwo, a young school mate of his. For seven long years he had not seen her, but daily she seemed ever closer to him. Across the seas, across the continent, her letters were always a source of joy and her picture, conspicuously displayed in his bedroom, was an ever-reassuring presence. Onuoha drew from his wallet a small picture of Yvette and looked at it. They had grown up together in the same street in Owerri. She attended the

Girls' Secondary School in Owerri while Onuoha was studying at the Holy Ghost College across the street. There was a river near their schools, the River Nworie, and each afternoon as the girls were returning from bathing, they used to meet the boys going to bathe after their daily games. They passed each other by the road and exchanged quick glances of love and sometimes messages. The boys continued their descent down the hill, the girls counted their steps up the hill, waiting for another evening to come. The Irish missionaries running the two schools did everything possible to keep them apart.

Then Yvette was just one of the many friends of Onuoha. But the times had changed. The years that passed by brought forth the best in her body, soul and intellect. Somehow, in the process of this transformation, Yvette stood out amongst others. She became no longer *a* friend for Onuoha but *the* friend; no longer one of many but the sum of all and life itself. Each letter from Yvette revealed her more to Onuoha and each revelation opened further his eyes, each vision in turn created a burning desire, a craving to possess, to own Yvette. Daily, though far away, their life appeared already linked inseparably. He planned for her, with her in mind, with themselves in view. Long days of distant contemplation alternated incessantly with short nights of beautiful dreams. But all evaporated in sorrow when he awoke, knowing her to be so far away.

Yvette's last letter had arrived on the day hostilities had broken out between Biafra and Nigeria. That was over two months ago. There was no guarantee Onuoha would see her again, none that she would write again or that the letter would come to him. The times were insecure, unsure, fluid. It was in this mood, choked up with work and emotion, with business apprehension and private love, wanting to open his heart to sing his love, anxious to write enough, to transmit enough love and warmth to keep Yvette consoled across the difficult times ahead, times of privation and temptation, times of silence and great doubts, it was to do all this and more that Onuoha took up his pen to give to Yvette in words, in images, his tormented and unfaltering love.

When Onuoha finished his letter, Dr Okeji and Jeff Edu were

still at their conversation. 'I am in a way happy,' Edu said. 'I might sound sadistic, but I am not at all. I hate blood, I hate fighting. I would like to see the whole thing come to an end. I am in a way happy that our government did not score a four-day victory as they hoped they would. Such a victory would have heralded the greatest tyranny in the history of our people, because the politicians advising or running the government once they had won the war without the people would also have ruled without the people, or with the outspoken ones amongst them in jail.'

'As I was saying before,' Dr Okeji added, 'what you are analysing now cannot happen again. Having mobilized the people when they realized that they could not win this quick victory, having politicized them to this extent, in the face of this crisis, they have forged, they believe, a new generation that would save them from defeat, that would uphold their banner, but in actual fact they have sown the very seeds of their destruction. After the war, the wounded soldiers will ask questions. Those alive will make sure that their comrades did not die in vain. These soldiers who were able to repulse the enemy with practically nothing, as they are trying to do now, surely will be able to overthrow the coalition of corruption and nepotism with the new techniques and ideas they have been taught. But this process does not in itself bring about sanity in government. You need a leader courageous enough to stand firm for justice and to stamp out inequity, a leader sensitive enough to feel the pulse of the people as he guides them with his creative imagination. You need such a leader for this unleashed power to be channelled into scientific progress, human happiness and peaceful prosperity.'

At that point, Onuoha intervened and said: 'Gentlemen, it is two o'clock. Arise and let us go, for the time has come.' Trying to be funny, Jeff Edu added, 'Before the cock crows thrice today, someone is going to let me down.' 'Which one of us, Lord?' Dr Okeji asked, assuming a less serious posture. Jeff Edu looked around and said that the coward was not yet amongst them.

Together, they descended the creaking wooden steps of Hotel Michel on Rue d'Odessa. Some two hundred metres away was the Inno garage. The truck drivers were already waiting downstairs.

At the garage, Dr Okeji's car would not start. The battery was low. But with a connecting cable attached to Onuoha's car, the motor roared in the silent morning, revved and the caravan moved along the spiral gangway up to the street floor. The gate-man saluted and locked his doors behind them. From there on to Boulevard Montparnasse, along Avenue Général Leclerc towards Porte d'Orléans, the cars moved along across blinking yellow street lights. There was little or no traffic on the way, just a few police cruisers and a handful of stragglers emerging from the cafés that had closed an hour earlier.

The Autoroute du Sud was foggy in the morning air and visibility was rather poor. After turning to Halles de Rungis, the caravan veered left towards Orly Airport. The rendezvous point was the Air Branco hangar in the Gare Industrielle Nord. Some-where along the way, the group took a wrong turn and found themselves in the precincts of Orly Hilton Hotel. Onuoha saw a man near the hotel and asked him where the Gare Industrielle Nord was. He said that he did not know. Trying to correct their bearings themselves, Onuoha and his group ended up in the premises of the Aeronautical Engineering and Research Centre located near Orly Hilton. The sleepy watchman gave them the directions. The fog thickened along the road and over buildings. While it misled them in their trip, it also kept them away from suspicious eyes. The agreed pass-word gave them easy entrance into the wired premises of the establishment.

A plane was parked not too far away from one of the hangars. There were still some workmen around but not many. The hired drivers were asked to unload the trucks. One of them was retained in case something had to be carried back to the city. A few minutes later Dr Eugene Fresco arrived and by his side was Colonel Ochar Lavignette, rubbing his fingers in apparent satis-faction. As the chauffeurs received the cheque from Jeff Edu, their leader pleaded with all earnestness that Edu should contact them if he had other materials to be moved another day, emphasizing that he was a man that could be trusted to keep secrets. He left his card with Jeff Edu. He must have thought that the business was a regular gold smuggling enterprise.

Dr Eugene Fresco protested when he saw the amount of luggage being off-loaded. It had not been anticipated and no arrangements had been made for loading it. At the same time, Obiora Ifedi and the rest of his squad arrived. He announced that Chief Iweka would accompany Lawyer Afoukwu and Samson Anele on the plane to Enugu. Chief Iweka had something very important to do at home. About fifty dollars overcame the protests of Dr Fresco and brought out two workers who loaded the luggage. One of the containers started to leak and when they saw that it contained glycerine, they were frightened. When Chief Iweka found out the explosive power of glycerine, he changed his mind about going to Biafra in the plane. Before long, Lawyer Afoukwu decided the risks were too great and changed his mind also. Samson Anele was Obiora Ifedi's cousin and the former was not going to let his Special Courier run unnecessary risks. But someone had to go with the plane at least from Lisbon to Enugu so that he could converse with the Enugu control in Igbo and identify the craft, since that was its first run. Mr Ifedi spoke about sending a message to Lisbon and asking one of the boys lazing around in the office there to accompany the plane. Lawyer Afoukwu spoke of sending someone back to Paris to get Ndubisi to travel with the plane, but they decided they needed him in Paris for typing their confidential materials.

Dr Clinton Okeji moved forward, faced all of them and said, 'I will travel with the plane!' It was a rare moment of love and courage. His face was radiant in the dark morning like that of a man about to die. Edu and Onuoha could not go because they were in charge of the Paris office, a vital chain in the daily operation of the government. There was shame and silence when Dr Okeji climbed up the steps of the plane to get in through the cockpit area. The cock crew in a farm under construction, not far away from Rungis. Dr Okeji turned and smiled as Jeff Edu said: 'The cock just crew, Clinton.' Lawyer Afoukwu burst out laughing also, and said, 'See him. Look at him. He is laughing. I knew he was not serious about travelling in that plane. Nowadays young boys love life more than we older ones.' Dr Okeji smiled again and waved good-bye. Onuoha ran up to him and got his car key and promised to return the car to the car-hire company. Dr Okeji was going to give him money to pay for the cost of the rental. Onuoha refused and instead gave him money in case he should need it along the way during his unexpected trip to Biafra.

The plane was delayed a few minutes as Obiora Ifedi and the others scribbled a few more lines of instructions for Dr Okeji about how to deliver the parcels they had put in the plane for their families in Biafra. Clinton came to the cockpit door again and waved. There were almost tears in the eyes of Jeff Edu as he turned away from the plane. 'I know you will be back here amongst us soon,' Onuoha shouted over the sound of the engine and added, 'Safe journey, Clint, and see you soon.'

The plane turned and taxied a bit, then took its place waiting for clearance to take off. As the engines roared harder and the ground near the group vibrated, the plane made its run. Then there was the lift-off. The wheels disappeared as it gained altitude and in the distance, on that cold misty morning around five-thirty, the Super Constellation looked like a grey ghost receding from mortal view.

There were tears of joy and tears of relief. There were a few handshakes and a few good-byes. Those around made their way separately back into the city. Jeff Edu and Freddy Onuoha left to begin their normal day's work. Obiora Ifedi and his group, together with Dr Eugene Fresco and Colonel Ochar Lavignette, left to have breakfast in the airport lounge. Chief Iweka spoke of their having an early bottle of champagne to give their satisfaction a concrete and tangible expression.

A Six Million Dollar Loan

The very day that the grey ghost left Orly Airport, as if contractors all knew immediately that the Ifedi squad had an independent means of transportation, five firm offers came from transporters who wanted to ferry goods from Lisbon to Enugu. One of the proposals came from Captain Boris Henk. Mr Ifedi knew him already and dismissed his application summarily. Professor Obelenwata overruled his decision and for the first time there was an open clash between them, a sort of struggle for power, for the control of the government in Paris. As a compromise, Onuoha was asked to go and interview Captain Henk in his hotel on Rue Clément Marot not far from the Paris building of the American Legion in the eighth *arrondissement* of the city.

Though Onuoha had not met Captain Henk before, at least, he thought to himself, the captain was by no means a stranger to Biafra. In October of the year before, at the beginning of the crisis that led to the war, Captain Henk had obtained a contract from the Enugu government to carry down from Stockholm about four tons of rifles, machine-guns and ammunition in his DC 3 aircraft. The negotiations had been concluded by Professor Nwoke during one of his earlier trips to Europe, but he had left a young man, Christian, to supervise the final details of the shipment, for he had to leave immediately then for a tour of the United States. The young man was a well-known writer and naturally no one would suspect him of smuggling arms across oceans. Christian intended to travel with Captain Henk on that journey from Stockholm to Enugu, but the Captain had asked him to fly by commercial transport because the plane was already overloaded. Christian had deliberately left his brief-case in Henk's plane, however, since he did not want curious customs officials going through his papers and discovering compromising documents.

On his way from Stockholm, he had stopped in Paris to wait for a connection to Douala from where he would continue his trip to Enugu. Being an old friend of Jeff Edu, Christian had spent the night at Edu's house. He was a charming fellow, very jovial in company. Edu and Christian had been drinking coffee after dinner that night when the radio announced that a DC 3 plane bound for Eastern Nigeria and carrying lots of arms had crashed in Camerounian territory. The Eastern Nigerian Government had naturally denied ownership of the plane or the cargo immediately, and had accused the government of Lagos of smuggling arms into the country to worsen an already deteriorating situation. The name of the pilot had been given as Captain Boris Henk. He was reported as being in fair condition.

The following day, the crash had been headline news in most European papers, in particular in Britain where journalists made capital out of it, predicting civil war; it had also made the headlines in Germany. But it had also been widely commented on in the French press and the incident had attracted the attention of Joel Bouchara, who had then decided to go to Enugu, Lagos and Kaduna to cover the start of the revolt against the Federal Government. Fortunately, no mention had ever been made of Christian's brief-case.

The circumstances of Captain Henk's release from the Camerounian prison and the way in which he had been smuggled out of the country assisted by his lady private secretary who had enclosed him in a huge wooden box, which was loaded onto a ship bound for Abidjan in the Ivory Coast, had astounded the very few people who had known about the incident. Arrested in Abidjan, Captain Henk had been released due to the intervention of the American Embassy there; His Excellency the Ambassador had issued him American travel documents because he was an American-protected person. These facts had convinced Mr Ifedi beyond all reasonable doubt that Captain Henk was in the employ of someone. Another puzzle was caused by the fact that the crash had not set fire to the plane, heavily laden as it was with ammunition, and had not killed or seriously injured any of the occupants. Captain Henk was of course an exceptionally good pilot, and he had told the story that he had run out of fuel and had to ditch in shallow water. Somehow, there had not only been fishermen around to save him from drowning in the lagoon, but there had also been American journalists around to film action pictures of the crash.

As Onuoha now entered the Hotel Franklin D. Roosevelt on Rue Clément Marot, there was a beautiful well-mannered young lady waiting in the lounge. 'You are looking for Captain Henk,' she smiled. 'Please follow me.' Onuoha followed her to the second floor of the hotel and was led into a suite and asked to sit down on a sofa in the lounge. Captain Henk appeared. To Onuoha's surprise, it was the man he had seen early in the morning at the Orly Hilton Hotel. They knew they had met before, but Onuoha was not anxious to tell him where and perhaps Captain Henk had not forgotten himself.

Captain Henk went straight to business as his secretary left the lounge to bring some snacks. The Captain was persistent, pleading, anxious to market himself and his services. He brought out his album and showed Onuoha pictures of the crash in the lagoon, of himself lying in bed in a Douala hospital, the remains of the plane. He repeated his own version of the story. He was armed with clippings of the reports that had appeared in newspapers in West Germany, France, England and the United States. Everything was orchestrated to show that he was solidly behind the Biafran cause. He was willing to help and had planes that could leave that night. He made it clear he was not a philanthropist but wanted to recover some of the money he had lost during his abortive trip to Enugu. He had a crew of seven pilots, co-pilots and flight engineers ready to put at the service of Enugu two planes every other day. He brought out his compass and his maps and traced the probable routes he would take to avoid Nigerian territory. This time, he would fly along the coast. With the DC 7s and the Super Constellations in his fleet, he could carry ten tons at a time and fly more than sixteen hours without having to make a technical stop. His offer was reasonable, he maintained, some $25,000 per round trip and only seventy-five per cent on take off, the rest on return from Enugu. He was able to guarantee eight flights a week to Enugu.

At that point, Captain Henk left the room as the secretary entered. He left her to complete the job he had started. The secretary offered Onuoha champagne, martini, Scotch, rum, but Onuoha did not drink. There were sandwiches and coffee on the table also, but Onuoha accepted only a cup of coffee. The secretary's name was Phyllis. She brought out her own album in turn and showed Onuoha pictures taken of her and Captain Henk when he was in hospital, pictures of her vacation once in Bar Beach, Lagos, dressed in bikinis, and at another vacation on Bonny Island, basking in the sun. She looked gorgeous in the pictures and Onuoha looked up to see if her figure and face had changed. His gaze upwards was rewarded with a warm smile and a deliberate brush of the breast on his chin. Onuoha was almost over-powered by the freshness of a Lancôme perfume. With charm, Phyllis announced that she was leaving for Lisbon that night.

When Onuoha reported the relevant parts of the discussions to the squad, all of them made up their mind that on no account would any other contract be offered to Captain Henk. He was an agent, some persisted. Wisdom required that they should not take a second risk. The following morning, Onuoha was going to pick up the telephone to call Captain Henk regretting that they could not offer him a contract, when the telephone rang. It was Captain Boris Henk on the telephone. He thanked Onuoha for his co-operation and announced to him with joy that he had got a contract for two months of flights to Enugu. Phyllis had just telephoned from Lisbon to tell him that the Biafran Special Envoy charged with signing contracts in Europe, Mr Everly Nwomah, had signed the contract and that he planned to start operation almost immediately. The Captain also said that the promissory note of half a million dollars would be in his hand that afternoon.

There was real consternation when Obiora Ifedi and Professor Obelenwata heard of this encroachment on their prerogative. They heard also that the grey ghost had arrived safely in Lisbon. After a few hours of instructions, Captain Lang, it was understood, had tried to take off and one of the engines had caught fire. He managed most fortunately to land again. After repairs, the Super Constellation had been able to take off again with Dr Okeji and Everly Nwomah on board. The story became clear to them. Mr Everly Nwomah was planning to go to Enugu and claim all the credit for the purchase of the first plane, since the contract had his signature alone. He would also claim credit for signing the Captain Henk contract. When he came back to Europe, he would come back with increased powers to rule and to control all operations. Mr Ifedi would not tolerate someone else trying to control Biafran affairs in Europe, and Professor Obelenwata was not going to sit idle and let Everly Nwomah take credit for a plane he had person- ally negotiated and which had only been sold to Nwomah because of the Chancellor's special relationship with Colonel Ochar Lavignette. The faces around became sour and confidence was broken.

It took Captain Boris Henk two full weeks to start operations once he had received the promissory note. As it turned out, he actually did buy his planes from Air Branco and ended up using the spare parts bought for the grey ghost to get his own planes in flying condition. Allegedly, the Super Constellation G planes cost him $80,000 a piece. Also the grey ghost had accomplished a suc- cessful maiden voyage to Enugu. On her return, she had been strafed by the Nigerian Air Force, but she had survived the few bullet holes. Dr Clinton Okeji had returned to Europe with more orders for chemicals and explosives for the Research and Produc- tion (RAP) division of the Science Group in Biafra.

One of the early assignments given to Captain Boris Henk was the flying out of one million pounds of Nigerian currency notes in denominations of five and ten pounds. During the negotiations that had preceded the engagement of Captain Henk, Everly Nwomah had persuaded him to agree to be paid partly in Nigerian currency, which would constitute substantial foreign exchange savings for the government. With the triple laurel—signature of the contract for the grey ghost, engagement of Captain Henk and securement of his payment in local currency—Everly Nwomah became the *de facto* controller of Biafran affairs in Europe. He arrived with Captain Henk and the load of Nigerian currency which was carried straight to the Zurich market for sale. Captain Henk wanted the entire amount deposited in his name. Everly Nwomah refused his suggestion and this disagreement was reflected soon in the refusal of Zurich brokers to change the currency. Nwomah had reason to suspect that Captain Henk had a hand in this. At almost the same time, the Nigerian Government imposed export restrictions on the Nigerian currency notes. This further complicated matters in Zurich. No headway was being made in Switzerland with the exchange of the currency: that may have been thanks to Henk. But there was no reason to suspect that Captain Henk had intelligence with the Nigerians and had given them the tip about the currency traffic.

In Paris, Jean-Pierre Dubien appeared again, and presented Ifedi with a proposal that would bring Biafra American dollars in direct exchange for Nigerian pounds at sixty per cent of the official rate. He wanted the money brought into Paris so that the banks could check and certify its authenticity. He emphasized to Mr Ifedi again that his field was finance and banking and not transportation. Jean-Pierre Dubien was also making arrangements for a loan of six million dollars from the Pluto Trust Bank in exchange for certain specified mining rights and monopolies in the country. Professor Obelenwata was also interested in the proposals. In the face of the new power bid and threat from Everly Nwomah, Ifedi and Obelenwata closed ranks and decided to strike a blow that would undercut the developing power base of Nwomah.

Jean-Pierre Dubien had provided them with the opportunity. Ifedi now sent for one million pounds of Nigerian currency notes to be ferried across from Biafra. Meanwhile he put the word around to his protégés abroad to start prospecting for other buyers also. Enugu replied that use should be made of the amount already consigned to Zurich. On this authority, Ifedi asked that the money be brought over from Zurich. Everly Nwomah was reluctant at first, since he wanted to retain complete control of this money. However, Dubien suggested that one or two people nominated by Ifedi should travel in a car or cars to Zurich and bring over the money with Mr Blanc, his associate. The suggestion sounded hazardous and full of risks, so Everly Nwomah, who still had full responsibility for the money, refused to agree and decided instead to charter a plane to bring over the money to Paris.

Dubien, who had connections all over Europe, readily suggested a reliable company that could rent a small plane to Everly Nwomah for the trip.

In Switzerland, Nwomah had little difficulty getting a small plane from the company Dubien recommended. The flight was set for a few days ahead. Once the arrangements were completed Nwomah hired security officers and went to the bank to collect the one million pounds. At Zurich Airport, the customs officials would not allow him to depart with the money; their reasons for this were not clear, since there were no currency restrictions in Zurich. The money had already been loaded onto the plane.

Meanwhile, back in Paris, the Ifedi squad was waiting for the plane that was supposed to arrive at Le Bourget Airport. They had all gone to the airport to wait. Edu took along his pistol. Professor Obelenwata once had a pistol in one of his suit-cases, but he was always afraid of being searched by the police. So he usually left the pistol in Onuoha's hotel room, Onuoha brought it along also. Dubien was at the airport with the squad.

Eight o'clock, nine o'clock, nine-thirty, ten o'clock, the airport control at Le Bourget said that no contact had been made with the plane, although it was scheduled to arrive at eight in the evening. Calls were made to the Paris office to see if Nwomah had contacted anyone by telephone about changes of plan. There was no message anywhere. Dubien himself was visibly worried. He knew the Zurich airport tower number by heart and he went to the small post-office at Le Bourget Airport and telephoned. Onuoha stood by him to overhear the conversation.

Dubien spoke in very fluent German to the Zurich tower. But Onuoha understood a bit of German, enough to make sense out of the conversation. Onuoha wondered why Dubien chose to speak in German instead of French, which would be understood also by the Zurich control. Onuoha thought to himself that Dubien was probably trying to hide something. Dubien was about to tell Onuoha what the conversation was about when Onuoha spoke to him in German, saying that he did not know that he spoke German as well as that. Dubien was frozen and paralysed as he looked at Onuoha, more like a thief caught in the act of crime.

In any case the news was that the plane was reported to have left Zurich Airport at eight o'clock that evening. Had it crashed? Had it been hijacked? No one could answer those questions, so after the long wait, the group decided around eleven to call off the vigil and go back home. Dubien drove straight to his house. The rest of the group drove to Jeff Edu's house in Neuilly-sur-Seine.

At Edu's house the proposal made by Dubien about the six million dollar loan was examined in detail. Dubien had flown to Enugu before the war to discuss this particular proposal and detailed arrangements had been made then. But later on, Enugu changed its mind, thinking that it was giving out a great deal for nothing. At that time, the war had not started and it was thought that with a four-day victory, there would be no need of the type of loan that Dubien was proposing. The oil companies had also promised to pay to Enugu about seventeen million dollars in royalties. With that amount expected in the treasury, there was no need for a six million dollar loan. However, the war had not been the short one expected and the oil royalties had never materialized.

Seasoned diplomats sent out by Enugu had concluded the tough negotiations that led to the capitulation of the giant oil companies on this royalty issue. Obiora Ifedi took part in the negotiations. He was bubbling with plans and pride the day he arrived in Paris from New York where he was assisted by a team of eminent lawyers drawn from the best firms and associates in the white world. Their advice reportedly cost half a million dollars. The oil companies were ready to pay fifty per cent of the royalties immediately after the negotiations while the other fifty per cent would be left in escrow pending the issue of the Nigerian struggle with Biafra. Obiora Ifedi was confident of victory. He wanted also to be tough with the oil companies, so he declared that he wanted all or nothing. Naturally if the companies accepted to pay nothing, then they would reap the results of their treachery after victory.

In the face of such menace, the companies, reportedly, after consulting with Her Majesty's Government, promised to show up in Enugu on Monday July 10th, 1967 to pay in total the oil royalties. As fate would have it, war broke out on July 6th, four days before the due date. The companies had every intention of coming to Enugu that day to pay the whole amount to the government in control. The Lagos regime had assured them secretly that they would defeat Biafra in four days and be in Enugu on time on July 10th, to receive the royalties. When war broke out, Enugu assured the companies that victory could still be achieved within four days.

When the fighting between Nigeria and Biafra continued beyond Sunday afternoon, with all its insecurity, uncertainties, claims and counter-claims, the oil banker took flight and tried to escape from Biafra, across the Mid-West Region of Nigeria. Caught in mid-flight on the River Niger with a British journalist, he was brought back to Enugu. His captor was a young engineer he sacked from his bank and who had become an officer in the Biafran Army. Put in detention at Aba, he later bought his ransom dearly with a promise to pay more after reaching London. Once the banker arrived in perfidious Albion, he never kept his promise.

Because of this, Obiora Ifedi was in no mood to miss Dubien's proposal for a loan of six million dollars. The way things were developing, he would even accept a loan of one thousand dollars. The negotiations were duly completed. The signature of the final contract followed by an initial payment of two million dollars—other instalments to follow in two weeks and one month—was set for the following day.

In the midst of the discussions, the telephone rang. It was the voice of a lady calling from Switzerland. She was telephoning on behalf of Mr Nwomah to say that the latter had left Berne Airport for Le Bourget and should arrive there around one in the morning. There was utter confusion and consternation in the house as Lawyer Afoukwu accused Everly Nwomah of running around with women instead of carrying out the very serious mission with which he had been entrusted. Obiora was furious himself. Chancellor Obelenwata, who answered the telephone, was sulky. He knew the voice. It was that of Judith Gatwick. She was married and her husband had entertained Obelenwata and Everly Nwomah once when they made a trip together to Berne. Judith and her husband were now all but separated. Obelenwata liked Judith and Nwomah liked her also. Judith was out to have a nice time and entertained either of the two whenever they were in Berne. But Everly Nwomah was more pushing about the whole thing.

Mr Gatwick had come to suspect what was going on and had issued a warning to both of them. He had threatened to report the matter to the Enugu authorities if the seduction continued. He was also thinking seriously about seeking a divorce on the grounds of infidelity. Obelenwata was frightened by the thought of the sort of scandal this would cause and the effect it would have on his professional reputation. To placate the injured husband, Everly Nwomah had secured a contract for Mr Gatwick who was given responsibility for having stamps printed for Biafra Postal Services. This kept the husband on the road quite often and whenever Everly Nwomah was in Berne (which was quite often) he used to go to Mr Gatwick's house to find out from Judith how far the printing of the stamps had gone. Before returning to Lisbon, he would stop by in Paris to show Obelenwata provoking pictures, mostly in colour, taken in the bedroom of Mr Gatwick. To get even with Everly Nwomah, Obelenwata had the contract withdrawn from Mr Gatwick and the payments due were delayed or blocked entirely. In anger, Mr Gatwick had made a trip to London with the stamp samples and there purposefully got himself caught by the 'vigilant' police at Gatwick Airport, as he was smuggling in the samples, hidden inside the army boots he was wearing. Judith had remained faithful to Biafra, however, and was thinking of going to Enugu after the war to find a job.

Obelenwata murmured something about how Everly Nwomah would burst into the house and recount what an intrepid exploit he had undertaken to bring in the currency. What pained Chancellor Obelenwata was having to wait more than three hours at the airport for his political rival, who had undercut him at home by claiming credit for a contract he had negotiated, a rival who was amusing himself in Berne and making a fool of everyone in Paris. He refused to go to the airport again to meet Everly Nwomah. Lawyer Afoukwu also refused to budge. The rest left for Le Bourget.

Obiora Ifedi, Tobias Iweka, Jeff Edu and Freddy Onuoha were

at the airport, together with Samson Anele. They did not contact Jean-Pierre Dubien. Onuoha could not help feeling that Dubien was aware of their plans and might have sent people to waylay them on their way home, and make away with the money. Perhaps there was no reason to suspect him so much. Nwomah arrived at one in the morning. He looked tired, exhausted, on the point of collapsing. He had with him about twelve suitcases, each of them as heavy as lead. The Zurich officials had not let him board the plane there and he had had to join another flight to Berne from where he joined the original plane, which had by then arrived in Berne also. The story he gave was rather confused and he could not advance any reasons why he was delayed in Zurich. In Berne, he had had difficulties too. Only the intervention of Judith Gatwick had made possible his being allowed to take the plane out of Berne with the currency on board. He had retained all along the six Swiss security guards, who had now gone back to Switzerland with the plane.

The suitcases were loaded in Edu's and Onuoha's cars and the rest were asked to take taxis back to the city. They were asked to stop at Place de l'Etoile, get off, walk a distance and then take other taxis to avoid any link being made. Such connections might lead to the discovery of the fact that the currency was being kept at Edu's place. The two private cars took different ways, through Saint-Denis and Saint-Ouen to arrive also at Neuilly-sur-Seine.

They stopped and were unloading the suitcases. From the description Everly Nwomah gave of his cloak and dagger operation, it was a real and amazing exploit of courage and intelligence. He spared the group all the details, for he was very tired that night. He asked about Obelenwata. With apparent comfort, Everly told Ifedi that, 'Judith said that I should greet Obelenwata warmly. She sends her kisses.' Mr Ifedi right away advised him: 'You had better keep the kisses to yourself and not tell Obelenwata that.' Once inside the house, the Professor had to smile when Nwomah, smilingly, embraced him and recounted his exploits of the day, as well as his hazardous trip to Enugu on the grey ghost. The Professor was not impressed. He accused Everly of going home to claim credit for a job he had accomplished single-handed after weeks of exertion. Voices were rising higher and higher despite the chairmanship of Chief Tobias Iweka. A few neighbours on the second floor started coughing to indicate that they were being disturbed. One even came out and knocked at the door and threatened to telephone the police if the disturbance continued. A moratorium on the subject was accepted. A few drinks calmed tempers as they faced the problem at hand.

After a brief silence Nwomah said that it would be wonderful changing the money in question. The proceeds would go a long way towards helping him pay the debts he had accumulated on behalf of the government. There was the money he owed to Judith and her husband for the work they had done for the government. There was also the one half million dollars he owed to Captain Boris Henk, half of which had to be paid in foreign exchange. Professor Obelenwata bitterly disagreed, pointing out that he would control the money which should be put in the bank account. After all, he was the Special Envoy and Permanent Personal Representative appointed by the government to Europe. Everly cut his statement short by saying that he had brought the money out from Enugu, that he had again suffered carrying it from Zurich to Paris and that he had committed his name and reputation, getting things on credit for the government. He wanted to control the greater part of the money realized from the exchange. Obiora Ifedi thought that the quarrels were unnecessary, since by right he should control the funds which would be needed for transportation of materials to Enugu. At that point, Chief Iweka struck a note of realism and shifted their attention to the practical problem of how to protect the money that night. Lawyer Afoukwu said that they should take turns keeping watch the whole night. Jeff Edu told them it was not necessary. He had a six-shooter pistol and a hunting rifle. They helped him move the suitcases to his bedroom. He did not think that any man would come that close to attack him in his own house.

After this was done, there was an air of euphoria in the house. For the people in the room, the war was almost over. With six million dollars from the Pluto Trust Bank and about one and a half million dollars from the Dubien exchange, the end of the war was a matter of weeks, perhaps days, depending on how fast equipment could be moved down. This was enough to ensure the reconciliation of all. Obiora Ifedi patted Nwomah on the back and told him: 'There is only one favour I ask of you and you can control all the foreign exchange you want.' Nwomah asked him to speak and he would grant it. 'I hope,' Mr Ifedi said solemnly, 'that you will allocate to me two thousand acres of land in the Rivers Province so that I can cultivate tobacco.' Everly Nwomah was the Commissioner of Lands and Survey and was a native of Bonny Island. Jokingly, Nwomah in turn made a request. He wanted Ifedi to get the government to assign to him during his travels abroad a nice-looking young Igbo girl to act as his confidential secretary. He was thinking in particular of Ebere Okafor whom he had seen in Paris during his last visit. 'No problem,' Ifedi said. 'That I can do with a stroke of the pen. You can have anyone but Ebere. She belongs to another distinguished ambassador.' On that rather light note, the evening came to an end. They were to meet again at nine o'clock in the morning at Edu's place for the rendezvous with Dubien over the currency exchange. Meanwhile, Edu was charged to call Dubien very early in the morning to inform him that the money had arrived after all the night before.

Onuoha was to make arrangements to get a Biafra Government seal made the following morning. The seal would be needed to legalize the contract with the Pluto Trust Bank. The General Manager of the B.E.B. in London would be attending the signature of the Accord. That morning before Onuoha went to bed he tuned into the B.B.C five o'clock news. It was announced that Biafran forces had again halted the Nigerian push towards the University town of Nsukka. The commentator suggested that the victory was due again to the single-handed feat of Major Chukwumah Kaduna Nzeogwu, who had led the overthrow of the civilian government in January 1966.

By seven in the morning, Onuoha was up again. It was not easy trying to get a seal prepared and made ready for the four o'clock signature of the contract. Onuoha gave the job to a friend. At nine o'clock the scheduled meeting convened at Edu's house and Dubien brought his business associates along. Onuoha was late for the meeting, just arriving at the tail end of it as the people present were dragging out the suitcases of money into the cars waiting outside. The money was going to be checked by the banks concerned and though the negotiations were tough, it appeared that all the difficulties had been solved. Everyone breathed a sigh of relief as the money was moved out of Edu's room. The cheques in dollars would be issued later that afternoon after the currency had been deposited in the bank vault. The buyers were unyielding and came down to fifty per cent of the market value instead of the sixty per cent Dubien had offered earlier on their behalf. The group went over to Hotel Splendid overlooking the Arc de Triomphe de l'Etoile on Avenue Carnot for a quiet and leisurely lunch, satisfied with the turn of events that morning, looking forward to the signature that afternoon of the six million dollar loan. There was no argument about who would control the money, for it would be paid directly to the B.E.B. in London. Onuoha promised to bring the seal at two in the afternoon.

Unfortunately, it was not possible for Onuoha to get the seal at two o'clock, for the workers could not forsake their lunch break even for extra pay. Therefore, he could not join them for the meeting. However, Edu left a message that Onuoha should bring over the seal to Boulevard Suchet. Onuoha could not believe his ears because he knew that the Nigerian Embassy was located in the same building. Françoise Schultz, the secretary, assured him that the number was right. With beating heart, Onuoha parked his car and approached the building. On his arrival at the door, there was someone waiting for him. The man, a well-dressed guard, said that Onuoha was being expected and he went in to call Jean-Pierre Dubien. Onuoha wanted to give the seal to Edu personally to assure himself that they were there and alive. So Dubien went in again and called out Edu. The three of them walked in. Onuoha felt uneasy as he stepped into the building. There were armed guards all over the place, as if they were guarding the entrance to the President's Palace.

The entrance to the building was magnificent, typical of most of the elegant and royal houses of the sixteenth *arrondissement* of Paris. Wall mirrors were all over the place, duplicating infinitely the graceful image of Madame de Pluto, who was deputizing for her brother who had had to go to New York City for a very important multi-million dollar contract. Strong rounded pillars rose up as in a medieval church. Tall chandeliers graced the ceiling above. Past the anteroom, the three had walked down a few steps to a beautifully decorated luxurious split-level sitting and reception room, turned into a conference bureau. Everyone sat down there stiff, serious, stern as if in a Council of War, the Ifedi squad on one side of the table and the members of the Board of Directors of the Pluto Trust Bank on the other. It looked as if the seal alone remained to sanctify the contract, for as the three entered, a steward also came round assisted by several hostesses to pass about glasses of champagne, caviar and sandwiches. Onuoha felt increasingly uncomfortable and had to excuse himself on the grounds that he had some very important unfinished business waiting for him in the office. It was actually when he got into his car to drive away that he realized he had two appointments around that time in the office not far from Champs-Elysées.

The Biafra Historical Research Centre was situated on the second floor of a commercial building, a large building that housed about fifty other small businesses. Somehow, it appeared that all the contacts and buyers and sellers the Ifedi squad dealt with had offices in that building or had some form of partnership with people having offices therein. Next door to the Historical Research Centre, a man sat down all day with his door open. He had moved into the office a few days after Onuoha had found the office space. The man seemed to speak every European language. He observed everyone that came in or went out of the Historical Research Centre. Once in a while, he received a few visitors and drank with them. Otherwise, it appeared that he spent the rest of his time either lecturing his several secretaries or discussing the upwards and downwards movement of the Parisian Bourse with his business associates.

One day, Joel Bouchara had come to the office to pick up some documents about the war. Bouchara was an exceptionally observant journalist. He came into the office and left almost immediately and went back to the elevator. Then he walked back again and came inside. Bouchara called Onuoha close to him and said: 'That man next door has no real business in this building. He is a member of the French Secret Service detailed to watch all your movements and operations. He observes every little pin that moves up and down the hallway with the corner of his eyes and his door is always open.' Onuoha had not worried about this too much, since as far as he knew, they were not plotting to overthrow the French Government. Besides, the host government had a right to find out what foreigners were doing on its territory.

The Historical Research Centre, itself, was a small two-room office. The building was just a stone's throw from the Nigerian Embassy though neither side was equipped with snooping gadgets. One of the secretaries in the office was Françoise Schultz, a beautiful young girl, half Senegalese, half German. Technically, she was still unemployed and was receiving unemployment benefits from the Ministry of Social Welfare. She was, however, working full time with the office. Onuoha used to watch her with interest as she telephoned the Employment Agency every Wednesday to tell them that the job they recommended to her was unacceptable.

One of the men that was supposed to come and see Onuoha that afternoon was Arthur Kutzenov. After failing to get anyone on the telephone about his money, Kutzenov had decided to come to the office and embarrass everyone. It happened that Françoise was the only one in the office when he came. The scoundrel did not spare any four-letter words that particular day. He had purposely got himself drunk before arriving for the marathon invective session.

Françoise was completely shaken as Onuoha entered the office. She was shaken not because of the four-letter words, but because Kutzenov had threatened to report to the police that the Historical Research Centre was carrying out illegal deals in arms and currency exchange. Françoise was afraid that a police investigation would expose her before the Employment Commission. Onuoha assured her that nothing of the sort would happen. Freddy

Onuoha said that Kutzenov would personally be afraid to bring the police into the affair. Kutzenov had written several times to the office threatening to bring his attorney to molest the Centre. When he started the barrage of letters, Onuoha had sat down and drafted a carefully worded letter to him, addressed to the 'Chairman, General Business Associates' and had mailed it to Kutzenov's address in the seventh *arrondissement* of Paris and had sent a copy to his London office. Kutzenov had introduced himself as the Chairman of General Business Associates and had said that he had branches in London as well. A return address was also put on each envelope. The post office returned the two letters after a few days regretting that no such company was registered at the address in question. Armed with this evidence of Kutzenov's fraudulence, Onuoha was ready to confront him anywhere and if need be make him pay back the $10,000 he had got from Obiora Ifedi by fraud. Not even that assurance could calm the nerves of Françoise. Kutzenov did come back later that afternoon, but he was a sober man by then, meek as a lamb. The effects of the alcohol had disappeared. He was like a child as he came in and asked if someone had picked up his wallet. No one spoke to him, no one looked at him. He looked wretched and miserable as he turned around and strolled out of the Centre.

Apart from Kutzenov, Onuoha had an appointment with two Biafran Navy boys who had been in Paris for more than one month, to make 'final' arrangements to collect warships and torpedo boats for which more than £1·7 million sterling had been paid to one Ulrich Merton. The latter had received the money directly from Enugu and no formal receipt had been issued since the operation was supposed to be classified and 'top secret', and the contract highly confidential. The vessels were supposed to have been ready some two months before the war started. But each day, Ulrich Merton had a different story to tell about why they were not ready. Finally, immediately after war was declared, he had sent word that everything was ready. He had said that Enugu could send people to come and collect the warships. A group of one hundred and twenty boys had been airlifted by the grey ghost to Lisbon to join the vessel from there. But after two expensive weeks, it had been discovered that the ships were far from ready.

Merton had sent work that the torpedo boats were ready. This time two Navy boys had been sent to examine them. On their arrival in Paris, Ulrich Merton had wanted to place at their disposal a chauffeur-driven Lancia car and had generously agreed to pay all their hotel bills including drinks. On Monday he would take them to Stuttgart, on Tuesday to Amsterdam, where the battleships were being prepared and equipped. He had said that he was willing to place at their service in Paris two private secretaries for their needs. Ulrich Merton had planned everything. He had planned to equip fully the two warships and three torpedo boats. Loaded with arms and equipment from Europe and accompanied by a cargo ship carrying supplies and fresh water, the new Biafran Navy would arrive near Port-Harcourt in two weeks and sink the Nigerian frigate, S.S. Nigeria. Once the frigate had been sunk, they could then isolate the other vessels one by one and sink them with torpedoes and rocket-fire. What delayed the ships, he had apologized, had been the fitting of launchers and anti-aircraft guns on the vessels.

Jeff Edu had tried himself to discuss the project with Merton on several occasions. Merton had always replied that certain specific individuals had given him the contract and that he was responsible to them alone. Edu had started suspecting whether there was a kick-back, as happens in the United States to some highly placed government officials. Protected by this complicity, Merton was perhaps doing all he could not to fulfil the contract. When Edu had approached Merton again about the deal, the latter told him that he was having difficulty fulfilling the contract because the Nigerians had been trailing him. He was sure that the Nigerians and the British knew every move he was making. No one except Merton, Edu had concluded, would have told the British and the Nigerians about the deal. Edu had begun to wonder whether Merton had been bribed by the Nigerians to delay the delivery of the goods in order to frustrate the Biafran war effort.

After consideration of all these aspects of the problem, when they came to the office that afternoon Onuoha advised the Navy boys to give back the Lancia to Merton and go back to Port-Harcourt and join their comrades in the sea front of the war.

Onuoha by that time was anxious to find out how the operations were moving along. So he got into his car, a Simca 1000 coupé Berline and headed towards Neuilly-sur-Seine. He got involved in one of the miserable traffic jams of Paris, along the Champs-Elysées. On Place de l'Etoile, nothing seemed to move. It appeared as if all the cars had stopped reverently for an aerial photograph. The French policemen could do nothing to get the traffic moving again. About the only things that moved were the arms of impatient drivers, thrown up in the traditional French gesture of despair and frustration. Then, through some kind of miracle the cars moved and Onuoha continued his trip to Neuilly. Rounding the Etoile, he took an extremely wide orbit and this way avoided being held up again. As he completed the curve for the final right turn on Avenue de la Grande-Armée, the red light on the circle exit came up suddenly and Onuoha had to stop, since there were already pedestrians crossing the street, more impatient perhaps than the drivers. There was a sharp bang behind him. A car had hit the back of his own.

He got out of the car to see a gesticulating Italian with a car registered in Naples. The man spoke no French or English and Onuoha's Italian was not fluent. Onuoha looked at the car and saw that the damage was not serious. He was in no mood to start taking down the man's particulars, so Onuoha told the man that it was all right. The Italian turned round and told him that it was not all right. The Italian was definitely in the wrong for not being able to stop in time. So when he started arguing, Onuoha decided to invite a policeman to examine the situation and file a report for the insurance companies. There was a tall, elegant policeman dressed in a white coat standing nearby. Onuoha asked him to assist them. The policeman turned round and said that was not under his jurisdiction and asked Onuoha to go to another policeman about one hundred yards away.

Meanwhile, with the two cars blocking the traffic, cars were packed bumper to bumper not only around the Etoile circle but on all the twelve Avenues leading into and out of it. Impatient at continuing to waste time in that way, Onuoha merely exchanged particulars with the man and drove off. He had been told that the French insurance companies normally did everything humanly possible to avoid paying compensation for accidents. The two companies would do nothing but exchange letters all year round relegating the responsibility to the other company until the entire case was forgotten in frustration.

It was a long way that day to Neuilly-sur-Seine. The traffic was no lighter at Porte de Maillot. Cars headed for Le Bourget Airport, going towards the Autoroute du Sud, coming into Paris or going out to Neuilly, all seemed to converge there and no one had the patience or the courtesy to let his neighbour cross the intersection. Every-one seemed to move when the street light was yellow thereby blocking the approaches to those who had the green light with the result that nothing moved, even at a snail's pace. The five or six policemen on the spot seemed to be working at cross-purposes. On days like this, the motorist wishes he could press a button, propel his car into the air and fly above the sea of cars. But if he had that magic power, others would soon discover it and there would be another traffic jam in mid-air. At moments like this, even the music coming from the car radio seems to annoy, the lungs appear choked and there is real suffocation. There is a criminal urge to abandon the car and walk the rest of the way. Onuoha did not even have the strength to walk even if he had the callousness to abandon his car there. The car driver resigns himself to his splitting headache, as he surveys with incomprehension the ad-vantages and inconveniences of modern inventions, the opulence of the many and the apparent selfishness of everyone. American rush-hour traffic is bad because of the number of cars. London traffic jams are worse because of the narrow streets, but Paris is the worst of all because of the sheer selfishness of its motorists in spite of the big boulevards and wide avenues.

Somehow, after an eternal delay, the cars moved. Onuoha even took advantage of the red light, in spite of the strident whistle of the policeman, to get past the bottleneck. Finally, he arrived at Edu's place in Neuilly. He had to circle four times before he could find somewhere to park his car. Fortunately a man was about to move out. Onuoha went behind the man's car with his indicator flashing to show he was waiting to park there. The man pulled out and Onuoha raised his arm in appreciation and edged forwards to park with reverse gear. He turned the steering all the way to the right and started edging in, when a nicely dressed lady in a Deux Chevaux came from behind and moved right into the parking space. Onuoha was irate, bamboozled. He could not understand such discourtesy. The French woman calmly rolled up the windows of her car, locked it and walked away as if she had done the most normal charitable act in the world. Onuoha had no alternative but to park on a pedestrian crossing. Of course, before he came out, there was a ticket stuck onto his car by a policeman who had stood by and observed everything that transpired.

When Onuoha entered the house, the members of the squad were all there. From the sullen look on their faces, Onuoha felt it would be unwise to start recounting his little adventures of the day. He merely listened for a few minutes to get the 'state of the union' message. It was Nwomah who spoke first. 'The Pluto Trust Bank wants the weekend to think over the affair.' The bank was having some second thoughts. They were apparently not satisfied with signing such a contract with the emissaries of the government. They wanted the government in Enugu to sign it. The concessions involved were quite important and committed the nation for ninety-nine years. They were also very uneasy about consistent reports appearing in London about Lagos's intention to attack Port-Harcourt. Such an attack, they argued, would make nonsense of the Enugu concession of off-shore mining rights in those areas. They wanted to consult their intelligence experts on the exact military situation and the relative chances of an invasion of Port-Harcourt. They were demanding in addition a total monopoly of gold-mining rights on the mainland, a concession that was not included during the preliminary negotiations in Enugu. This concession, Mr Nwomah knew, could not be accorded to them since another California-based company was interested in it and had made quite attractive proposals. What was disturbing was that the agreement had been signed and the seal embossed on their copy. The objections were after-thoughts following signature of the contract. They were disquieting after-thoughts, for it had been hoped that the Pluto Trust Bank would pay at least one million on the signature of the contract.

As for the currency exchange, Jean-Pierre Dubien had rung to tell Jeff Edu that it had not been possible to convert all the currency that day and regretted that no advances could be made that Friday. Since the bank was closed on Saturday, he could either bring back the currency, in which case the conversion operation would start all over again on Monday, or he could keep it in the vault of the corresponding banks pending completion of the operation on Monday. A substantial amount of money had been expected from that source too, but again hopes were dashed at least for that day. The rugs appeared to be slipping from under the feet of all those present. So much money had been invested in the financing of the two deals and future hopes rested with at least their partial success.

The Ifedi squad sat down thinking over the events of the day. Edu's house boy served the squad some supper. He served mai-mai and gravy for hors-d'oeuvre, foo-foo made out of fine wheat flour cooked in milk and butter, together with egusi soup laden with mutton and seasoned with ground shrimps steeped in a delicious sauce. That was the main course. He prepared a side dish of jollof rice and for dessert he served oranges, bananas and other fruit. It was news time.

The British Broadcasting Corporation announced that Nigerian troops claimed to have killed Major Kaduna Nzeogwu and that they had finally broken through to Nsukka. Biafran soldiers were trooping back to Enugu in a disorderly fashion. It mentioned that pictures of Nigerian soldiers entering the University town of Nsukka had been shown in London and that the burial with full military honours of Major Chukwumah Kaduna Nzeogwu, for whom the Nigerians had the greatest respect and whom they considered to be the greatest officer the country—in fact, Africa—had ever produced, was being organized in Kaduna. During the news commentary, the commentator added that most diplomatic observers in Lagos agreed that the capture of Enugu was imminent and would signal the end of the rebellion that had been going on for more than two months. The Biafrans, he concluded, were expected to make a final stand at the Nine Mile Corner, the gateway to the Miliking Hill. The battle promised to be murderous and was considered the Waterloo of Biafra's coming defeat.

The squad was struck with stupor. The initial reaction was to disbelieve such reports coming from the London agency, that had consistently supported the Nigerian side. A call was booked immediately to find out from Lisbon if they had received any confirmation of the report. They said that the Biafran Radio had denied the reports and said that a communiqué would be issued later. They would call back if there were further developments. Within minutes, Ndubisi knocked at the door and brought a telex message that had just arrived. The message issued by the Biafran Ministry of Information said that Major Nzeogwu burst out laughing in Enugu when he was questioned about London reports of his death. There was something laconic about the release. It did not categorically deny the death of Major Nzeogwu and the tendency in the room was to believe that Enugu was trying to console the soldiers, for whom Major Nzeogwu meant a lot and whose death would have demoralized the entire army.

It was saddening to feel that Major Nzeogwu might be dead. All of that night and most of the following day, London was vicious in its broadcasts. It read out reports supposedly by eye-witnesses and foreign correspondents in the Nsukka area confirming that the Nigerians had finally taken total possession of the city. London announced that Nigerians had succeeded in landing troops on Bonny Island, which controls the channel leading to Port-Harcourt. The reporter was absolutely sure that the island would be overrun within the next two or three days.

Two days passed and there was no word from the Pluto Trust Bank. The general feeling was that they had decided because of the military situation not to honour the deal. It was a sad blow to hopes and morale, and Obiora Ifedi left the city with a broken heart, swearing he would not come back to Paris. For the first time in his life perhaps, his face lost its smile of optimism. Not a word was heard from Jean-Pierre Dubien and his associates either. No one had been able to get in touch with him on the telephone. Gradually, the impression was gained that he also could not deliver the goods. Finally contact was made with him over the telephone and he asked Onuoha and Edu to come to his home and carry away the money, since it could not be exchanged now.

Jean-Pierre Dubien lived in the fifteenth *arrondissement* in a second-floor apartment. It was with fear that Edu and Onuoha stepped into Dubien's room. The money was not there. He had put the suitcases in an old truck in a disused garage as if to emphasize his contempt for the money, to underscore its total loss of value. The money was brought into the apartment and counted. It was just two thousand pounds short. Dubien said that the two thousand was still in the bank and that he would get it the following day. As Edu and Onuoha drove off in their car, they imagined all sorts of things that could happen to them on the way home—encounters with gangs of robbers, being arrested by the police for the illegal possession of the Nigerian patrimony. Was Dubien working in collaboration with the Nigerians? Onuoha suddenly realized that no one really knew anything about the background of Jean-Pierre Dubien, except what he had said about himself. The first contact Edu had with him was a letter of introduction from officials in Enugu instructing Edu to give Dubien all due co-operation because he was working for the Biafra Government. Edu remembered feeling very uncomfortable after the first meeting with Dubien, and he did not make any further contact with him until Obiora Ifedi arrived in Paris.

That same day, when Onuoha and Edu had returned to the office, a man came and introduced himself as Albert Bondieu. He described himself as a very good friend of the Minister of the Interior. He confided to Onuoha that Ulrich Merton had taken £1·7 million from the Enugu Government, pretending that he was able to give them two warships and torpedo boats. He said that he knew also that two Biafran seamen had come to Paris and that Merton was taking them around Europe supposedly to show them the shipyards where the vessels were being built. He said that it was a big show. He said that Merton had actually taken the naval boys to a yard where torpedo boats were being built for a movie company shooting movies about wars. The vessels Merton showed the navy officers belonged to a demolition company. They were Second World War vessels being dismantled because they were no longer sea-worthy. 'A thirty-eight calibre pistol could sink any of those ships,' Bondieu said. He further went on to say that Merton had no intention of delivering the ships and had received substantial amounts of money from the Nigerians and was working with them. He was working for the destruction of Biafra so that the Enugu government could never come to claim back the money given to him. Albert Bondieu said that he was touched by these revelations which he got from very reliable sources and had, therefore, come to offer his services to help Biafra get out of the predicament and its difficulties.

Albert Bondieu's proposals were simple. He wanted to set out with a team of three frogmen and go to Lagos or to Port-Harcourt and from there organize the sinking of the Nigerian frigate, the S.S. *Nigeria*. It would have cost the Enugu government, he argued, at least two million pounds to equip effectively a Navy that could destroy the Nigerian frigate. Then there was no guarantee of success. Precious lives of the few Navy officers from Biafra would be lost and some of the torpedo boats could be sunk. For a paltry sum of one hundred and fifty thousand francs, he was willing to blow up the Nigerian frigate and he would charge an additional fifty thousand francs for every other vessel he blew up. He would purchase all the equipment needed in Europe, and carry along the needed explosives, since Enugu did not have enough to wage the war and since he knew that one Dr Okeji was in Europe buying explosives for the Biafra Science Group. It was understood of course that the Centre would pay for the cost of the needed equipment but he did not think it would be more than five thousand francs. Onuoha asked him to come to Hotel Michel some evening so that they could discuss it in greater detail. He advised him also to bring along concrete proposals that could be used as the basis for a contract if there was agreement in principle

That afternoon also Jean-Pierre Dubien telephoned again. He wanted to see Obiora Ifedi immediately. He said that all he needed

was Ifedi's signature and the Enugu government could get immediately about $200,000 in cash. The company in question was
asking for a deposit of one million pounds of Nigerian currency
with them. Onuoha and Edu had not told Dubien that Ifedi had
left Paris. Onuoha felt that Dubien must have known about it to
make this proposal. Onuoha thanked him for his proposal and told
him that he would transmit the message to Mr Ifedi, who had gone
to Enugu. Dubien of course was mad that Ifedi should have left
the country without telling him when he, Jean-Pierre Dubien, had
staked his reputation to obtain for almost nothing valuable foreign
exchange for Biafra. Onuoha asked him to write down his proposals and send them to him at the Centre, so that he could transmit them to Ifedi. Onuoha regretted also that the money had been
taken out of Paris and exchanged. Onuoha just added this to cut
short any insistence on the part of Dubien. It was difficult and
Onuoha only ended the conversation by threatening to hang up
on him.

4

A Pound for a Silver Dollar

At the Centre, Edu and Onuoha were sorely in need of some good news, and when it duly came it amazed them and was received with great joy. Biafran troops had taken over the Mid-West Region of Nigeria. Edu could not believe it. He jumped up and down like a child. He cried. It was a feat, a veritable *blitzkrieg*. An entire region had been taken over in less than ten hours of fighting. There had been little or no fighting even during the first ten hours, for Nigerian defences had collapsed like a castle of cards.

A German journalist, Friedrich von Mueller, was one of the first to report the incident in Europe, with all the details about how Biafran militia had moved in after the regular soldiers to set up radio stations and man the local newspapers. Von Mueller mentioned in particular the bravery of Tudor Opara, a veteran of the Nsukka front who with firmness mixed with a human touch pacified the Binis who were trying to rebel against the newly installed regime. But as the Biafran soldiers marched towards Lagos, the Nigerian capital, the Nigerian soldiers claimed they were within hours of Enugu, the Biafran headquarters.

It was difficult to tell who was dishing out propaganda or whether the two governments were both right. From the outside, there appeared to be no real advantage in installing the Biafran capital in Lagos and the new Nigerian capital in Enugu. In other wars armies had been more interested in defending their own capitals than in taking over those of their opponents.

Meanwhile at Hotel Michel, Onuoha was having a cup of tea when the telephone rang. Picking up the receiver, he asked who was on the line. The receptionist answered that there was a man downstairs who wanted to speak to him. The visitor in question was Albert Bondieu. Onuoha asked him to come up. Onuoha had just finished his tea when Bondieu knocked and entered the room. He was followed immediately by Jean-Pierre Dubien.

Freddy Onuoha was visibly embarrassed, but he did his best to control the situation. He asked them what they wanted to drink and ordered beer for them. Onuoha was going to introduce Bondieu to Jean-Pierre Dubien when the latter told Onuoha that there was no need. Jean-Pierre and Albert Bondieu had known each other for more than fifteen years. They had served together with the French forces in Indo-China. They were parachutists and had co-operated on several occasions together since the war. They were good friends, on as good terms as any two friends could be.

Jean-Pierre Dubien talked about everything. Bondieu was silent most of the time. Dubien was annoyed that he had prepared a deal for the signature of Mr Ifedi and that the latter had left Paris without telling him. Onuoha protested that he had nothing to do with the negotiations. This was apparently the chance Dubien was waiting for. He accused Onuoha of pretence. 'You say,' he continued, 'that you have nothing to do with these negotiations and yet you prepared the seal for the signature of the contract at Boulevard Suchet for a six million dollar loan. You say that you are nothing but a student and yet you are here recruiting mercenaries to go and blow up the Nigerian frigate. You have nothing to do with all these and you carry around in your car more than one million pounds' worth of old Nigerian currency. If you pretend any further, I will denounce you to the police.'

Onuoha did not know what to say. He merely offered Dubien and Bondieu some more beer to drink. They were staying too long and it was getting too late. Dubien threatened next time to bring people to the hotel to beat up Onuoha. As Dubien was saying this, two men came to the half-open door and entered. They had come at the invitation of Bondieu who had made a rendezvous with them at Onuoha's hotel room. They were members of the team that would blow up the Nigerian frigate. The two of them knew Jean-Pierre very well also.

Onuoha had to find an excuse to get the visitors out of the room. He asked Bondieu to prepare for him full details about his two friends and send these over to him. He told Dubien that he would contact him the following day, even though Dubien had insisted on getting an immediate reply to his proposal for the new loan. Dubien refused to leave and wanted to find out where Mr

Ifedi was. He said he knew he was not yet in Biafra. Onuoha went to the closet in his room, put on his overcoat and put his hand in his pocket and pulled out a ·38 calibre twelve-round pistol, an air pistol, as a matter of fact, he had bought not long ago. Dubien was the first to raise his hands and his friends stood up and followed him to the elevator. With a steady face, Onuoha watched them get into the elevator and leave that floor of the hotel.

The following day began with a new resolution by Onuoha, *Beware of Unscrupulous White Businessmen*. He started paying more attention to his movements and to the cars following him. He always tried to avoid coming home very late and, before he drove off in his car in the morning, he made it a point of duty to make certain verifications before starting the engine.

When he arrived at the Splendid Hotel, he met another Biafran named Samson Ogbuefi. Ogbuefi was an exceptionally well-dressed man. Tall and elegant, handsome and fluent, he could very easily pass for an honours graduate from one of the Ivy League Colleges of America. His manners were correct, almost impeccable. He was the in-law of Jeff Edu, though they were not on speaking terms. Edu had absolutely no confidence in him and refused even to see him, still less to talk to him. It was not quite clear how Samson Ogbuefi had managed to get out of Biafra and get involved in arms purchases. Maybe it was the triumph of the school of thought in Enugu that maintained firmly that the best way to get something out of unscrupulous European businessmen was to send out unscrupulous characters to deal with them. As a result, two or three ruthless characters had already been sent out to Europe to confront some of these dealers. Perhaps it was under this assumption that permission was obtained for Samson Ogbuefi to leave the country. Samson had a criminal record in Biafra and had been to prison at least three times before the war broke out on charges of robbery and theft and on one occasion for forgery of the elementary school leaving certificate and the Cambridge School Leaving Certificate.

That morning, Samson Ogbuefi was in a terrific hurry. According to him, he had barely ten minutes to stay in Paris. He was on his way to London. He had to leave almost immediately to collect his air ticket from the Air France office on Avenue des Champs-Elysées. He was anxious before his departure to introduce some of his contacts to Onuoha and Chancellor Obelenwata.

There was a bank in Paris that was willing to change Nigerian notes at very good rates. The bank in question had connections with some important groups of companies operating in Nigeria. The idea was to buy the currency notes in Paris and ship them back into the Nigerian market as bales of Java cloth. In Nigeria, the money would be used to buy local products and raw materials like cocoa, cotton and groundnuts. That way they would recover their money without having to go through the tedious process of contacting the Bank of England. Onuoha had become highly sceptical after recent experiences. Everyone was cautious. Chief Iweka took Ogbuefi out of the room while the rest discussed the matter.

The decision was taken to decline the offer, but Onuoha wanted to investigate the matter further and discover which was the bank in question. When Samson Ogbuefi came in again, he was informed that Onuoha had some money with him and that they wanted to try to get that changed first, since Ogbuefi had indicated that the exchange could be made on the spot. Samson was elated. He regretted he had to leave immediately for London. He had absolutely nothing to do with the deal, but he readily agreed to introduce Mr Roundseason who would organize the affair and who was downstairs at the moment. Roundseason was an American Negro businessman. Immediately after Samson had left in a taxi for his London trip, Roundseason invited Onuoha, who was carrying a rather big and heavy bag, to join him in his car. Onuoha declined, preferring to drive his own car.

The two cars drove off along Rue Tilsitt, round the circle towards Avenue Friedland and Place Saint-Augustin, stopped near Avenue de Messine. Roundseason asked Onuoha to wait. He disappeared after double-parking his car and reappeared five minutes later with a middle-aged white man. The new addition again asked Onuoha to park his car there while they travelled on in one car. Onuoha thanked him, but regretted that he had another meeting around eleven-thirty and would like to proceed to it straight from the bank.

Roundseason left his own car and joined the other man's car. After meandering through a maze of streets, five or ten minutes later they signalled to Onuoha to park his car in an open space nearby. They parked theirs a few yards further down. It was a one-way street. Onuoha brought out his bag as they joined him. But before leaving his car, Onuoha scribbled the name of Roundseason, his description, that of his friend and the numbers of their cars and left this in the glove compartment of his car. He was exceptionally apprehensive about the situation. In front of them was the Akaba Bank. The first question Roundseason asked him (for the fourth time) was whether he had the one hundred thousand pounds here with him. Onuoha said that he had. Roundseason said that the bank had been informed and that they were expecting them.

Inside the bank, they went past the tellers' counter into the administrative lounge right inside. The manager of the bank was sitting there with two other people whom he introduced as his assistants. Onuoha sat down also, together with Roundseason and his friend. Earlier Samson Ogbuefi had explained that the bank would change the money immediately, but no one of course took him seriously. The manager of the bank wanted the one hundred thousand pounds for deposit. Onuoha wanted to know how much he would get immediately, at least as an advance, and at what rate of exchange.

The manager explained that Onuoha should open an account with a number. No name was necessary. The account could even be in the name of Roundseason. They would then on the basis of the deposit try and sell the money in the market and turn over the proceeds as they became available. There was to be a regular rate of exchange. He brought out a paper he wanted Onuoha to sign. Onuoha asked him to fill in the necessary details himself. He did this and gave it to him to sign after Onuoha had reaffirmed his willingness to deposit one hundred thousand pounds. Onuoha took up his pen. Everyone around him smiled. Onuoha paused and asked what would happen if the Akaba Bank failed to change any of the money deposited there. The manager said he could give no guarantee that the money deposited would be changed. In addition, he confirmed that Nigeria had just issued a decree stating that Nigerian currency exported out of the country after August 21st, 1967, would not be redeemed by the Nigerian Government. But the bank was willing to backdate the deposit slip to cover it from that clause of the Nigerian decree.

Onuoha suddenly saw the risk he was running, incriminating himself if he signed the document. He felt that everything he said was being recorded. It was difficult to say whether or not the bank was acting in concert with the Nigerians. The bank manager appeared even to be pressuring him into signing the document. Roundseason added a few words of assurance. Samson and Roundseason did not know beforehand that Onuoha spoke French. The idea was that Obelenwata would have come alone. If it had been Obelenwata who had come, Roundseason would have been able to do all the translating in his own way, making any misrepresentations that he wanted.

If Onuoha had told them that he was backing out of the deal, this would hurt feelings and create a sour impression. Pretending that he never said beforehand that he had the money with him, he informed them that he had no money in Paris, but that, having found out about the possibilities of exchange, he would now contact those concerned in London and elsewhere to see if they would be interested in the Akaba Bank proposals. It was one of those scenes where the participants all knew that the others were lying, but because of this, no one dared accuse the other, for fear of being unmasked himself. So, Onuoha exchanged a smile of confidence with them and left.

Smiling to himself, Onuoha whistled happily as he went back to Hotel Splendid to inform his colleagues. For him a new era had begun and he was determined to drill round all unscrupulous businessmen he saw. He was barely two minutes in Hotel Splendid when Samson Ogbuefi reappeared with Roundseason. Samson was furious as he spoke to Chief Iweka. He asked him to warn Onuoha, who was behaving like a secret service agent or a private detective, pretending to have money to change when he was only interested in unmasking the group. Onuoha was surprised to hear this because he thought that Samson was already attending a meeting at the Dorchester Hotel in London. Onuoha called him aside and reasoned with him. They should be working together to make sure that they were not swindled by foreigners. It was disappointing to see that Samson was siding with foreigners without even trying to find out what had happened. Fuming with rage, Samson warned Onuoha to be careful, that he was not like Jean-Pierre Dubien, so Onuoha could not threaten him with guns and get away with it. Samson Ogbuefi said that he would deal with anyone who stood in his way.

Samson Ogbuefi was known to be a dangerous man who could do anything, and even get rid of anyone he believed to be standing in his way. He had connections in Nigeria and had apparently developed contacts since his arrival in Europe. It was Ferdinand Flatula who later revealed to Onuoha that Roundseason was connected with several spurious American organizations in Paris commonly believed to be front-organizations of the Central Intelligence Agency. Flatula said that Roundseason had also fought with the American forces during the Korean war. Though a director of a bar in Paris, he was also in the pay of about three other organizations. Flatula was willing to give more information about Roundseason but had to leave that night to meet a Katangese friend who was travelling the following day to Algeria to pay a visit to Moise Tshombe. In a lower voice, Flatula indicated that the friend desperately needed about one hundred dollars to complete his round-trip fare to Algiers by way of Russia, since evidence of a recent visit to Russia would make his entry into Algeria easier. Flatula said that he did not normally like begging but asked Onuoha to lend him one hundred dollars on behalf of the African black brother. Flatula promised to pay it back within four days. Onuoha gave him fifty dollars instead and assured him, despite his protests, that there was no need to pay it back.

Flatula then opened his mind and spoke at length about how the French led them astray during the Katanga revolt. They promised everything but gave them nothing. They relied on them and were defeated. Even when they made up with the others, the

French kept on urging them to continue their struggle. They sent them a team of mercenaries that finally brought about the ruin of Katanga. Flatula warned Onuoha about the French. They were nice people, he insisted, but he concluded, 'I would not encourage you to put too much trust in them.'

While Flatula's friend was going to Algeria, Joel Bouchara was on his way back from there, after covering a news story. His reports did not do much to comfort the squad. He said that in Algiers he saw about seventy-four Russian technicians who were in transit to Nigeria where they were supposed to take part in an exchange programme. Most of them were engineers and several of them had worked in the Russian Air Force. Joel Bouchara gave the squad the numbers of the new passports of the Russians, all in series, together with their names and fields of specialization. They had travelled by way of Czechoslovakia and, perhaps to avoid making a direct flight to Nigeria, were to stop a few days in Mauretania and Guinea. From Guinea, they were to join an Aeroflot flight to Bamako and Ghana where a regular Nigerian Airways flight would take them to Lagos for their cultural exchange programme. Lagos and Moscow had signed a Cultural Pact a few weeks earlier and it was reported that one of the clauses included the supply of MIG fighter planes and Ilyushin bombers.

In the face of the complications with the Akaba Bank, the squad decided to find buyers immediately for the money or else to find ways of getting it out of Paris. Joel Bouchara was again very helpful. He had very good connections with the banks in Paris. By that time, Nigeria had also decided to change its paper currency by introducing new designs. A time limit was set for the redemption of the old notes in circulation at home and abroad. That day Samson Anele came from London and carried away about one hundred thousand which he was going to exchange in Germany. Ruddy Nnewi also appeared for the first time in Paris and took another one hundred thousand to change in Germany also. Joel Bouchara decided to try to exchange the rest through the Sahara International Bank (S.I.B.).

Joel was frank: he was not absolutely sure that it would work. Chancellor Obelenwata was afraid to get involved and Lawyer

Afoukwu decided to lead the negotiations. Contacts were made with the directors of the bank and, after days of negotiations, the bank agreed to accept one million pounds. Since they had a branch in Lagos, it was thought that they could justify the possession of large quantities of Nigerian currency abroad. They wanted to keep the deal strictly legal. They planned to present the amount they acquired thus to the Bank of France which would in turn through normal channels ask the Bank of England to redeem the money in question. In that way, the full value would be recovered and the S.I.B. would only get its legal commission for the exchange.

Lawyer Afoukwu was full of optimism when he reported this and arrangements were already being made to get some more money into Paris. The Accord was supposed to be signed the following day. But at the last minute, the S.I.B. announced with deep regret that it could not go ahead with the operation. Bouchara was quick to recommend other people. These people, he said, could help exchange the money at thirty per cent of its market value. He was not personally interested in money affairs and would just introduce the people in question and leave the discussions to the two parties. A meeting was arranged for this purpose. There was now a sense of desperation as the deadline for the currency switch announced by Nigeria approached. Chancellor Obelenwata wanted to give Bouchara's people a chance and agreed to meet them. At nine in the morning on Saturday, Bouchara came along with two of his compatriots, Michel Rottier and Pierre Richier. Onuoha was present at the meeting at Edu's house.

Joel Bouchara left the house before the meeting began. Pierre Richier spoke at length about the difficulty of trying to get banks like S.I.B. to change the notes. Richier said that there would firstly be interference on the part of the cautious French government. It was conceivable, he indicated, that pressure was brought about by the British on the American management of the S.I.B., since the Desert Corporation of America owned about forty-nine per cent of its stocks. Matters of that nature required a political rather than a financial decision. Richier said that the franc and the pound were linked and France would not indulge in any game that might boomerang. The Bank of England could also do the same thing to France should trouble arise in French-speaking Africa. He indicated that in spite of superficial squabbles the interests of white Europeans, political, economic and ideological, were basically the same.

Richier spoke also about Samson Ogbuefi and seemed to know quite a bit about him. He informed the group that Samson Ogbuefi was carrying no less than one hundred thousand dollars in traveller's cheques in his small brief-case. The money had come from deals he had made on behalf of the Biafran government and gifts from foreign organizations who bought him over. Samson had been trying to buy torpedoes from Richier. The latter had done his best to dissuade him, telling him that the boats he bought for the government from another dealer were rotten and could never make the trip from Europe to the West African coast, less still confront the Nigerian Navy. Richier promised to co-operate with Chancellor Obelenwata if the latter wanted to recover the money from Samson. Richier said also that Samson had bought a cabaret in Paris and was operating jointly with Mr Roundseason a rent-a-car service, financed by the money they made collectively from their deals.

Coming down to the business of the day, Richier said that he had banking connections in Switzerland who were willing to take the risk of changing the money. Richier said also that the Nigerian Government through the Nigerian Embassies in Germany and Switzerland had written to all the major banks telling them about the decree and about the refusal of the Nigerian government to buy back notes illegally exported from the country. In addition, the Bank of England, which backed the Nigerian pound, had also written to major banks in Europe asking them to declare immediately the approximate amount of Nigerian notes they had in their possession before the closing date, so that arrangements could be made to redeem them.

Their bank in Geneva, Richier said, was not one of the big ones and did not receive the note from the Bank of England. The big banks, he emphasized, whose annual business index ran into millions of pounds would not risk spoiling their reputation and credit-worthiness with the Bank of England. The price of the Nigerian currency had gone down so much in Europe because the Nigerian Government and the Bank of England had sent powerful agents to Switzerland, France, and Germany. The aim of these agents was to try to buy over at the minimum possible rate all the Nigerian currency available. He strongly criticized the Biafran sale effort. Biafran envoys, Richier said, had not made the matter easy. The law of supply and demand weighed heavily in this case. The prices of shares in a company go down when too many start offering the sale of their shares. Buyers become wary and the prices go down. The difficulty in selling the Nigerian notes arose from the fact that there were too many Biafrans offering the sale of the same notes, often to the same buyer or to different agents of the same buyer. If ten people start offering agents of banks the sale of one million pounds of old Nigerian currency notes, sooner or later the impression is created that there are actually ten million pounds for sale and this is enough to bring the buying rate down from seventeen shillings to the pound to less than five shillings. At that price even, buyers are afraid they might not recover their investment.

Richier's arguments were so impressive that Chancellor Obelenwata asked him what he wanted him to do to save the situation. Richier suggested that Chancellor Obelenwata confide to him all the money there was for sale. In that way there would be a collective offer to a single buyer. In anticipation of this development, Richier said that his bank had sent a message to the Bank of England saying that they had some Nigerian notes and wanted instructions on what to do with them. This procedure had a double advantage. Firstly, the amount in question was not stated. Secondly, because the letter was sent before the deadline, the Bank of England could not refuse payment, since the statute of limitations would have been met by the notification. The accuracy of the man's information impressed Chancellor Obelenwata even more. The latter asked how much money Richier could handle. Jeff Edu quietly suggested, in Efik, to Chancellor Obelenwata who was a native of Arochukwu that the man be tried first with fifty thousand pounds. Obelenwata would not listen and called Lisbon immediately to make available for him about £7 million. It was decided that Onuoha should travel with Rottier to Geneva to complete the negotiations. Following his report, a decision would be taken either to transfer the money in Lisbon to Geneva or to keep it in Lisbon for the Geneva bank to pick up.

Onuoha and Edu did not share the Professor's optimism. It was agreed between them that Onuoha should just take along with him one hundred thousand pounds. The tickets were bought that Saturday and Onuoha was put on the waiting list for the direct flight to Geneva on Monday morning. Onuoha and Michel Rottier agreed that should anything happen and they did not travel together, they should get together at Hotel Europe on Monday evening.

On Monday morning, Onuoha collected the amount in question and drove straight to Orly airport, where he was to join Rottier for the Swissair flight to Geneva. Onuoha drove straight to the departure entrance of the terminal. Despite the protests of the policeman, Onuoha left the car there and rushed inside to deposit his luggage. He was one hour early so as to have time to check in the luggage and then park his car in the overnight parking lot which was then quite a distance from the airport. Rottier was there already. He helped Onuoha with his luggage and told him that there was no room on the direct flight to Geneva. Onuoha checked immediately at the Swissair counter and this was confirmed. Swissair told them that the next best thing was a flight going to Zurich and assured them that a Zurich-Geneva flight could be confirmed for them that morning. This was acceptable.

The plane was due to leave within half an hour and Onuoha had to hurry. At the Air France check-in counter where luggage was normally checked in for European-bound flights, the same hostess that had informed Obiora Ifedi that he had a phone call on the night that the Toulouse flight was cancelled, was at the counter. The lady refused to check in Onuoha's luggage because he had no Swiss visa. Onuoha had to lie that he was going to Frankfurt and was making a brief stop in Geneva. Nigerian passport holders did not need visas to enter Germany. The air hostess insisted that Onuoha buy a Paris-Zurich-Frankfurt-Paris ticket. Onuoha agreed.

The lady then proceeded to calculate and find the cheapest flight plan for the journey. Onuoha thanked her for her efforts and asked her to give him the fastest even if it turned out to be more expensive. He had to be in Geneva that day, for in two or three days the deadline would expire for the currency change. Having got the ticket, he went back to check in the luggage. The lady told him that he had excess baggage of over thirty kilograms. She gave Onuoha the bill, but naturally refused to hand him over the ticket until he had paid for the excess baggage. Anxious and enervated, Onuoha stood in a long queue with others who were also waiting to pay their excess baggage charges. He made out a cheque and had everything ready. Time was running out fast. With the receipt, he rushed back to the check-in counter and claimed his ticket. Rottier was waiting for him and asked him to hurry. Just as Onuoha was about to go and park his car, Rottier told him, 'Please, meet William Spenser, my associate. He will be travelling with us.' Onuoha had barely time to reflect on this new element. He told them he would join them in the plane and rushed out to park his car.

There was already a police warning slip on the windshield. There was no parking space in the nearest lot facing the airport, with the result that he had to drive another seven hundred yards to the next lot. He almost crashed through the iron gate which would not open until he picked up the time-check ticket. The door swung open and he parked his car, locked it and took to his heels.

He looked at his watch, and saw that it was already ten, take-off time for the plane. But normally he used to set his watch about five or eight minutes fast. So he still had at least five minutes to go. He looked at the big clock in front of the terminal, which read five to ten. He ran as fast as his legs would carry him, clutching his abdomen and dragging along his heavy brief-case. He had his ticket and boarding pass. He dashed through the gate, tearing out his boarding pass to make it easier for the lazy guards manning the

ntry to the upper platform. He had forgotten the exact gate. His
rst inclination was to run to the main customs entry gates of the
eparture platform and ask, but it was the wrong gate. As it
urned out, French immigration for those Switzerland-bound was
andled at the Swiss end of the trip.

Onuoha rushed over to the Air France information desk and
vas asked to run over to gate twelve. He was running, sliding
lown the banister, jumping five steps at a time and at the gate
resented his boarding pass to the hostess. 'Sorry, Sir, it is too
ate!' Onuoha pleaded and almost cried. The lady repeated her
tatement. The plane was taxiing out and would be taking off any
econd from then. Onuoha almost fainted. 'What about my lug-
;age?' he asked. There was evidently nothing that could be done
bout it. He tried to open his mouth to plead again, but he did not
ave the courage to do so. Naturally, he could not explain his
reoccupations to the lady. He went down again to the Swissair
ounter and explained the situation to them. He looked like a fool
s he walked back slowly to the ground floor of the terminal.

When he arrived at the Swissair counter, he reported that he had
nissed the plane to Zurich and that he would like to get back his
uggage. The young lady at the desk was very sympathetic and
old him that there was no problem. She asked to see the baggage
laim ticket numbers. Onuoha almost collapsed. He had never felt
o stupid in his life. How on earth could he prove that he had two
uitcases on that plane? The baggage ticket was not attached to
he ticket he was holding. Then he remembered and produced the
xcess baggage payment receipt. The Swissair hostess was very
o-operative and promised to do her best to trace the luggage.
)nuoha briefly described the suitcases for her.

Since they were not his and he had just dragged them into the
ar without taking great note of them, his description was very
pproximate. Then she asked him what they contained. Onuoha
vas highly embarrassed as he said 'Personal effects'. With a broad
mile, she asked if Onuoha could mention one or two of the items
1 the suitcase, just for identification purposes. 'Personal effects,'
e said with greater embarrassment. She wanted to find out the
alue of the personal effects for the purposes of claims and

insurance. Onuoha simply told her that they were of gre
sentimental value. The hostess laughed.

When she learned that Onuoha was going to Geneva instead o
Zurich, she informed him that there was a direct flight to Genev
leaving almost immediately. Onuoha said he knew about it, bu
had been told that there was no seat available. 'No problem,' th
hostess replied. 'There are lots of seats.' She telephoned to veri
and this was confirmed. 'Would you like me to confirm a seat fc
you on the flight?' she asked. 'Yes please, if you can,' Onuoh
replied, rather morosely. As for the luggage, the hostess promise
to send out a tracer right away and said that the luggage would b
put on the first plane going to Geneva, where Onuoha coul
claim it. Onuoha was asked to report to the Swissair counter fc
missing articles on arrival at the airport. The hostess also cable
a message to Zurich and Geneva. Onuoha went to the uppe
platform again and went to the telephone booth to inform Edu tha
he was about to leave. He dialled the number, it rang a couple o
times and Onuoha hung up again. He did not know what to te
Edu.

Once on the plane, Onuoha thought about his luggage an
about Rottier and his friend William Spenser. The name of th
latter sounded English or American. But his accent was neithe
English nor American and his complexion was Mediterranean. H
seemed also to speak French with a foreign accent and the trace o
a stammer. Onuoha was quite worried by this situation. He wor
dered if the two of them could claim his luggage. Were they i
possession of the claim ticket? Was the entire morning a carefull
planned succession of events? Would Rottier and Spenser com
back to Paris for him, wait for him in Zurich or proceed on t
Geneva? How could he explain the whole incident to his co
leagues?

The Geneva flight was barely fifty minutes, but it seemed lik
hours as they flew over the mountains of southeastern France
There were a few storms on the way, but they landed safely a
Geneva. Onuoha experienced a feeling of satisfaction and appre
hension at the same time. He passed through French custom
without trouble. At the Swiss immigration, the officer told hir

that he could not enter because he had no visa. Onuoha told him that he was in transit and would be continuing to Frankfurt within six hours, but just wanted a sight-seeing tour of Geneva. He showed the officer his ticket and was granted leave to enter Geneva, but was asked to leave his passport at the airport office.

Onuoha went straight to the baggage claim section to see if he could recover his luggage without attracting attention and without having to meet airport officials again. He looked around and watched the various conveyor belts. There was nothing. Anele was supposed to be in Geneva to meet him at the airport. Onuoha did not have the courage to telephone him at the Hotel Intercontinental to tell him that he had arrived. He decided to find his suitcases before going anywhere. He made a few inquiries about the location of the lost and claims department at the airport and was directed to the second floor of the building.

They had not received the cable from Paris and he had to start filling out forms again to identify the approximate size and appearance of the missing cases. Messages were sent immediately to Zurich instructing them to fly the cases over to Geneva on the next available plane. At noon, the connecting flight from Zurich arrived and Rottier and Spenser were not on the plane. The suitcases were not there either. Onuoha's head was reeling with ideas, with fever, with headache. He forgot that he had had nothing to eat all day. He hoped the luggage had not been sent back to Paris or sent on ahead to Frankfurt. He was glued to the airport. He knew that Anele would be anxiously waiting for him and would probably call Paris and report Onuoha's absence.

A second flight, a third flight and a fourth one arrived from Zurich. He saw neither Rottier nor the cases. He was tempted to call Hotel Europe to see if Rottier and Spenser had arrived there by a mysterious route and checked in with the two suitcases. But he did not want to call and set off an embarrassing alarm. There was a plane leaving for Zurich in half an hour at 3.50 p.m. Onuoha wanted to travel to Zurich and locate his luggage himself. Then, on second thoughts, he considered what would happen if he went to Zurich and the plane arrived in Geneva with the luggage. Once the cases got into the hands of the police, he would have to identify the contents.

He was looking completely lost in the customs area when an official came up to him and asked if he could help. He explained his case to the officer. He was given more customs forms to fill out reporting the loss. He complied. This officer was not the one in charge of the luggage department, but he promised to pass on the papers to his colleagues who had gone out for a cup of coffee. Within minutes, they were back. The official responsible asked Onuoha to come along. He took him to the office and there Onuoha saw his two suitcases waiting for him. 'Your suitcases have been here since noon. They were moved straight from the plane into the office here on special instructions from Paris and Zurich. I have been waiting all this time for you to come and claim them.' Onuoha thanked him for his kindness, took a caddie and moved the cases out of the customs zone. He telephoned Intercontinental Hotel to tell Anele that he would be over shortly. Anele was not in his room but Onuoha left a message for him. A ten-minute taxi ride brought him to the doors of the fabulous twelve-storey hotel on the banks of Lake Geneva.

He checked into his room on the fifth floor, facing a motor-park. It was a great relief to be able to sit down. He opened the cases and everything was there just as they had been packed. He locked the cases inside the closet, locked the outside door and hung a red sign on the door—DO NOT DISTURB—then went downstairs to look around. He entered the elevator but it went upstairs instead of downstairs. This was nothing compared with the other inconveniences of the day. Finally the lift came down. Whom did he see at the check-in counter of the hotel receiving keys but Rottier and Spenser. He was dumbfounded. He told them that he was just planning to call them at the Hotel Europe. They replied that they were just planning to call him at the Hotel Europe also. Onuoha discovered also that they were on the fifth floor and were occupying a suite just next to his room. The coincidence was too much. He promised to meet them upstairs in a few minutes for discussions. They went into the elevator and Anele appeared and was told what had happened. Onuoha also told him about his fears and suspicions. It was agreed that Rottier and Spenser should not be told that Anele was staying at that hotel. Anele was also to pass as the Biafran banker in Europe.

Anele told Onuoha how influential Yoruba elements in the Lagos government had come personally to Switzerland or had sent their trusted emissaries to purchase at very low rates old Nigerian currency notes. These would be smuggled back to Lagos in diplomatic bags and exchanged at par for the new Nigerian notes. The end of the war would give birth to lots of Nigerian millionaires. It was not known immediately whether the money was being accumulated to start an insurrection in Western Nigeria or whether the buyers were just shrewd businessmen.

Apparently, old politicians and their cronies were feeding on the sufferings of the peasants. The rich were getting richer, the poor poorer, in obedience to the gospels. The rich were speedily sending their children out of the country to study in exclusive schools and universities while the sons of peasants were shedding the last drop of their blood for the survival of all. The politicians stayed in Europe making money and opening new accounts in every city, making allowances for the rainy day in case the battle was lost, while the poor workers and cocoa farmers at home were being forced to contribute money and their services for the comfort of the soldiers.

In press conferences in every capital abroad, from their bunkers away from the war zones, the politicians proclaimed the determina- of the people, their people, to fight to the last man. In the tropical bush, the peasant saw his sons perish one by one in a never-ending battle over some marshy piece of terrain. But there was also another side to the war. There were the heroes who gave their lives willingly so that others might survive. There were others who sacrificed their lives and personal careers for a cause they believed in. There were others who did not have the heart to abandon their people, women and children, old and young who could not fight and who often did not quite understand what the fight was about, but ran when the enemy approached so that they should avoid the rapacity of demented soldiers. There were others who genuinely understood and believed in the cause to which they had devoted their lives.

Beyond the zones of combat, beyond the parties concerned, there were also men and groups whose zeal and support for one group or the other was dictated by what they could grab, how much they could make out of a deal. These were often ruthless in their approach, impersonal in their business, brutal in their treatment of human beings in great suffering. Without conscience and hardened, they would kill an infant or rape an old woman in order to snatch the last farthing from the shivering hands of a famished body, a homeless soul, a bereaved heart.

Beyond the zones of combat, outside the parties in conflict, there were also genuine souls who could not stand the suffering of human beings irrespective of their race or the colour of their skin. They would share their earnings, give out their clothing, donate their blood and sometimes offer their services, fully aware of the risks involved, in order to save the life of a suffering child they did not know and had not seen.

There are various kinds of people in the world, each one has his private motivation. Behind fervent zeal often lies a personal wish to have power. Behind verbal boldness and flaming courage often lie barefaced cowardice and moral bankruptcy. Sometimes inside the tender-hearted, soft-spoken man that shirks violence lies a strong mind, an unwavering commitment. The world is full of many and diverse voices. Human intentions are several and unclear; so too are states of mind changing. The world is a mystery, an understatement.

Onuoha sat on his bed brooding over these thoughts. The thought that high government officials would send emissaries abroad to make profit out of the people and the government they were serving, out of the savings of the young men they had sent to fight in the fields of battle, over the dead bodies of the people whose cause they were supposed to champion, filled Onuoha with disgust. As Flatula had once told him, European businessmen had been made into the crooks by the envoys sent from the warring nations. If the Europeans succeeded in bribing the envoy with ten or twenty per cent of the contract money, the European often fled without fulfilling the contract. The embarrassed and stained envoy would forever lament the dishonesty of European contractors but naturally, he would think twice about bringing the European to justice or justifying his embarrassment before his home government.

Rottier and Spenser rang Onuoha's door-bell and came into the room. They wanted to meet the Biafran banking representative and find out also how much money there was available in Switzerland. Onuoha was more interested in getting specific details about their proposal, since its feasibility alone would determine the availability of money. At that point the story changed. Rottier said that his bankers wanted to find out how much money would be deposited. His bankers were surveying the possibility of flying the entire amount into Great Britain by landing at a quiet country airport. They were also examining the possibility of smuggling the currency across the channel in boats overnight. Once in England, the money could be presented to the Bank of England by individuals hired for the purpose. It turned out that Rottier had no particular bank in mind. In fact, he gave Onuoha the impression that he was only going to make the contacts the following day. The meeting was then arranged for the following morning.

Onuoha took the elevator to the twelfth floor restaurant with its red lights, red carpet and red table cloths. Beyond its glittering windows lay Lake Geneva, flat and quiet. It was a glorious sight by night. As Onuoha sat down to eat, Spenser came and joined him. He appeared anxious to talk about himself as they began their dinner. Spenser said that he had worked as a journalist for *Paris-Match*, investigating traffic accidents and insurance claims. His family was very rich, but he was anxious to gain as much experience as possible before taking over the management of the family property. He had just returned from New York after spending six tough hours there on a business meeting. He had gone there the day before to sign a contract with an American machine tool company. He and Rottier were setting up a machine tool factory on the outskirts of Paris, just one mile from Orly airport, where they would manufacture divers gadgets on licence from America.

They were also negotiating to manufacture car parts for one of the major American car manufacturers. In all, they employed about one thousand workers.

William Spenser had also worked as a guest observer with the Chase Manhattan Bank. His father had sent him there to help him observe financial transactions and operations. The contacts he had made then were valuable and they had aided his business prospects. He had lots of experience in currency exchanges. It was because of this that Rottier had cabled him to come down from New York. He said that an exiled Panamanian leader had deposited over three million dollars worth of Panamanian money with the Chase Manhattan Bank. Though the date for the switch had expired, his lawyers had been able to recover a substantial part of the equivalent of the old currency in dollars. Drawing the logical conclusion, Spenser said that in the Biafran case, even after the expiration of the deadline, a legal case could still be initiated and he was very sure of recovering at least a percentage of the total amount deposited with the bank.

At the end of the long monologue, Onuoha asked Spenser about his nationality. Spenser said that his father was French and his mother American. When he had finished his short autobiography and there was no more to be said, the two of them left the restaurant, pursued by the sweet mellow voice of a young lady singing to the accompaniment of the piano and a flute. As they bade each other goodnight, Onuoha reminded Spenser of their early morning meeting. He promised not to forget and, on that note, they parted.

The following morning at seven, Onuoha knocked at the door of Spenser and Rottier. There was no answer. He went back to his room and telephoned them and there was no reply. As he hung up the phone, Anele came in and together they surveyed the situation. It became evident that no headway could be made. The plane-load that Professor Chancellor Obelenwata had requested to be sent to Geneva had arrived. The crew and all concerned were in such a hurry and so disorganized that the two security men on board had not brought their passports. Since the crew could not say who owned the money and were unprepared to make any customs declarations or even hand over the cargo to the customs for safe-keeping for the owner, Geneva officials would not let them off-load the cargo. News of the misadventure was already in the morning papers, in spite of the efforts of the Biafran lobbyists in Geneva. While Anele and Onuoha were discussing all this, Rottier and Spenser arrived and together the four of them left for the proposed meeting with their bankers.

The bank in question was the People's Bank in Geneva. They took the elevator to the third floor of the building to meet the assistant manager. Like most bankers, he was affable and business-like. He invited the group to come down to the vault and see where the money would be kept, if Onuoha and Anele decided to keep it with them. As they descended to the vault, he told them that he could handle any amount, one thousand, one million, seven tons. The amount was immaterial. Asked if he had received any letter from the Bank of England about his cablegram, he said that he had not sent a telegram to England. On the other hand, he had received a letter from the Embassy of Nigeria stipulating that after a certain date, Nigerian currency notes still floating around would not be redeemed. He was planning to write to the Bank of England about the possibility of changing the money that Onuoha was bringing.

The bank manager showed Onuoha and Anele the various compartments of the vault—the control room, the safe-deposit section for clients. He was willing to rent a large vault at a modest price if Onuoha decided to leave the old Nigerian currency there. Asked about how he would write to the Bank of England without compromising himself and his clients, he said that it was simple. He would inform the Bank of England that he had a long-estab-lished client who had quite a substantial amount of old Nigerian currency he would like to convert to sterling. Because of profes-sional secrecy, there would be no need to name the client. He could even say that several clients were involved. But he wanted to know the exact amount involved in the operation so that he could inform the Bank of England should they ask him how much over the telex. He confessed that his bank would look ridiculous if it informed the Bank of England that he had seven million pounds and later it turned out to be just half a million. He would be accused of indulging in speculation. Asked if the Bank of England would not be suspicious and question how he came to possess so much money in old Nigerian currency, the assistant manager then explained that his bank had lots of business in Northern Nigeria and in fact they had an associated bank in Lagos itself. Besides, he added with confidence, the People's Bank of Geneva was the senior partner in the Bank of the North in Kaduna, the official bank of the Government of Northern Nigeria. Within seconds, it dawned on Onuoha and Anele that they were actually right inside an enemy vault and at the total mercy of their enemies.

Pretending to be unmoved, Onuoha asked what would happen if after all his efforts, the Bank of England was unable to do anything. The manager smiled and said, 'Then you still have your money.' Onuoha asked him if he was aware that after a certain date, the currency would cease to be legal tender and it would be a criminal offence to transport it from one country to another. The bank manager said that they could keep the money for him until the end of the hostilities. 'As you know,' he continued, 'in civil wars, whether there is victory or failure, there are always negotiations and, as a banker, I know that one of the points to be negotiated would be what to do with the national patrimony. It could then be decided that a certain percentage would be paid as compensation for each unexchanged pound.'

Finally Onuoha asked him what effect on his business discovery of the notes would have. The manager did not think that the discovery of the notes by the Swiss, English or Nigerians was possible. Concluding, he said, 'As a banker, I have absolutely no knowledge that there is old Nigerian currency in my bank.' Onuoha asked him what he meant, pointing out that the bank would naturally give an official receipt for the deposit. 'Certainly,' he said. 'I will give you an official bank receipt for the package deposited. As far as I am concerned, I have no knowledge of what it contains. As far as the bank is concerned, we can receive from our clients anything, except explosives, for safe-keeping in our deposit vault. It could be sand, but it is usually not worth anyone's while to pay to keep a bag of sand in our safe deposit. It could also be jewellery. We are not interested in the value. We make no guarantees except that we promise to produce on the client's demand the package he confided to us.' Put in other words, the bank manager said that what he could receive from Onuoha would be a certain number of cartons or suitcases, so many centimetres long, wide and deep and weighing at that particular time so many kilograms. 'Even if the cartons were filled with ordinary useless paper?' Anele asked, with a smile. Everyone laughed.

Onuoha thanked him for giving up so much of his time and assured him that he would bring the proposals immediately to certain Biafran businessmen who were interested in the exchange. They were already on the street level of the bank. They said goodbye to the manager and left. Everyone was quiet. Rottier and Spenser stopped a taxi and invited Onuoha and Anele to join them. They thanked them, but said they were going somewhere else. 'We shall see you then at the hotel,' Rottier said. 'Certainly,' Onuoha smiled.

Onuoha telephoned Jeff Edu to tell him what had happened. Jeff asked him to carry the money to Lisbon that afternoon where final efforts would be made to change it at two shillings for a pound. It was obviously impossible, even in Zurich, to exchange the Nigerian pound for an American silver dollar. After lunch at the hotel, Onuoha went to the desk to check out of the Intercontinental. The floor manager called him and said that his friends in the suite next door had checked out a few minutes earlier and said that Onuoha would pay their bill because they belonged to the same company. It turned out that they had given false names to the hotel and given out Onuoha's Paris address as their company office. Anele and Onuoha left the hotel amused, after giving the floor manager what they knew to be the Paris address of Rottier and Spenser. Onuoha reclaimed his passport at the airport and together with Anele boarded the plane, a TAP flight to Lisbon, in search of a buyer who would pay a silver dollar for an old Nigerian pound.

. . . .

When the plane landed in Lisbon, they went through immigration. When the officers saw their Nigerian passports, the Portuguese authorities stopped them. They explained that they were Biafrans, and were allowed entry only after the immigration officers had checked with the Biafran office in the city. Security was quite tight. They went through the customs area to claim their luggage. Onuoha located the two suitcases and handed one to Anele.

Rather mechanically, the customs official was going to mark okay on the suitcase when he stopped and asked Onuoha if he had anything to declare. He said he had nothing but personal effects. Anele was already shivering. With calmness, Onuoha watched the officer who asked him to open the suitcase. Coolly, Onuoha brought out the key, fiddled around a bit and opened the suitcase. He opened it slightly. But the officer, as if to show the people around that Onuoha was not carrying any contraband goods opened the suitcase completely. He almost fainted when he saw what it contained. He shouted. He was not satisfied with this personal visual ingratiation. As if to prove he was not egotistical, with typical Latin fervour and exuberance, he called the other four or five officials around to come and satisfy their eyes also.

Within seconds, they were all there. The Lisbon luggage room was unlike other luggage claim halls elsewhere. It was oval-shaped and had a balcony overlooking it as in a medieval theatre or even Roman arena. The balcony was always full of tourists and the jobless. That particular day, it seemed as if all Lisbon had been given a day off to come and watch a customs official open a suitcase full of currency notes. It was impossible to listen to all the varied remarks and reactions of those above. Apparently pleased with this diversion, the official asked Onuoha to open the other suitcase also. Onuoha told him it contained the same kind of personal effects. Fortunately, Portugal has no restrictions about the import or export of foreign currency and there were bold signs proclaiming this liberty on the walls of the customs room.

The official, still amused, asked Onuoha where he planned to stay, perhaps for his own private information. Onuoha was not sure, but lied to him, 'Hotel Don Carlos'. 'Don Carlos?' the man asked again, shaking his head. 'Don Carlos,' Onuoha repeated and the name of the hotel was echoed by some people on the balcony. Outside the luggage room, Onuoha and Anele took a taxi to the Biafran Office in Estoril, on the outskirts of the city.

5

From the Frying Pan to the Fire

The Biafran Office in Lisbon was located barely twenty yards from the river with its magnificent El Ponte Salazar. The area was an ideal resort place, cool all the year round, quiet, calm. Since the Biafrans had moved into the building, an American businessman had acquired a house across the street and a British firm had luckily found a home for one of its newly Lisbon-based executives. He lived next door to the Biafrans. Naturally there were foreigners around there most of the time, while Portuguese soldiers patrolled the area night and day. There was also a Frenchman who spent his time walking up and down looking for a house in the neighbourhood. It also meant more jobs for taxi drivers and the same cars and chauffeurs seemed to park there every day waiting for customers. Long antennas and complex wireless masts sprang up on the roofs of the houses around.

The Biafran office itself was well furnished, in exquisite taste, with chandeliers floating down from the ceilings and Persian rugs decorating the floors. The lounge looked like a palatial anteroom and the officers there seemed to have a penchant for dry rosé during their meals. In one small corner, in a room adjacent to the kitchen was located the Operations Room, the tiny life-vein on which the destiny of Biafra hung. It contained the telex link between Biafra and the outside world.

After he had completed his mission, Onuoha left Lisbon for Paris. His arrival there coincided with the beginning of the student disturbances in the French capital of May 1968. At first Onuoha that that the radio was exaggerating, until he drove himself one evening to the Quartier Latin and saw thousands of students prepared to fight, facing hundreds of law-enforcement officers, the famous French C.R.S. (Compagnie Républicaine de la Sécurite). At first nothing happened: they just stood around and looked at each other with suspicion. It was drizzling a little, but that did not seem to bother any of them. There were crowds around Boulevard Saint-Germain, but the concentration seemed to be around

Boulevard Saint-Michel. Students stood around Place de la Sorbonne and harangued one another, posing for photographs and for television groups in front of the dominating statue there, with a background of the hammer and sickle, Viet-Cong flags and Mao Tse-Tung emblems.

The entire neighbourhood was littered with papers, flags, garbage and posters. Thousands of copies of campaign literature passed from hand to hand. The statue of Montaigne looked across from Rue des Ecoles, pensive and unabashed. Here there was a lad with a jerrycan, there a kid with a walkie-talkie. There were some kids wearing helmets, others merely stood and watched. The feeling was that anything could happen at any time. Meetings were taking place everywhere—in the cafés where poor students sat and drank one cup of coffee all day; on the side-walks where myriads of legs trotted up and down in opposing directions; in front of stores, where those who had no money stood and admired the affluence of the bourgeoisie. It was difficult to say who was directing the movement or even whether it had any direction at all.

Sometimes, from what the students said and from what the press reported, it was impossible to find out exactly what they were fighting for or against, what order they wanted changed and what new regime they would like to see installed. It looked like the eve of another French Revolution, this ritual dear to the French people, with all its terror, uncertainty and bloodshed. Everyone knew there was something wrong. But no one knew exactly what to supplant it with. The intention seemed to be to destroy existing institutions and then later call a Constituent Assembly that would establish the new dictatorship of the new generation. There were students in Quartier Latin that could stand, high in physique and eloquence, side by side with Marat, Danton and Robespierre. The Internationale replaced the Marseillaise. Meanwhile, the everyday life of Paris was paralysed.

Barricades went up everywhere. Riots broke out everywhere. Soon the strikes began. Petrol became scarce and newspapers appeared irregularly. But the radios kept everyone informed about the atrocities being committed, about police brutality and the vandalism of the mobs. Then came the dash to the supermarkets.

Within hours essential items were scarce as hundreds of house-wives and concubineless bachelors rushed to the nearest stores. Soon big grocery stores had no more powdered milk, dried bread, sugar, salt and dried vegetables.

There were rumours of a state of insurrection, of anarchy, of a civil war. Post offices were closed and telephone communications became difficult inside the city and impossible outside the country. Transport came to a standstill. Soon life itself came to a standstill. The only news on the radio was a repetition of new bomb attacks on public buildings, clashes between the police and students. Then came the sharp rumours of the resignation of the French Government. Politicians from various groups, left of centre and right of left, already declared their willingness to take over power.

The Army appeared on the streets of the capital. At first it simply patrolled the main boulevards. Gradually, it took over the banks, the communications centres, the airports, the railway sta-tions. Then came the mammoth traffic jams. Cars moved at the rate of one mile in three hours. Then the small stores closed their doors. The streets became deserted. Even the Americans and the North Vietnamese vacated the conference rooms of the Hotel Majestic with its curved four-sided tables. Army trucks and tanks alone remained on the streets. Army Red Cross vans and ambul-ances followed each convoy of trucks. Blood banks were set up in various parts of the city. The nation was bracing for the worst.

The heavens and the minds of people were filled with premoni-tions. At night, the rain fell with the sound and fury of shovelfuls of clay thumping over myriads of graves. The sleeper was haunted by real and imaginary sounds of explosions and gun shots. Money became scarce and the few businesses still open refused to accept cheques drawn even on Paris banks. Warnings and counter-warnings came from political, student and professional groups. Man felt helpless in the midst of the impending disaster, in the midst of the catastrophe gradually taking possession of his body and soul.

The cruel and putrefying evidence of disaster lay at every corner. The pigeons in the parks disappeared. Vultures took possession of the roof tops. Guns boomed in the night, Molotov cocktails cracked in the darkness and during the day, piles of garbage and filth stood staring menacingly at the tenant from across the street. Radio reports of clashes and mass demonstrations increased. Radio announcements of student and worker resistance doubled. Complaints about police brutality tripled. The nation seemed not to heed the appeals of those that thought themselves its leaders. The leaders seemed to lose control of the nation. France woke up on the brink of an internecine war, a war without boundaries, a war where the combatants live in the same building and are housed under the same roof; a war that would divide the nation and the citizens, the army and the armoury.

Biafran operations were also at a standstill. Paris had grown to be the centre of all Biafran activities and the crisis seemed to have affected Onuoha and his friends even more than the French people. With the telephone not working and the telex out of order, it was impossible to get anything done.

Meanwhile, Enugu, the Biafran capital, had fallen and the Mid-West Region of Nigeria had been lost again by the Biafran troops. The Nigerians had landed their troops in Calabar on the south-eastern corner of Biafra and they were pressing steadily from the north of the country towards the centre. Meanwhile, a final attempt to smuggle out about eight tons of Nigerian currency with the help of a Yoruba businessman, in Lomé, ended in a fiasco. On the eve of the operation, the protector of the Yoruba businessman fell out of favour with the Lagos government and was placed under house detention. The Yoruba man was supposed to stay in Lomé and collect by lorry a plane-load of seven million Nigerian pounds which were due to arrive from Lisbon. The airport police seized the money and later on the Nigerian government bought it over from the bankrupt Togolese Treasury for one million pounds sterling, which the latter used in paying its workers who had been on strike for three months. Funnily enough the operation was mounted by Samson Ogbuefi. After the fiasco, some people thought that Samson was actually working hand in hand with the Nigerian government.

Meanwhile, Edu and Onuoha were like a flight of birds with

their wings clipped, grounded on the desert island that was Paris. With no petrol available, it was impossible to move out of the house. Electricity supply was no longer regular and gas for cooking was becoming more and more scarce. The break-down of law and order was complete. The situation demonstrated both the power of the individual and the weakness of the single man. Onuoha could not help thinking that it was one man alone, a Cohn-Bendit, a Jacques Sauvageot, who appeared to have galvanized the whole movement.

People as individuals then felt helpless in the face of a protest that had assumed the dimensions of a revolution. No amount of goodwill seemed enough to stem the impending disaster. The man in the street looked intoxicated and became impervious to reason, displaying a ruthless logic that implies a total refusal to argue. Prophets and moralists sprang up overnight. Everyone had an answer to the entire problem, but the problem could not be solved entirely at once and no one seemed able to provide an answer to any of the problems facing the entire nation. Looking back, Onuoha thought that a few little steps earlier could have prevented the existing state of disaster. A few little concessions could have saved the nation from its seemingly impending demise. A little bit of humility, personal, corporate and ideological, could have saved the nation.

However, it appeared that a conjuncture of forces, perhaps irresistible, perhaps fatal, seemed to have united, converged as if in a planned and predestined way, to bring down the nation and its people. The gods, the Greeks would have said, were angry and no amount of pacification short of human blood would placate them. And blood was flowing already in the streets of Paris. The rioters killed a policeman in Lyon. The policemen shot a demonstrator somewhere else. A young boy running away from the police and the demonstrators was pushed into the River Seine. Life continued to flow. Criticism of the police made them more irritable. The strain on their loyalty seemed to complicate the problem. For those in power, it was a matter of life and death, of personal and physical survival. They used the power in their grip to protect themselves, their political power and their physical safety. For the opposition, the time had come. They had arrived at the Rubicon and there was no going back. Their own survival was also at stake.

These thoughts took Onuoha back to that Friday afternoon on July 7th, 1967, when Edu touched his shoulder and asked him to kneel down and pray for peace at home. He asked himself whether the war was inevitable, whether a few concessions here and there could have prevented a disaster, whether some humility on the part of some could have saved the lives of millions. The fact was that a war there was and questions about its inevitability were pointless, futile.

About this time, word got through to Onuoha and Afoukwu asking them to go to Sierra Leone to explain to the government there the latest military and political situation. Getting out of Paris was a difficult job. With no air connections between France and the outside world, the trains and road transport stopped, Onuoha and Afoukwu looked around for another means of transport. Air France was then operating from Brussels and was providing buses for passengers going abroad. That morning, Onuoha and Afoukwu obtained their visas from the Belgian Embassy to enable them to cross the territory. Tickets were bought on the morning of their departure. Onuoha put away his car, somehow feeling that he might never come back to Paris. He cast a final glance at all the fresh vegetables and provisions he had bought in preparation for a long drawn-out strike and closed his door. Jeff Edu drove them to the old Gare d'Orsay. There they joined about two hundred other people also waiting for buses to go to Brussels. It was drizzling and the organization of the trip, despite the best efforts of the hostesses, was deplorable.

They waited in the rain for more than ninety minutes. Their suitcases travelled in one bus and they in another. Fortunately, they were not carrying Nigerian currency this time. The bus was so crowded that some people had to stand. Slowly they drove past the River Seine. Edu followed them for a while and then waved them goodbye from his car. It was a very sad way to part from friends. Somehow, Onuoha felt something fatalistic about the journey. Each goodbye, each look, each turn looked like the last one for him. The Place de la Concorde was quiet and deserted. Around the Eglise de la Madeleine, one had the impression of visiting the remains of an ancient city with its columns of brick and stone. Past the Galeries Lafayette they took a roundabout course up north towards the Autoroute du Nord. They were soon out of Paris.

As they drove past Le Bourget Airport, Onuoha cast a final glance at the air field and relived within seconds the anxious moments he had spent on the second floor of its terminal. From there onwards, undulating valleys, interlocking hills, green corn-fields spread out over the deserted countryside. The normally crowded road up north to England and Belgium was deserted. Onuoha had been on that road several times as he drove to the coast to cross the English channel for a brief stay in foggy London. He was not sure he would ever be on it again.

It appeared that everyone had left France at that crucial moment of trial. All along the route, factory doors remained shut. There were no trailers going back to the provinces after delivering their cargoes of fresh fruits and vegetables at the Halles market. There were no caravans taking vacationers to the south of France. That night must have been a dreary one at the Halles market. The few cars they saw on the road were military vehicles moving in formation, searching the few passers-by who dared the desolate road. They were searching them for arms, weapons and jerrycans for the sale or possession of petrol, which had been declared pro-hibited following a series of bomb attacks on government build-ings. About half-way along the terribly slow journey, the hostess served them cold chicken sandwiches and soda. They stopped somewhere along the road to ease themselves and stretch out their limbs. It was a painful experience for those who had not taken public transport by land for a long time. Though they left Gare d'Orsay at midday, they only crossed the Belgian border three hundred and forty kilometres away towards evening.

After spending most of the morning running around to get pictures for their Belgian visas, they came to the border only to discover that it was not necessary after all to have a visa, since they were in transit. But the border police removed one of the passengers in the bus. As rumour had it, he was accused of setting off explosions in Paris and trying to run away to Brussels. There were lots of people crossing the border. Quite a few French people went across to buy food and petrol.

Once in Belgium, it took them almost as long to get to the airport, which was not too far away, as it had taken from Paris to the border. Things were in almost total chaos when they arrived at the airport of Brussels, which was carrying its own traffic in addition to that of Orly and Le Bourget. Several buses lined the approaches to the airport, waiting to take travellers back to Paris. Some of the passengers were arriving from London, others from Europe, Africa and America. No one at the airport seemed to know when any plane was arriving or departing. After their luggage had been checked, they were asked to wait. The delay seemed interminable and, though their flight was finally announced for eight in the evening, it was postponed from hour to hour until well past midnight when they were informed that they could then assemble at the departure lounge. Then at last they boarded an old rickety DC 8 cargo plane chartered by a makeshift company operating on the Europe-Africa run because of the strikes of the other airlines.

It was a long and circuitous journey to Sierra Leone. They had to stop at Saint-Etienne, Nouachott and Conakry, Abidjan and then go back to Dakar before heading for Sierra Leone. It was during this trip that Onuoha learned a little more about Afoukwu. When the latter learned that they might be stopping briefly in Mauretania, he became sad and throughout the journey never said a word to Onuoha. Other people had remarked to Onuoha that Afoukwu lived in daily fear of being kidnapped. And if any Biafran was to be kidnapped, he would be the first one.

When the plane stopped in the early hours of the morning in Nouachott and the passengers disembarked while two sweepers came on board to clean the floor, Afoukwu sat elongated in his chair and covered himself with blankets, thinking that spies had come to seize him. When the two cleaners tried to sweep round his row, he rose up startled. Later on he told Onuoha that he thought he had seen the face of the cleaners before in Paris. The stop-over in Conakry was more than one hour. Afoukwu refused to budge from his seat although the cleaning and the arrival of mechanics and technicians to check the plane did not make things easy for him. When one of the technicians discovered that he did not understand French, he addressed him in pidgin English, but Afoukwu feigned total ignorance. Later on, he claimed that he recognized the face. He swore the technician was a Hausa man who had been sent to spy on him.

When the plane took off, Afoukwu narrated a strange encounter in an African airport. His passport had almost been seized at the airport. That very day, the local Nigerian ambassador had made a speech attacking the government of Biafra. On Afoukwu's arrival at the airport, several soldiers armed to the teeth had come on board the plane and searched for him. He believed that the Nigerian ambassador had told them to arrest him. Fortunately for him, he declared, he was travelling that day with a United Nations Refugee Committee Certificate instead of his regular Nigerian passport. His fear was great that day, and it was only by great luck that he had escaped their attention.

Afoukwu believed that he was known all over the world. Sometimes in a spirit of generous self-immolation he would turn round and say that his bravery and courage alone had kept him still travelling on behalf of the country at war. He acknowledged that the government at war had invited him to come home several times and give an account of his more than one year stay abroad, which had originally been supposed to last for only two weeks. Each time, Afoukwu regretted that he was unable to go back to Biafra because of ill-health and high blood pressure. He also firmly believed that his presence abroad was indispensable and more important for his people than his stay in the war zone. Europe and the rest of Africa were also war zones as dangerous as Enugu and Calabar.

Arrival in Abidjan was a great relief. They had to spend the night there. They checked into the Hotel Ivoire. Afoukwu requested a room facing the lagoon. Onuoha took a room facing the main street of Cocody, Boulevard de la Corniche. From his room,

Abidjan spread out before him in all its splendour. Directly in front, Onuoha could see the presidential palace towering into the sky.

Afoukwu wanted to relax a bit after the dangerous and hazardous trip through enemy territories. They hailed a taxi which drove them to a good night spot in Treicheville, the people's section of the city, the African section. They stopped by a night club called Café Le Refuge, a sort of white island in an African night world.

Afoukwu was full of apologies to Onuoha. He let him know right away that he was not used to going to places like that. But he remembered that he had once been to the Lido in Paris, the Folies Bergère in Pigalle and also to the Moulin Rouge in Montmartre. Two young ladies came and sat by them and proposed drinks to them. Afoukwu looked away when he saw them coming, but when one of them sat dangerously close to him, he turned and offered a wry smile and gave Onuoha the green light to order drinks for everybody.

The young ladies preferred champagne. Before long, they had emptied four bottles. Afoukwu seemed to relax more whenever Onuoha was on the floor dancing with one of the girls. When later on Onuoha suggested that they go after the fifth bottle of champagne, Afoukwu confessed that one of the young ladies had been insisting that he take her to his hotel that morning. Since the young lady could not leave before the closing of the club, they were compelled to wait until four in the morning. The young ladies when their turn came left to perform a strip-tease show on the floor but always came back for another bottle of champagne. They drank the champagne like water. They seemed to have learned the science of making the gaseous elements of the drink evaporate with the help of a spoon. Once the effervescence had gone, they gulped the liquid like water, swallowing an aspirin tablet at the same time. Afoukwu was feeling more relaxed after the drinks.

The singing was good and the floor shows were interesting, especially the acrobatic stunts and the man dancing with a mannequin. Afoukwu clapped as hard as anyone around, especially when the lady looked at him and came embarrassingly close to him still dancing with frenetic movements of the hip and the waist. Fifteen minutes before closing time, the bill came and Afoukwu nearly fainted. Having used up all the cash that he had on him, he had to issue a cheque on his London bank for the remaining amount. The young ladies took the money and the cheque with a broad smile and kissed Afoukwu on both cheeks. The one that had invited him to spend the morning with her at the hotel raised two fingers which Afoukwu understood to mean that she would be over to see him in two minutes' time.

Onuoha and Afoukwu waited until everyone had left the club. Finally the young lady appeared and the lawyer smiled as he adjusted his pants. The lady came near the lawyer. He tried to hold her hand but the lady was coming to bid him goodbye for she walked out of the club and entered the car of a young man waiting for her outside. When Afoukwu rushed out and asked her what was happening, she said something about her maid being very sick. She had to rush home immediately and promised to be at Hotel Ivoire to meet him that afternoon at four o'clock.

Lawyer Afoukwu waited in vain. The cabaret girl never showed up. The same afternoon they continued their journey to Sierra Leone via Dakar.

The air hostess announced that they were flying over Conakry and were about to take a north-easterly course, which meant that they would arrive in Dakar within ninety minutes. Parched landscape, burnt and dry, replaced the vegetation they had seen earlier. There were no rivers again. No trees could be seen below. The area was desolate. A few misleading clouds here and there, but, by and large, the journey became dreary and after a while the flight itself became very uncomfortable. The stewardess asked them to fasten their belts as they were expecting to run into a storm. Afoukwu ordered some more cognac and rum. Then the air hostess announced that they were entering Senegalese territory. They circled a few times waiting for clearance to land. The sea was beautiful, the coastline majestic. Dakar looked like a beauty from above. The streets appeared well-planned and, as dusk approached, street lights were going up one by one. To watch this from above was a wonderful experience. The plane landed. Unfortunately there was no connecting flight that day to Sierra Leone. As chance would also have it, Lawyer Afoukwu saw, at the airport, the Senegalese Chief of Protocol, an old school friend. The latter invited the two Biafrans to spend the night in Dakar as guests of the Government. The Chief of Protocol hurried them briskly through a back door and asked them to wait in a car outside. He took their luggage tickets with him. A few minutes later, the driver of the black Citroën, marked SO (Service Officiel), signifying that the car was on government service, sped off towards the city.

The road from the Dakar-Yoff airport looked like the Appian Way, beautiful, large and decorated. It was a divided highway and in the centre was a strip of flowered shrubs. The city looked quiet on the outskirts and there were only a few people walking along the streets. The cars on the road were few. As they reached the centre, they saw a military vehicle loaded with soldiers. As they rounded a block, they saw more soldiers armed with rifles and bayonets and dressed in full battle attire. At another corner they saw broken window panes, smashed plate-glass windows and up-rooted street pavements. The area was guarded by the police and the army. The doors of a neighbourhood post office had been smashed. Onuoha and Lawyer Afoukwu looked at one another and said nothing. The driver continued speeding along until they arrived at the Medina Palace in the centre of the Moslem section of the city.

Medina Palace was the residence of Mamadou Dia the first Senegalese Prime Minister, the man who wrote *African Nations and World Solidarity*. In his book, the writer spoke about the uncertain course of world history and the impossibility of forecasting anything, The surest predictions of yesterday fall like a castle of cards tomorrow. He was right.One day he had tasted the summit of power. The following day he was locked up in a miserable prison serving a sentence of life imprisonment. Onuoha had some personal admiration for the brilliant economist who had inhabited the house where he and Afoukwu were lodged.

Afoukwu had cabled Ebere Okafor, still in school in Dakar, telling her about his arrival. Onuoha was to go and locate her whereabouts. Onuoha got into the car with the driver, Dadah Sène, and just before they drove off, a security guard, Alioune Dia, joined the driver in the front seat. They were heading towards the girls' dormitory at the University. The driver hesitated a little bit, but the security man told him it was all right.

There were more and more soldiers on the road. They crossed the first street and ran into a barricade of soldiers. They stopped and the security man told them that Onuoha was a government guest. With reluctance, they let them pass, but warned them that they were taking a dangerous risk, adding that there was another checkpoint further down. A little before the check-point, Onuoha saw a huge crowd in front. Sène did not even wait for the soldiers to turn him back. He reversed and headed straight back to the Medina Palace. Molotov cocktails thrown by the crowd exploded not far away. Gas bombs hurled by the soldiers burst in the distance. Rifle shots cracked all around. A straying bullet shattered the windshield near the security guard. Dia asked Onuoha to lie low as they sped back into the compound. The situation was serious.

Afoukwu was sitting down in the living-room deeply worried. He was relieved when Onuoha reappeared, rubbing sweat from his body. Afoukwu then told him that they said revolt had broken out in Dakar amongst the students of the University and that the unrest was extending fast to other sectors. Rumours were circulating that more than forty students had been killed in the clashes and hundreds of others wounded. The army had been called in and the University campus evacuated. A decree had been issued ordering the repatriation of all foreign students to their home countries. There was immediate concern over the fate of the two young Biafran girls known to be at the University. The thought of their being repatriated to Lagos disturbed the two of them.

Phone inquiries were made about where the foreign students were. A lady at the girls' dormitory gave the address of a military camp in the city. The camp said that the students had been handed over to their respective embassies or had gone to friends in the city. Others were at the central police station. The police station said that the students still there had gone to the nearby prison for their dinner and would be back shortly. Onuoha, who did not know either of the two girls, entreated Afoukwu to come along. The latter refused to move out of the sitting-room of the Medina Palace, so Onuoha had to go alone.

Onuoha got into the car, followed as usual by Dia, the security man. Driving through the streets of Dakar that evening required special skill. The crowds in the streets were thickening, their looks were menacing. Apparently their main objective, as Onuoha soon learned, was to destroy government cars and property. In the black government Citroën, Onuoha was an easy target. Because they were in a government vehicle, the army and police assisted them, warning them about which areas to avoid. As evening wore on, more and more windows were being broken and passers-by were uprooting more stones from the pavement as if they were storing up arms for a night battle.

When the driver realized that he could no longer hide the truth, he tried to explain to Onuoha that the situation was not really serious. A group of students in the University had revolted, like the students at the Sorbonne. The revolt happened to coincide with general worker dissatisfaction. The workers encouraged the students and supported them, and together they planned to organize a strike that would start the following day. Students in the secondary schools were also on strike and several of them were moving in just to create confusion. Deteriorating economic conditions had destroyed the unsteady and simmering political *status quo*. Money would not buy much anywhere again. Workers in Dakar were asking for a major salary increase comparable to the demands of the French workers .n Paris. The students, for their part, were demanding a change in the statutes of the university. They were protesting against the fact that after eight years of independence, the University of Dakar was still essentially a French university and the professors were all French. The examinations were all oriented towards the French system of thought and had very little African content. The great majority of the students were French also. The students wanted an increase in their scholarship stipends and a drastic change of the Law, Arts and Science Faculties.

In addition to the student and worker discontent, there appeared to be, Sène said, growing evidence of political unrest, which had led to political murders of government members of Parliament and an assassination attempt on the life of the President of the Republic, who had escaped miraculously. The assassination attempt led to arrests and trials as well as to cabinet reshuffles and more strained nerves and loyalties. The army was also purged and this made the supporters of the purged officers very unhappy. Onuoha, after hearing the comments, remarked that the people were probably expecting anything to happen. 'Nothing will happen,' the security officer said. 'The people are cowards,' Dia continued. 'They will run once they hear a gunshot. And the army has received instructions to shoot to kill if the situation deteriorates.' Crowds jeered at them as they passed. Some shook their fists at them as they drove to the central police station.

The police station was crowded with people and the police were searching some and preventing others from approaching the vicinity. Physically, it was not possible to drive the car any closer. Sène stopped the car and Onuoha asked him to reverse and stay inside. Onuoha came out, followed by Dia. Dadah Sène kept the motor of the car running so that they could pull out at a moment's notice. The police officers around were too busy to listen to anyone. They were too busy controlling the crowd trying to surge up the steps towards the offices of the Department. When Alioune Dia succeeded in explaining to them that Onuoha was a guest of the government, the doors were opened wide for him. When he asked about the two Nigerian girls in question (he dared not mention Biafran girls since the Senegalese were very sympathetic to Moslem Nigeria) he was told that they had been repatriated by their embassy to Lagos that evening. Onuoha was concerned, but was unable to explain the source of his worry to the police chief or even to Alioune Dia. He was advised to contact the Nigerian Embassy for further details.

As Onuoha turned sadly to go, he saw a young lady with tattered dress and bruises from her encounter with the soldiers.

she looked lost and appeared to speak English. Onuoha was right. She was a Sierra Leonean. Onuoha asked her if she had seen the Biafran girls in question. She had seen them last about six hours earlier when a band of marauding soldiers had poured into their dormitories and started beating up and raping the girls who had done nothing. Everyone ran away helter-skelter and she could not tell which way Ebere Okafor and Titi Duru had run. It had not been possible for the girl to go back to the campus to bring her luggage out and, with the tribal shootings and riots in Sierra Leone, her embassy was not very interested in helping, since she came from the 'wrong' tribe. The army, she continued, just bundled all the girls into wagons and shipped them off, some of them wearing no more than towels and bathing suits. It was not until that evening that the foreigners who had not been repatriated and who had no place to go had been moved into the barracks at the central police station. They marched over to the local prison for dinner. There they had been given a bowl of soup and some grains of groundnuts. The young lady, Cynthia Clark, was almost sure that the Biafran girls had not gone to Lagos with the Nigerian plane.

Cynthia accompanied Onuoha again to the courtyard behind the police office where some students were lying down in various stages of desperation. Cynthia Clark, as they entered, pointed to a young lady in front and said, 'That's a Nigerian girl. She might help us.' Cynthia introduced Lola Ajayi, the Nigerian girl, to Onuoha. Lola knew Ebere and Titi very well. Lola confirmed that a Nigerian plane had come to take home Ghanaian and Nigerian students to Accra and Lagos. Lola said with all certainty that Titi and Ebere had not gone with the Nigerians and must still be staying somewhere in the city. She was not sure of the exact place, but thought that they might be taking refuge in the home of an Ivoirian who lived at number fifty . . . something of a certain street. Lola said that the house in question faced a mosque and was on the same street as the Hotel Croix du Sud. Lola remembered that the apartment was located on the second floor just facing the staircase.

Onuoha thanked her for the information and asked if he could help her in any way. Lola said that some of her Dahomean relations living in Senegal would come over to take her away. As for Cynthia Clark, she begged Onuoha to drop her off at the British Embassy on his way out. Lola said that she had no intention of going back to Nigeria so long as the war continued. She opposed the war. News from her home indicated that her two brothers, Akin and Tunde, had been conscripted into the Nigerian Army and nothing had been heard of them since then. Both of them had been assigned to the Second Division under Colonel Murtela Mohammed and Akin was believed to have been killed in Abagana, Titi's home town, when Biafran forces wiped out an entire brigade in a few hours. Lola was daily praying for the return alive, of the younger brother Tunde who was still believed to be alive.

Lola sighed as Onuoha turned to leave. 'War is a bad thing,' she said. 'Since our days at Ibadan University, Titi and I have been good friends. We have always been together. We came to Dakar together. Now the war has divided us. Titi has never forgiven me because my brothers joined the war against her people. I tried to explain that it was not my fault, not their fault. I might never see her again. Some day perhaps, she will understand. Please give her my love. Oh, Titi is such a tender friend. Please give her my love. Take good care of her. Ask her never to forget her good friend Lola.' With heavy hearts, Onuoha, Cynthia and Dia left Lola and went back to the car. Cynthia said as they got back to the car, 'Strikers and agitators might have legitimate reasons for their claims. People certainly have a right to defend themselves when attacked. But a state of war certainly causes incalculable suffering to innocent parties. Wars ought to be avoided at all costs.'

Dadah Sène fortunately knew the street where the Hotel Croix du Sud was located. He named the street when the hotel was mentioned. Cynthia was dropped off at the British Embassy. As she left, she shook Onuoha's hand and thanked him a million times and said, 'I do not want to create another scene like Lola. But give my love to Titi. She has been a wonderful friend. The dress I am holding in this parcel belongs to Titi. She gave it to me as we all ran away almost naked. She was about the only girl that

ared defy the soldiers and run back to her room to take away all
er suitcases and belongings which were already packed. Give her
1y sincere love. And I hope you can help her as you have helped
1e.'

When Dadah Sène was told that the house faced a mosque, he
aid that he knew the building and that several foreigners lived
1ere. Onuoha climbed up the building to the second floor. Dia
vanted to follow him. Onuoha asked him to wait in the car.

As Onuoha climbed up the stairs, the smell of home cooking,
1ore specifically Egusi soup, filled the air. It was reassuring for
)nuoha. He knocked at the door that Lola had described. There
vas no answer and no movement. Onuoha knocked again and
zain. There was no reply. He was worried. Then he followed the
dour of the cooking and it took him to the third floor. The door
vas half-open. He knocked and someone answered in English,
Vho is it?' A young mother appeared at the door at the same time.
1e was Mrs Grace Eyo, an Efik woman from Calabar. Her hus-
and was away in France and had not been able to get back to
)akar because of the strikes. Onuoha explained to her his mission.
;race informed him that the Ivoirian family had left the country
)ur days earlier for Geneva but that Titi and Ebere were staying
ith them. The two of them had gone out to get some milk for
1e baby. She promised to tell them of Onuoha's visit. Grace was
:companying Onuoha down the stairs when they saw Titi and
bere. Onuoha had not seen them before, but somehow, instinc-
vely, he guessed which one was Titi Duru, tender rather than
legant, attractive rather than beautiful. After a brief stay in the
ouse, they all left for the Medina Palace. The maid was left to
)ok after Mrs Eyo's baby.

: was dark and the streets were getting dangerous as they drove
ack to the Medina Palace. Stones were hurled at them from dark
)rners, but they reached it safely. Afoukwu was full of smiles when
e saw the three young ladies. They all sat down and talked about
ome, the events of May in France and Senegal. Ebere described
1e brutality of the soldiers, how the students were pushed down
) the floor and beaten by the drunken soldiers. The students—at

least the girls—had done nothing and were nowhere near the scene of the riots. Ebere said that they were preparing for their examinations when the rioting started. As if they knew where it would all lead to, they had packed their belongings and, because of Titi's presence of mind, they had been able to drag out their suitcases.

Ebere and Titi were worried about events in Biafra. Ebere was crying. What could she do? She was formerly a student at the Ibadan University, together with Titi, when the crisis broke out in 1966. They all had to return to Eastern Nigeria to enrol at the University of Nsukka. From there they were sent over to the University of Dakar for a junior year abroad, since they were French majors. They were getting ready to go back to Biafra in July 1967 to continue their studies, their final year, when war broke out. In fact, they had boarded a boat in Dakar to go to the Camerouns and from there via Douala and Mamfe to Biafra. The boat had been berthed in Accra, Ghana, when they had learned that the land route leading from Mamfe and Ikom as well as the river route from Ekang to Biafra had been sealed off by the Nigerians. Ebere and Titi had had to come back to Dakar to try to pursue their studies. The French Government had refused to give them any financial aid, insisting that they had to apply through the Nigerian Embassy. Other Biafran students under French Government scholarships had seen their stipends withdrawn by the French Government also at the request of the Nigerian Embassy. The German Government through their Embassy in Senegal had come to the aid of Titi and Ebere. The German Government had offered them full tuition and board scholarship at the University of Dakar with an option to continue their studies after the school year in a German university. After one year of studies, just one week before the examinations, the University of Dakar was closing its doors against them. They had nothing to show for their four years of university studies.

Titi Duru said that studies could wait. Titi emphasized that there were students at home in the same predicament. But events at home worried her. Since she had left Biafra, she had not received a single letter from her family. Before they were separated by the war, her parents were living in Enugu. But Enugu was completely evacuated some nine months previously. She knew that her parents would have returned to Abagana, their home town. But Abagana had fallen to the enemy three months ago. Titi knew also that Abagana was the theatre of the greatest battle of the war where more than twenty thousand Nigerian troops had been wiped out. Titi did not know where her parents were, since they had lost everything in Enugu and Abagana. She had been reading and listening to daily reports about the plight of refugees in Biafra, how they were dying in their thousands. Some, she also learned, had no tents. And now the rainy season had come. These thoughts filled her with sorrow. Titi was doing her best to check her tears. Afoukwu tried to comfort her, saying that newspaper reports about starvation were exaggerated in a desperate effort to win world sympathy and support for the Biafran cause. Afoukwu said that he received letters every week from his wife and, according to her, things were quite normal in spite of the difficulties.

.Mrs Grace Eyo told how she and her husband managed to escape from Lagos after the war was declared. Being Easterners, their homes were watched and searched quite frequently. Every night, they listened to Radio Biafra to find out what was happening. They had to lie with their ears to the ground and their transistor radio tuned very low so that people outside would not overhear the voice and signal of Radio Biafra and report them to the police as collaborators. Several Igbos, Efiks, and Ogoja people, especially the intellectuals, were being imprisoned in horrible cells.

One day a Yoruba woman saw their predicament and volunteered to help them get out of Lagos and out of the country through the back door by avoiding all the check points, manned by the police or the army. Since they had known the woman for quite a long time, and she had demonstrated that she could be trusted, they decided to risk it. The woman had helped them safely to the Dahomean border and from there they made it to Senegal.

Since he was fond of dramatizing his own part in the war, Afoukwu told about his encounters with the enemy in Conakry and Nouachott, how Nigerians were setting spies on him everywhere. He repeated the story about the near seizure of his passport. When Titi asked him about his flight from Abidjan to Dakar, Afoukwu merely said that the flight had been wonderful and then cracked some jokes about Titi's beauty and teased her about wearing wigs. In actual fact, Titi had very long hair and she told him that she was not wearing a wig. Ebere Okafor, half smiling, half resentful, accused Afoukwu of throwing around condescending jokes about women. Afoukwu slapped her fondly on the back. Ebere pushed away his hand and in an effort to hold on to her, Afoukwu knocked off the wig Ebere had on her head. The evening turned sour immediately, and Ebere rushed into a nearby bathroom to tidy her hair. Titi went in to help her friend and Grace Eyo mildly chided the lawyer for what he had done.

Afoukwu tried in vain to exonerate himself by accusing modern girls of putting on make-up and lipstick. Grace Eyo was irritated. She wanted to go back and look after her son and it was nearing curfew time. When Titi and Ebere came out, they also wanted to go and have some rest.

Onuoha accompanied the three ladies into the car. They stayed in the back seat. Onuoha, Sène and Dia stayed in the front seat. The gateman opened the gates of the palace for the car to come out. The car had just come out of the gates when a huge crowd charged from about one hundred yards away. Sène, throwing the car into reverse, brought it right back into the compound. The gates were locked again. Shouts were heard from the crowd. 'It is an official car. Get it! Smash it to bits!' Stones fell all around them. Gun shots cracked all around further down the street. Smoke bombs exploded and store windows were smashed systematically. The atmosphere was tense and restless. The darkness made it more treacherous.

The ladies could certainly not be taken home in the official car. That would be murderous. The gateman, the security man and driver advised against it. 'Then we shall take a taxi,' Titi suggested. 'We cannot leave young Eyo alone tonight with a twelve-year-old nurse.' Onuoha stepped out of the gate with them and hailed a taxi. Onuoha wanted to see them home safely. The taxi driver said he could take the risk and take them home, but he would not risk bringing back Onuoha to the palace. 'Besides,' he added, 'I can only take three passengers.' Onuoha stood there and watched the taxi leave, praying that the girls who had suffered at the hands of soldiers that day be spared the molestations of the rioters that night. He walked back to the palace impressed by Titi's strength of character. Later that night their proposed trip to Sierra Leone was cancelled because of large-scale riots in that country. With planes in Dakar grounded, Onuoha and Afoukwu decided to take a charter flight carrying wounded foreign students home to their countries.

Onuoha and Afoukwu could not leave without telling Grace, Titi and Ebere. Onuoha went into the city with the driver and the security guard. The road was quieter now and the rioting had subsided. A big demonstration was being organized in support of the government but most of those present were men in uniform. On the same day, a million people were demonstrating in Paris in support of the French President. Radio Senegal estimated the crowd assembled in Dakar at about one million also. With tanks, Landrovers and half-tracks mounting guard at the Place de l'Independence where the demonstration was supposed to be taking place, a careless observer might think it was a military exercise. Grace, Ebere and Titi were relieved when they saw Onuoha. Briefly Onuoha explained the situation to them and offered to take the two students out of Senegal. They accepted the offer. Ebere wanted to continue on to Germany and complete her studies there. Titi Duru was not sure what she wanted to do.

Once again, Onuoha and Afoukwu were on their way to Abidjan. Onuoha felt as if he were in a Red Cross plane evacuating people from the field of battle. Some of the students had lost their hands, others their eyes. About seventy-five per cent of the students in the over-crowded DC 8 were injured. Some had plaster on their legs, others had their faces completely bandaged, except for their eyes. Some could not walk, others could not sit down. Their nerves were all frayed. Some moaned the loss of their comrades. Yet the radio announced that only four students had been killed and forty wounded. The statement even said that the dead students were Marxists, masochists and followers of Mao Tse-Tung who were learning how to make Molotov cocktails when the mixture exploded in their faces, killing them. About three other planes had left the day before carrying other groups of wounded students back to their own countries.

On arrival in Abidjan that evening, the local newspaper had already announced that peace and quiet had returned to the streets of Dakar after the people had refused to follow the calls for a strike issued by a few extremist elements.

6

The Merry-go-round

Onuoha was sitting down in his room in the Hotel Ivoire when someone knocked at the door. He opened the door and saw Titi Duru standing there timidly. Onuoha was taken aback and when she saw the surprise on his face, Titi asked if she could enter. 'Please do,' Onuoha entreated her. Onuoha tried to order some drinks for her but she refused. She asked Onuoha to continue what he was doing. Onuoha was typing a report of his journey to trouble-infested capitals. The proposed trip to Sierra Leone had been cancelled because of tribal riots in that country. Onuoha assured Titi that her presence was welcome. She felt at ease.

Titi had come to thank Onuoha for all he had done for her. She said something about her inability to recompense Onuoha for all his help in Dakar. Her mind was a bit troubled. Onuoha assured her that he would have done the same thing for anyone. Titi looked at him with a slight air of disappointment. 'So I am just anyone,' she thought to herself. She wanted to say something, but could not say it, and instead started crying.

Onuoha was overcome by her grief. He could not fully under-stand what was going on in her mind. Titi started leafing through a copy of the Biafran publication, *Pogrom in Nigeria*, a series of shocking pictures about the atrocities committed against Biafran civilians in Northern Nigeria. Onuoha, who could not quite picture what was in Titi's mind, concluded that she must be worrying about the events in Biafra, the suffering at home and the fact that she had not seen or heard from her parents.

Onuoha tried to console her, emphasizing that she was not alone in the situation. There were others in her position too. There were other Biafrans who had been cut off from their families, who had had to abandon their schooling because the Nigerian Govern-ment had cut off their scholarships. There were young married mothers abroad who were separated from their husbands in Biafra. There were parents abroad who had left their children at home. In Biafra also, there were several young ladies who three days after their wedding had seen the life of their young groom and love snuffed out by an enemy bullet. Titi listened attentively as he told her various stories about the war.

She listened patiently, but there was not much she could say in reply. The long sermon appeared to have had its effect. Titi picked up courage and spoke. She had been thinking of what to do. She had already decided not to go to Germany and study. She wanted to contribute directly to the war effort. She had spoken to Afoukwu about it and he had invited her to be his private secretary, since she spoke French and English. Titi had lots of respect for Afoukwu but she did not like the idea of being a private secretary, afraid that she might be expected to perform some extra-secretarial duties. She could never quite feel at home with him. She asked Onuoha for his advice. Onuoha told her that she alone could make the decision. Titi said that her mind was made up after listening to Onuoha. She wanted to go to Biafra and help somewhere, somehow. She felt that she would be more useful serving the nation, her people, than serving the whims of a man, married with children almost her own age.

Titi was frank. She was torn between the material necessity of support, moral and financial, and the desire to be herself and independent. Afoukwu had called her over to his room the night before, immediately after Ebere's departure for Germany, and offered her the post of his private secretary. He had offered Ebere that post before, but after the wig incident in the Medina Palace, Ebere was not very happy with Afoukwu again. Though Titi and Ebere were friends, Titi did not always approve of the way Ebere flirted with men. The atmosphere when she had entered his room the evening before had been unrelaxed. Her heart was panting as if something was going to happen to her. Normally she was not a nervous girl, but she felt nervous whenever she was alone with Afoukwu. The latter had invited her again to his room that morning. When she arrived, he told her that he would like to have dinner with her that night and go out alone to a movie afterwards. Titi did not want to go out alone with him and was asking Onuoha to join them. She was in a great dilemma: if she refused to go out with him, it might appear insulting and ungrateful to someone who had devoted his life to the service of her nation. This was more painful because of the war. If she accepted to go out, she was afraid that something might happen that would make it better if she had not gone out at all.

Before Onuoha could say anything, there was a quick knock at the door and Afoukwu entered without waiting for an answer. The expression on his face was one of shock. Onuoha kept on wondering how long Afoukwu had been standing listening at the door and whether he had overheard the last stages of his conversation with Titi. Afoukwu tried to ease the situation by cracking a few jokes about two young people falling in love already after only a few days of acquaintanceship. There was an expression of jovial jealousy on his face and in his voice. Titi stood up and was walking out of the room when Afoukwu regretted abruptly interrupting her tête-à-tête. He asked Titi to come over after lunch and take down in shorthand some letters he would like to send out. Titi walked out without saying a word.

Afoukwu then told Onuoha that he had just been talking with Biafran offices in Europe. He said that the situation in France was coming back to normal and that some of the strikers had gone back to work. The Paris office was functioning normally again. Afoukwu said that it would not be necessary to go up to Lisbon before taking a plane to Biafra as they had proposed. They had agreed to continue on to Biafra to see things for themselves. Lisbon was then the only place in Europe where planes going to Biafra could land. One of the charter planes that normally took supplies to Biafra for Caritas and the World Council of Churches, a Super Constellation belonging to Captain Boris Henk, had just then landed in Abidjan because of radio and engine trouble. If the plane was repaired in time that evening, they could take it to Biafra. Onuoha asked Afoukwu if Titi could come alone, but the latter wanted her at first to stay in Abidjan and wait for him to come out of Biafra. Later he said that he would think about it.

Afoukwu then said that the Biafran government was deeply worried about the mishaps that had befallen several of the planes carrying supplies to the Port-Harcourt airport within the past few weeks. One of the planes belonging to Captain Boris Henk which was carrying more than six tons of spares for military vehicles and equipment bought in Czechoslovakia was impounded in Athens when it landed there, supposedly for technical reasons. The spares were urgently needed and there was no means of getting replacements immediately. Afoukwu mentioned also a series of trials and errors, incredible expenses incurred in the purchase of fighter planes, monies tied down by counter-agents who promised to buy planes for Biafra when in fact they were agents of the British government; after all these problems, Biafra had finally succeeded in purchasing three fighter planes. The planes had been dismantled and sent to Biafra in pieces. Everything had now arrived, except for one plane-load of fuselages and spare parts and sections of the wings. The Super Constellation carrying these had made a re-fuelling stop in Bissau. While the crew and the two Biafran passengers had been having their dinner, there had been an earth-shaking explosion which had destroyed the plane completely, rocking and shattering in the process the glass windows of the airport installations. The fire could not be put out in time, because the initial explosion set off secondary fires amongst the few boxes of ammunition and shells in the aircraft, as well as in the fuel tank of the craft which had been holding almost twenty thousand gallons of aero-fluid.

It was difficult to say whether this had been sabotage or an accident. Afoukwu did indicate that an investigating team made up of Biafrans and Portuguese had left Lisbon and Umuahia, the new Biafran capital, to conduct the necessary inquiries. Some people thought that the explosions could also be the result of the shelling of the airport by one of the Portuguese Guinea Liberation fighters that constantly attacked Portuguese installations in the colony. They could have scored a direct hit on the plane, thereby setting off an immense explosion. Fortunately, no other commercial craft had been around at the time. Fortunately also, there was no loss of human life, but the material loss was put at more than two million dollars. In military terms, the loss of the fighter planes, since the parts could not be purchased again, could mean the loss of Port-Harcourt airport, leaving Biafra with only the Annabelle landing strip near Uli.

While Onuoha and Afoukwu were being besieged in Senegal by rioting students and strikers, another Boris Henk plane had left Lisbon carrying two million pounds of the new Biafran currency in notes of five and twenty shillings, as well as three-quarters of a million pounds worth of assorted guns, bazookas, ammunition and a few 105 millimetre shells. Half-way, the captain had complained of engine trouble. Samson Anele who had been travelling with Captain Henk himself in the plane had begged the crew to land in one of the friendly countries that had recognized Biafra's independence on the West Coast of Africa, so that the engine could be repaired or replaced. Captain Henk had refused and had opened the creaky window of the Super Constellation and thrown into the Atlantic Ocean more than half of the load of Biafran currency and more than three-quarters of the load of arms and ammunition. These things had happened when Biafran forces most needed equipment for the defence of Port-Harcourt, industrially and economically their most important town. To confound observers, the Henk plane had come into Biafra and circled three times around the airport, then had flown back and later landed on the island of São Tomé, a Portuguese possession off the West African coast. From there he had sent a message to Lisbon that he had not been able to make radio contact with the control tower at Port-Harcourt or Annabelle airports. And unfortunately, because of engine trouble, the plane had not been able to leave the island.

During all this time, the battle of Port-Harcourt was raging and it was a matter of life and death. Relying on the arrival in time of the fighters and the loads of ammunition, bazookas and shells expected, an order was issued by the Army High Command that no one should leave Port-Harcourt, because Biafran troops could defend it successfully. As a matter of fact, Biafran forces scored more amazing victories than ever in various sectors of the Port-Harcourt zone. The Biafran Navy in a very successful manoeuvre re-empted the attack of a Nigerian invasion force along the Bonny channel and captured intact two boat-loads of ammunition, Oerlikon automatic anti-aircraft guns, food supplies and power-

generating plants. On land, Biafran armed forces struck deep
behind enemy lines in the Port-Harcourt sector and seized th
brigade headquarters at Umuagbai. The equipment captured from
the retreating Nigerians included bazookas, several dozen boxe
of mortar bombs and artillery shells, ferret ammunition an
hundreds of automatic weapons and ammunition: some thre
hundred and eighty rounds of eighty-one millimetre morta
bombs, twenty-two thousand rounds of ·303 ammunition
105,200 rounds of ammunition for Browning guns and vas
quantities of artillery shells and other military stores. They als
captured or destroyed several trucks and staff cars, containing
large supplies of tinned food and cigarettes. The Biafran force
turned back to eliminate the forward troops of the enemy facing
Aba on the one side and Port-Harcourt on the other. The Biafra
Air Force was also itching for action, waiting for the arrival of th
fuselages and spare parts for their machines.

Then came the various bits of news about the plane coming
from Czechoslovakia detained in Athens, the destruction of th
Super Constellation in Bissau, the casting into the Atlantic Ocea
of Biafran currency and much-needed equipment, the grounding
of the other plane in São Tomé. Finally even a plane carrying foo
was grounded in Abidjan. It was hoped that, after it had lande
in Biafra, the Biafran government would then charter it and use
to move into the country some military equipment stranded i
São Tomé. Very few people believed that all those mishap
happened just by chance. Afoukwu said that he had felt from th
beginning that at the vital moment, the moment of life and deatl
Captain Boris Henk would just abandon Biafra. He appeared t
be doing it then. The end now appeared to be in sight. From a
angles, structures and fabrics were collapsing and the entire worl
seemed to have turned against the Biafran cause.

Afoukwu and Onuoha agreed that they must hurry the engir
eers to work on the plane so that they could leave for Biafra. A
they were talking, Lisbon telephoned to inform them that it wa
unsafe to go to Port-Harcourt. The airport there had fallen int
the hands of the Nigerians. They were advised to land at Anna
belle airport instead. If the plane could land that night and mak

the shuttle flight for the arms in São Tomé, there was a chance that the situation in Port-Harcourt could be arrested, and the Nigerian advance towards Aba stopped. Afoukwu was saddened as well as Onuoha. The former went over to his room while Onuoha went to the pavilion of the hotel for a quiet lunch near the swimming pool.

Onuoha had barely sat down when Titi came and joined him on the terrace. Onuoha told her about the possibility of going to Biafra that night if the plane that had landed in Abidjan could be repaired. Titi was intrigued by the prospect. She wanted to go to Biafra and stay there if possible. She would like to try to locate her parents and see if she could do anything to assist them if they were still alive. Titi said that she had no intention of going that afternoon to see Afoukwu in his room after lunch. Just as she said that, Afoukwu appeared. He was walking towards them along the corridor joining the hotel to the pavilion. Titi was almost sure that Afoukwu had seen them dining together from his hotel window which faced the terrace overlooking the pool and the lagoon.

It was a quiet lunch and not much was said by anyone. Afoukwu said that Titi could come along with him to Biafra, as if the plane personally belonged to him. He invited Titi to come along so that he could buy food supplies for his family from the local shops. Afoukwu was worried about the trip to Biafra. After the series of mishaps on the last five planes that had tried to get into Biafra, Afoukwu was not sure that the Abidjan plane could make it into Annabelle that night. He said that he had lain down and tried to sleep a little, but that he had premonitions telling him not to take the plane. But he was determined to risk it. He would only stay a few minutes, an hour at the most in Biafra, and come out again, since he had very important business to do abroad, especially now that the war was getting more difficult. He was anxious to get back to Europe and join Obiora Ifedi, Chief Tobias Iweka, Chancellor Obelenwata and the rest, who were now all back in Europe. Their joint presence there was becoming more urgent with the near collapse of the regime. Onuoha could report on the situation in West Africa should he decide suddenly not to go to Biafra at all. In that case, Titi would continue to Europe with him.

That evening, they went out to the airport, Port Brouet. Afoukwu had collected more than fifteen suitcases of provisions, four ten-gallon containers of petrol, some kerosene, candles, batteries for torches and cars, as well as transistors and tyres for bicycles and cars. It was dusk when they arrived at Port Brouet airport. The engine of the plane was roaring already. Everything was ready. At the lawyer's insistence, the workers loaded the suitcases on board. The plane was over-weight, but everyone climbed on board and soon afterwards the plane taxied off to the runway and was quickly air-borne. There were only four seats in the plane. The rest of the space was filled with cartons of milk, bales of stockfish, boxes of drugs, hosts for the the churches and mass wine for the priests. Titi came and sat down with Onuoha, since the seats were in twos, but as darkness fell, Afoukwu asked Titi to bring her pen and come over and take down a few notes beside his seat.

The Super Constellation was an old rickety plane. Onuoha remembered travelling in old and rickety cars before, but never had he tried boarding an old plane. The craft had no heating system and no proper ventilation. There were no partitions in the plane except for the cockpit, which was separated from the rest by wooden boards. Cold and rarefied air rushed in through the open vents, which could not be regulated. The plane was so cold that not even a sweater could make the situation comfortable. There were some blankets on the disused coat-racks and, when Titi complained of cold, Afoukwu brought two of these blankets and covered his and Titi's legs.

The plane's platform vibrated as if it were going to disintegrate at any moment. From where he sat at the back of the plane, Onuoha could hear the rattling and the vibration of the instrument panel in the cockpit and started wondering how accurate the readings could be and how the pilots ever managed to land in Biafra on a direct flight from Lisbon or Bissau when they could not contact any of the intermediate stations along the route for weather information and direction control. After flying along the coast for a while, they veered into the Atlantic Ocean to avoid the Ghanaian coast. The engines vibrated as if they would break apart and fall into the ocean at any moment. Whenever the engine sound changed and the propulsive power increased or decreased, or the plane lost or gained altitude, Onuoha got the uncomfortable feeling that anything could happen. At certain moments, he thought that he was developing stomach ulcers as the plane bumped up and down through the clouds. After a while, without really getting used to it, he tried to resign himself to the inevitable. He knew that death could come at any time, but he would rather have it over Biafran territory so that he could have the satisfaction of having died in his own country. Death over the Atlantic Ocean seemed to be a lost and meaningless sacrifice, especially if it was not due to hostile fire but to faulty engines or mechanical trouble. 'If I am destined to die in this war,' Onuoha said to himself, 'I would at least like to die a hero in the service of my country and be buried with due respect in my village.'

They were flying at a height of about thirty thousand feet and cruising at a speed of about four hundred miles an hour. They maintained an easterly course along the fourth latitude, thereby avoiding the whole of the West African coast, and were heading directly towards Douala in the Camerouns. Abidjan was exactly four degrees west longitude and the Biafran Annabelle Airport was located at about seven degrees east longitude. As they approached the delta of the River Niger, Onuoha could see in the far distance the lights of the Oloibiri oil wells and Nigerian search lights along the Bonny Island complex. He knew that Nigerian soldiers had anti-aircraft guns in those positions. Not far away also was the island of Fernando Po. There were also lots of Nigerians around its airport since the International Red Cross was operating shuttles to Biafra from Santa Isabel, its capital.

The lights in the plane were completely turned off. The pilots read or tried to read their bearings using a low-powered red flashlight that looked more like a red lighter flame than anything else. They flashed this intermittently to avoid any form of indiscretion that might betray their position to the enemy. After bypassing Fernando Po, the plane came down lower, probably to avoid high radar detection. It was practically lost in the clouds. There was still the sound of the motor, but not much else. The wing lights were put off and the position of the plane was only betrayed by infrequent spouts of greyish and bluish lights from the engines. There was total silence inside the plane as if the crew and the passengers thought their mere voices would betray their presence to the enemy.

The plane started curving and veering at an angle of almost one hundred degrees to the left. They were moving into Biafran territory, through the back door, not too far away from Calabar. Calabar at the south-eastern coastal tip of Biafra was under Nigerian control and was also one of their Air Force bases. They had about seven MIG fighter planes and two Ilyushin 28 bombers stationed there. It was at that point that Onuoha discovered that the captain of the plane, Patrick O'Donnell, was a new man and had not made the trip to Biafra before. He had been thoroughly briefed before his departure from Lisbon and while in Abidjan he had telephoned Lisbon to find out the current situation in the war zone.

Captain O'Donnell was an Irishman who had just joined the service of Captain Henk. He spoke with a deep Irish accent. The co-pilot was a Rhodesian and the flight engineer came from South Africa. The plane they were piloting was a Super Constellation made by the Lockheed Aircraft Corporation of America and the wares in the craft included a mixture of goods bought in Czechoslovakia and some drugs donated by Biafran students in Russia. In that small plane, one could see the complexity of the whole operation and the international character of the war and the smuggling effort, designed to keep the Biafran troops alive and well-armed with food and equipment. Scattered round the plane, one could see boxes of used clothing from Western Germany, Super-lait dried milk from France, reams of printing paper from Portugal, an Imperial Executive typewriter bought in England and a French Japy machine for the Translation Bureau in Biafra.

Captain O'Donnell came over to Onuoha and asked him to come to the cockpit and assist him with some information about directions. Onuoha almost fainted when he heard this and felt that they might end up in the wrong airport. The captain told him that they were over the Camerouns and would be moving into Biafra soon. Captain O'Donnell knew the exact location of the Annabelle airport, but wanted to find out from Onuoha the dangerous zones that should be avoided, the zones controlled by Nigerians or where there was fighting. He said with a wry humour: 'You see, I do not want to be shot down like a duck.' For the first time, Onuoha felt that he was facing a man who was also human and who certainly did not want to die. This gave him some consolation. Onuoha realized more profoundly that the flyers, mercy pilots or mercenaries (the names often ceased to matter once they were air-borne and in the zone of fighting) were human beings with families and friends who expected to see them back alive. The pilots were human beings who had ready-made plans as to how they intended to spend the future, with the money they were earning during the Biafran war. Of course there were those who wanted the war to continue a little longer so that they could continue making quick profits. Generally this was not because of their love of adventure or their courage in the face of imminent death, but because of the very quick cash they could make in a short period of time.

Onuoha brought out a map of Biafra he had in his pocket and explained to Captain O'Donnell the military situation as he knew it, warning however that the situation could change within minutes. He spread out the map and showed him where the original boundaries were. The Nigerians had taken Enugu, the capital city with an international airport, which they could use and were using as an air base. Enugu was in the northern part of Biafra. They had also taken Ogoja, the north-eastern corner of Biafra, and they had constructed another military airport in that area. They had taken Calabar on the south-eastern corner and had enlarged the existing airport there for their bombing operations against Biafra. They were also occupying Ikot-Ekpene. The latter city, Onuoha emphasized, changed hands at least twice every day. The Nigerians had practically assured themselves of Port-Harcourt and were moving towards Aba in the centre of Biafra. To the west, they had taken Yenogoa and had massed their troops along the River Niger. They also had a large concentration of forces in Onitsha, but Biafran troops were holding their ground in that area. Summarizing, Onuoha told Captain O'Donnell that it was impossible to fly into Biafra without traversing a zone of at least one hundred miles of territory controlled by the Nigerians. Onuoha suggested what he considered to be the safe routes. Captain O'Donnell could fly until he was over Ikot-Ekpene where the Nigerian contingents were not very strong and were constantly being harassed by Biafran troops. Once the plane went beyond Ikot-Ekpene he could then come down lower and fly straight along the Owerri-Oguta road and from there make contact with Annabelle tower.

Captain O'Donnell spoke at length about the hazards of the enterprise. He said that Biafrans should try to obtain a few jets to escort the supply planes and protect them against Nigerian threats of destruction. He told Onuoha that he had been a war pilot during the last world war and that he thought the Nigerians were fools. If he were in their position, he could easily shoot down a Biafra-bound plane at night. Onuoha told him that it was not easy for the Nigerians to do so, since the planes were sometimes Red Cross planes and Nigerians certainly could not risk an international incident which would be bound to arise if one of these were shot down. Captain O'Donnell laughed at the idea, saying that the Red Cross would just protest, and the United Nations might pass a resolution condemning the cowardly raid against humanitarian international voluntary operation. To avoid shooting down a Red Cross plane, Captain O'Donnell said that if he were a Nigerian pilot, he would follow the planes as they took off and mark out the ones that belonged to Biafra, follow them out to sea and just shoot them down over the Atlantic Ocean. 'No announcement would be made about it,' he said. 'And I assure you that if it happened two or three times, no other pilot would dare go into Biafra.' Onuoha told him that the Nigerians did not have equipment for night flying and that their mercenary crew of pilots from Egypt and the Arab countries were cowards and would be afraid to fly at night. Onuoha told him also that Biafra was in close touch with the situation and would not let the pilots serving her run that type of risk. Captain O'Donnell was greatly reassured after the conversation. As the plane started its descent, Onuoha went back to his seat in the rear of the aircraft.

Titi who was sitting next to him again asked Onuoha if everything was all right. Onuoha told her that they would be landing shortly. Afoukwu's face was very sad. He was almost pouting like a child. He did not even care to ask Onuoha what had been discussed. Onuoha felt that there had been some misunderstanding while he was gone, but he did not ask any questions. Onuoha just saw Titi shaking her fists silently in anger and shaking her head in deep disappointment and muttering: 'He is a terrible man. He is a terrible man.' Onuoha looked at Titi with surprise and she added, 'I had to slap him to teach him basic manners and standard decency.'

After this, the time seemed interminable. Onuoha thought that they must be flying very low. He could see a few lights down below, even though there were frequently black-outs in Biafra. For a while, they seemed to be circling interminably in the Biafran sky. He could not tell why they had not landed. He was afraid even to walk up to the pilot and find out what was happening. The plane went up and down in the dark sky. It veered sharply right and left as if it were being pursued by another craft. It appeared to be flying right over the trees and the next moment it was climbing up into the clouds and beyond. Then it would come down again and describe circles about three miles in diameter. Onuoha could not tell what was going on. Suddenly, Onuoha realized that his watch had stopped, probably because of the drastic changes in temperature during the past days. He knew that they were supposed to land around 10 p.m. He did not want to ask Titi what the time was, for that would give away his fear, his growing worry and deep anxiety. With the corner of his eye, he saw in the darkness the sparkling dial of Titi's watch and knew that it was about midnight.

Onuoha sat glued to his seat, motionless. The plane stopped its up and down movement and levelled out again. After ten or so minutes, the pilot put on the lights again. The three passengers looked up with surprise and despair. They could not understand what was happening. Were the pilots acting in collusion with the enemy? Before Onuoha could recover from his fright, he saw below him the sea, a lighthouse and an airport. He sighed with relief when the lights of the airport went on—green, white and red. They circled round and he could see below several planes parked on the sides of the runway. Some looked like fighter planes, others like rescue planes and transport craft. He was surprised and dumbfounded. Onuoha had not come back to Biafra since its declaration of independence. The airport did not look like what he had read about in the papers—a widened road that was being used as a landing strip. Onuoha knew that some improvements had been made to the airport, but he did not think the improvements had gone to that extent. He was filled with joy when he saw what looked like fighter planes waiting at the airport. That might be why the authorities had left on the airport lights without fear of enemy raids. Normally the Annabelle airport lights were on just for a few seconds before a plane touched the ground and, once the wheels touched the runway, the lights were put off. For Onuoha the sight was a mixture of joy, relief and surprise.

Afoukwu spoke at that point and broke Onuoha's reverie. 'Please put off the lights,' he pleaded. 'The Nigerians might come over and bomb our plane and the airport.' The pilots did not seem to hear what he was saying. He shouted again that they should put out the light and open the door and let him out of the plane. Hearing such a commanding voice, the pilots put out the lights in the interior of the plane. Afoukwu thinking out loud asked why the airport lights had been left on, and blamed everyone for carelessness and for trying to imperil the lives of people who had devoted their time and efforts to serving the country. 'The boys responsible for this ought to be court-martialled,' Afoukwu concluded.

As they moved toward the plane door, they suddenly saw with alarm that the airport was not Biafran. There was a gigantic terminal, well lit, sticking out in the dark night and the radar screen was rotating confidently with its coloured beams in the distance. A car manipulated a ladder towards the plane. Two police cars followed closely behind. It was certainly not a Biafran airport where everything was done in pitch darkness and where there was no terminal, no tower and no radar control for approaching planes. Captain O'Donnell came up to the door as Afoukwu hesitated to descend: 'I am sorry. I am awfully sorry. I did my best. I circled several times but we could not land in Biafra. I know how you feel. I feel the same way too.'

In his heart of hearts, Onuoha wished that they had not landed in Lagos. It was dangerous, disastrous. 'We had to land in Lagos —I am sorry, Libreville,' Captain O'Donnell added. With immense relief, Onuoha realized that they were therefore in safe hands, amongst friends in a country that had recognized Biafra. But again personal disappointment spread over Onuoha's face at 'the thought that they had been unable to land in Biafra that night Captain O'Donnell repeated the fact that he had done everything possible. He knew what the whole thing meant for Biafra. He wanted to help. He mentioned then that Ireland at one time also had fought a war of independence against the British. Captain O'Donnell had been sure he was right over the airport. He had circled at least four times, called on the radio, given the code word and signal, but there had been no reply, no contact. He had done everything that he could. Since there had been no contact with the Annabelle tower and no lights on the runway, he had decided to land at the nearest friendly airport, Libreville. He was also running short of fuel after circling for such a long time at low altitude. He could have landed even without lights at the place he thought was Annabelle. He was sure of it. He had come very low and had even seen the limits of the airport, but he had remembered what Onuoha had told him about the military situation being liable to change from minute to minute. Afraid that the Nigerians had perhaps taken the airport, he had flown over to Libreville in Gabon. Onuoha had no reason to doubt the sincerity of Captain O'Donnell. He was the type of man in whom you could not help having confidence. Though seriously disappointed, Onuoha accepted his explanation. He was sad, as he thought about it. It meant that the plane could not land that night and therefore could not go to São Tomé to make the requested shuttle to bring in the tons of ammunition there.

After going through the customs and immigration, Onuoha contacted the Biafran Special Representative in Libreville and also booked accommodation for all of them at the Hotel le Gamba not far away from the airport. The Biafran Representative promptly came over to help them. When they told him that they had not been able to land at Annabelle that night, he said that he knew about it. It was regrettable. The airport in Biafra had contacted him already by radio. The Annabelle tower acknowledged seeing the plane. With a feeling of disappointment, he said, 'The vandals came again tonight.' By the vandals he meant of course the Nigerians. Nigerian planes had bombed the airport about three-quarters of an hour before Captain O'Donnell tried to make the first contact with the tower. The vandals, the Representative continued, had bombed the airport and the bombs had made deep craters on the runway. Planes could not land under such conditions. He said that the airport could have been repaired almost immediately while Captain O'Donnell was still circling. However, just when they had filled up all the craters dug by the bombs and a roller had been brought to run over the surface and smooth it, an explosion had occurred as the roller approached one of the craters. Ten of the workers around had been killed on the spot and twenty-one sustained varying degrees of injury.

The Special Representative assured the captain that word had just that moment come from the airport that all was clear and that planes could now land. Some Red Cross planes from Santa Isabel had actually landed already. He tried to encourage the captain to go back immediately. Titi was anxious to go to Biafra that night. Captain O'Donnell complained that he did not have enough fuel to make the trip to Biafra and back that morning, and unfortunately there was no Super Constellation fuel in Libreville. It could only be obtained from São Tomé. Besides, it would soon be dawn and he would not have time to land in Biafra and get the plane off-loaded and out again in safety. The trip had to be put off till the following night. Afoukwu was feeling very ill and decided to go to bed immediately. Titi accepted the invitation of the Special Representative to spend the night with his family. His wife was an old school friend of hers.

Onuoha went to bed and tried to snatch a bit of sleep. It was refreshing in the cool night. Five floors below him, he could hear the waves of the Atlantic Ocean beating relentlessly on the sandy beach adjoining the hotel. The inward and outward lashing movement of the waves, the darkness and serenity outside were enough to remove the cares and worries from his troubled mind. Onuoha thought of Titi. He hoped that she was sleeping peacefully after the tumultuous events of the last few days. Somehow he could not quite define his attitude towards her. Even in his sleep, he tried to keep some kind of distance from her, but her image kept on coming back, creeping in on his thoughts. Unconsciously, he felt that Titi was beginning to rely more and more on his advice. Somehow too, Onuoha began to miss her presence. Gradually Titi was becoming a part of the scenery. At about the same time, Yvette Okonkwo was becoming a memory of the past, a rather hazy and unsure image of adolescent years.

Onuoha thought of Lawyer Afoukwu also before he slept. Afoukwu was fond of taking sleeping tablets. He would probably take an extra one that night to help him forget that, if their Super Constellation had come across the Biafran sky three-quarters of an hour earlier, it would have been shot down in the sky or set ablaze by the explosions on landing.

7

The Umbilical Cord

In the morning, instead of waking Lawyer Afoukwu by telephone, Onuoha decided to walk down to his floor and see if there were any signs of his stirring. On his door was hanging a red sign in English and French: *Do not disturb—Ne dérangez pas*. That was enough warning: Onuoha did not even knock at his door. He decided to invite Titi over to the hotel for breakfast. Titi was already breakfasting with her hosts, but wanted Onuoha to take her round the city that morning.

When Titi arrived at the hotel at ten in the morning, Afoukwu was still not up. They took a drive round the city of Libreville. Everything looked new and open. The city looked like a one-street city with houses on one side of the street and the ocean on the other side. It was beautiful and small and more lively than one would expect in the capital of a country of only half a million people. It looked like an ideal place for a honeymoon or even for an ordinary vacation.

For lunch, they went to a Chinese restaurant in the centre of the city. The Chinese seem to carry their restaurants and their food to the remotest corners of the world: they seem to be everywhere. That afternoon Onuoha and Titi arrived as the man was roasting a fat pig in the open air. The Chinese man also did about four or five other odd jobs like engraving, laundering, typing and store-keeping. And every morning he roasted a pig Chinese-style. Titi enjoyed the meal. The Chinese are generally good cooks. It seems that there is something they put in their soup and dishes that makes people want to come again. After a while, it becomes a habit and whenever the initiated person goes to any city, the first thing he asks is where to find a Chinese restaurant. And there always seems to be one around the corner.

When they came back to the hotel, Titi and Onuoha saw Afoukwu sitting down in the lounge looking miserable and sick. At first, Onuoha was frightened to see him in that state. When he spoke to him, Afoukwu could only reply in whispers and Onuoha thought that something really bad had happened. Back home in the villages of Biafra, people would say that he had been visited or touched by spirits, by evil spirits. Such a visit usually signalled the loss of a limb due to paralysis and sometimes also the temporary loss of the power of speech.

Asked if he had had anything to eat, Afoukwu whispered that he could neither eat nor drink anything. He had already sent for a doctor who had told him to stay quietly in one place. The doctor had also recommended that he should not go to, or stay in, a place of tension. Since Biafra was an area of high tension, the doctor had advised him not to go there. He lamented how much it pained him that he would not be able to get to Biafra that night. He had looked forward to it. He had planned on staying a long time there to see what was happening, to visit the soldiers at the front and encourage them, but he had now been struck down by this illness. Afoukwu expressed the profound wish that he would get better before dusk and be able to make the trip to Biafra. He might be able to convince his doctor to let him go. Lawyer Afoukwu was even willing to disobey the doctor and go if he felt better.

Afoukwu saw the presence of Titi as a blessing. Titi would stay in Libreville and nurse him. She could take down some important notes about his experiences during the Biafran War. He had been thinking for a long time about writing what he called Lawyer Afoukwu's History of Biafran Diplomacy in Europe and how it was deciding the fate of the war. More than anyone else, he had seen it grow and to a large extent he was responsible for shaping this diplomacy. If countries ever recognized Biafra, it was because of his indefatigable zeal and world prestige. It was precisely this zeal and hard work that had now struck him down with exhaustion. Afoukwu moaned to emphasize both the intensity and the location of his pains, mostly in the ribs. Lawyer Afoukwu wanted to put down in black and white his memoirs before anything happened to him. He also planned to hand over his confidential papers and documents to the Biafran National Archives, with the simple instruction that they should not be opened for three hundred years.

Afoukwu wrote a short note he would want Onuoha to take to

his wife in case he did not travel with the plane. He asked Onuoha to deliver the provisions and supplies immediately on arrival. Titi was not going to yield. She wanted to go home to Biafra for at least a few days. If she was going to become the private secretary of the itinerant ambassador, she would also like the appointment to come officially from the government, with defined responsibilities. Knowing the firmness and determination he could expect from Titi, Lawyer Afoukwu did not raise further objections, but merely expressed the desire to see her back very soon so that they could start work on his memoirs. 'The world knows nothing of these experiences: I should like to bring them to the knowledge of the world as soon as possible.' He advised Titi to get enough rest in Biafra, because, when she came back, they might have to work night and day, mostly at night.

By afternoon Lawyer Afoukwu had decided that the best thing for him to do would be to go to Geneva for a complete rest. So, around four o'clock Titi and Onuoha went to the airport again to board the Super Constellation. They would fly to São Tomé, refuel and then fly directly into Biafra. While they were waiting at their airport in Libreville, three French Red Cross flights left on their way to Biafra. A French Colonel was directing the French Red Cross operations. In fact, their Red Cross seemed to be entirely run by Colonels and Generals.

There was something admirable and brutish about man's behaviour. Man does not hesitate to commit genocide against his kind. The same man appears willing to run incalculable risks and to sacrifice his own life in the service of his neighbour. Some build and others destroy in this world of individuals, with their cowardice and their bravery, their callousness and their generosity. Before departure, instructions were given to Captain O'Donnell and Onuoha to try and off-load the Church Aid goods in São Tomé and load on about ten tons of ammunition and rifles. The situation in the Port-Harcourt and Aba areas was considered desperate, and pressure was building up around Ikot-Ekpene and Okigwi.

When the plane landed in São Tomé, Onuoha and the captain spoke to the Reverend Patrick O'Keefe who was in charge of the operations of the churches in São Tomé. They explained to him the necessity of off-loading the Joint Church Aid supplies and carrying ammunition to troops in Biafra. Father O'Keefe refused to allow that to happen. He had strict instructions never to let a trip paid for by the churches be used for carrying arms to Biafra. Onuoha explained to him the desperate situation in Port-Harcourt, the need for ammunition, the uselessness of food if the enemy overran the area and massacred the population. Father O'Keefe sympathized with him, but refused to allow the transfer of cargo. Nothing would make him relent. With a sad look, Onuoha went back to the plane after refuelling.

Titi was feeling as free as the air. The thought of going home to Biafra to see the situation for herself and maybe to see her parents again filled her with joy. The beauty of the island and its tropical atmosphere gave the occasion an even greater air of homeliness. Titi could not contain her joy and suspense. The absence of Peter Afoukwu seemed to remove all her inhibitions. She was a young girl all over again. She talked about one and a thousand things, about the parting emotions she had felt when her mother bade her goodbye on a rainy morning as she took an early bus to the local inner-city station. Her mother had assured her that she would come back safely to them. Her mother had been crying as she told her that she would come back to see them well and sound. Little had they known that there would be war. Little had they known that they would be forced out of their own village where they had lived for generations, where they had maintained their own farms and where they had always been sure of finding something to eat and drink, even after her father had lost his job in the city. The village had also gone now. It was heart-breaking when a family was forced to abandon a house where they had lived for more than ten years, but when in addition they had to abandon their final refuge, it was like digging a dead man out of the grave and leaving him to rot under the moist of the rain and the heat of the sun.

The trip to Biafra was cold, as usual. This time Onuoha was able to doze for a while, but the distance was shorter than it had been from Abidjan and soon they were inside Biafran territory. Deep within him, he prayed that there would be no bombing again that night. He could not bear the thought of having to go back again and make another try. As the plane lowered its altitude when they approached the airport, Onuoha could hear a small beep, beep, beep sound indicating that contact had been made with the tower. The clearance for landing was given.

The Annabelle airport was a two-mile-long highway that had been turned into an airport. Since then, the roadway had been widened and lengthened and several parallel tracks had been constructed. The pilot of the plane only had to line up his craft along the road and follow a straight course until he overflew a red blinking light indicating the beginning of the runway. Before, the runway used to be lit with hurricane lanterns, but the place had recently been electrified. However, because Nigerians used to hover in the sky until they saw one of the Biafran planes approaching the runway, the electric lights were only switched on immediately before a plane landed and then switched off at once. Even then, the Nigerian fighter would dive in like a kite and try to rocket the plane as it was landing and try to bomb and rocket the runway and terminal. It was because of these possibilities that the lights only went on some thirty seconds before the plane headed downwards to make contact with the runway. Immediately the wheels touched the ground, the lights were switched off.

On receiving the clearance to land, Captain O'Donnell circled the airport and made for the runway, nose down and lights off except for the pair of wing lights which flashed down and lit the roadway ahead like a pair of powerful stationary searchlights. After the plane had crossed the red signal, the lights on the ground went on and Onuoha looked down with joy as he saw the landing appear. Suddenly, the plane went right up again. The lights were still on. Normally when an enemy plane was in sight, the lights were blinked and then turned off and the pilot had to take off again, regain height and run for safety while the airport guns dealt with the intruder. At that moment, however, the lights were not turned off, indicating that there were no enemy planes in sight. The Super Constellation circled again, tried to land, but failed again and took off for the second time.

Onuoha did not know exactly what was happening, but felt

that something was wrong. As Captain O'Donnell told him later, he was determined to take all the risks in the world and land at the third attempt. One of the engines was over-burning and the captain was afraid it would catch fire as the plane landed. He took the chance. The plane scraped the ground, the lights went off and the Super Constellation taxied in the darkness to Ginger Sixteen, as the airport staff referred to their particular landing and parking zone. As they came out of the plane Captain O'Donnell was swearing in the name of St Patrick that if ever he got back alive, he would never try to land at Annabelle again. It was sheer luck that he was able to land that time. 'An explosion would have blown everything to bits.'

The staff at the airport were always very pleased when they saw the Super Constellation arrive, for more often than not it carried arms and ammunition. The Red Cross and the Joint Church Aid generally used DC 7s and other carriers. 'Man does not live by bread alone,' the airport boys used to say to Red Cross pilots. 'A bullet for a soldier is better than a ton of powdered milk for a battalion.'

Captain Umuofia was the Air Force officer in charge of Ginger Sixteen. He came forward to clear the passengers, who indicated where they were coming from. Captain O'Donnell gave Captain Umuofia a duplicate copy of the manifest, containing details of the articles in the plane. The passengers were invited to descend. For a ladder, Onuoha and Titi used two long poles and wobbled down to the ground while dutiful soldiers below waited with their hands outstretched in the darkness to catch the young lady so that she should not take a false step and land on the ground the wrong way. Captain Umuofia was a little disappointed when he read the manifest with the aid of a flash he had with him. He ordered the soldiers to remove personal luggage first. This almost filled up one of the trucks.

Two lorries were moved into position to receive the goods as they came down from the plane. The operation was carried out in total darkness. Occasionally a torch flashed here and there but this was greeted with a chorus: 'Out that light.' The visitor could see without being told that the nation was at war. The boys knew what was expected of them and did their work with amazing speed. Planes were landing almost every ten minutes. The lights came on and off. As each plane plunged downwards in the darkness, making for the runway, one of the tyres usually distorted the position of the wing lights, giving the false impression that the plane was going to crash-land. Somehow the plane always straightened out and landed safely, taxiing to the middle or the end of the runway, depending on the size and weight of the particular plane. It turned and headed to its assigned ginger where transport lorries and private cars stood waiting for the passengers and the cargo.

As one plane was landing, another was taking off. Often, they made use of the same light period with one taking off in an easterly direction, another landing from the west. That night, a few minutes after Onuoha and Titi had landed, a plane was taking off from a ginger next to theirs. The engines roared in the silent night, carrying away Titi's scarf. They could not stand the force of the wind, or the suffocation from the gas (especially the carbon monoxide) coming from the exhaust. Newspapers, light materials and boxes as well as hand luggage were blown into the surrounding bush that rustled like the wind cutting a bush-path through the savannah. The night air was filled with noxious smoke and clouds of fume curling out of the engines of the plane. It was a great relief when the plane taxied out and Onuoha and Titi with the help of Captain Umuofia found their belongings again at the edge of the surrounding bushes.

Captain Umuofia asked Onuoha and Titi to get away from the plane because it was dangerous. He told them to stand off a little, indicating that the planes were always the main targets of the bombing and rocketing of the airport. He advised them that if there was a raid while they were still at the airport, they should make for the nearest concrete shelter usually near the bush. 'If the shelter is far away,' Captain Umuofia said, 'just dive below a trailer with a reinforced steel platform. There are always one or two permanently placed at each ginger.' Onuoha and Titi listened seriously, but they could not quite appreciate the importance of the instructions.

Captain Umuofia added that he was supposed to have been on

duty the day before but could not come because of a mild indisposition. He had been replaced by another captain, who had been killed by the explosion that occurred when one of the unexploded bombs dropped by the Nigerian pilots blew up. Several of his men had been killed or injured. So most of the people working with him that night were new people. Captain Umuofia broke off his conversation abruptly and ordered the men around to hurry up because the plane had to leave immediately and try to make a shuttle flight from São Tomé before dawn. He told the loading crew to stand by and load copra and palm kernels into the plane for export. His men complained that they did not have enough hands. He called a second lieutenant assisting him to go to the base and get about fifteen more fatigue men. The lieutenant saluted and departed.

Returning to Onuoha and Titi, Captain Umuofia told them that they should avoid running into the bush. He explained that the first inclination for visitors was to run into the bush for cover. But Nigerian pilots were usually scared to death themselves, with the result that they just dropped off the bombs at random. Only a few of them had fallen on the runway. About ninety per cent of the bombs fell into the neighbouring bushes. Some were napalm and incendiary bombs that often flamed for days. They did have some special liquid for combating the flames, but not in sufficient quantities, so they reserved what they had for major fires.

Captain Umuofia pointed out in the distance a flicker of flame still glowing. 'That was lit early this evening by the vandals,' he said. 'Night bombing is not easy, though, especially when you are not equipped for it. The Nigerians sometimes use a DC 3 for bombing. They sometimes use those flickers you see there as direction finders at night. Quite often we have to camouflage them or even set up misleading flickers a few miles away from the airport right below our gun positions.' Captain Umuofia explained that the Nigerians hovered in the sky and, just as the Biafran plane was nosing down to land, the 'vandal' plane would dive to bomb. The visiting pilots of Caritas, the World Council of Churches and the Red Cross, were used to it. The Biafran pilots handling a few DC 3s and 4s had taken even greater risks while airborne. A couple of times, they had tried to shoot the enemy planes in the sky. The following day, Nigeria had announced that Biafra had bought some fighter planes. One of the Caritas pilots, Captain Umuofia said, claimed that the Nigerians followed his plane as he was landing and still threw their bombs into the bushes around. The Caritas pilot boasted thus: 'The Nigerians are as bad as the Egyptian pilots. The runway was lit like a two-mile-long Christmas tree. They could not light a candle on it, even with their heavy bombs.'

When Nigerian pilots were in sight, friendly planes were asked to hover in the air in certain safety zones. The funny thing was, he continued, that the Nigerian plane often joined the queue, in a sort of an 'unmerry-go-round', circling like a kite, waiting for a landing so that it could make its own dive and release a bomb. He said with a smile that they had recently devised new means of isolating enemy planes in the sky and dealing with them successfully. 'How?' Titi asked, rather naïvely. 'That's a military secret,' he smiled. He was asked about the risks of inadvertently shooting a friendly plane down. He said it was minimal—almost nil. Great precautions were always taken. Gunners could not just shoot when they saw a plane in the air. Often an alarm was sounded to give the workers time to take cover and the gunners were then given instructions from the control room when and where to shoot.

Captain Umuofia had barely finished his comments when Onuoha heard the streaking in the air of a jet plane. 'That sounds like an enemy plane,' Captain Umuofia said. 'But wait. Do not run yet until we find its exact direction.' Titi and Onuoha were instinctively going to jump into the bush when Captain Umuofia held them. 'Keep cool. There are no shelters in this ginger. It is still under construction. Keep cool. There is no alarm yet.'

It appeared that the jet streak had faded in the distance. But then there was a warning shot followed immediately by an alarm. Captain Umuofia said briskly: 'Follow me.' They all dived under one of the trailers nearby. It had a steel platform. They were barely beneath it when a rocket whistled right over their heads and exploded in the bush not far from where they were. Guns boomed in the dark night as the plane turned and made another pass. Titi

clung on fast and hard to Onuoha. Onuoha held tightly the vibrat-
ing steel rod below the trailer. It seemed as though Titi would
squeeze Onuoha to death. A Biafran gun position barely five yards
from where they were hiding boomed and fired a rocket. Its
sudden explosion, more frightening because unexpected, made the
atmosphere more unnerving than the explosion of the enemy
bomb. Other gun positions in Ihiala, Mgbidi and Oguta—two
miles, three miles, five miles away—continued to boom in the
dark night. For the first time it dawned on Onuoha that they had
arrived in Biafra, a nation at war. They were also in a war zone, in
the war front. The gunning died down. The rocketing had caused
no damage. A few minutes later, planes continued to land and
take off.

From that moment onwards, however, the sound of planes
ceased to be innocuous. Each plane taking a position to land
appeared like an enemy plane and whether one was sitting, standing or dozing, one was seized by a sense of constant alarm. One's
heart jumped, leaped up high in a futile flight. It was a tiring feeling, and from that moment, Onuoha began to lose weight. At
first it was a mere sensation but it would become a reality later.

The young captain helped himself, because of the scarcity of
petrol, to the aero-fuel. He said he would mix it later with engine
oil to reduce its volatility. The other workers helped themselves to
the stockfish and dried milk. Those who preached the gospel quite
often lived by it as well.

Finally, Onuoha and Titi entered a car that would take them to
the State House, the passenger and luggage terminal of Annabelle
airport. As Captain Umuofia bade them goodbye, he asked
Onuoha in a rather embarrassed way, if by chance he had some
cigarettes. Onuoha did not smoke, but he had some cigarettes and
felt guilty that he had not offered them to Captain Umuofia without his having to ask for one. Onuoha gave him two packets of
Craven A. The face of Captain Umuofia lit up like that of an
adventurer who had struck a gold mine. Onuoha and Titi waved
goodbye and promised to bring him some more when next they
visited the outside world.

.　　.　　.　　.

At the State House, the officials off-loaded their luggage. When they realized that the suitcases belonged to an itinerant ambassador Peter Afoukwu, they did not search or weigh them. About the same time, a young woman had arrived with her little son from Libreville, coming from America to join her husband and other children in Biafra. She had arrived with quite a bit of luggage as if she had bought enough provisions abroad to last her during the war of independence, but certainly less than Afoukwu bought to last his wife a few weeks.

The transportation officer on duty made her pay the cost of transportation from Libreville to Biafra for the excess baggage. Further down the line, the customs official made her pay import duties on all the articles, including salt and pepper. There were no standards or scales and the charges seemed to be at the whim of the officer on duty. By the end of the charges, the young mother cursed herself for ever thinking of importing articles of necessity into a blockaded area. She had nothing but British pounds on arrival. Too soon she discovered that the Biafran pound had not been devalued. Hence she only got eighty-five per cent of the real value of the devalued British pounds.

Onuoha felt guilty as the woman watched him imploringly begging him with her eyes to intervene and come to her aid asking probably how Onuoha managed to avoid paying a penny for all his luggage. Before Onuoha left the State House, the officials around quietly and discreetly begged for cigarettes, salt sugar and soap. Such requests, Clinton Okeji had warned him were usually indices of what people lacked most at home. An attractive young lady, well dressed in spite of the war, who was working in the customs office, asked Titi for some hair thread for plaiting her hair. Titi said that she had none.

As for the young woman returning from America to join her husband, in spite of all that she had paid in cash or kind, she discovered that there was no way of carrying her luggage to Umuahia where she planned to take her husband by surprise. Overnight petrol had become scarce since the evacuation of Port-Harcourt Onuoha felt guilty again as he could not help her. Onuoha had at his disposal a small truck and a station wagon filled up with

Afoukwu's goods. He could probably have taken along the lady and her child. On second thoughts, he advised her to stay there and be patient until she could herself remove every bit of her luggage. As Onuoha left her, he could not help realizing what must be going on in the mind of the woman. She would probably be thinking that in Biafra there were also many mansions and her suite was rather low on the scale.

Finding herself in Biafra was not the joy that Titi had anticipated. Already she had seen enough to make her pensive. The desire to locate her parents became an overriding preoccupation. But the search had to wait until Onuoha had delivered the message he had for the government. They drove in the dark night, putting on the headlights once in a while to make sure of their bearings. The headlights even were shaded. They took the Onitsha-Owerri road. Occasionally they saw groups of people on bicycles carrying bags of rice and garri, who seemed to be moving to the Onitsha front about thirty miles further north-west. They drove in the middle of the road and with the fresh breeze of the morning it was difficult to tell that there was a war going on in the country.

There were no lights along the road or in the houses they passed by and all along the road the houses were camouflaged. The zinc-roofed structures were covered with palm-fronds to give the air of an unending chain of forests. But here and there from the bush a small lantern signalled a stop and their car screeched to a halt as young soldiers walked out majestically from the bush to check on their identities. 'State House—From the airport,' the driver, Emeka Diogu, said. This scene was repeated at each stop on the way and on each occasion they were allowed to pass.

Onuoha drew Titi's attention to a river they were passing at that moment. She hardly recognized it. 'It looks so small,' she exclaimed. It was the Njaba River. She told him how several years earlier she used to be terribly frightened to cross the bridge that used to be over the river. Those were days of murderous accidents on local roads when transport vehicles that were rarely taken to the garage to be serviced, lost their front tyres or wheels, plunging vehicles and passengers into the nearby rivers while the driver lay safe and sound on the bank because he had jumped out without making any serious efforts to save the lorry and the lives of his passengers. In those days, that particular bridge, the Njaba River Bridge, was so small and so old that cars would never dare to cross it loaded.

The car sped along the road past Ogbaku, Orogwe, Irete. Around here, only one side of the tarred road was in use, the other shut off with oil drums, as if they were planning to tar the area again. Onuoha did not bother to ask Diogu what they were doing there. Firstly, Onuoha suspected that he might not know why they were there, and secondly, he feared that the driver might think that he was being too curious about military secrets.

The few schools they passed by on the journey were completely covered with bushes. The bushes and grass had been purposely left to grow over the establishments for camouflage, giving the impression to enemy planes from the air that the area was deserted. It was difficult even for someone who had known the area before to recognize turns along the roads. The familiar signs were gone. The petrol stations on the roadside were covered by overgrowth. The pumps were sheltered with palm-fronds and the entrances were barred with barrels.

The night was cold, even in the tropical atmosphere, and there was a little drizzle. A scanty rain-coat barely covered the soldier who brought out his rifle at the next check-point before they entered Owerri. His companions were taking a nap under a structure of palm leaves erected at the corner to provide some shelter from wind and rain. A hurricane lamp burned dimly beside them. Who knows how long they had been there at that post? Who knows how many people they had searched? Who knows how many saboteurs they had apprehended? The soldiers stood or sat there waiting from morning till dusk. Another group would relieve them from twilight until dawn. They stood and waited, as if for a Godot. Their uniform still had some freshness left about it, but the visitor could not help feeling that before long, before the end of their long wait, the crispness would have gone. Perhaps then the war would take on another more arduous phase.

Onuoha could hardly recognize the Holy Ghost College just on the outskirts of Owerri. The college was his alma mater. On the other side of the road was Assumpta Cathedral. Further down the road was Owerri Girls' Secondary School where Yvette Okonkwo used to go to school. The three institutions, even in the breaking dawn, seemed to have discovered newly-found age and antiquity because of the laurels that decked their roofs and walls. To the right was the tarred road that led to Port-Harcourt. On both sides, the road was beautifully lined with oil-bean trees, like a French departmental highway. There was a difference, though, for the openness of the French countryside was replaced in Owerri by the dark richness of the tropical forest, forests that sent tons of lumber, snails and staple food to the local and overseas markets. But there was war in the country and Onuoha did not know for certain if the peasant hands were still there toiling.

Pointing to the Port-Harcourt road, Onuoha asked Diogu how far away the war front was to the right. 'About thirty miles,' he sighed. 'The enemy almost pushed into Owerri two days ago. But our soldiers fought back and pushed them right back to Igrita. There is no menace from that side now.' 'So we really have lost Port-Harcourt?' Titi asked. Diogu shook his head and said, 'It was really a shock. Up till the last minute, the last second, we were told we could defend the city. It is not worth the trouble recounting what loss we suffered there. One colonel I drove back to Umuahia yesterday at about this time, also from the Onitsha front, was telling me that if we had had just one plane-load of arms, just ten tons of ammunition and about three hundred extra rifles, we could have saved Port-Harcourt.'

There was silence for a while as everyone pondered the importance of Port-Harcourt. Diogu continued talking, half-lamenting, half reminiscing. The government had been determined that what had happened in Enugu would never happen in Port-Harcourt. During the attack on Enugu, the civilians had all run away and the soldiers left alone had not been able to guard the city which had easily been infiltrated by the enemy and taken from the inside. Experience had also shown that it was very difficult for an ill-equipped army like Biafra's to recapture a city easily once it had been lost to the enemy. When the Port-Harcourt boys had heard of the fall of Enugu the year before, their militia had sent three thousand men to help recapture the city. When therefore Port-Harcourt itself was menaced, the civilians were determined not to evacuate the city and not to give it up to the enemy. They argued that evacuation demoralizes both civilians and soldiers. The latter often see no point in defending a city that has practically been handed over to the enemy.

'*Port-Harcourt must not be evacuated* was the password in the city,' the driver continued. 'Even when the enemy was about fifteen miles away and the shells were falling on the outer perimeter of the city, courageous militia boys manned the checkpoints leading in and out of Port-Harcourt to prevent its residents from leaving the city with their cars and from taking so much as a pin out of the city. A big businessman approached the government quietly with a proposal to dismantle and move by night the essential elements of his aluminium industry, since the situation was deteriorating. The government answered back that the movement of such heavy equipment would set off a series of rumours that might give the impression to the wavering that the government had no firm intention of defending Port-Harcourt to the last man.'

The loss of Port-Harcourt, Diogu went on, was therefore a national tragedy. Even on the morning of the total evacuation, soldiers were still firing bullets over the heads of civilians who wanted to leave the city. The soldiers were trying to force them to remain. But when the critical time came, everyone, soldier and civilian took to the road. Cars were abandoned not only in the city but along the road because of lack of petrol. But there were two million gallons of refined petrol unevacuated in Port-Harcourt and more than ten million gallons of crude oil. The fall of the city seemed to have happened in a few minutes. First one battalion collapsed completely after running short of ammunition, then another collapsed somewhere else. Biafran troops were cut off in various sectors. The brigade headquarters was suddenly being moved within minutes at the same time as more than five hundred thousand civilians were struggling to leave the city. Pedestrians could hardly move, let alone cars. Passenger lorries were packed full and were overflowing with civilians. There was no time to evacuate the wounded soldiers in the General Hospital. The Nigerian troops massacred four hundred of them. Shells claimed the lives of hundreds and thousands of civilians as the enemy cut off the Port-Harcourt/Aba road leaving the civilians nothing but the Owerri road exit. The Nigerians seemed to direct their shells purposely with unusual accuracy, on the Owerri road. The range increased as the civilians surged out of the city. It was a massacre.

The stories were atrocious and some of them should never be repeated before the coming generation. A young woman for instance had just gone outside to get some powdered milk for her baby when the exodus began. A shell fell on her house and killed her baby sitter. The husband was at work and probably killed there or was running towards Owerri like lots of other family heads that were forced by circumstances to abandon their families. The frantic woman rushed into the bedroom to grab her child, and, wailing and almost unconscious as shells fell around her, made for the Owerri road, her bottle still in one hand. About five miles from the city she joined a long and interminable queue to get some water for the child from the nearby tap. After waiting for half an hour, the young mother bent down to get some water for her child. She fainted on the spot when she realized that she had grabbed a pillow instead of the child in the cot. She never recovered from her shock.

It is needless to repeat such stories or to mention the number of women that went into premature labour on that fateful boiling afternoon because of the trauma, the massacres, the rockets, the explosions. The stories were shocking and each evacuee from Port-Harcourt had his own tale of horror, of sorrow, of bereavement. A few desperate husbands dared back that night into the city in search of their wives and children. Some never came back to their villages. Others were sent away by the Nigerian soldiers, castrated as a lasting mark, the Nigerians reportedly said, of their great imprudence. Children who were not sure of the whereabouts of their parents ended up in refugee camps. Parents who lost everything including their young ones languished miserably back home in the villages, that is to say, those who were still lucky enough to have a village to which they could return.

At the check-point just after the Nworie Bridge, there was a courier waiting for Onuoha and Titi. There was no need to go to Umuahia that night. Someone had been sent to Annabelle airport to tell Onuoha this but the messenger might have crossed them around the airport. A radio message from Libreville said that Lawyer Afoukwu had been urgently flown just after their departure to a summer resort in Geneva so that he could recuperate quickly. There was no need for Titi to go and join him again. The courier in question was a young lieutenant and an aide-de-camp at the State House in Owerri. He confirmed that Port-Harcourt had fallen completely into the hands of the enemy. With a breath that almost choked him, he added that word had just arrived that Aba, forty miles north of Port-Harcourt had fallen that very night. 'Thank God, we were able to evacuate the city in time, for once,' the lieutenant added. When the lieutenant mentioned Aba, Onuoha immediately thought of Lawyer Peter Afoukwu, and his beautiful mansion. The young lieutenant stopped his reverie when he said that if the Super Constellation had come the day before with about ten tons of ammunition, they could have prevented the fall of Aba. If the ten tons had arrived a week or so earlier, they could have retaken Port-Harcourt completely. Speaking quietly to Onuoha, Titi said that one got the impression that every city in Biafra had been lost because ten tons of ammunition failed to arrive at a certain moment. 'But we are not discouraged,' the lieutenant said. 'The morale of the soldiers is high. The people want to continue the war and we have no alternative but to defend ourselves. The important thing is that we are sure of final victory.' Together, they left for the State House.

Onuoha and Titi spent the night in the same hotel as the famous Captain Tudor. They discovered this in the morning from Emeka Diogu. Titi wanted very much to meet the young man about whom she had heard so much, whose courage and dedication were almost proverbial. After the Onitsha campaign, Tudor had been asked to be an aide-de-camp at the State Office. He refused.

saying that he wanted to go to the front and fight the enemy. His presence at the State House was not necessary. There were other people who could do the job equally well.

Tudor, Titi and Onuoha had breakfast together. They exchanged views about lots of things, including the turn of the war at home and abroad. They had many views in common. Tudor then informed them that he was specializing in activities behind enemy lines. He was in charge of a group of boys who plied between Nigeria and Biafra for trade and other assignments. Though the two zones had changed their currencies, the coins had not changed as yet and some sort of illegal trade was still going on secretly across the borders. Tudor mentioned that he would be leaving with a group that evening for Enugu and planned to be back within two or three days. Titi could hardly believe what he was saying. She wondered how he could go to Enugu when it was completely under the control of Nigerian soldiers. The idea was intriguing. Onuoha wanted to go with Tudor if it was possible. Titi asked to come along. Tudor asked them to think about it during the day and if they still felt like coming along, they should meet him at the Brigade Headquarters of the Biafran Army a few miles from Ogidi which was near Onitsha, before six o'clock. Emeka Diogu knew the brigade headquarters in question.

Later that morning, Onuoha and Titi set out with Diogu for Mgbidi. They were going to Nempe, a small village near Mgbidi, where Peter Afoukwu's wife was living, in order to deliver the supplies to her. They had to cross the Nworie River again. As they crossed the bridge, Onuoha saw a young lady who reminded him of Yvette Okonkwo. Somehow he associated the swift flow of the river with Yvette's quick gait. Moreover, they had passed lots of sweet moments along that road. Without really expecting an answer, he asked Diogu if he knew Yvette Okonkwo. The reply was quick; everyone in town knew Yvette Okonkwo. Yvette was an exceptionally popular girl. She had been married to an army officer about three weeks earlier. The driver added philosophically, 'The beautiful girls are all running over to the army officers nowadays. Army boys are about the only people who have everything now. They alone can satisfy the thirst of our girls.' Of course, Diogu did not know of Onuoha's previous relationship with Yvette. Onuoha was silent for most of the journey. Titi knew that something was wrong. She appeared to understand but said nothing. Out of the corner of her eye, she observed Onuoha's dejected face. She knew trying to cheer him up would just complicate matters, so she kept quiet.

Lawyer Afoukwu's wife lived near a hospital for wounded soldiers in what seemed a beautiful house, when compared with what was left in other parts of the country. She was delighted to receive the supplies from the head of the family. Onuoha did not tell her about the sudden trip of Peter Afoukwu to a resort in Geneva. As they chatted, she handed them other lists of important articles she wanted bought for her abroad. She wanted some perfume like the one Chief Tobias Iweka had mailed to his wives. She was intrigued by the mini-dresses Obiora Ifedi had sent to his wife and children. She complained that she was running low on Cutex, lipstick and hand cream. She pointed out a few new models she had picked up from some of the women's magazines which her husband had sent her earlier. She insistently begged Titi to do the shopping herself, adding that men were often embarrassed to go into women's sections and ask for panties, girdles, bras and Cutex. She asked Onuoha to remind her husband that his family had not seen bread and butter for some time, while the Ifedis and the Iwekas were getting a steady supply.

Titi asked her how she found her new house after leaving their fabulous official mansion. She complained about the insensitivity of the government. She had lodged a complaint since she moved in there four weeks earlier, but no one had done anything to change the curtains in the house. The material was very flimsy. 'They look very cheap and I really feel embarrassed receiving you in a place like this,' she apologized. She had stopped complaining because she was thinking of moving out of the area. Recently, after the fall of Opobo and Yenogoa, a brigade headquarters had been transferred to the neighbourhood. The soldiers had become a daily nuisance. They were too talkative. The brigade either had to move or she would.

Mrs Peter Afoukwu was afraid also that because her house was only a few miles from the airport, Nigerian planes might bomb it by mistake, not knowing that she was not really one of those fighting the war. Her house was one of the most imposing in the area and would normally attract attention from the air. She was already making arrangements to rent another villa in the heart of the country. As a matter of fact, she had rented several villas already and had been paying for them monthly. One of the villas was in the Nnewi area, another in Mbaise and a third in the Orlu area. She worked out that she was absolutely sure to have a house to move to, irrespective of the direction from which the Nigerians came. They could not, she concluded, take those towns all at the same time. And if they succeeded in taking them all, then the independence bid would be finished and there would be no reason to run again.

As Titi and Onuoha left her house, they stopped by a Red Cross depot a few miles away. It was a pitiful sight. The store that housed the entire provisions of the local Red Cross was smaller than the living-room where Onuoha and Titi had just been talking to Mrs Afoukwu. The drugs they had for the community there could be counted in five rapid minutes. They had some milk, but only just enough to feed some one hundred children for two days. But these provisions were to be distributed to several refugee camps. The powdered milk in the store was packed in half-torn cement bags, partly soaked by rain, partly moistened by the humidity which spares little in the tropics. The local Red Cross director invited Titi and Onuoha to join his group on their weekly visit to the war front. The invitation was tempting, but they already had another commitment. They decided to take him up on it another time.

They drove off towards Onitsha. At Awomama, Diogu wanted to stop for a while and cash some money at the bank. It was getting late and Onuoha suggested that he could do it some other time. Onuoha had seen more than two hundred people lined up in front of the counter waiting to cash their cheques. Diogu said that it would take him less than three minutes. Onuoha did not want to start arguing with him, so he let the driver out of the car and, to Onuoha's surprise, he was back within two minutes, with ten pounds in his pocket. As he explained later, one of the Port-Harcourt branches of his bank had moved over to Awomama. Diogu knew some of the girls working there. Because of the critical shortage of Biafran currency notes, the bank was only paying one pound to each depositor. Some of the depositors had been waiting there for the past six hours, but in vain. 'I know a young girl who works there,' Diogu said. 'Every week, I get her about two gallons of petrol for her Mobylette from the State House. And whenever I go to the bank, all I have to say is how much I need and she will give it to me. Today, I asked for ten pounds, so she gave it to me. I could have asked for more, but I did not need it.' In Biafra, as in any other country, it pays to know people who matter and who are working in important places.

They drove straight on to Ihiala and from there to Nnewi. They turned to the right past Nnobi and Adazi and headed towards Agukwu. Thus they bypassed Onitsha, which was still being disputed by the Nigerian and Biafran forces. They were on their way to Titi's home in Abagana. They drove along roads that had not seen cars for years. All along, Onuoha feared that they might run into an enemy ambush because one was never completely sure where the fighting had reached. Most of the villagers beyond Agukwu and Nri had been evacuated. A wrong turn in the woods could lead one straight into an enemy camp.

Interlocking chains of hills spread interminably along their route. There seemed to be spring water spouting out from rocks every two or three miles. Their mouths gaped like the legendary lions. The vegetation was dense, very dense and rich with lusty undergrowth. But it was not too difficult to follow the ancient paths once trodden by ancestral feet. They had survived the war better than the modern roads. Then Biafran troops were in control of the stretch of road between, eight miles from Onitsha and Nawfia about ten miles beyond Abagana.

Diogu said that just two or three months earlier, that whole zone was impassable. The Nigerians had attacked in full force and had pushed down into Onitsha after they had failed to take that city from Asaba across the river. Biafran forces had succeeded in cutting off their supply lines and their communications links between Ogidi and Awka. During that fight, a very young Biafran engineer, who came back from Germany, Major Madu, was killed in an air raid near the war front. 'I had just brought him back from Aba that day. The government issued a special communiqué saying that Major Madu had died in a motor-cycle accident on the Onitsha road. It would have given too much credit to the Nigerian/Egyptian pilots of the Russian planes and their British bombs to announce that Major Madu was killed in an air raid.'

Back in Paris, Onuoha had heard the rumour that the young Biafran engineer was dead but he never was sure of the news or of the circumstances of his death. 'He certainly died in the service of his country,' Titi said. 'Yes, he died in the service of his country,' Diogu added. 'But the same thing,' Diogu continued, 'could not be said about one Doctor Xavier who died in another air raid a few days later in Aba.'

Titi asked Diogu what had happened in that case. Diogu smiled and said that the doctor worked in Queen Victoria Hospital, Aba. One evening, Dr Xavier had left his wife and children and told them that he was going to the hospital to look after wounded people. Diogu himself was in Aba that day and had transported some wounded soldiers to Queen Victoria Hospital from the Ikot-Ekpene front. Dr Xavier was supposed to be on duty but he could not be found in the hospital. They looked for him for two hours, but he was nowhere to be found.

Diogu was sent with one of the nurses at Queen Victoria Hospital to go and look for Doctor Xavier in his home at University Road, Aba. When they arrived, the wife of Dr Xavier told them that her husband had left home for the hospital about two hours earlier. The nurse could not understand it, since she had been on duty all afternoon and had not seen Dr Xavier in the wards and there were urgent cases that required immediate surgery. They turned to go back to the hospital. Diogu and the nurse were still at the door when a policeman drove up and asked for Mrs Xavier. The mystified wife and children then learned that the head of the family had been killed in an air raid. Naturally, the family asked if the hospital had been bombed. The policeman, full of embarrassment, said that the hospital had escaped it that particular day.

It was on their way back to Queen Victoria Hospital that Diogu and the nurse learned that Dr Xavier had gone to the house of Yvette Okonkwo instead of reporting for duty. He was reportedly lying in Yvette's bed while she went to the kitchen, in typical Aba fashion, separated from the main house, to make a cup of coffee. 'The vandals,' Diogu said, 'chose that particular moment to visit the neighbourhood. Dr Xavier was killed on the spot apparently. As for Yvette, she later ran out of the kitchen looking as beautiful as ever and without a scratch.'

The hilarious thing about the incident was that somehow the Nigerians had monitored Biafran Army Defence radio saying something about the death of Dr Xavier. That evening, Radio Nigeria while announcing their supposed capture of Ikot-Ekpene town, which was still in Biafran hands, claimed also that they had killed several Biafran officers, including a young medical officer, Dr Xavier, during a fierce battle that had raged for four hours. Titi could not help smiling, tragic though the incident was. 'So you can see,' Diogu concluded, 'that Dr Xavier naturally died in the service of his country.'

They had reached Abagana. There they were confronted by horror. For miles on end, they saw the carcasses of an entire Nigerian brigade—lorries, ferret cars, saladins, empty and un-exploded shells, full and decapitated skeletons, were littered over a space of two miles or more. The story was simple yet miraculous. At first, there had been an encounter at Udi, Oji River. Ugwuoba and more than six thousand Nigerian troops had been killed dur-ing the battles which had raged for several days. The Biafrans had captured several ferret cars intact and destroyed at least ten vehicles.

Titi said that they had arrived at their destination. Diogu stopped his car and opened the glove compartment, then gave Titi a military communiqué issued by the Biafran Army Headquarters during the Abagana episode.

In the past few days [the communiqué said], Biafran Land Forces in and around the town of Onitsha have encompassed and completely destroyed one of the largest armies ever assembled in Africa—the twenty thousand strong Nigerian Second Division commanded by Colonel Murtela Mohammed. A total of fourteen thousand men under Colonel Mohammed set out from Enugu in late January with the aim of capturing the river-side stronghold of Onitsha from the rear, after three attempts to take it by sea had failed. Subsequently, this force was backed by another six thousand men sent from the Enugu Garrison after repeated requests for reinforcements.

Along the sixty-eight mile stretch of road between Enugu and Onitsha, Mohammed lost close to twelve thousand of his men in ten weeks of the fiercest and bloodiest fighting of the war. Two days ago, the remaining two thousand men made a wild dash for the last eight miles to Onitsha. Surrounded in the outskirts of the town, the Nigerians are in the throes of being wiped out after having senselessly tried and slaughtered over three hundred civilians who failed to flee in time.

The final destruction of the force came on Monday, 25 March, 1968, when the six thousand reinforcements were intercepted in a one hundred and two lorry convoy heading west for Onitsha from Enugu. The thirteen thousand gallon petrol tanker accompanying the convoy was hit by mortar. It blew up and drenched over sixty of the vehicles in blazing petrol. The surviving troops were destroyed as they attempted to force a passage back to Enugu with two hundred and fifty tons of artillery pieces, mortar bombs, shells, guns and ammunitions contained in the convoy.

Over one third was captured intact and the rest totally destroyed, as were also the escorting armoured vehicles. At Onitsha repeated attempts by Federal forces at Asaba to cross the water by canoe and relieve the surrounded remnants of the second division have been repulsed, often by the fire from the heavy machine guns captured from the Nigerian troops. As a fighting force, Colonel Mohammed's 20,000 men have ceased to exist.

The story was simple, miraculous and tragic. The debris of the entire brigade was still there to tell how simple it was, proclaim the nature of the miracle and show the extent of the tragedy. One had to see the horror to believe that it could happen, that it had actually happened. From the road, they branched off to the village to see if they could pick up notes or see signs of Titi's home. Titi sighed as they walked and said that it was there probably that Akin Ajayi, Lola's brother, had been killed. She cried as they approached the village. It was impossible to recognize the tarred road that used to be there just before she left for Dakar. The entire roadway had either been dug up purposely or else been destroyed by explosions. The roads were completely covered by moss, as if the area had been abandoned for more than twenty years, for more than one generation perhaps. It appeared also from the number of common graves around that at least one whole generation of villagers had been wiped out. It was difficult to say if there remained anything of anyone.

House after house in the area had been destroyed. It was difficult even for Titi to recognize which road led to her home. When an army had gone through a neighbourhood, it made no difference whether the army was Biafran or Nigerian, both left behind death and desolation. Soon, too soon, the feeling of death had disappeared but the stench of desolation still persisted. At Abagana, two armies had gone through the village, each of them twice, and the destruction in the area defied all description. In another area, Ngwoma, not far from Ulakwo where the enemy stayed less than one week, a young doctor went back to his home to see its state after it had been recaptured by Biafran troops. Two miles from his home, as he hurried on foot since it was still not possible to drive in the area, he started picking up his wedding pictures. Closer to home, he saw littered on the road articles of furniture and cutlery embossed with his family initials. He did not have the courage to find out what the main house looked like.

Titi Duru that afternoon would have paid any sum, would have sacrificed anything for the luck of being able to pick up somewhere along the road to her family house, an old picture, the picture of her childhood, of herself in her mother's arms or in white with her father and mother on the day when she had received her first communion. She would have paid anything to recapture again in a black and white image the picture of her ageing mother. But nothing could be found. The rainy season had come and was going and ants, the tropical myrmidons of desolation, had wrought their havoc on the few structures that had escaped the bombing and the shelling.

In a village where the landmarks are gone, it becomes difficult to recognize houses even when the street names are there. In a village that never had streets as such, looking for a family mud house lost in the thick undergrowth is like searching for precious jewels in the bottom of the sea amidst coral reefs. Titi did find what looked like her family house. The roofs were gone. Where there used to be a bed, it appeared that a shell had dug a hole after exploding. What remained of the walls were riddled with bullets. There must have been hand-to-hand fighting in the vicinity. There was nothing that could be picked up in the way of relics of the past. It was difficult for the most optimistic being to believe that anyone could have escaped from the house alive.

Beside the fire-place lay a cluster of bones. They could have been the bones of anything, a huge animal, of human beings, a friend, a foe, perhaps a parent. It was difficult to tell. It was heart-rending to look at them. With her eyes dry but laden with sorrow, Titi picked up a stick and made holes here and there as if looking for something. About the only thing left in the house was a cooking tripod, a steel tripod laden with dirt that stood there to mock time and age. Titi turned it. The tripod fell over something that made a ringing noise. Titi and Onuoha bent down and there saw, half-hidden by clay, a ring. When Titi saw it she started crying. Onuoha looked at it. It had engraved on it the name *DURU*. Onuoha could barely control himself as he tried to console Titi. Diogu came nearer, his eyes also filled with tears.

The ring was Titi's parents' single wedding ring. Her father had given it to her mother. Titi remembered how much her mother had cherished it. Her mother had promised to pass the ring on to her before dying. As far back as Titi could remember, the ring had very rarely left her mother's finger. Could the mother at the moment of death have left the ring by the fireside hoping that some day after the sorrowful war, Titi would come home to discover the parental relic of love? Somehow, Titi could not believe that the bones by the fireside were the remains of her parents. But who in her position would believe it or even want to believe it? The idea was too shocking to be plausible. She wiped her eyes, took the ring and put it in her small handbag. Titi was weak and could scarcely stand on her feet as she moved to go. Onuoha offered her a hand.

With sorrow, with deep reluctance, they turned. Titi knew perhaps that that was the last time she would cast her eyes on the family property that went back several generations. Titi felt like someone who had just attended a funeral ceremony, the funeral of a very beloved one. The last funeral hymn is sung. The coffin is lowered. Each beat of the heart marks the stroke of a shovel enclosing forever in deep earth the body of the beloved one. Stricken, the bereaved turns her back to go. The tears are gone, but a new kind of sorrow begins—more painful, more excruciating because it can no longer find solace and comfort in tears.

8

Behind the Enemy Lines

That evening, Tudor was there waiting for them at the Brigade Headquarters at Awkuzu. The BEL (Behind Enemy Lines) squad was there also with their diesel lorry. In spite of the war, there was some smuggling still going on between Nigeria and Biafra. In Biafra, it was not quite the private affair that it was on the Nigerian side. It was a legal operation sponsored by the Army and the BEL brigade was specially trained and divided into squads to carry out the trade.

The network was a gigantic one stretching from the coastal areas in the south around Yenogoa provinces, along the south-eastern areas in the Calabar provinces, to the Ogoja war zone, where meat was purchased quite often. To the north, there was a lively trade around Nsukka and along the Anambara River. The trade across the River Niger via Aboh was perhaps the most flourishing. Since there were Biafran troops operating secretly in the Mid-West, it was quite easy to conduct an extensive trade with the Mid-West and through the Mid-West (where sympathy for Biafra was not lacking) with the rest of southern Nigeria.

Unfortunately, though the business was carried out under government supervision, with money issued from the government bank, in old Nigerian currency, which was still being used in those border areas, and in coins which were still being used by both sides, the products purchased, which were normally destined for the armed forces and the refugee camps, quite often found their way into the hands of unscrupulous highly placed public servants. These often used agents to resell the products at exorbitant prices in the black market, or hoarded them for the benefit of their relations and friends. Tudor had complained several times, but in vain. He employed a few boys to watch the profiteers and accumulate evidence for their arrest. Some army officers involved in the traffic imprisoned the boys one by one for more than two weeks without trial, until Tudor discovered what was happening.

Some of the profiteers were even threatening Tudor's life, saying that they would ambush him some day. Tudor had to suspend his investigations for a while.

The procedure for the journey was simple. The lorry was taken as close to the enemy territory as was safe. The BEL Squad walked the rest of the way and there purchased what they needed, or simply carried away materials their comrades already behind the lines had bought and stored for them. They set out on the journey around seven in the evening.

The days had gone when motor vehicles roared along the road. There were no roads now in the war areas, nothing but footpaths. The going was difficult. It was a military order that the BEL Squad should not use the same road for two consecutive trips. In short, for each new trip, there was a new route and an entirely new experience. Sometimes it was long, sometimes it was rough, but, as Tudor said, it always turned out to be exciting and, once the individual had a taste of it, he always wanted to come back, again and again.

Young as the Biafran war then was, there were already in the BEL Squad that evening veterans of several battles. There were those who had fought in Calabar. They spoke of the bombardment of the city by Nigerian artillery. The Nigerians had set the Bulk Oil Palm Depot on fire and the entire city had been burned, sending the civilians scuttling away. The Nigerians had lobbed shells into the local prisons and had set free the criminals as well as the political detainees. Some of the latter had retired into the forest, taken up their hidden arms and helped organize the infiltration of the Nigerian troops. One of the BEL boys spoke of the various attempts made by Nigerians to get into Calabar dressed like fishermen in small groups of ten to fifteen, using fishing vessels. But each time, the infiltrators had been discovered and arrested.

The vehicle continued to move along through the farms which had seen nothing but a blood harvest that fateful year. The relics of the gruesome war were everywhere in the dark night. There was a moon that night and a few zinc-roofed houses shone in the bushes. Most of the time, the aluminium roofing lay in masses on the ground. Small market-places had been burned down as the armies exchanged fire. History will never be able to tell how many villagers died in the process.

In those zones, new valleys had been created by shells and heavy bombs. Rugged hillocks had been levelled by the war machines that grazed the vicinity. The old roads had been covered by debris. And, as the complex equipment of modern warfare moved along the plains to consolidate new grounds, new roads had been fashioned out of farm ridges. Everything appeared to have changed. The system of nature seemed to have been reversed. With brazen insolence, animals jumped in front of the slowly rolling car. Human beings, savage from want of company, disappeared in the bushes when they saw in the distance what looked like a four-wheeled devil of destruction. No one has so far been able to advance figures of the number of villagers who took to the bushes at the approach of the Nigerian army.

True enough, the battles were over, won or lost. The front had shifted. But Nigerian war materials continued to move, compelling the frightened civilians to stay in the bush. In the night, each car looked like a ferret and each ferret car was a vehicle of destruction. Even in his wildness, in his savagery, the hungry civilian hiding in the bush dreaded the voraciousness of the British Saladin. Tudor said that, on previous occasions, he had been able to bring back to Biafra-held territory some civilians who had been hiding in the bushes, emaciated, famished, petrified. Like a child, they had to be initiated again into the mysteries of food and water, bit by bit, drop by drop. The mere odour of food had led to the death of several of them. A glass of milk, too eagerly given, had sent many a refugee to his grave too soon. Others had died of diarrhoea because of a sudden overdose of protein.

After a while, Tudor decided that the squad could proceed no further. The lorry stopped at Ndiagu near the Nnana River. It was carefully parked in a cave specially built for the purpose. It was then a no-man's land. Behind was Biafran-held territory. In front was territory occupied by the Nigerian troops. Biafrans did not have enough forces to occupy the area. The Nigerians feared to patrol that stretch of land. They never quite knew what was waiting for them in the bushes, death from a snake bite, a land-mine, a booby trap.

Time was running out fast. The BEL Squad had to leave the lorry there and venture into the unknown. They checked the petrol. It was barely enough to take them back to Biafra-held areas, but enough to destroy the vehicle if need be. Sometimes they did purchase petrol in Nigerian-held territories, but this was not always easy, since the sale of petrol in cans was strictly forbidden.

The BEL boys and Titi also had to leave their clean clothes with the car and put on the garb of miserable refugees returning to Nigerian-held territory. That naturally presented a problem they had not thought of before. It was not clear immediately what they should do with Titi. The essential thing was to pass off as local refugees under Nigerian control, once inside Enugu. They had to put on tattered clothes. The presence of a young lady in the group made it a little difficult. Someone suggested dressing her up like a boy. But the rough Nigerian soldiers when they really searched, examined every bit of the body. Discovery of Titi's impersonation would spell death for every one in the group.

Some suggested that Titi should stay with a group of five marksmen who looked after the vehicle during the trip to Enugu of the other BEL members. Titi would not be bored. The marksmen had their binoculars and rifles with telephoto lenses and, from their observation post, could pick out enemy troops one by one, when necessary. The BEL loner sometimes even operated without his gun. When a visitor looked suspicious, the BEL loner would present himself looking like a famished refugee in dire need of salvation. If the visitor had strayed from other Nigerian soldiers, the BEL loner knew how to get rid of him easily. If the loner were taken by surprise, well-trained in the techniques of judo and karate as well as in modern guerrilla warfare, he let himself be captured only to surprise his captor with a stroke of his hand or a kick of his toe. The captured weapon belonging to the imprudent Nigerian soldier became part of the growing arsenal of the BEL armoury. If there were a number of Nigerians around, the BEL loner could also easily communicate with his friends through a combination of falls and coughs to let them know when to open fire to liquidate the intruders. With larger groups of Nigerians, the marksmen simply took note of their movements and direction, waiting for a better time to engage them.

Titi was ready to stay with the marksmen in the face of the difficulties, but she did not want to stay away from Onuoha. It was not because of her love for adventure, but because of her fear that the squad might not make it back safely from Enugu. She had travelled together with Onuoha. It was because of her enthusiasm that Onuoha had decided to undertake the trip. She wanted to stay with him to the end and, if need be, also die with him. Onuoha represented the small world that had suddenly become her own.

By the same token, aware of the dangers that the marksmen incurred by staying behind, Onuoha did not want to leave Titi there alone. Titi was under his care in a way. He would like to feel that he had personally done everything possible to protect her. Though she did not mention it, Onuoha knew that Titi entertained a very faint hope that perhaps in one of the Refugee Camps in Enugu, she might run into someone she knew, a parent, a relation. It was Tudor who took the decision. Titi would accompany them to Enugu. 'Girls,' Tudor said, 'have funny ways of saving people in difficulty. Maybe it is not just coincidence that we should have with us a member of the fair sex.'

Titi shed her shoes and her long nails. She had fortunately plaited her hair before leaving Owerri. Also, because of the strain of the past few days, she had lost some weight. With a little bit of a grimace, she could pass off after a while as a haggard and weak woman. Should it become necessary, Onuoha and Titi would pretend to be husband and wife. On their feet, the BEL group had worn-out canvas shoes that had abandoned their original white colour several trenches earlier. One or two in the group carried walking-sticks. Almost all the members knew every inch of the neighbourhood. They could also speak the local dialect. They were either local boys or people who had lived in the surrounding villages before the war.

There were about twenty-five altogether. Some would stay on

in Enugu, while others already in Enugu, who had completed their tour of duty, would come back with Tudor. Those remaining in Enugu would, of course, be responsible for the purchase of merchandise to be taken away during the next BEL trip. Normally the BEL boys operated in groups of five, but the presence of Titi and Onuoha created two groups of six.

The BEL boys carried no papers, no pens and no written instructions. They carried all their instructions and plans in their heads. These instructions were often many and diverse. Local headquarters and meeting points were created in Enugu and these rotated every night. Only the date and place of the first meeting was given at first, then future dates and meeting places were set at each subsequent meeting. If for some reason the representative of a group could not make it to one of the meetings, he had instructions what to do to find out the place of the next meeting. But discipline was such that no representative had so far missed a meeting. Somewhere in the suburbs of Enugu, the BEL boys also had the BEL bank, from which they drew the Nigerian currency and coins needed for trading. After final instructions given by Tudor, the groups fanned out in the bush and each took a separate direction towards Enugu.

Titi, Onuoha and Tudor were all in the same group. As they walked along, Titi leaned on Onuoha. She felt so tired that Onuoha began to wonder if she would not fall ill along the way. They walked most of the night. As they trudged along, Tudor, who knew every inch of the neighbourhood, named the villages one by one: Umueze, Iwollo, Achala-Owa, Amankwo-Oghe, Amansiodu-Oghe.

Towards three in the morning, somewhere between Eke and Ebe, they lay down beneath a huge Iroko tree and slept. Onuoha had wanted to mount guard while the others slept, but Tudor told him that it was not necessary. No one would disturb their sleep. Generally the Nigerians never fought at night. None of them would dare come into that part of the countryside at that hour. The BEL boys roamed freely in the night and controlled the bushes around. Onuoha therefore lay down. Titi rested her head on him. Onuoha tried to sleep, but without success. For the first time since he had met Titi, he wanted to be alone with her. The fact was that he wanted to tell her something, something that she alone should hear, but Titi was already asleep.

Onuoha thought about Senegal, Abidjan, Libreville, Owerri. And he thought about Yvette Okonkwo. When Clinton Okeji had returned to Paris from Biafra he had not said much about Yvette. He was brief and terse. 'Oh! Yvette is an awfully nice girl. But do not pin your hopes on her. She is not worth the trouble.' Clinton Okeji had refused to elaborate when Onuoha pressed him for details about her. Onuoha had not seen Yvette since his arrival in Biafra. He was almost afraid to see her. Onuoha thought also of what Diogu had said about her—the wedding and the story of the young doctor who had been killed in the bombing incident.

He felt some regret when he thought about her, a deep regret that things were not different. He had looked forward with emotion and love to meeting her again, but that was now a thing of the past. On second thoughts, Onuoha tried to understand. The circumstances were difficult. The times were trying on loyalties and emotions. When there is war and insecurity reigns, the tendency in young women, the ordinary ones amongst them, is to grab what they have at hand. Only the few heroic ones would brave the advance of the invading troops, endure the evacuation of their homes, and defy the daily aerial bombardment that killed friends around them, to wait for the love abroad and far away, the love whose intentions they did not quite know and from whom they had not heard for months, because of the war and the blockade. Yvette Okonkwo might be a very nice girl, but she was definitely not one of the heroic ones. It was only then that Onuoha realized the full meaning of what Clinton Okeji had said. 'Do not pin your hopes on Yvette.' He remembered later that Clinton also added: 'Yvette is the type of girl you would fall in love with at first sight. She must be an entirely new girl for me to love her.'

When his reverie had reached that stage, Onuoha could not tell whether he was awake or dreaming His meditations merged with the hazy dreams about realities that were or that could be. Titi looked beautiful in her sleep, in spite of her transformation. Onuoha was dreaming about slowly moving his lips to kiss Titi

when the latter almost shouted and woke up with a start. Onuoha
recoiled.

In actual fact, it was nothing of the sort. It was Tudor waking
up Onuoha and Titi and telling them that it was nearly five in the
morning and that they had to continue their journey and make
their entry into Enugu. Though not a soldier, Onuoha realized
that he had to obey. He was only then beginning to enjoy his
sleep, a peaceful sleep. He wished Tudor had just allowed him to
complete the little dream that seemed so pleasant. They ate their
last ration of food and moved into the city empty-handed. They
crossed the Enugu-Nsukka road near Ikenga and descended slowly
towards the former capital of Biafra.

Even in the midst of war, though ravaged by destruction, Enugu
had not completely lost its beauty. The grass grew with greater
abandon, as if nothing had happened or was happening. The
undulating valleys and interlocking chains of hills continued their
graceful daily rise and fall with the sun. From the top of the hill,
one could look upon what used to be the splendour of the city,
partly lost in the morning fog, a war fog. They moved along the
bush tracks that linked the outlying villages with the main city.
The brooks were still running, perhaps a little bit cleaner and
faster than they used to, because there were fewer people now to
soil their sparkle, and block their flow with daily garbage from
the city.

There was a time when Enugu had a population of more than
two hundred thousand. That was just before the war. After the
civil servants that used to live in Lagos had descended on the
regional capital, Enugu became the city of traffic jams. The Enugu
Presidential Hotel accomplished alone the functions of the Lagos
Federal Palace Hotel, Ikoyi Club and Kakadu. Soldiers and civilians, intellectuals and workers, drank and discussed in its bars
and along its corridors. The famous bands had also descended
from Lagos to take refuge in Enugu: the Fractions, the Hikers,
Erasmus Januari, Pal Akalonu. The times had now changed.
Enugu was left with a paltry population of about five thousand
people, including the soldiers garrisoned there. Several thousand

soldiers had also passed through the streets of Enugu, the Biafran soldiers who had failed to defend it, the Nigerian Second Brigade on their way to the slaughter house of Abagana. Enugu had seen thousands of Nigerian soldiers pass. Thousands of them had never come back. A few, a lucky few had been carried back to Lagos— maimed, wounded, more dead than alive.

Such was the fate of the Second Division of the Nigerian Army, formerly the crack battalion of the Queen's Own Nigerian Regiment. They had met part of their Waterloo at Ugwuoba, south of Enugu. More than seven thousand of them had been annihilated by a powerful remote-control weapon developed by the Biafran Science Group. The mass killer was called 'Ogbunigwe'. The Ogbunigwe pulverizes everything within its range, whether tender flesh or reinforced steel. The success of the experiment had changed the entire course of the war and the Ogbunigwe became an impenetrable defence against the invaders. Clinton Okeji used to refer to it as 'the black devil that spurts out red flames'. He might as well have simply called it 'the red devil.'

On the hills of Ugwuoba, when the red devil had spoken like thunder and lightning combined, several of the Nigerian soldiers had still been in their defensive positions, guns in hand, helmets in place, fore-fingers on the trigger, satchel bags swung over the shoulders and eyes still gazing wildly in front. But the figure in front was nothing but a pulverized statue that collapsed with a merciless rustle of the tropical wind. Unfortunately, Titi and Onuoha could not go to Ugwuoba because it had been retaken by the Nigerians. But Tudor told them that there they could still see the remaining carcasses of the Nigerian war machine. After the battle of Ugwuoba, civilians had been paid five shillings for each enemy corpse they buried. The government had miscalculated. When Biafran officials saw the number of the dead involved, they cut down the burial fee to two shillings and authorized the digging of common graves for the crack battalion of the Queen's Own Nigerian Regiment. Even then it took several civilians working day and night to complete the burial job, while Biafran troops pushed on ahead to consolidate their positions.

Tudor led his group towards Enugu-Ngwo. He pointed out

not too far away the Nine Mile Corner, the famous road junction that controls the narrow entry into Enugu. British experts had predicted that the greatest battle of the war would be fought there before the collapse of the Biafran regime. After the fall of Nsukka and the Opi Road junction, the Nigerians had been in no haste to press on for the attack on Enugu. They feared that resistance would be insurmountable around the Nine Mile Corner. Instead, they concentrated on building up and consolidating their rear. Tudor confirmed that they could have taken Enugu the same day that they took Opi. They could have taken Enugu that night with all its population. The army had been totally disorganized. The people had not known enough at the time about the danger ahead and had not attempted to evacuate the city.

When the Nigerians had finally advanced, the expected great battle at the Nine Mile Corner never did take place. Suspicion and fear crept into the ranks of the Biafran army. Everywhere there was talk and rumours of sabotage within the army. Tudor had then been on the Onitsha front, defending the bridge-head and the riverside city. Enugu had been evacuated quietly but very little property had been taken out. The Nigerian soldiers had taken the Nine Mile Corner without a fight to their incredible surprise and stupefaction. Afraid of a ruse and an ambush, they had not moved into the city until some thirty-six hours later.

Enugu had been empty when the Nigerians arrived. In their communiqué, the crack division of the Nigerian army boasted that when their troops showed up before the Biafran rebel capital of Enugu, 'the city defences collapsed like a castle of cards.' In spite of the boast, they could not understand why a leader should abandon his political capital and army headquarters without a fight. With sorrow, Tudor remarked that a suicide squad of about five hundred commandos could have successfully defended the Nine Mile Corner and destroyed the Nigerian brigade attack on the city. 'We abandoned the city without a fight,' Tudor lamented. 'Since then we have lost more than five thousand people trying in vain to recapture it from the entrenched Nigerians.'

Tudor and his group were approaching the Miliking Hill. The hill had always inspired Onuoha with awe. It was not an ordinary hill, but a steep cliff that rose sharply, high into the tropical sky on the right as one entered Enugu. It was also at the same time a deep valley, a steep precipice that descended equally suddenly about half a mile deep. Within the gorges of the valley flowed a slow rivulet. A small road barely six metres wide separated the bottom of the hill and the top of the valley and provided the precarious entrance into the city of Enugu. The road itself meandered perilously like an ever-coiling, three-mile-long snake, with gaping ridges and sticky edges. In peace time, bold signs used to warn motorists who dared it into Enugu at sports-car speed, 'Better late than the late'. The sign was perhaps superfluous. Even the most intrepid motorist could not help being overpowered by the splendour and treachery of the natural combination of a rising hill and a sinking valley drawn together in a vertiginous pull by a narrow mountain pass. The Denver Pass in Colorado, even if it surpasses it in height, cannot be compared to the treacherous splendour of the Miliking Hill. Before colonial times, few if any ever returned safely from the Miliking Hill, a type of Oracle.

Tudor, Onuoha and Titi walked together and talked as they descended towards one of the villages of Enugu. One of the boys in Tudor's group was a few steps in front, the other two were a few yards behind. Once in the village, Tudor, Onuoha and Titi sat down beneath a coconut tree. The others continued walking up and down. Within minutes three people came out from nearby mud houses. They were dressed in tattered clothing. They wore beards and were walking barefoot. They performed a few movements quite innocently, but these movements were apparently signs. Two of them joined the groups walking up and down. One of them moved towards Tudor and recoiled when he saw three people sitting down there. Tudor made some signs on the ground. The visitor winked and made another sign. 'Okay,' Tudor told him. 'They are friends.' They erased the signs on the ground and they all moved towards a hut not far away. Once they were inside, the doors were closed. The others continued their innocuous parade outside, watching and greeting the village men and women going to the Central Market in the City.

Their host was Captain Ofor, the leader of the BEL company

in Enugu. He had been waiting for Tudor for the past two days and had been getting worried. Tudor replied that certain repairs had had to be done on the car in Umuahia before their departure. Captain Ofor was anxious to find out about the situation at the home front. 'All is well,' Tudor assured him. Captain Ofor in turn told Tudor that his men in Enugu were safe and doing well. They had done a good job and some of them had asked to stay longer. Tudor told him that he had brought replacements along who should also be given a fair chance to contribute directly to the war effort. 'If your boys have done a good job,' Tudor added, 'then they deserve a good rest.'

Ofor also told Tudor that his load was ready and that he could leave that night if he wanted. Ofor wanted to stay a little longer in Enugu. There was something bloody in human nature. He seemed to derive immense fun from his forbidden adventure behind the enemy lines. It is normally so in life. There might be dangers ahead, the risks involved might be great and small mistakes fatal, but each new success whets the appetite of the adventurer, be he a lone sailor, a racing driver, a matador, a BEL boy.

After he had given them a brief review of the highlights of his three-week stay in Enugu, Ofor invited the group to the village market that morning. After a warm meal they set out towards the new market where the refugees did their buying and selling. There were lots of soldiers in the market. Most of them, Ofor said, were there to look for Igbo girls and women. Some young Igbo girls from conquered zones had been kidnapped and brought to the city. A few fortune-seekers who had stayed on in Lagos after Biafra had declared her independence were also around. That day there were not many around 'for the comfort of the Nigerians', to use a Nigerian expression. Unfortunately for the Nigerian soldiers, that type of comfort often proved a bane for them.

Ofor said that there was no telling the number of times a co-operating Igbo girl had given a double rendezvous to two competing Nigerian lovers, only to have them ambushed and killed about fifty feet from each other. In the Nigerian camp, the commanding officer was usually reported as saying: 'There goes another pair of brilliant officers, who have killed themselves off in a chivalrous duel.'

It was a busy day at the market. As they stepped into the market-place, rumours flooded the area about some moves planned by the Nigerians. Lots of Nigerian soldiers were reportedly being moved up towards the Onitsha front. Tudor and Onuoha made a few ordinary purchases—kola nuts from the north and alligator pepper from Western Nigeria. They talked to one or two of the refugees in the market. Tudor saw some of the boys who had fought under him in the Onitsha front. They smiled back knowingly. One of them even made the mistake of forgetting where he was and saluted Tudor. The latter turned his face away. A Nigerian second-lieutenant standing nearby accepted the salute, however, and tossed a shilling to the refugee in appreciation of his friendliness.

One of the refugees Tudor and Ofor spoke to was Mr Oti, a teacher the Nigerians captured when they first landed in Onitsha. He was a respectable man. It appeared that he refused to leave his home because of family problems. The other members of the family fled when the Nigerians were approaching. He had however anticipated the event and had stocked up enough food and drink in the ceiling of his room. He climbed into the ceiling and waited. He saw every villager leave the city as news spread around that the Nigerians had entered the city. He watched them leave the town as shells fell on the thatched roofs around and set them ablaze. Suddenly, he was afraid and wanted to run; but it was too late. He lay down where he was. Soon the firing died down and all was quiet.

Oti heard rustles, the following morning, inside a cluster of banana stems behind his house. At first, he thought it was a wise villager who had come back secretly to the village just outside Onitsha to loot his property. Oti crept out to see who was the intruder standing there and munching his ripe bananas. It was a Nigerian soldier dressed in battle attire.

When the Nigerian soldier, for his part taken unawares, saw someone coming, he started apologizing. The soldier had apparently been hiding there during the night to avoid pushing ahead with the forward lines. The soldier pleaded that he was not run-ning away, that he was not a coward, that he had just stopped to pick a few bananas for the other soldiers. He thought his visitor was a Nigerian Army Officer. Mr Oti for his part was profuse in his apologies. He did not mean to disturb a Federal Government soldier exercising his legal duty. Oti even pointed out that he had some more bananas inside his house and a bottle of wine also. When the Nigerian soldier saw that his visitor was a shivering villager, he regained his courage and arrested Mr Oti. The latter raised up his hands and the Nigerian commando marched him to his commanding officer. He explained that he had captured the villager. After interrogating him, Oti was taken to Enugu and used as an interpreter for the villagers, and for the Igbo broadcasts from the Nigerian radio station in Enugu.

Since his arrival in Enugu, Mr Oti had earned some respectability both with the Nigerian soldiers and the local refugees. He had become a sort of middle-man between the government and the refugees. He became an example of one of those Igbo leaders who refused to collaborate with the secessionists and had crossed freely over to the Federal-controlled territories. But Oti had changed his mind since his capture by the Nigerians. Oti thought for a while and said: 'I would love to go back. But if I do escape, several of these refugees you see here will suffer and will pay perhaps with their skin. You must remember that though under the control of our enemies, these refugees are still our brothers and sisters. We should not increase their misery.'

Mr Oti begged Tudor instead to carry a message, a letter back to his sons and daughters in Biafra. He took out his pen but suddenly changed his mind, frightened by the thought that the letter could be captured. 'Tell them instead that you saw me. I believe they are in a refugee camp in Ekwulobia. Tell them I miss them. And if you do come back here, bring from them an embrace, a word of forgiveness, a word of love.' The old man put his sun glasses over his eyes. He informed them that he would be going over to the neighbouring villages to inform the Igbos living there that they should assemble immediately at the market place to receive foreign visitors. Mr Oti strode to a vehicle waiting to take him to the villages.

. . . .

After they had been there for about half an hour, a bell was rung in the market square. A crier was telling the villagers around that the Red Cross team would be distributing 'welfare' in the market. 'There goes another propaganda stunt,' Ofor said. 'They always do this when there are visiting journalists around. It is mostly for overseas publicity and consumption.' Rightly enough, within half an hour, a long queue had formed before the Red Cross Office located in one corner of the market. More than twenty-five visiting journalists had arrived. What Ofor did not know was that there was also in Enugu that day a team of International Observers, who had come from Lagos to satisfy themselves that there was no genocide in Biafra.

Caught in this situation, Tudor and his group had no alternative but to join the queue and also get some 'relief'. As the line progressed, there were Nigerian soldiers around dusting some refugees and powdering others, making them more acceptable to the camera lens fixed in front of them, making sure that the refugees looked a little happier and cleaner before the international audience they were about to face. As she passed, Titi was singled out and given a pair of sandals and a scarf. She was ushered into a room nearby and given a mirror to dust off and powder her face. Before Onuoha realized it, he was sporting a hat and a walking-stick and a raincoat to cover his dirty clothes. Tudor and Ofor got less majestic treatment.

Titi, as a matter of fact, recovered her lustre to such an extent that the Commonwealth Member of the International Observation Team, Admiral Timothy, gave her a gentle kiss as she passed along to the Red Cross stand. Admiral Timothy's courtesy earned Titi a double ration of milk, cheese and stock-fish. The Nigerian officers around eyed her lustfully. The eminent generals around cast their own share of adulterous glances. They whispered a few words amongst themselves, as if deciding who should take care of and adopt the young refugee beauty.

A British television team came round to interview Onuoha and Titi, who sounded more articulate than the others. They asked them to express their views very frankly for a British audience that supported Nigeria, to say what they thought about the treatment being given to them by the Nigerian soldiers. Admiral Timothy was there—tall and smiling mischievously as if to warn Titi and Onuoha to be careful about what they said. The Nigerian officials also stood around, ears sticking out, but pretending not to be listening to what was going on.

Onuoha told them in broken English that they were all happy and that, if given the opportunity, they would like to get their parents on the Biafran side over to Enugu with the Nigerian soldiers. Not to give the impression that they were being insincere, a bit smart, Titi pretended that she did not want the Nigerian officers to overhear her, and said that the soldiers did not always treat them well, the girls in particular. She said that they felt much happier with foreign journalists and members of the International Red Cross around. This balanced judgment seemed to please the Nigerian officers around, for it gave the interview a dimension of spontaneity and thus made it more plausible for the outside world.

Titi was chosen to read out, as the 'Secretary-General of the Igbo Women's Association of Enugu', a statement of thanks to the International Red Cross, the Nigerian government, which was giving them and their children protection, and particularly to the British government, which had provided 250,000 pounds worth of food through OXFAM. The Igbo women reaffirmed their belief in the principle of the territorial integrity of Nigeria and their acceptance of the twelve state formula as the best way of preserving the freedom of all the peoples of Nigeria. They finally dissociated themselves from the mad ambitions of the ruling clique in the so-called Biafra and reaffirmed their absolute confidence in the good judgment and honesty of the Head of the National Liberation Council and the Supreme Commander of the Nigerian forces. The resolutions were handed to the Commonwealth Admiral Timothy on behalf of the Igbo Women's Association of Enugu by Titi.

In his reply to the resolutions, Admiral Timothy said a few things about the desire of the British government to maintain the territorial integrity of Nigeria and the fact that Great Britain, faithful to her commitment to defend freedom everywhere, was giving Nigeria most of the arms to make victory possible. The

Admiral pledged that back in London he would recommend to the Commonwealth governments—and he had every reason to believe that they would listen to him, since he had been a veteran of several hot seats—that they should join Britain in pouring in more equipment to help liberate areas still under Biafran control. The Nigerian soldiers roared in applause. The refugees who were waiting for the translation also roared in applause at the same time as the Nigerians.

There were also demonstrations of Igbo dancing—the war dance, the Atilogwu and the Amakefu. The dances were performed by Igbos supposedly living in Enugu, but Ofor thought that the dancers came from Lagos. The music was, however, accurate. Television cameras flashed and recorded the scene; they would transmit the pictures through the Comsat to all the capitals of the western world. The dances made a great impression on the International Observers. Admiral Timothy said that as a navy man, he knew that people could be forced to read out messages of support for a government they did not like. 'But it is not easy,' he said to his colleagues, 'to get people, even island savages in the hey-days of colonialism, to line up and appear cheerful before cameras. Also the zest, art, dynamism and vivaciousness I saw in the women dancers and the men performers can only come from hearts, souls and muscles that are spontaneously convinced about the righteous-ness of the Nigerian cause. Gentlemen, you will agree with me, therefore, especially those of you who are still hesitating, that we should adopt my report that there is absolutely no evidence of genocide in the Nigerian war.'

Admiral Timothy concluded by saying that he had seen enough. He would ask the Commonwealth Secretariat to withdraw him at the end of the month from the International Observer Group. He had not seen any sign of massacres of Igbos by the Nigerian soldiers. From his observations at the front, he was convinced that the policy of the 'quick kill' was the best way of bringing to an end the rebellion and the secession. On a more humorous note, Admiral Timothy added that only in Igbo land could one find a beauty like Titi in a refugee camp. The Admiral edged his way quietly towards Titi and and in a whisper volunteered to take her back to Lagos and lodge her at the Federal Palace Hotel and, if it could be arranged, put her in school in London. Titi merely told him that she would think about it.

As the show came towards its end, almost all the Nigerian officers wanted to take Titi to their residence. Some were timid. Others were bold. Onuoha and Tudor and Ofor watched with interest and deep apprehension as the Nigerian officers moved forward when their colleagues were not looking and introduced themselves as Captain Abiola, Colonel Ademola, Lieutenant Shuwa, Major Waziri . . . and offered to take Titi to dinner that night and to the night-club later. To all of them, Titi gave a single answer: 'Sorry, Officer, I have a date already with Admiral Timothy.' Each one of them recoiled when he heard of the Admiral's interest, afraid to create an international incident that might have repercussions on their arms supplies.

Several of the British journalists around were also anxious to invite Titi out, to take her to dinner, to interview her at their homes more extensively for this and that women's magazine, for British television. Some even promised her front-page coverage in the leading magazines. Titi looked like a beauty queen in the setting sun as the journalists and photographers stood up, bent down, drew forwards, climbed the tables around, withdrew backwards, to snatch pictures of her, her legs, breast, profile, arms, hips—alternating their normal lens with filters, wide-angle and telephoto lenses.

Titi was sedate, smiling, composed and luscious. Onuoha was half-amused, half-irate. Titi moved towards Admiral Timothy and the journalists and Nigerian officers started to leave. Titi stood there talking to him for a while. The other eminent general respectfully drove off in their common car. There was another car waiting for Admiral Timothy. He got inside the car and opened the door discreetly for Titi to enter. Onuoha and the rest stood watching with anxiety. Titi put her head inside the car and told the Admiral that she could not make it that night. Admiral Timothy behaved like a typical British-trained gentleman. 'Tomorrow, then. Tomorrow morning at six o'clock. In front of the Presidential Hotel. I shall be there waiting for you.' Titi said that

that would be wonderful, as Admiral Timothy gave her a double kiss and waved as his car pulled out. Titi later said that the Admiral had told her she looked like a young girl he used to know in the Gold Coast a few years back.

They walked back towards the village. For Onuoha the evening revealed another aspect of Titi's character, the luscious young lady who draws the eyes of every normal man who passes. Onuoha saw her for the first time in that light. As they strode back home later that evening, Onuoha moved to congratulate her for her performance that day with a kiss. For a brief second as he held Titi's hands and drew her close to himself, he forgot where he was. Not in the streets of Paris, Dakar or Libreville, but in war-torn Enugu. Their lips never met, for an imperious voice ordered: 'Hurry back to your homes!'

It was a Nigerian soldier on patrol. Onuoha recoiled and there was silence. The soldier approached nearer. Titi smiled and invited the soldier, 'Officer, come give me a kiss!' The Nigerian soldier looked backwards and saw that the other soldier patrolling the zone with him had turned his back towards him. He accepted Titi's invitation. Darkness was descending on the valleys of Enugu after engulfing the hills. The Nigerian soldier put his gun on the ground and opened his arms to embrace Titi. Titi let herself go completely and the intoxicated soldier lost control of himself, unzipped his pants and raised Titi's wrapper with shaking fingers.

Titi connivingly put her hands around his neck and stroked his back. A few seconds later, the soldier was a dead man, strangled by the tough arms of the two companions of Tudor. They pushed him under a bush. Another member of the Tudor group picked up the soldier's rifle and started patrolling in place of the dead man. The other Nigerian soldier had turned by this time. He was approaching and walking towards them. He too walked into a kiss of death. Titi smiled and said: 'There goes another pair of brilliant officers who killed themselves off in a chivalrous duel.' Ofor shook his head and said: 'You catch on fast. I think we need more women like you behind enemy lines.'

To remove any trace of suspicion, one of the Tudor boys zipped up the pants of the first soldier and two bullets were pumped into their dead bodies and their guns were put near their hands, lying a few inches away from them. Tudor's boys searched them for documents. Onuoha and Titi were going to start running when the shots were fired. Ofor told them not to move, adding that when shots like that went off in the dark night, the Nigerian soldiers in the camps dared not move out. Those still patrolling the neighbourhood or on their way home in the evening had instructions to shoot anything running. The safest thing was therefore to walk as if nothing had happened. For someone going through the experience for the first time, it was difficult to feel that nothing had happened.

'It will be morning before their bodies are discovered,' Ofor said. 'They dare not come out at night to look for them. They are human beings and they are more afraid to die than we are. We are fighting to defend ourselves. They do not know why they are here or what they are fighting for. During the day, we oil their guns and walk amongst them. At night we control the city and choose where and when to strike. During the day, we cook for them and buy their food. At night we lay mines on their paths and strangle them during their patrols. We rarely operate with arms except when we move in for a suicide operation.'

Ofor mentioned as they walked home that a few days earlier, when rumours started circulating that the Nigerians were about to move large amounts of equipment and men towards the Onitsha front for a major operation, he and his men had attacked the Enugu armoury. It had been set ablaze. Their attack had delayed at least for one week the mounting of the attack on Onitsha. Ofor thought the Nigerians were thinking of attacking Agulu and Adazi. The Nigerian Brigade in Enugu would have to wait for new equipment to arrive from Lagos and by rail through Northern Nigeria. If his men were in the mood, and if the new equipment arrived at night, Ofor planned to attack the railway depot with rocket launchers and machine-guns from the top of the hill. In that case, the Nigerians would open up with their heavy artillery and fire thinking that there was a Biafran Brigade invasion of Enugu. The Nigerian artillery would pound all night in the direction of the shelling. But, as Ofor put it, 'We shoot and leave the position immediately. Within minutes, as the armoury or the depot blazes, as the office buildings flame, we are back in our homes through our underground tunnel, home drinking merrily some beer and coffee, courtesy of the International Red Cross.'

On arrival at Ofor's headquarters, they had some coffee and beer to drink. Tudor mentioned that he was afraid he would not have enough petrol to take him back to Biafran-held territory. Ofor called two of his men and asked them to go and get some petrol from a nearby station. Other groups arrived for the meeting. Some of them had been at the market that morning. They had all accomplished their specific missions and assignments. Tudor decided to leave Enugu that night and go back and warn the army about the threatened invasion of Agulu and Adazi by way of Awka. Tudor was also thinking of having some radio communications equipment installed in the tunnel so that Ofor could contact Biafra army headquarters when issues of great military importance came up again. Tudor promised to make a strong recommendation to the headquarters in Umuahia to that effect.

About half of Ofor's men would go back with Tudor while twelve of those who had travelled out with him would remain in Enugu. They compared memory notes and certain important decisions were taken about targets to be attacked. Meanwhile the two people who had gone out to get petrol had arrived back. They had on their heads two earthenware pots, as if they had come back from a village stream. They had actually fetched the petrol from a local petrol station where one of them worked during the day. For a siphon, they had used reeds from a nearby river. The petrol was immediately transferred to kerosene tins hidden in a compartment of the mud house.

Tudor asked Ofor if the escape tunnel was clear. Ofor went outside and came back after a while and reported, 'Sound and safe!' Then Ofor led them to a patch of carefully protected undergrowth. He left two of his men behind. They stopped when he signalled. Ofor moved forward with his torch and made some signals into the dark tunnel. A small greenish light flashed inconspicuously in return. Ofor then said that all was safe and they moved into the tunnel.

The main tunnel was nearly half a mile long. But it appeared that there were other routes branching off from the main axis in other directions. There was no need to stoop, for it was high enough to allow an average man to enter with a kerosene tin on his head. Ofor's torch went on and off as they moved along. Titi stopped at one corner and changed her red OXFAM trappings for her real refugee clothing. Ofor motioned to them to stop. They did so as a figure emerged from a small cubicle in the tunnel. Ofor made a few signs with his flash and the figure disappeared again. The man was one of Ofor's aides who guarded the tunnel.

The tunnel led them underneath a small brook at the bottom of Eva Valley and they emerged into the open at an obscure point on the other side of the bank. The other groups were there already. Each group carried their own luggage and now went by different routes to meet again at the diesel lorry several miles away. Before Ofor bade farewell to Tudor and the rest, he put his hand in his pocket and gave Tudor an envelope. 'Here you are, in case the private lives of your victims interest you. It is a letter the boys discovered in the pocket of the second Nigerian soldier bumped off this evening.' With that Captain Ofor shook the hands of everyone and disappeared again into the tunnel.

Tudor brought out the letter from the envelope. He spread it out. Onuoha and Titi came around and read it with the help of a flash:

My loving Tunde,

I miss you. I hope you are still alive. I hope this letter gets to you. Please drop me a line to assure me that you are still alive. Oh when, when will this war come to an end, this war that separates families and friends.

My dear brother, I have often told you about Titi, that college friend of mine. You have not met her, but I have told you often how dear she is to me. Now we are barely on speaking terms because of the war. Now, I have just learned that she has gone home to Biafra. I cannot bear to feel that something bad might happen to her. When I told her about the death of Akin in Abagana, somehow she held me personally responsible for anything that happened to her home and to her refugee parents. I have tried to convince her that there is nothing personal in war, that it is not the Yorubas as a whole who are fighting against them. She would not understand.

Oh Tunde, I should be asking you about your health, your plans instead of talking about Titi, whom you might never meet. Oh Tunde, I give you my love. You are all I have left now. I kiss you a thousand times. Every day, I pray and cry that this war will come to an end and that you will come back safely to your darling sister,

Lola

Titi sobbed uncontrollably as she read the letter. Onuoha understood her sorrow, but Tudor did not quite know what was happening. Titi sobbed and sobbed as they walked back away from Enugu. The letter had been mailed in Dakar, the very day that Titi had left the city. It was signed by Lola Ajayi.

Some were carrying sacks of rice and beans, agbonu and crayfish. Others were carrying cartons of soap, batteries and matches as well as other articles which were badly needed in Biafra at that particular time. The return journey from Enugu was almost a repeat of their entry except that they followed, separately as usual, other tracks. Titi herself was carrying a bag of crayfish, which she balanced comfortably on her head. Their walk was as brisk as the road they carried would allow. Everyone had something to carry. It was not easy ascending the hill with the luggage and they had to stop several times. Fortunately for them, they walked along the valley most of the time as they edged their way back to Biafra. They rarely exchanged words, not out of fear, but because of the heavy loads on their heads. Talking does demand a great amount of supplementary energy at moments like that.

As they ascended the hill to come up to the road, Tudor suggested that they stop. They lowered their loads, each one helping the other. Tudor indicated that all was not right there. He raised his hand mechanically in the air and moved it round and round before finally pointing towards the east. He lowered it again and tried the same movements moving around like someone drunk and a little bit unsteady on his feet. His hand pointed again immobile in an easterly direction. Tudor had a highly developed sixth sense and could find hidden things in the bush no matter how thick the undergrowth or how inaccessible the location of the lost object. Locally, he was often referred to as the 'hound of hounds', and not in a derogatory sense, either. There were lots of others like him in the Biafran army. A 'hound' always accompanied any BEL expedition. On several occasions, the 'hound' had been able to warn his companions in advance about impending danger with a very high degree of accuracy. The 'Hound Associates' had given a smattering of their cult to every member of the Biafra Organization of Freedom Fighters, a guerrilla brigade that lived in the area where the Nigerian front-line troops were now operating.

When Tudor therefore stopped, there was no telling what it was. He asked everyone to lie low. He moved forward alone. One of his aides asked to accompany him. Tudor said that it was not necessary, declaring that his premonitions indicated that there was nothing really dangerous. He just felt that there was someone around not far from where they were, someone not belonging to their squad. Tudor took a few steps eastwards in the darkness. His friends heard a slight rustle of the wind and the sound of an owl. There was a response which came from Tudor. There was another squeak and another response from Tudor. Tudor squeaked again and within a minute there were two men standing with him. Soon the three of them rejoined Onuoha and the rest.

The two comrades who had joined them were part of the group that had travelled under Tudor's command the night before and who had stayed on in Enugu. They were already at work laying mines in a desperate effort to ruin the Nigerian brigade if it ever tried to get out of Enugu. They had almost completed their work but were running short of explosives. Tudor gave them some of the explosives his boys were carrying. Jokingly, Tudor remarked that they were faster than he was in giving the bird call. They said that they had also perceived the presence of people in the neighbourhood and wanted to give them a call in case they were comrades. There was an exchange of farewells as they left to continue their work. The following morning, they would report to Captain Ofor who would give them a brief note to take to the Biafra Underground Bank in Enugu. At the bank, they would be given some Nigerian money to start their lives as loyal traders in the local market in Enugu tunil their tour of duty expired and they were called away to serve their nation on another front.

The Tudor group picked up their luggage again and set off on the long trek homewards. The moon was up and gave them its welcome light part of the way, until it disappeared into the threatening clouds. As they walked home, Onuoha could not help thinking what would happen the following day, or the day after or even in a week's time, when the Nigerian military convoy rolled down the Miliking Hill. The Nigerian foot soldiers would move towards the Onitsha front singing with confidence: 'OSHEBE! OWE! OSHEBE! OWE!' They always resounded their pledge to keep Nigeria one. Sometimes they marched along singing the Nigerian National Anthem.

Nigeria, we hail thee our own dear native land
Though tribes and tongues may differ in brotherhood we stand.
Nigerians all are proud to serve our sovereign motherland.
Our flag shall be a symbol that truth and justice reign,
In peace or battle honoured and this we count as gain,
To hand unto our children a banner without stain.
O God of all creation, grant this our one request,
Help us to build a nation where no man is oppressed.
And so with peace and plenty, Nigeria may be blest.

For the past few years, there had been neither peace nor plenty and the people appeared to have decided to build a country where every writer, artist or intellectual of any importance was put in prison. God seemed to have refused all the requests and prayers intoned in supplication by the faithful and infidel alike, by Christians, Pagans and Moslems. For years, the national flag had been hanging at half mast, stained with the blood of heads of government, supreme commanders, premiers, army officers and thousands of civilians. The army defenders of justice and the security of the nation seemed to have sown the seeds of butchery and turned the entire nation into a human abattoir. The country appeared to have easily lost its sovereignty again to a new form of colonialism. Young men were being forced into the army and at the battle front old men and women were being used as human fodder. The nation separated into tribal cliques, new brotherhoods were being formed to divide and slaughter. It was difficult to see in such a land a fatherland. It was more of a murderland.

Lost in thought, Onuoha continued the trek with the others, forgetting somehow where he was and what he was doing. After a long distance, they stopped again to rest and relax a bit in the cold morning. It was dewy all over the farms they crossed. For some time, they had expected it to rain at any moment. As they were resting, one of the other groups caught up with them. The leader was Lieutenant Ihenacho.

Lieutenant Ihenacho told them some of their exploits the previous day. Some of his boys had gone with him to the Enugu Regional House of Parliament as vendors of groundnuts. Under the pretext of going to the toilet, they had entered the building and put explosives in various parts of the ground floor. They left the building and from a nearby store, some fifteen minutes later, they watched the offices explode and the papers and files inside go up in flames. The men in the building all rushed out. Very few of them ever again delayed on the upper floors, for fear of air-raids and bombings.

One of Ihenacho's companions remarked that in civilian times cabinet ministers in Lagos and Enugu used to haggle over who should occupy the highest floor in a government building. The times had changed and officers and civilians were struggling now as to who should have his desk on the ground floor. At the Provincial Library in Umuahia, the fear of bombing was such that there were more than twenty senior officers and thirty assistants and secretaries crowded in the undivided ground floor lounge of the building, although there were enough rooms on the floors up above to house three times that number of officers and assistants.

Others in Ihenacho's group had collected useful information about the movement of Nigerian troops in the Nsukka area and the general condition of the refugees there. One of the groups staying in the upper Enugu area had organized a suicidal attack on the enemy positions in Nsukka. They had caused real terror on the campus of the former University of Biafra. OXFAM and Red Cross officials had to evacuate their personnel from the area and withdraw to the Northern Nigerian borders. The Nigerians thought that it was a brigade attack on their position. Even their ammunition dumps had been destroyed: charges had earlier been laid by the refugee workers at the University campus and at night a concerted attack from ten different points had set the entire area ablaze at the same time as the campus had been subjected to a barrage of rocket and bazooka fire. Fleeing Nigerian soldiers had been cut down. One of the boys said that the great Major Nzeogwu reportedly used to employ techniques like that to destroy enemy formations at the very beginning of the Biafran war.

When they had rested for long enough, they trudged on towards their lorry. The rest of the journey was made in the dewy morning. Titi and Onuoha could hardly believe that they had just been behind enemy lines. After the experience at Enugu, Onuoha had now lost part of his fear of the war front and the war zone. Already there was an urge in him to return some other day, or better still go to other areas behind the Nigerian lines in Yenogoa, Opobo, Calabar, Ogoja, Kwale or perhaps even go deep inside actual Nigerian territory. The difficulty seemed to lie in crossing the border. But once behind the enemy lines, one's identity became lost in the land of refugees.

When they got there, the other groups were already waiting beside the lorry. It took them a little over an hour to load their cargo. At the very first light of the morning, they made their way back to Biafran land, to begin another kind of life in front of enemy lines.

9

Our Lady of Mount Carmel

Some days later, Titi and Onuoha were on their way to attend a meeting of the Provincial Refugee Committee which was to take place at Umuoma, about ten miles from the centre of Owerri and slightly off the Owerri-Port-Harcourt road. Since the fall of Port-Harcourt, the 'Garden City', the refugee situation in the country had been deteriorating. Titi and Onuoha stopped at Owerri that morning. The streets were crowded like New York, Fifth Avenue on a busy Saturday morning. All the banks, or most of the banks in Port-Harcourt, as well as other establishments, had been moved over to Owerri. Young boys and girls paraded the streets looking for a place to rest their heads. There were no more rooms available. Hundreds of families were sleeping on the floors of school buildings. Prices also had rocketed very high. Before the war, a cup of salt used to cost three pennies. Now it was being sold for thirty shillings. The same proportional increase was common with other commodities if they could be found. A chicken in the villages used to cost three to five shillings. A good ten pounds could not buy a small sized chicken now.

In front of banks, customers lined up at doors that never seemed to open. Every now and then a sullen young teenage girl would walk up to Onuoha to ask if he by any chance knew the whereabouts of her parents and her younger brother. She had not seen them since the fall of Port-Harcourt. A father walked up to Titi in desperation and asked if she had seen a tall fair-complexioned woman with a four-year-old son looking for Obi Dike. 'I am Obi Dike', he emphasized. The encounters were heart-rending

Grown-up men and women walked the streets carrying small plates on their way to a food distribution centre. In normal times, they had lived happily in houses of their own. A few of the refugees were trying to busy themselves doing something so as to avoid death from sheer boredom. They were cutting the lawns in front of St Paul's School Owerri and the Immaculate Conception Girls' School not far from the Owerri-Aba road junction. The statue of the Virgin Mary looked as serene on the girls' school campus as it had back in 1954 when the structure had been built to celebrate the Marian year.

A few stores were making desperate efforts to remain open. Behind the counters stood neatly dressed young ladies. But their counters were a mockery to the retail trade—empty, dry except for a few old items which no one wanted to buy and which perhaps had not been in demand since colonial times. A few empty Star Lager beer bottles indicated what a bar used to sell in normal times. The chemist shops presented the same visage. Quite a few were open, but they did not seem to have anything in stock. The few bottles on exhibition were old, so old the contents would make a healthy man sick. They contained cures for diseases which no one suffered from then ... dissolving pills and mouldy mixtures for weight-reducing.

Thousands of people were aimlessly walking up and down the streets. Some who still had their cars had run out of petrol and could proceed no further. They walked from garage to garage looking for black market vendors. There again a gallon of petrol had gone up from the pre-war price of four shillings and sixpence a gallon to ten pounds a gallon. Masses of human beings walked up and down, down and up, aimlessly, morosely, looking, searching, thirsting, for a familiar face to talk to, to discuss their problems with, a face to share their sorrows, their expectations.

Titi and Onuoha stopped by Tudor's chalet. As was common with most young men during the war there was a very attractive young girl staying or rather living with him. Tudor needed company and the young girl, a beauty from Abonema on the coast of Biafra, needed food and shelter. Those bonds were enough to unite them while they were away from their families. Her name was Mabel Peters. She sat down in the living-room and talked with Titi while Tudor and Onuoha retired to an adjoining room.

Tudor told Onuoha that Mabel Peters was just one of a series of girls that had passed through his apartment. Before her, there was another young girl called Yvette Okonkwo, who had left Aba after the house in which she was living had been bombed and some people had been killed. She had met Tudor several times before in Aba. When she arrived in Owerri, she had begged to spend a few days with him until she could find something to do and a place to stay permanently. Tudor had given her shelter and a few days later had offered her a job as his secretary and accountant. Soon Yvette had cancelled all plans of moving out of Tudor's house.

As a result of propinquity, the attachment had grown daily. Yvette admired Tudor's courage and her beauty and femininity added a soothing flavour to Tudor's life at the end of each hard long day. Yvette had everything she could desire, including things that no money could buy in the country, like cold beer and Mambo wine. The latter had been shipped before the war from Europe to Port-Harcourt, in transit to the Chad Republic. Then hostilities had broken out between Biafra and Nigeria and the railway line up north had been disconnected. The Chad wine had been stranded in Biafra and was frequently used in the Progress Hotels to toast Chad-Biafra friendship. Military and paramilitary personnel had easy access to bottles of it as well. Generally, then, Yvette had everything she wanted. What Tudor had not been able to buy for her in Owerri, he had bought in Enugu or Ogoja during his trips behind the enemy lines.

One day, an old friend of Tudor's, Fabian, had been stranded, like many other people running away from Onitsha. Fabian had come to Owerri in a state of desperation. Tudor had been driving past the Post Office one day when he had seen Fabian and stopped. With head bent downwards, Fabian had been on the point of giving up his soul to the heavens. Tudor had taken him into his car and driven him to his house. Later on he had given Fabian a room in his apartment and a job in his office to make him feel independent. Soon Fabian had given up all ideas of moving out.

Gradually they had established a *ménage à trois*. Whenever Tudor had left for one of his excursions behind enemy lines, he had handed over his account books to Yvette and had left office administration to Fabian. When Tudor returned to town it gradually took Yvette a little longer than usual to open the door when he came home in the evening. As Tudor entered the room,

Fabian would usually be sitting in a chair reading with deep concentration the *Biafra Sun*, the *Mirror*, the *Times* or any one of the many daily newspapers printed on very rough exercise books then being circulated in Biafra. Fabian had appeared to discover every day a new newspaper five by eight inches in dimension and containing four pages of uniform news. After a while, Tudor had started to sense that something was going on between Yvette and Fabian. But he had no concrete evidence on which to base his doubts.

One day, Tudor had decided that he was going to Umuahia with his police escort. Fabian had wanted to accompany him and, before the car set out, Yvette said that she was coming along too. Tudor and the police escort had sat in the front of the car, Fabian and Yvette in the back. Tudor had been driving and, as they moved along, they had talked about a thousand and one things. Each time Tudor had asked Fabian a question, he had discovered that he had to repeat it. Fabian had apparently not been paying attention to what Tudor had been saying. Tudor had not quite been able to see from the rear view mirror what was happening behind. He had heard all kinds of funny noises behind him and then some panting. Tudor had eventually ground his car to a halt and turned his head. There he had caught Fabian and Yvette locked arm in arm, legs inside one another and lips and hips wet in an adulterous embrace. Tudor had not been able to control his anger at the insult. He had pulled out his service pistol and had raised it as Fabian and Yvette dived below the seats, ashamed and petrified at the same time. Tudor had then tossed his pistol in the air and laughed.

He had then turned his car and headed back to Owerri. He had nothing important to do in Umuahia. For a while, he had felt like throwing Yvette and Fabian out of his chalet that night. But he knew that they had no other place to go in the crowded city. He had let them stay until the following day. In the morning, Tudor had paid Fabian two months' salary in advance and had sacked him from his job. As for Yvette, he had given her one hundred pounds and asked her to leave the house. Tudor had been rather mad with himself because he had a wife and a lovely child in his village.

But in his kind of job, he rarely had any time for his family as he moved from one dangerous zone to another. He had loved Yvette with a different kind of love. He never would have married her, but he had not been averse to having her as a friend while he was away from home. Yvette and Fabian were single and had appeared to be in love. They might have been able to start a new life. Perhaps Tudor had been the divine instrument of their union. It had been with tears that he bade the two of them goodbye in the morning. Yvette had cried and pleaded with Tudor but the latter had made his decision. She had cried and said that she was not in love with Fabian. Tudor had bid her farewell. Fabian had begged and pleaded with Tudor to let her stay on, but Tudor would not listen to him either. The two of them, Yvette and Fabian, had left like a married couple being driven out of the Garden of Eden. But each had gone his separate way. Yvette had later secretly married an army officer, but he had been killed shortly afterwards on the battlefield.

Tudor himself told Onuoha the story. Diogu had told Tudor that Onuoha was perhaps interested in Yvette at one point. Because of their new mutual respect for one another, Tudor felt compelled to explain what had happened. It was better that Onuoha should hear it from him rather than differently from other people. Onuoha asked Tudor the whereabouts of Fabian. He had known Fabian too sometime in the past, a very quiet young man then, a little shy. The vicissitudes of war had apparently affected his attitudes to life. Tudor sighed and said that Fabian had become a tramp again. They went back to the living-room and listened to a few records before Titi and Onuoha left for the meeting at Umuoma.

It made no difference those days in Owerri which bush path one took or which major road, the long line of stragglers and refugees continued. It looked as if an entire nation had woken up one morning to find that everyone had lost his job. From the midst of this crowd, in the height of this concentration of human beings in the small area that was Owerri, Onuoha and Titi heard the sound of an enemy plane in the sky and later saw it appear below the clouds. The plane droned closer and closer as people ran helter-skelter, trying to take cover.

There was no safe place. There were no ditches and no sewage system in the city. About the only thing that could provide some shelter appeared to be the frequent mounds of unburnt rubbish in the midst of the city. But a direct hit on a dump would turn the refuse into a grave. At moments like this, fatalism takes over human reasoning. Wherever one went or looked, one found crowds, as many as two hundred people, looking up in anticipation, hoping that the bomb would not fall on them, fearing as the plane droned round and round that the pilot above was specifically looking for them, out to put an end to their life that particular day.

The few activities that were still going on in the city came to a standstill. Bank tellers rolled down their gauzed windows and closed for the day and ran out to take cover. Market women who were selling salt and other commodities, frightened, abandoned their wares and dived into the nearest cluster of shrubs for safety. The wise among them coolly collected their products and started walking home to their villages outside Owerri city.

The plane circled round and round, like an albatross, like a vulture. A few guns were fired, but the anti-aircraft gunners appeared to be saving their shells and ammunition. The long line that formed in front of the petrol station disappeared as car-owners abandoned their vehicles and ran into the bush for safety. Some of the drivers had been there for more than two days waiting to buy their one gallon ration of petrol. Those inside buildings ran down the steps and sought safety below the cement arch formed by the staircase and the wall.

The plane circled and circled, sometimes low, sometimes high. But it dropped no bomb and disappeared. There was a sense of relief. But it was not the type of relief that sent people back to work. It was the type of deep breath that carried them home as fast as they could make it. Once the plane had passed on any given day, all businesses closed: markets, banks, shops. The appearance of an enemy plane was usually considered a serious warning. If it did come again and someone was killed in the ensuing bombing, people often tended to blame the individual for trying to tempt the patience of the gods.

Onuoha and Titi continued their trip towards the meeting place. Diogu was driving their station-wagon. A few miles away from Owerri City, they saw long lines of people moving back towards Owerri. At first it looked like the normal stream of refugees, but the crowd thickened. Soon they saw large groups of soldiers running back towards Owerri, their guns in their hands, running as fast as their feet could carry them. Several people tried to stop Onuoha as their car passed. Onuoha could not quite understand what was happening and the reason for the mad rush towards Owerri. But the crowd increased more and more and the number of soldiers running back doubled, tripled. At one point about ten soldiers, when they saw Onuoha's car moving along, formed a barricade and stopped him. They informed him that the Nigerian troops had taken Obinze and were heading towards Obigwe, Ihiagwa and Egbelu. Onuoha could hardly believe what he heard. Ihiagwa was just a mile and a half beyond Umuoma where the refugee meeting was to take place. The car moved again. Onuoha turned his head and saw the soldiers still looking at them in bewilderment, unable to understand why people would want to drive to their death like that.

They arrived at the Umuoma school building where the meeting ought to have started. Diogu was going to park the car when a burst of gunfire greeted them. Looking in the direction of the shots, Onuoha saw a group of soldiers coming forward from the other end of the compound, surrounded by smoke and firing as they approached. Titi was scared. Onuoha was too. Diogu had lost his nerve and was already some one hundred yards away, running back to Owerri. Onuoha jumped into the car with Titi. Diogu had gone off with the keys in fright. With the scissors that he saw in front of the car, Onuoha cut the wires leading to the starter, pressed them together and the car started. He sped off as the soldiers continued firing in his direction. Diogu was still running when they caught up with him. He got into the car and they headed home to Owerri. Another evacuation had begun.

Other people jumped on to their car as they slowly moved through the crowd towards Owerri. It was impossible to believe that Biafran troops could have lost twenty-five miles in a single day. It was impossible to believe what was happening. Their car could barely move through the dark mass of human beings running back, trekking back to Owerri, fleeing the approach of enemy troops. Onuoha honked and hooted, but no one seemed in the mood to give way to them. They too had a right to be saved, to move in front of others. Some of the civilians and soldiers who had warned Onuoha about the presence of enemy troops in the vicinity jeered at them. Some said: 'Brave man. Did we not tell you? You thought you were different from us. Why did you not go and confront the enemy. See him now in his car, running faster than we can. Wise man! Wise man!'

Behind the refugees guns boomed. The arrival of the refugee mass in one village was the signal for the next village to vacate its homestead. Like the invading army, all the refugees were pushing on ahead towards Owerri. Onuoha could not imagine that the Owerri they had seen that morning as crowded as it was, could contain the approaching mass of human beings pouring in, descending like an avalanche. Looking at the crowd in front of him and behind him, he wondered how long they could continue to move from one temporary home to another. Some carried their bamboo beds on their heads. When their loads became unbearable, they tried to sell them for a few pennies. If the effort to sell failed, they simply abandoned them by the roadside. Thus they had lost not only their property but also suffered the pains of three or six miles of effort, intense effort carrying it to a future refugee home.

It was difficult to know whom to pity most: the old man bent in two by age and farm labour, the old woman with withered breasts crawling along the refugee road at a snail's pace: the old woman had probably never before gone more than three miles beyond her home. There was the young mother carrying an eighteen-month-old child behind her back and holding a six-month-old baby in her arms. There was the young man, trying to bear on his back, like Jesus on Mount Calvary, all the belongings of his family—including a six-year-old girl too big to be carried on the back of the mother, too young and tender to undertake alone the fifteen-mile-long race for life and safety.

It was impossible to know how many times they would be forced to move again. They had run, some of them, from Lagos and Ibadan, from Kaduna and Kano, from Jos and Maiduguri back to Eastern Nigeria. They had run from Nsukka and Enugu, from Awka and Abagana, from Onitsha and Awgu to Port-Harcourt, Aba. From those areas they had run again, to seek refuge in towns bordering Owerri. Again they were being forced to pick up what was left of their belongings to run once more for safety. The area of refuge was becoming smaller and smaller. No one seemed to know exactly where the enemy was. Sooner or later, the eternal wanderer would run right into an enemy camp or enemy-controlled village. It appeared that the Nigerians were only twelve miles from the centre of the city. If their progress continued for another four or five miles, their shells would be falling on Owerri City. Then that town also would have to be evacuated.

After the fall of Port-Harcourt, Aba and Okigwi, most of the refugee camps in the country were located in Owerri and its neighbouring villages. Owerri was also the food depot for organizations like Caritas, the World Council of Churches and the International Red Cross. Owerri was also the granary of the country. It would be impossible to evacuate completely both men and products. Worse still, the loss of Owerri would lead to the loss of the outlying villages, which would mean the loss of precious and fertile farms to Nigerian soldiers.

Fever was fast catching up on Owerri as the refugees poured in. It was impossible to know which way to run under such terrible circumstances. Owerri was the centre of the country. Its capture could mean the subsequent division of the country into two—the East and the West, since most of the areas north and south were practically in Nigerian hands. Thus a quick decision of a refugee to run east or west could mean that he would not, for years perhaps, again see his relations who would be separated from him by a wall of hate. It was difficult for those living in Owerri and who had property there to know what to take or what to leave for the ravaging and rampaging Nigerian soldiers. The fall of the city had become imminent much sooner than anyone could have anticipated.

In the tropical world, the weather could be anything at any time. As evening drew closer, it started raining, at first slowly, then more rapidly and finally torrentially. Misery stalked the lonely and crowded streets of Owerri. Men and women individually, collectively, pondered what to do with their lives. A young woman who had given birth three days earlier, stood shivering in the cold evening. The doors around were all locked. Onuoha was approaching the Owerri post office in his car when he saw the woman trying to cross the street. The poor mother took a false step and fell into one of the ugly gutters that had for years mocked the streets of the city. She struggled out, crying, wailing, her body shaking from cold, vainly trying to brush off the dirt and filth from her body and her child's, her tattered dress greedily holding more water than usual. Onuoha rushed to her help and put her in the car. Titi held the child. Together, they made for the Provincial Office. It was closed. The workers appeared to have left the offices and the city and taken refuge in villages further away. Refugees from the Obinze, Umuoma, Ihiagwa, Okuku and Avu areas surged into Owerri congregating in open spaces in the city. The rain poured down more heavily than ever. The thunder pealed, redoubling the intensity of the Nigerian artillery barrage in the distance. There was nothing there for the refugees to eat.

Onuoha was after all a stranger in Owerri. Not knowing what to do to help the mass of suffering humans lying out in the torrential rain, he rushed over to Tudor's house to ask for advice, to ask for help. As Onuoha and Titi arrived at Tudor's place, the latter's car was about to pull out. Tudor had been worried about Onuoha's safety and was just going to look for him once he had deposited outside Owerri all the confidential documents he had in his possession. Tudor was convinced that Owerri would fall to the enemy. Onuoha explained to him the refugee situation. Tudor said he had been trying to do his best.

Together, they went back to the Provincial Office. Since there was no one there to open the Provincial Hall for them so that the refugees could move in, Tudor decided to blow open the door with a rifle shot. The immense crowd standing outside in the rain rushed inside as the doors swung open. A few died of suffocation as they struggled to get a place to stand. Titi and Onuoha stood around and administered first aid to the most urgent cases. Tudor went back to his office, commandeered four vehicles and rushed down to the food depot. With the help of some of the refugees, he packed provisions to be distributed to all of them in Provincial Hall and in other refugee centres. He had to force the depot guard at gun point before the latter would let him remove some of the food. Food was distributed to the starving masses in the town hall. Some extra food was given to each refugee in case Owerri had to be evacuated that night.

Men cried like babies, babies wailed like animals, the sick just groaned and groaned. Those who did not know where to find other members of their families moaned for them. It looked like a gas chamber or a detention camp. Some would probably have preferred mass execution to the mass excruciating pains they were being subjected to then.

Among the people a young mother stood beside her two children. The kids were anaemic, almost bloodless. Though aged about two and three, they could hardly move their limbs. If one had the courage to look, one could discern the flow of blood or a white mass that looked like blood in their veins. The two children looked jelly-like, just like slimy fish. As one tried to handle them, one feared that they would just melt and turn into some other shape in human hands. There were scores of such mothers in the hall and three times as many children. The City Hall became some kind of a hospital. A few volunteers, mostly nurses organized by Tudor with the help of Mabel Peters, arrived. Food and water were being served to the refugees. Soon they were divided into small groups and various nurses tried to take care of the individual groups. One or two priests arrived to administer Last Sacrament to some. The stronger refugees were sent outside to dig a common grave for the dead. When some order came into the Provincial Hall, Onuoha and Titi left to see other refugees in other parts of the city.

The entire city was flooded. And in the growing darkness, the rain had awoken all the mosquitoes that had been breeding since the beginning of the cruel war. The situation at the St Paul's Boys' School was no less tragic. The few bush lamps in the centre of the building were covered by all kinds of insects. They buzzed and buzzed interminably on the ears of the wretched, as if to remind them of their hopeless situation. The anaemic and the children suffering from kwashiorkor could not even raise their arms and fingers to drive them away. Flies crawled on their bodies and mosquitoes danced in their ears as if the children had been dead for days in a putrid swamp.

Outside, the crickets opened their voices in concatenation. The frogs from the nearby Nworie River intoned their songs of happiness. The toads from the same river croaked in total disagreement, with a persistent cacophony. As the beatles chirped, the raindrops continued beating relentlessly on the zinc roof of the building with the solitary monotony of a lost drummer. St Paul's School was overcrowded. The nearby refugee store had been mobbed and the food stolen. Stolen is a very unkind word, but the sick and the dying had helped themselves to a final gulp. Unfortunately, the experience of eating again had finished the lives of some of them, the weakest amongst them. Nurses had assembled in the hall also. Some of them were Biafran religious sisters who were trying, trying desperately to help everywhere, to help everyone. The stronger amongst the refugees tried to assist the children, the most needy ones amongst them.

Onuoha and Titi were also doing their best, trying, trying with tears in their eyes to assist: to bandage a few people with open sores; to feed a few children who could not even hold their drinking cups; to encourage mothers who looked as if they wanted to collapse and die; to say a few words of kindness to husbands who wanted to strike their heads against the wall and get over with it all; to listen to a few, quite a few old men that talked and talked without knowing what they were doing or saying. They were trying to make sure that the water got to everyone, that the milk reached every child, that the pills reached those who needed them most. They were still there trying to do all those things when Tudor arrived.

Tudor had been invited to the Provincial Security Council Meeting called to examine the new Nigerian offensive and decide what measures to take to push them back and prevent their coming into Owerri. Tudor announced that the vandals had not moved beyond Umuoma and that three battalions had been detailed to wipe them out with Ogbunigwe. The Biafran troops were taking up their positions and would attack the enemy around midnight. According to the Divisional Commander of the army, everything was fine. Just one battalion had failed and, because of communications difficulties, had been unable to contact the brigade head-quarters. It took them some twenty-four hours to contact the brigade command and report their failure to hold back the enemy in that sector, although they had sent messages earlier saying that they were in complete control of the situation. The other batta-lions of the brigade were continuing their push towards Igrita, towards Port-Harcourt. This situation became clear a few minutes before the meeting scheduled at Umuoma. During the Provincial Security Council Meeting the Divisional Commander had been confident that his boys would arrest the situation that night. Consequently all the ammunition in the Owerri depot, which was not much to begin with, was being poured into the brigade attack against the enemy that night. Militia boys were going around the town asking people not to leave the city, which was going to be defended at all costs. Tudor was not very confident of the out-come of the battle. The consoling thing was that the miserable refugees might not have to leave Owerri that night for an un-known destination.

Titi and Onuoha did not sleep that night. They continued their round of refugee centres. The whole city was in a state of expec-tancy. Towards one in the morning, firing was heard and within seconds several guns had joined in. The artillery boomed. Shells took off and fell not too far away. A little farther away, one could hear the crackle and rattle of rifle fire, faint but consistent. A few of the refugees on hearing the sounds started to leave the town hall. The nurses had a difficult time trying to convince them that the firing came from Biafran troops. 'Yes,' one of them scorned. 'That is what they tell us always. The enemy has been contained.

The enemy has been bottled up. We will fight inch by inch to defend our territory and our people. We must never evacuate our dear city. That is what they tell us. And every time the vandals have attacked, we have had to run away from the cities. The rest of you can stay here if you want. I am going out again.' The man picked up his bag and walked out. About twenty people followed him out onto the refugee road.

Elsewhere, the sound and crackle of Biafran guns gave an air of assurance to the civilians. Those still in the city were able to breathe again. Some were diffident, saying that it had happened in Enugu, Onitsha, Port-Harcourt and Aba. The people were becoming more and more cynical. Some complained that government officials wouldn't let them go away from the city while there was still time. A few stole away through the bushes where they had smuggled their prized belongings. Others, once the guns started sounding closer and heavier, left everything. A small exodus had begun towards Orlu, Ikeduru and Mbaise. But the firing died down after two hours. Some were reassured. A few hiding in the bush came back to their homes. Even the refugee who had walked out of the town hall returned there later in the morning.

Dawn breaks early in tropical Biafra. By six in the morning, people were up again. A few of the refugees were even able to smile a good morning. They had never thought that they would live through another day. Civilians who had money in the banks were lining up before they even opened to withdraw all their money if they could. Those who had had no place to sleep the previous night were up early looking for accommodation in the city. The sun was bright and lovely, the type of beauty that breaks out after a rainy night. The atmosphere was clear and the air soft and refreshing. There was a feeling of rebirth. If the night had been a quiet one, people would normally have got up refreshed and smiling, greeting their neighbours with arched smiles as if the Saviour had come. The town was filled with happy and reassuring rumours about how Biafran commandos had wiped out completely with Ogbunigwe more than two thousand enemy soldiers in the Umuoma area.

At exactly one minute to ten, heavy artillery and rocket fire broke out again. Shells, bazookas, recoilless guns fired, cracked, thundered, in the heavens, on the earth. The fire power far exceeded anything Biafran troops could muster. The night before, people in Owerri had heard the nearby sound of the shell taking off and its explosion far away a few minutes later. That morning, they heard the shell take off far away and explode later on the outskirts of the city. At the same time, four planes appeared in the Owerri sky, pounding houses and streets, schools and churches, military bases and refugee camps. 'The vandals have come again,' women cried throwing up their hands in despair. 'The vandals have come in full force,' they gasped in desperation.

The shelling appeared to be coming from right inside the city. Another wave of four planes came as people started running for their lives. They took cover as the planes flew over their heads, but then stood up immediately and continued their race outside the city. The planes seemed to be aiming particularly at the petrol stations. Several cars lined up in front of them were set ablaze. From the top of the hillock where Titi and Onuoha were dodging the planes, they could see bullets flying out of the wings of the jets. The planes seemed to be spitting fire from their noses and bellies.

It looked like the sack of Jerusalem, or the sack of Rome by the vandals. The voices of the frightened were confounded with the shrieks of the wounded and the dying. The sun added fear and lustre to the wings of the planes as they dived low to spout out bullets and unload their bombs. There were soldiers directing the traffic at various cross-points, and the pedestrians leaving the city. Some of the refugees said that the soldiers in question were not wearing the traditional Biafran rising sun emblem on their shoulders. They feared that they might be Nigerian infiltrators. It was the whitest Monday in the history of Owerri. All was blank. No initiative was forthcoming from any quarter.

The long-delayed exodus from Owerri had begun. From Owerri about twelve important arteries lead in various directions. The refugees did not know which road to take. From information available, it appeared that the Nigerians would try to head for

Umuahia some forty miles away. This fear led to the evacuation of everyone who lived along the Umuahia road, up to seven miles away—in Egbu, Awaka, and gate villages of Emekuku, Ezeogba and Exedibia. Others thought that the Nigerians would head towards the Onitsha road and either link up with their troops in Onitsha or try simply to seize the Uli-Annabelle airport. This supposition equally led to the mass exodus of people along the Owerri-Onitsha road—from Irete, Orogwe, and Ogbaku. A few people were convinced beyond doubt that the Nigerians were aiming at dividing the reduced Biafra into two, in which case they would move along the Orlu or Okigwi road. As a result more than fifty thousand people living in Ubommiri, Akwakuma and the villages of Mbieri and Uratta abandoned their homes. There was no sense of direction anywhere.

Owerri was therefore empty, like Enugu, Onitsha, Port-Harcourt and Aba when the Nigerian soldiers entered it in a leisurely fashion during the day. The Biafran government had all along advocated the scorched-earth formula and policy in the case of the evacuation of a city. But in the general pandemonium, people seemed to have forgotten to burn down their houses. Perhaps they did not have the heart to do it, half hoping that sooner or later, they would be able to move back to their homes, victorious or conquered.

Onuoha and Titi were still standing paralysed with fright on the hillock when Tudor appeared. He had been driving from one refugee camp to the other, looking for them. They hailed him and almost had to run in front of his car before he saw them. He was relieved, but looked desperate and disappointed. He threw his hands up in the air and shook his head in very deep sorrow. Titi and Onuoha asked him what the matter was as if they had not seen enough that day to make a heart of stone cry. Tudor kept on saying, distraught: 'I cannot believe it. I cannot believe it!'

About three Biafran battalions had been sent out the evening before with instructions to seek out and destroy the enemy troops. The Biafran troops had taken up positions just outside Owerri and had fired shots and shells for more than two hours. They had come back at five in the morning and reported to the brigade commander that the enemy had been liquidated. The brigade commander in turn had reported to the Divisional Commander that the assigned mission had been accomplished. At nine o'clock on the Monday morning, during the session of the Provincial Security Council Meeting, the Divisional Commander had announced that his boys had wiped out all enemy presence in the Owerri area and that they were continuing their push towards Igrita and Elele-Alimini. The news was received with cheers and arrangements were being made to encourage refugees to go back to Obinze, Mbirichi and Ihiagwa. Tudor during the meeting interrupted the commander and asked him how many enemy soldiers had been killed or imprisoned. The Divisional Commander had said that the Nigerian battalions which had entered Umuoma had all been wiped out. He had not been able to advance any figures. Tudor had asked him how many of his own men were killed or wounded. The Divisional Commander had not got those figures either and had said that he thought the questions were rather insulting and should be addressed to a battalion commander and not to a local Brigadier. He had barely finished his harangue when new firing had broken out on the outskirts of Owerri.

It had been only an hour later that the entire story had come into the open. Apparently some officers had sent out Biafran soldiers alone into the night weather, without any reconnaissance being made. The Biafrans had fired all night without making contact with the enemy. Entrenched on the safe side of the river, the Biafran troops had fired into the dark forests for three full hours and had naturally come back when they ran out of ammunition. The Nigerians had refused to return the fire or to be drawn into a fight at night in an area which they did not know very well. They had also been waiting for some reinforcements from their men in the Obike-Okpuala axis. The Nigerians had been sure that the Biafrans would soon run out of ammunition. The Biafrans had stopped firing around four or five in the morning. The Nigerians had waited until eight, when, since there had been no Biafran movement to occupy forward positions, they had rightly concluded that the Biafrans had run out of ammunition and withdrawn to their barracks for breakfast.

The Nigerians had opened fire as their other troops had arrived around ten in the morning. As they had fired and shelled, their ferrets had moved forward to clear the area. Their infantry had also moved in to occupy forward positions. Within one half hour, they had been within shelling distance of Owerri. Their half-tracks had moved into the bush to clear obstacles. Transport planes had flown in from Lagos to air-drop further supplies to their troops. These measures had not really been necessary, because there had been not a single shell left to defend Owerri.

Meanwhile in the city, the Nigerian fighter planes had sown pandemonium amongst the people. They had set fire to most of the fuel dumps in Owerri, so that there had been no fuel anywhere to help evacuate government property, let alone that of ordinary citizens.

Now that Tudor had found Onuoha and Titi, he could control himself no longer. 'It was only yesterday, yesterday, that I went to the Provincial Secretariat and begged them to give me leave to evacuate the produce in Owerri stores and the provisions at the Caritas depot. With Falstaffian confidence, they assured me that Owerri would not fall. Thousands of refugees will starve on their way today. Hundreds will collapse on the way for lack of food while we leave in the abandoned city enough food to keep the Nigerian brigade here for six months.'

Later that afternoon, Onuoha volunteered to go to the food depot with Tudor to evacuate as much food as they could. Tudor did not have enough petrol. Onuoha had a full tank, however, and within minutes, they had siphoned out about three gallons which they put into the station wagon. On the way, Tudor rounded up at gun-point about fifteen fleeing Biafran soldiers and forced them to come along with him in his jeep and Onuoha's station-wagon. Along the way, they saw about five mammy wagons, which the drivers were about to abandon because of lack of petrol. Tudor put an armed soldier with the driver of one and forced him to join the caravan to the food depot. Within half an hour, he had about ten lorries. He put some petrol in each of them, just enough to take them to the depot. Beyond that, he did not know what to do.

About one hundred yards in front of him, a petrol station was ablaze and the petrol drums buried underground as well as those in the main dump were exploding one by one. As Tudor and the rest drew nearer, they saw a man trying to move a drum from the filling station at the risk of his life. The man was apparently a thief trying to make money with the petrol in the black market, for he abandoned the drum when he saw the army jeep approaching, and took to his heels. The drum was rolling back towards the elongating tongues of flame. Within seconds, Tudor was there with Onuoha and about three other soldiers. They pushed with all their strength, their backs to the flames. The heat was such that they could feel the petrol in the drum evaporating into the hot air above.

Just then a plane came overhead. The group dived into a nearby house for cover. Titi and the rest crawled under one of the trucks that was reinforced with steel. The plane dropped no bombs but just rocketed and strafed the area around. One of the shells hit a truck and set it ablaze. The driver jumped out of the flaming vehicle as the others rushed to their lorries and moved them away from the flames. Soon the air was clear again. Tudor and his group rushed back to the station and rolled the drum into one of the lorries.

They headed directly for the General Depot. In the absence of a key, Tudor broke one of the windows. A soldier climbed in and then opened the door from inside. The loading of the lorries was done quickly. Some of the soldiers filled up the tanks around and poured the petrol from the drum into the carburettors of the mammy wagons. Help was soon there. For a fee of two or three heads of stock-fish, passers-by willingly helped load the lorries. When the wagons were loaded, Tudor gave them instructions to move on towards Emekuku. A soldier accompanied each load. For a while, Tudor stood there and pondered what to do with the provisions still lying there and in the other stores. He did not want them to get into the hands of the Nigerian soldiers. He would rather blow up the entire store. On further reflection, he thought that perhaps he could organize a team and try to come back a second time to evacuate what was left or at least some of it. He decided to let the supplies remain there until they could be evacuated. He figured that the Nigerians would be so busy consolidating their positions that they probably would not have time to look into such details.

The three of them descended the hill in their station wagon on their way to Egbu which was about three miles from Owerri. The crowd thickened as the people in Egbu had started to move as well. As the Egbu people moved, so the people in Awaka, a mile further down the Umuahia road, also started packing their luggage, ready to move. The people of Ezeogba, the first village of Emekuku, did not wait for the Awaka people to arrive before they vacated their homes a mile further down the road. Half a mile beyond Ezeogba and exactly six miles from Owerri was located Our Lady of Mount Carmel Mission, Emekuku. The lorries carrying the provisions were waiting a mile and a half beyond across River Okitankwo. Facing the Catholic Mission was the Holy Rosary Hospital, Emekuku. Tudor and his group had just arrived there when instructions came for its evacuation.

The hospital, under the supervision of an Irish Matron was one of the largest in the country. It was a tragic sight to watch the evacuation. First of all the patients were moved out. The wounded soldiers were amongst the first to be evacuated. A lesson had been learned from the tragic incident in Port-Harcourt when Nigerian troops had massacred over four hundred wounded Biafran soldiers who could not be evacuated from the General Hospital. Military vehicles and civilian cars were lined up for the job. Some of the anti-aircraft guns were moved down from Umuahia to protect the hospital during the evacuation.

After the destruction of many hospitals in the country, and the evacuation of several cities, the equipment at the Holy Rosary Hospital was as complete as anywhere in the nation. The hospital had started some thirty years earlier, just before the second world war. There had been several German doctors serving there then, but they had been forced out by the British during the war. A few Irish doctors had also been sent home. To this very day the villagers still regret the departure at that time of their revered Dr O'Connor, whose name was synonymous with miraculous healing.

The villagers stood around and helped and cried as the hospital was being evacuated, momentarily forgetting their own miserable condition. After the wounded soldiers had been evacuated, some of them in makeshift oxygen tents, it was the turn of the kwashiorkor children, infants suffering from varying degrees of malnutrition. The sight was pathetic; in a single moment one could see all the tragedy of the war in its stark reality, sorrowful and miserable.

Discipline amongst the nurses and the workers was superb. The co-operation of the villagers was magnificent. The Irish Matron in charge of the hospital personally supervised the operation and the general evacuation. Box by box, the drugs were evacuated. Piece by piece, the hospital equipment was dismantled and put into vehicles standing by. The women left the maternity wards. Children were put in mammy wagons with beds of soft mattresses. The nurses folded the linen. The villagers helped evacuate the last Vono beds and mattresses. As darkness fell over the city, the Matron made one more round of the hospital buildings. She satisfied herself that there was nothing left there of importance, and walked over to the residence of the nuns. All was cleared including food supplies for the refugees. She cast a final look at the hospital, at the chapel in the Sisters' residence. Tears fell from her eyes. She made the sign of the cross and entered the car. She was one of the last to leave the premises.

One man refused to leave the Catholic Mission. He was the parish priest of Our Lady of Mount Carmel Church, Emekuku. For thirty full years he had lived in the same room, on the same floor of the same presbytery in Emekuku. He had seen the town grow up from nothing. He had seen several of his faithful flock die and be buried in the cemetery not far away. He had baptized most of their children. He had seen them grow up and administered their first communion, as he had to their parents. He was always by the Bishop's side when they were confirmed. He was determined to live, die and be buried on Emekuku soil. Already in his seventies, he refused to leave his parish as the Nigerian soldiers approached.

He personally supervised the evacuation of the refugee children under the care of his Mission. He had packed up all the documents of the Mission since it was established at the end of the last century. Our Lady of Mount Carmel had seen its golden age. At one time, it had been the only centre of education and the Catholic faith in the area. Its bush missions and substations extended as far as Ogoja and Port-Harcourt. The parish priest had the church vestments and chalices packed up, but he refused to leave the premises. His brother, also a missionary, pleaded with him in vain. His Bishop sent word. He still refused to move or be moved.

The parish priest went into the new church, the magnificent Cathedral of Our Lady of Mount Carmel, with its medieval towers and frescoes, statuettes and stained-glass windows. As the Ezeogba and Ezedibia members of the parish passed by the Mission on their way to take refuge across the Okitankwo River, they stopped by the church and knelt down for a hurried prayer. On their way out, they begged their parish priest to follow them into exile. The priest would not leave his house of prayer. On her way out, the Matron also stopped at the church to make a parting sign of the cross. She managed to say a few words to the parish priest. Nothing would make him change his mind. Everyone was sure that the vandals would kill him if they saw him in the church. With sad eyes also, Titi, Onuoha and Tudor turned to go, leaving the parish priest alone in the church. The sound of bullets from Nigerian guns was approaching dangerously close.

Three-quarters of a mile further down the hill, a few soldiers were mining the Okitankwo bridge and were preparing to blow it up. It was depressing seeing some twenty miles of straight road lost in one single day without a fight, without a single shot. The area between Ihiagwa, Ogbaku, Mbieri, Akabo, Emekuku, Agbala and Emeke-Obibi happened to be one of the most heavily populated in the country. As a few soldiers on the bridge prepared to lay their mines, some citizens of Emekuku sternly forbade them to do so. If the bridge were destroyed, then the only route of escape for almost one million refugees, cut off in the Nekede sector, would have gone. Some fifty young men from Ezeogba and Ezedibia stood on the bridge and refused to move, telling the soldiers: 'If you cannot defend us, at least let us alone, leave the bridge alone so that those who have not escaped can come over safely.'

Tudor agreed with the civilians. While they were disputing the issue, a crowd of people came crying and running as fast as their legs could carry them. 'The vandals have entered Emekuku,' they said. The women announced that they had seen a Nigerian Ferret about one mile behind them. As they passed the Mount Carmel Church, a shell fell on the roof of the Cathedral. As they were still talking, Tudor saw the Nigerian Ferret up the hill, slowly levelling everything on its way and heading straight for the bridge. If it succeeded in crossing the river, there would be absolutely no other obstacle in its way. There were no barricades. There was little resistance until about seven miles before Umuahia at the junction of the Owerri-Okigwi-Umuahia roads.

About the only way to stop the Ferret was to blow up the bridge. Tudor could not bear to see more than one million Biafrans cut off behind enemy lines. They would be massacred without being given any chance to escape. Tudor decided that the bridge must not be blown up. If it were necessary to play Horatius and defend the bridge as long as possible and only blow it up when every Biafran refugee had crossed to safety, Tudor would have done it and sacrificed his life for it if need be. But it was not necessary.

There were fox holes already on both sides of the bridge by the roadside. It was decided that the bridge must be defended. There were about fifty rifles around and some hand grenades. Everyone took his place on the other side of the bridge. Meanwhile the Ferret descended the hill as slowly as it could, spitting out fire and death along the way. Fear seized everyone as it came closer and closer. The Ferret covered every square inch of the bush around with bullets, spraying them as if ejecting insecticide.

Titi almost shrieked as she saw the monster, the flaming monster. Tudor covered her mouth with a handkerchief and warned her not to make the slightest noise. She was panting and out of breath. Turning and whispering to Onuoha, Tudor said: 'We must stop that Ferret car before it crosses the Okitankwo River.' With that, the two of them rose quietly and crawled towards the river. Still crawling, they moved along the river for a while. Onuoha and Tudor glided into the river, holding up the barrels of their guns.

'The idea,' Tudor explained, 'is to move close enough to the Ferret and launch tear gas and hand grenades inside the turret of the Ferret guns, right inside it. We have no bazookas and it would be folly to try to stop a Ferret car with mere rifles.' They swam across the river. Tudor opened his bag and gave Onuoha some grenades. They were crawling in the bush. There was a well nearby. Tudor and Onuoha rounded it and made their way through the undergrowth so as to attack the Ferret from behind. There was silence on the other side of the bridge. Nothing seemed to move but the Ferret car. There was no other sound but the splashing of bullets. Tudor and Onuoha got into position to attack. Tudor asked Onuoha to stay behind while he jumped forward close to the Ferret to attack it. They fixed a point on the road. Tudor would make his attack once the armoured vehicle reached there.

Five yards before the point they had chosen, the Ferret stopped and turned. The bridge was a few yards farther down. The Ferret stopped shooting. It was incomprehensible. Perhaps it had run short of ammunition. Perhaps the driver was afraid that the bridge was mined. Perhaps he was afraid of being encircled in the increasing darkness. Perhaps he just wanted to give the infantry time to consolidate their positions behind. Tudor and Onuoha were so stupefied that they could not even move. The Ferret was ascending the hill again and moving back towards Owerri. Tudor and Onuoha crossed the river again to rejoin their comrades.

While they were there wondering how best to utilize the opportunity offered by the retreat of the Ferret, they saw about five hundred Biafran soldiers at the top of the hill on the Umuahia side. They were coming back from Uzoagba. Tudor made every effort to let them know that his group was Biafran. Otherwise the soldiers would start shooting in panic. When they came nearer and arrived at the bridge, it was discovered that they formed part of a larger force that had tried to retreat to Umuahia by way of Mbaise. The people of Mbaise had lined up their local militia along the road. The boys had been armed with rifles and machine-guns and had refused to let the retreating Biafran soldiers pass through their town. They had ordered them to go back and face the Niger-ians.

The Biafran soldiers had turned around and tried to get to Umuahia through the Uzoagba road, but met the same obstacle. The civilians everywhere were deeply disappointed with the soldiers who had let them down so easily. They refused to let them pass or even let them set up their brigade headquarters in Uzoagba. The soldiers had therefore decided to try and camp that night near the river, not knowing that the Nigerian Ferret was within sight. They could hardly believe the story Tudor told them about the reaction of the Ferret car a few minutes earlier. The soldiers were ill-equipped. Not all of them had rifles. In any case, they decided on the spot to pursue the Nigerians and try to push them out before they dug in in the area.

Tudor volunteered to lead a group of about two hundred soldiers in the attack against the Nigerians. The soldiers were excited and all of them wanted to participate in the attack, even though they did not have enough ammunition. Tudor decided to use a technique that had been employed elsewhere with success. In the absence of ammunition, shells and artillery, this technique consisted of using loud speakers to blare out the sound of shelling, rocket, artillery and rifle fire over distances of about two to four miles. This was usually accompanied with sporadic rifle fire and occasionally a real shell or two. The brigade band was there to join in the march.

The fifty boys from Emekuku, who had been standing by the bridge all the time, explained to the commando unit all the secret paths in the area and accompanied them also. The formation started. The band was in the middle. The commando groups moved into the surrounding bush and fanned out. Up the hill, the band played military music, the sound of heavy artillery blared and the crackle of small arms deafened the ear. For some of the participants it was lots of fun, but the seriousness of the performers made it more than real.

The band marched straight along the road, protected by ten

rows of armed soldiers. The other commandos started closing in around the hospital from the Umuawuka road, the hospital perimeter bordering the river. Others approached the Mission from the Mount Carmel College area and the Catholic Mission grounds. Some went as far as the Boys' School gardens and the neighbouring villages and closed in around the Mission. The Commanding Officer of the brigade deployed his men, giving them instructions to occupy immediately any ground liberated.

When the Nigerians who had occupied the hospital compound heard the sound of fire closing in around them, they took to their heels, abandoning equipment and arms. They were just trying to dig in when they were surprised. Everywhere they were on the run as the sound of war music and blaring artillery pursued them. Tudor and his group pursued them for three good miles, right back to Egbu. The infantry moved forward and occupied the grounds regained—Emekuku Mission, Ezedibia, Ezeogba, Awaka. Tudor and the Commanding Officer decided that they should not over-extend themselves at that moment and their forward lines dug in around Awaka. The push changed the course of the war that night and foiled the Nigerian dream of capturing Umuahia from Owerri. With the restoration of morale and fervour, the soldiers deployed around the area were more than determined to relaunch a real attack to recapture Owerri.

As Tudor and the rest pushed towards Ezeogba and Awaka, Onuoha's first concern was to see what had happened to the parish priest. He was there still praying as Onuoha entered the church followed by a few other soldiers. Their boots knocked discordantly on the floor of the church. The parish priest was still bent down at his prayers as the soldiers confronted him. He made the sign of the cross and said: 'I am ready if you want me now.'

As he said that, he looked up and saw Onuoha and the Biafran soldiers. He could not believe his eyes. He looked at them again and his eyes were filled with tears of joy. He motioned to the soldiers present and they all knelt down and recited the Magnificat Anima Mea Dominum. By the end of the psalm, Tudor and Titi had arrived there, one from Awaka, the other from the bridge.

Turning to everyone, the priest said: 'I was here, kneeling down right here. The sounds came closer and closer. Shells started falling all around the church. I heard some women outside running towards the bridge, crying and moaning. At the same time, one of the shells fell right on the roof above my head. I prayed and prayed. My heart jumped up. I thought that all was over. But there was no explosion. I prayed to God to save my parish, to save all the faithful, to save our city from the scourge of war. I promised Our Lady that we would erect in Her honour a grotto, the Grotto of Our Lady of Mount Carmel. She heard my prayers, my supplications.

'In a few days time will be the feast of the Holy Rosary, the patron of our hospital. I hope it was not damaged. I prayed. Shells were falling all around. Bullets were falling all around the church and on the walls but apparently not a single object or glass pane was damaged. Nothing in the church was touched. War . . . War . . . War is horrible. It is horrible. All the suffering; all the misery; all the humiliation. If only the soldiers would spare civilians, leave them alone in their villages, in their towns, in their churches, to worship their God in peace instead of making the whole nation one big holocaust, one big concentration camp, one big refugee camp. The Second World War was not like this. For six months during that war, I was a chaplain for West African soldiers fighting in Burma. I was a young man like you people during the Irish War of Independence and I can assure you it was not as bestial as this. When the Nigerians were coming, I was bent on asking them to kill me if they wanted, but to leave alone my church, to leave alone my parishioners.'

Nothing was damaged at the Holy Rosary Hospital. There was, in actual fact, no real fighting in the area. Only a few mud houses had been burned down by shells and rocket fire. These were a few old and dilapidated bars and brothels. Their destruction left the city of Emekuku a cleaner place. The parish priest then agreed to leave the church, when he was assured that there was no longer any danger to it.

People all over the country were impressed when the story was told. Already the faithful and unbelieving alike were filing daily to the Mount Carmel Church to see for themselves the miracle of prayers, and as they departed they left donations for the realization of the vow of the parish priest. The faithful looked forward to the day when the promise of their priest would be accomplished. Others could not help comparing this phenomenon to what happened in Onitsha. There the English Archdeacon of Otu Onitsha abandoned his flock immediately fighting broke out in July 1967 and took refuge in England. The very first shell the Nigerians lobbed into Onitsha from Asaba fell on his presbytery and completely destroyed his church and burned down his library.

As the Biafran soldiers descended the hill towards their temporary brigade headquarters around Nkwo-Emeke, they all agreed that the top of the hill just after the Mount Carmel College campus would be a good site for the grotto. From there, Our Lady of Mount Carmel symbolically could spread her arms wide and glorious to protect her children and the children of the world. She could wear on her head a crown of glory to signify that her children will rise again from the scourges of war, that her children have survived with increased faith the massacres by the infidels. Around her feet will be a wreath of palm leaves, a sign of renewed peace and prosperity. In addition to her traditional colour of blue for love will be also the colours of red symbolizing the blood of her children, black proclaiming her remembrance of those who suffered and died, and green to demonstrate the richness of sanctity and courage. She will stand facing the East, decked with garlands like a beautiful golden yellow rising tropical sun.

10

Behind the Rising Sun

When Tudor and the rest arrived at Nkwo-Emeke market where mammy wagons carrying the provisions were waiting for them, they discovered that some army boys, who had run away from Owerri, abandoning the civilians, had stopped the lorries on the road and made away with more than half of the load of stockfish and milk. He was depressed when he discovered it. It was too late now to go back to Owerri to rescue what was left.

There was no time for recrimination. The situation in the villages around—Umuocham, Ubowala, Umuakuru, Uboegbelu, Okwuemeke, Azaraowalla—was well nigh catastrophic, that night in particular. The situation had been bad enough in Owerri where there were large school buildings in which to put up the travellers and immense town halls to house the refugees temporarily. But in these villages, there was nothing. Some of them had never seen more than two thousand people, even on large market days or during times of festivities like the famous Ugo-Uzo Festival of Alaukwu Emekuku. That night the population in each one of those villages was more than fifteen thousand.

There was not enough food to go round and not enough beds to rest tired heads. Some of the refugees did not know where they were. They just followed the crowd as it moved out of besieged Owerri. They stopped when the movement stopped. Others stopped when darkness fell or when they tired of running. Even families could not take in all their distant relations, cousins, great-grandchildren, all kinds of in-laws and friends-in-law. Some families were separated into three or four groups. The man went to a refugee camp. The children stayed perhaps with the relations of the mother. The mother went to another family. Sometimes the grown-up children roamed from camp to camp, from house to house, waiting for darkness to fall.

In one single day, Biafra had lost more than fifty per cent of its remaining food-producing area. In anticipation of the suffering from the war, the farmers had been storing all the food they could grow and preserve. It was heart-rending for them that fateful day to have to abandon all the food they had stored up in their homes and take to the road, a long painful road that led them to a refugee camp. Unable to carry their goats and fowls, or lead them along during the exodus, the farmers, most of whom had pinned their future on the sale of their cattle after the war, abandoned them in their deserted villages. They left abundance at home to starve for want of food in an unsanitary refugee camp.

The fate of the villagers who had not run and had welcomed the refugees was not any better. Most of them depended for their food on the evacuated villages. In a matter of a few days, they knew that there would not be enough for everyone, even if there had been before. Even amongst the normally independent farmers in the undisturbed villages, life would become gradually more impossible. They too would begin to die of starvation, as prices began to rocket higher and higher each passing day because of the increased new demands, because of the growing scarcity of essential goods like salt and meat.

Perhaps the greatest miracle of the day was the evacuation of the little food at the Owerri depot. That night, Onuoha and Titi went around with Tudor distributing the meagre rations to the refugees in the camp who were worst off. Barefoot, bare-bodied, pot-bellied, wide-eyed, the children looked on. Not even the sight of food could move them any longer. One could see mothers and children shivering each time the door banged or the wind rustled. The few school buildings in the area around Uzoagba, Ikeduru, Amaimo, Enyiogugu, Nguru and Ekwerazu were overflowing with new arrivals from all directions.

There was not even enough fresh air to go round. Some of the refugees had not had a bath for weeks. Fortunately, it was not raining that night and people could sit or lie outside on the ground, on the grass, beneath a tree, below a small market shed, thinking and thinking about nothing, looking fixedly at the sky, the un-happy stars in the heavens that also seemed to mourn their misery, their new errant life. Some fell asleep with their eyes still open, but their senses had lost the power to concentrate again on the body's misery. Several would never wake up from their unrestful sleep.

A refugee village is a miserable place. It is like a concentration camp where people from divers places are brought together to be punished. They develop new relations based on common sufferings, common lacks, common wants, common expectations. There is nothing to do during the day. There is nowhere to sleep at night. The farms are gone. Separated from their age groups and familiar surroundings, they look like a group of lost pilgrims at the close of life. Not much happens except a death or two next door almost every other day. Life loses its present meaning. Death has lost already its ancient glory.

A Biafran refugee village was a particularly miserable place. There were not enough coffins to go round. Well-to-do farmers were buried without the traditional ceremonies. They were lucky if they had a coffin, even if they still had families that could afford coffins in which to bury them. At every turn of the road, there was a new grave. There was a time in the village when every farmer knew who was buried where and each villager knew the owner of each new grave. That was no longer possible. There were too many graves around. At night, people dug up recent graves to add more bodies. A family woke up in the morning to discover that in the dead of night, a refugee had buried a brother or a wife in front of their house. The identity was immaterial. It was just a grave. A housewife went to the market in the morning, early to avoid the Nigerian traditional air-raids on village markets during peak periods around noon. On her way home around ten, the apprehensive housewife would wade through five or six new graves.

More unbearable than the thought of death for a man was the painful and mortifying experience of seeing his age group slowly disappear. Such was the case with Egbula, a member of the refugee village. All of a sudden, he looked around and saw that his mates were all gone. The younger men had their preoccupations. Egbula had no longer any particular reason to wish to live but the thought of imminent death destroyed the little joy existence could still have for him. Egbula daily saw his life confounded and misery com-

pounded by the disappearance at an increasing rate of his grand-
children. Sometimes, it was a daughter who died, leaving perhaps
eight or ten children behind.

Death by hunger is slow, very slow, very excruciating. It is a
slow torture that minute by minute eats up all the fat and energy
a man has accumulated during his life. There is often no headache.
There is often no stomach trouble. Life moves on ahead. Only the
neighbours saw the change taking place in Egbula: he never heard
them talk about it. On their lips they had a sympathetic smile
whenever he was around. The change was slow, barely perceptible.
Egbula of course forgot his mirror as he packed his luggage to run
for dear life. Gradually Egbula began to notice that his clothes did
not fit any more. At first he thought it was a passing phenomenon.
The neighbours talked about it but they found it difficult to tell
Egbula that he looked like a scarecrow in his Sunday suit. His
morning wrapper became unusually noisy. He wobbled back and
forth inside it on his daily round to the village square for a
refugee meeting. His neck seemed to elongate. At first he attri-
buted it to an illusion, due to loss of weight. Slowly, Egbula got
bored having nothing for breakfast, for lunch and, when he could
afford it, for dinner as well.

Egbula smiled at friends in the morning. In the evening, he
was gone ... eyes wide open gazing into space exploring the
moon, the stars and the planets with abject incomprehension.
Egbula was dead. There were no women around to cry for him.
No gun shots announced his death. There were no young men
around to spend four carousing nights mourning for him. Worse
still, there were no mates to vaunt his glory. Added to all this was
the fact that Egbula would be buried in a strange land. He who
could not sleep in peace in a strange land during the day, should
not expect to find solace in the stranger land above or below during the night, eternal night. Egbula carried with him to the under-
world those symbolic gazing eyes, cursing the world and society
that had brought so much suffering on him during so short a life-
time. His tales of horror and massacres, of suffering and misery
were not stories that could entertain and amuse his ancestors in the
world beyond. Egbula went to them poor and dispossessed, as he

had lived during the last days of his life. He went to them bearing a glowing testimony of the life he had never lived.

Beyond the refugee village, lay the deserted village. This was a village bordering on the war front. There were no enemy soldiers there, but the villagers refused to return to their homes. The enemy was still within shelling range, though, and the villagers did not want to go through the experience of running away from their homes yet again at the approach of the enemy. The deserted village was occupied by Biafran soldiers. Once in a while, those villagers who had the courage went back to cast a glance, a mournful glance from a distance, at the houses they could not sleep in again. After a prolonged moment of contemplation, they returned to their camps to sleep on the floor with the other refugees.

The Biafran troops had taken up their positions after the Nigerians had come and gone. The area had been evacuated a few days earlier, perhaps a week, perhaps a month earlier. The place was in ruins already. Tom, the village's artful dodger, had been able to come and revisit all the homes. Tom worked in league with the billeted soldiers and some of their officers. Together, they shared the booty recovered from the deserted village. When the fortresses of a village farmer were locked and barricaded, the billeted soldiers blasted the door open with a hand grenade or forced the lock with a bullet.

Sometimes, the soldiers found it easier to jump in through the broken windows to 'liberate' every movable object and destroy what they could not carry. The 'liberated' objects usually included radios and sewing-machines. They used books to make fires for cooking. On the farms, they uprooted yam tubers and cassava roots. In the gardens, they cut down vegetable plants, pumpkins as well as melons. A few wise villagers—and some of them had uncommon wisdom—had before their hurried departure taken the precaution of burying in the ground their cherished dining sets and other precious belongings. They had carefully covered the spot with dry sand and grass. Some had even put a cross over it as if a dear child, a very dear child was interred there. But Tom, the village dodger, had 'washed' his hands and as a 'hound' could easily lead the soldiers to the location of those precious articles, buried or unburied. Piece by piece, the heritage of the deserted village, the billeted village was looted and sold in the black market.

Sometimes families were allowed to go back to their houses and take some of their belongings to 'liberated' areas. Several had been known to have died of heart-attacks on seeing their homes ransacked. One Biafran mother saw a soldier playing her gramophone which her son, who had since been killed in the war, had bought for her during the civilian regime. She plucked up courage and asked the billeted soldier how he came by the gramophone. The brave soldier, in very neat uniform and clean-shaven, replied with a wry military courtesy: 'I captured it today from the enemy trench, madam.' Naturally the right of conquest took precedence over the law of ownership. The weeping mother turned her back, afraid to penetrate further into her own house, afraid that once inside she might discover that the greedy Nigerians had stolen and later abandoned in trenches her other prized possessions. She returned to her refugee village, her heart heavy with sorrow and deeply lamenting the death of her son, her only son, killed in the same war, defending other lands.

In the billeted village, in less than one week, the once shiny village market, swept once every four days on the market day, was covered with grass. The visitor could hardly recognize the place where more than five hundred chattering women used to congregate once or twice weekly to buy and sell products made at home or cultivated on their farms.

Beyond the refugee village, beyond the deserted and billeted village, lay the new village organized by Onuoha, Titi and Tudor. The last now lived with his wife and child in the new community. Among others who had joined the group were Yvette Okonkwo, Dr Clinton Okeji, and Onuoha's own parents.

The misery of the refugee camps greatly affected the lives of the villagers. Life there had no meaning. People sat down all day and lay down all night in expectation of nothing more than their diminishing supply of food. Those who survived the marathon battle against hunger and sickness often succumbed to boredom. Human life could not be organized under such circumstances. It was this realization that led Onuoha to establish a pilot programme that grew within a short period to a large community of villages.

For the people, the war was no more. The past was a receding nightmare. The rising sun was a dream; its zenith, a dark noon. Behind, lay the ruins of youth and the remains of age.

The new community was an attempt to build in the bush from nothing a new life for the refugees. About two hundred families were put in each compound and there were about ten compounds in each village. Houses were erected for them and, if they were physically able, they participated in the setting up of their homes. Each family had its own unit. Once constituted, the village elected its own representatives. People originally from the same area were placed together so as to give them the notion of some continuity with their former lives. The citizens were re-allotted plots of land and given crops, sometimes sold on credit. They were expected to reimburse the community from the proceeds of their new farms. This way employment was created for them, as well as a new sense of being. They would not only be self-sufficient, but would contribute materially to the survival of the less fortunate ones. They had something to work for, something to look forward to also. They had their farms, their harvest, their market and above all their children whom they could watch grow without fear of starvation.

At first, it was a simple idea but like a germ it spread, and like a gem its brilliance shone all over. Its effect on health, sanitation, morale soon became evident. Food production and distribution increased. The new villages grew up one by one, giving a feeling of rebirth. New forest areas were cleared to set up new communities. Schools were built again and instruction started at all levels. The rudiments of civics were given to the young. The young who had been out of school for years learned again to read and write, at first with great difficulty, but later with renewed joy. This way, the physical and intellectual extinction of a once happy race of people was avoided. There was a partial return, a temporary return to a more primitive life, the quickest way of facilitating progress and building the new society on solid and tried foundations.

The new citizens turned their minds away from the past period of chaos and social upheaval. They looked forward with confidence towards peace and progress in the future. The new community meant a new life for them. The citizens were content, in poverty as well as in wealth, content that everything was shared, baths, schools and quite often fireplaces. They shared all in common because experience had bitterly taught them that they were nothing individually. At first, they had nothing to buy or sell because the harvests were not due yet and the fruits were not ripe. Their rations of milk, flour and garri were distributed to each according to his need and each worked without questioning, according to his ability, in the collective farms and gardens, giving of his best and putting his talents at the disposal of the community.

Because of their system of life and in honour of their founder, Onuoha, they called the new community Umuoha, the communal children, for Oha in their language meant community. By a strange coincidence, they chose as their leader and spokesman, Onuoha, whose name stood for the voice of the community. Onuoha declined their offer, preferring to remain a simple citizen. The village belonged to the community and each member of the community felt himself responsible to the people. Each citizen saw himself as a tenant called upon by the community to make good use of what the community had placed at his disposal, and to leave it in good order when he was called upon to leave the community for other duties or when he had to join his ancestors in the worlds beyond. Life did not belong to him personally. No individual then had the right to lord it over others. Neither could the individual give up his rights as a tenant or assign them to another.

Onuoha let the citizens run their affairs as their forefathers had done in former days. During their meetings they sat down in a horse-shoe fashion and elected as chairman the oldest and the wisest, Onyewuchi. When decisions were to be taken, the matter was discussed in detail. No votes were taken. A consensus was drawn from the general sentiments and views expressed by the individual experts in each field. But once a general consensus had been reached, everyone accepted the decision. Since there was no voting and no decision by majority rule, there was no need to impose anything on the unwilling minority.

In the evenings, before the citizens retired, they sat down and told stories of their past and expressed openly their aspirations for the future. They sat around and also told fairy tales until they felt like going to bed. When the moon was up and the evening refreshing, they stayed in the open and dozed all night until it was time to go to work. Some women would go to the streams to fetch water, others would go to the woods to fetch wood for their cooking and for making fires at night. The men and the boys went to the farms allotted to their group. The women, seeing how their husbands and sons were sharing their labours and their duties, decided that it was not necessary to prepare meals separately again. Those who worked together should also eat and share jointly in all their affairs. They remembered also that the children played together and went to school together.

At harvest time, after the farmers had paid back to the community their dues, that is to say what the community had advanced to them, they exchanged products for other things. Those who needed vegetables gave up some of their yams and cassavas. In turn, the community gave each his protein needs by continuing to furnish them their weekly rations of those products like milk and stockfish not produced by the community. As more compounds grew up, the citizens decided to have consultations with the representatives of the other groups around. Their farms were very fertile and they had been producing lots of vegetables, but they were unable to produce enough yams for their compound. They wanted to exchange some of their products for other articles. Emissaries were sent to a few of the other villages around. These responded with haste, adding that they had been thinking along the same lines.

A general meeting was called. Onyewuchi was there to chair the occasion. Agreement was reached that each village should co-operate with the others, exchanging labour, information about techniques, predictions about weather and, after a harvest, a redistribution of products to ensure that each community had enough of everything available to all. At the end of each planting season, each village was to declare its surpluses so that these could be stored in the common granary for use during times of national crisis and emergency and, if need be, for the use of other villages in the community that had a less fortunate harvest. An old man stood up and said that, if by any chance, one village had for example yams and others did not have enough during that particular season, though the first village might not have enough to declare a surplus, the community in question should make a serious effort to share equitably what it had in its possession. Others saw in the reasoning of the man golden words of wisdom. Those present cheered his statement and the principle was adopted without much further discussion.

Another elder stood up and apologized for having to remind people around about what they had gone through during the past few years. He suggested that each village should bring forth its youth so that they could build a ring of defences around their community. He suggested that their young men should be drilled daily so that they could defend their system of life when their security or interests were threatened. These thoughts were weighed at length. Some argued that war was a bad thing. Others maintained that self-defence was righteous. Some maintained that strong moral values were the best safeguards against invasion and threats of invasion. Others strongly argued that the alertness and preparedness of a community constituted the greatest deterrent against aggression. The opinions were varied and many.

Finally, they decided to call upon experts in various fields to come and testify before them. They invited Tudor Opara, Freddy Onuoha, Dr Okeji (one of their best men in the sciences) and also some philosophers in the community. All of them wanted to see the end of wars and strife amongst men. But they recommended the establishment of a defence system. A consensus was arrived at and the community adopted the initial suggestions of the old man who had introduced the topic. Tudor was commissioned to study the defence needs of the community and to submit his recommendations to a special committee appointed for the purpose. His recommendations were approved with a deep sigh of relief, though they strongly wished that war could be avoided completely. They felt that this could be done, if men would mind their own business and put away their personal ambitions and the mad desire to rule other people's minds and souls. Onyewuchi stood up and concluded thus: 'The only lawful domination is that of one's mind and instincts, a personal domination that looks for the good of others. This way alone can man avoid the brutal temptation to settle family affairs with the sword, for beyond Umuoha, our community, the entire world is one big family.'

Marshal Tudor set up civil protection units to draw up plans for the defence of the communities. Shelters were built around the communal schools and markets. Detailed plans were drawn for the quick and safe evacuation of the women and children and old men in case of a sudden invasion. The young men were to stay in the community and defend their homes, farms and ideals. The Defence Report concluded that the presence of civilians and their encouragement of the defending forces improved the morale of the defenders. The report indicated that those fighting for the people ought to be looked after by the community. The report was adopted by the assembly during its regular meeting.

The reputation of the new experiment in communalism spread far and wide. People came from other lands to see the citizens, talk to them and visit their farms. The visitors watched them in the evenings as the villagers held their dance rehearsals in the moonlight. The men and women danced together. The older ones beat the drums while the children watched the dancers and the players and joined them when they felt confident enough. When it was time for the children to retire, their parents took them to their communal sleeping homes where nurses looked after them.

Some of the visitors brought their cameras along. The members of the community refused to be photographed. They argued that they were not museum pieces or ethnic curiosities for the amusement of people abroad, but normal people living their normal lives, normal people having no need to advertise their existence, their prosperity or their misery. A few of the visitors wanted to take some of the communalist children abroad where they could be fed better and sent to other schools. The people's assembly met and, after due deliberation, decided that it was not right for their children to be allowed at very young ages to go abroad for their education. Abroad, they would be subjected to different customs and on their return would pose great problems of integration. Not quite having assimilated the foreign customs, unable to adjust to their communalist way of life again, they would be like lost children belonging to no culture at all, without standards to emulate or roots on which to grow.

During one of the community assemblies, Onyewuchi stood up and moved to the front of the horse-shoe assembly and greeted the people in the traditional form:

Umuoha Kwenu!
He!
Umuoha Kwenu!
He!
Kwenu!
He!
Kwenu!
He!
Kwenu!
He!
Kwezuo-nu!
He . . . !

After the rallying cry, the people started shuffling their feet, knowing that something important was about to be announced. 'Elder, come down to the point,' the younger men pleaded anxiously. 'Come down to the point, Elder, whether it is good or bad.' Onyewuchi would not be tempted. He asked his helpers to come forward to distribute kola-nuts. They also served palm-wine and they passed round plates of salad made from ugba, oil bean fruits sliced and mixed with cooked melon seeds and seasoned with a thick oil dressing.

When the people had all taken something and were in a festive mood, Onyewuchi came to the point. 'The parents of Onuoha,' Onyewuchi said, 'whom you all know have been living amongst us for sometime now, have asked me to inform you of the planned union of their son and Titi Duru. In the absence of the parents of the young lady, Titi has asked me to act on her behalf and ask for the blessing of the elders and the community on this union.'

One by one the elders came forward and declared their support for the union, invoking the blessings of the heavens on their future offspring. One by one, they came forward and voted to celebrate the wedding on their Harvest Festival Day. They decided to invite people living outside the community to come and rejoice with them as they celebrated their Thanksgiving Day. They decided to have games, wrestling matches and organized dances. They wanted to make the harvest festivities a great occasion so that all those there would have enough to eat and drink. After the meeting, the news spread all over the lands and far beyond the community. There was a spirit of joy everywhere when the day came.

Compounds and villages brought out their choice wines, the women prepared their best dishes. Fortunately each compound declared a surplus that harvest season. Collectively women fried yams, others prepared mai-mai, chim-chim, agidi, akara and groundnuts. There was egusi soup as well as okra soup and vegetable soup for the mighty basins of pounded yam, garri and cassava. They had plenty of vegetables spread along the tables in the communal dining-hall. Files and files of women and children moved from table to table to celebrate the great day. Young boys and girls specially chosen for the occasion served the people and the visitors.

Outside the buffet hall, the sun shone in all its glory. There were all kinds of exhibits. The farmers proudly exhibited their products. They displayed yams as tall as human beings and livestock as healthy and gay as the season. The scientists demonstrated their new techniques and productions for farming and industry. Congregations of men and women went from one exhibit to another. Women of the community were elegantly dressed in wrappers made from the looms belonging to the community and

woven from the cotton produced on their farms. Arts and crafts
were on exhibit too. Members of the community who were thus
talented produced beautiful figurines of ancient gods, others painted gorgeous images on calabashes grown on their own farms.

A stage was erected in the central park of the community and
beautifully decorated. Surrounded by the luxuriant trees that the
community had planted in the grounds it looked like an arena of
nature. There men and women played and performed the various
dances of the community: Odimma, Nwaokorobo, Alija, Abigolo.
The music and dances were a combination of grace and elegance,
of harmony and melody. Beautiful teenage girls from the community let themselves go with the joyful rhythms of the traditional
beats of the xylophone, the blaring trumpets, the jingles of the
castanets, solos of female voices, the chorus of young men and the
sweet variety of sounds from empty water-pots. The young
dancers seemed to flutter in the air, their arms bedecked with
bracelets and their legs with trinkets designed by the community.
There was joy everywhere, a feeling of rebirth as the crowds
surged from one enthralling dance to another artistic exhibit.

There was newfound joy, the type of laughter and ease and cheer
the community had never seen before. Women and children stood
around and just looked, looked and talked. Tudor led the Defence
Corps in a gigantic parade. Each unit exhibited its judo techniques
and each company gave a different performance. The battalions
paraded in their colours and paratroop uniforms. Everywhere
there were cheers and cheers for Tudor. His head was erect, eyes
slightly bent to the left as he marched past the communalist flag.
The march music was soft and brilliantly executed by the Communal Orchestra. It was a great day watching the school children,
boys and girls, dressed in their uniforms, marching past the communalist flag, singing songs of victory and glory, hymns of joy
and rebirth. A whole generation was reborn. The fruits of their
toils could already be seen in the happy faces of their children,
buds that were waiting for time to bloom. After the march-past,
Onyewuchi presented the new couple to the people. The crowd
cheered and cheered. Titi was bashful, preferring to remain behind
the scene. She retired with Onuoha and they joined the others

going from one exhibit to another. But the crowd recognized them everywhere and cheered them.

It was as if the entire world attended Umuoha Harvest Festival. Families who had been separated by the war found each other again and immediately recovered lost tears and laughter. Friends who had thought each other lost saw their faces again. Children who had never seen a smile before, for the first time saw the faces of their mothers light up with joy and laughter. Those who had looked sick as they came to Umuoha seemed to recover their health and ease. It was a symbol of new hope, a hope generated by a community for the community. It was a hope generated by the people for the people. For the first time in a long while, the people seemed to participate fully in life, their life, a joyful life.

As the citizens of Umuoha rejoiced, they knew that the following day they would go back to their duties: to their farms, schools, factories and centres. But they were determined to enjoy their free time and their Festival as joyfully as they had worked hard in their respective duties during the previous seasons. It was also a day of thanksgiving for the fruits of their labour, a day of thanks for their deliverance, also a day of reflection and meditation.

During one of the tours around the exhibits, Onyewuchi came to Onuoha and Titi and informed them that there was a couple that would very much like to have a word with Titi. The latter left with Onyewuchi. The elder left Titi beneath a tree and disappeared. Titi was there chewing some akara bulbs when she saw an old couple approaching with Onyewuchi who left them a few yards away from her. The wise old man had decided to leave them alone. Titi looked for a moment in astonishment and then rushed forward to embrace her mother and father. The parents could not contain themselves either. There was a very brief moment of joy, then tears flowed. Titi cried. Her mother cried also. The father merely stood and gazed with bewilderment.

They had walked round and round all afternoon looking at Titi. They knew that they were not mistaken, but they were not absolutely sure and did not want to make fools of themselves. They concluded that Duru was a common name. They did not want to approach Titi directly. They knew that raising vain hopes would cause them untold pains. They did not believe that Titi could still be alive or could have come into the country. They thought that their only daughter was dead or had been kidnapped and sent away somewhere. From a safe distance, they walked around looking at her. She was a little older and more beautiful. They were not quite sure. But they felt something in their blood.

The father was sure that the child standing there and receiving the applause of the community was their daughter. Would she recognize again her withered parents? The father had lost the power of speech. Several times, they had turned to go home when they could not bear the apprehension any more. But each time, they had decided to stay a little longer and watch again the child in front of them, the impeccable double of their own daughter, more mature, more beautiful, more elegant. When they could no longer resist the temptation, they decided to approach one of the elders who took them to Onyewuchi. 'We were still far from you,' the mother concluded, 'when, adorable child, you rushed forward to confirm all our glorious expectations.'

Titi cried again and, putting her hand in her pocket, she showed her parents the wedding ring she had picked up in their home, adding that she would explain how she got it later. The mother heaved a sigh of wonder and relief. She had cried and cried for the ring. She knew that she had lost it in their home but could not go back for it. Every day, she saw herself still sitting by the fireside in her old kitchen in Abagana. She could still imagine the shells falling down all around their house as she sat in the kitchen preparing dinner. It was nothing, the militia boys had told them. Then the shells had approached closer and closer and the bullets had fallen nearer and nearer.

She had removed her ring as she washed the pots and peeled the yams while preparing dinner. She had gone to the back door to get some water from the water-pot behind the kitchen. She had never stepped into her kitchen again. A shell had fallen on the house and blown up the thatched roof. Her husband had been away. He had gone to the village square to find out what they were supposed to do and what other people were doing. She had run away from the premises when she heard the explosion. She had been running out of the gate when she had seen her husband rushing back home in search of her. He had lost the power of speech. A shell had exploded in the village square killing several people. Together, they had cast a final glance at their burning home and walking and running they had left the village.

At first, they had stayed for a few days in a refugee camp not too far from their village. They had been told that the situation would improve. It had been reported that there would soon be a counter-attack to recover the area. The days had passed by and it had become evident that the situation, far from improving, had gradually deteriorated. They had moved from one refugee camp to another as the enemy had pushed them farther and farther away from their homes. Old men had withered away and died for want of consolation. Small children had pined away and died for lack of food.

From village to village, they had wandered like a bunch of Hausa beggars. There had been no place to sleep or to lay their heads. As they moved farther and farther away, the sound of shelling had moved closer and closer. Every day, they heard that another village had fallen to the enemy. Every day, they had been joined by new groups of refugees. Every night, they had discovered that they had to run once again from their new place of abode. In the market place, in the home, in the camp, planes had flown over their heads. The next moment there would be people dead beside them, a house near them levelled.

Titi's mother continued her lamentation. Titi let her continue considering that it was healthy to let her get the whole thing out of her mind. She had been apparently looking for someone to talk to since her husband had lost the power of speech. 'War is a hopeless thing,' she continued. 'You can never tell when it will be your turn, when the plane will strike, when it will bomb your house, your office or simply strike you in bed. It is worse than a pest, worse than an epidemic. There used to be vaccines against pests and epidemics. But there is no remedy against the misery and insecurity of war. Even in days when there were no vaccines once a plague attacked an individual and he survived it, he became naturally immune to it. With air-raids, there is no guarantee that if you escape it narrowly today, or if it wounds you seriously today in the office, it will not come again tomorrow or the day after, in the hospital, in the restaurant or while you are in bed, to get you again with a rocket, a shell, a bomb.

'I will never forget it,' she continued. 'I will never forget the day your father and I arrived in Umuahia after the fall of Okigwi. Your father was put in a hospital along the School Road not far from Azikiwe Avenue. They wanted to see what they could do for him. You remember the small clinic facing the Progress Hotel and the Provincial Assembly? I was going back to my camp after visiting your father. I missed my way. I saw a young man passing by. I stopped him and asked him the way to the camp. He told me that I was heading in the opposite direction. He himself was coming back from an office near my refugee camp.

'The nice young man decided to accompany me back to the camp and show me the way. We were just passing the clinic again when I saw the planes in the sky. It seemed as if they were looking for me. I raised my hands up in despair. The young man held me by the side. "Be calm, Mother. Be calm," he entreated me. "Jump into the bush here with me and lie down flat." I was too frightened to understand what he was saying then. I cried and called upon heaven and earth to come and take me away. The young man stood up again and pulled me towards the bush at the edge of the road as the planes turned again. Frightened more than ever, I snatched myself from his grip and fell unconscious on the un-tarred road.

'It appeared as if the heavens fell on me, as if the earth under my feet caved inwards. A thunderous explosion rocked the ground beside me. I did not know exactly what happened. But I think I opened my eyes and then saw this young man lying there dead. Did I say dead? His body was shattered to bits. I did not know where I was again or what I was doing. The next thing I knew was that I was lying in a hospital bed beside your father. The nurse there later told me that I ran into the hospital shouting "Pour cold water on me! Pour cold water on me!"

'My mind was blank for two full days. It was only then that I began to recollect what had happened. I was not sure whether what I had seen that day really happened, whether that young man was really killed, whether the entire episode was a mere dream. When I fully came to myself, Titi, they told me that the young man was buried that morning. The nurse told me also that exactly three months earlier, the father of the young man was killed in another air-raid on Umuahia.'

Her head was clear. It was like an exorcism. She looked relieved. There was even a smile on her face, as she repeated, 'Child, Child! Tell me where you have been!' Daughter and mother shed tears of joy. 'Enough! Enough!' Titi's father signalled with his fingers. Titi turned to her mother and said: 'Those days are gone, Mother.' Half crying herself she continued: 'Let us retain the memories, but let us rather look ahead into the future. It is clear and bright.'

Onuoha walked in right in the midst of this scene which seemed like the work of some French Romantic painter. There was a child weeping on the lap of her mother and the father looking on with tears hanging from his eyelids. Onuoha could not control himself when he saw the image that told its own story.

As darkness fell, the Festival closed with fireworks. It had all the brilliant colours Clinton Okeji had been able to imagine. His exhibits carried the day.

As they all sat down in the evening in an enlarged family reunion, Yvette Okonkwo sat by Clinton Okeji. She was a new girl. Onuoha remembered what Clinton had said about Yvette: 'She must be a new girl for me to fall in love with her!' Tudor's wife was there also. Yvette was carrying one of her children. They talked about all and nothing. Tudor spoke rather seriously about paying some tangible tribute to his comrades-in-arms who had sacrificed their lives for the people. He was thinking of a historical work that would be faithful to fact and figures and the real characters of the various participants in the struggle, the struggle they had been through.

Titi thought that a historical study would be dry and impersonal and would not do real justice to the social situation that prevailed during the crisis, especially the general moral climate. Clinton Okeji was more interested in the strides made by science and engineering and how they had contributed to the survival of the people. Onuoha had no strong opinion. He was only interested in a fair account that would expose the strength as well as the weaknesses of the noble revolution.

Yvette agreed with him and concluded: 'That way, every reader will find something to make him happy and something to make him sad, for so life was and is both inside and outside Biafra—a mixture of joy and sorrow, of goodness and evil, of moments of heroic sacrifice and mean cowardice, though most people, most actors, would rather have official history immortalize their greatness while ignoring the most natural and human aspects of their lives, their tragic faults. We owe it as a duty to tell our children nothing but the truth, the entire truth.'

40-302